CHARLES NODIER

JEAN SBOGAR
AND OTHER STORIES

TRANSLATED AND WITH AN INTRODUCTION BY
BRIAN STABLEFORD

I0591184

THIS IS A SNUGGLY BOOK

Translation and Introduction Copyright © 2021
by Brian Stableford.
All rights reserved.

ISBN: 978-1-64525-079-1

JEAN SBOGAR
AND OTHER STORIES

CHARLES NODIER (1780-1844) was one of the pioneers of French Romantic prose; his salon at the Bibliothèque de l'Arsenal, begun in 1824 and known as *Le Cénacle*, brought together many of the key figures in the Movement and spun off other *cénacles* in which it was anchored, including Victor Hugo's. His best work consists of short stories and novellas.

BRIAN STABLEFORD's scholarly work includes *New Atlantis: A Narrative History of Scientific Romance* (Wildside Press, 2016), *The Plurality of Imaginary Worlds: The Evolution of French roman scientifique* (Black Coat Press, 2017) and *Tales of Enchantment and Disenchantment: A History of Faerie* (Black Coat Press, 2019). He has translated more than three hundred volumes from the French, mostly in the genres of *roman scientifique*, *contes de fées* and Romantic and Symbolist fiction. His recent fiction includes the visionary science fiction novel *The Revelations of Time and Space* (2020) and its sequel *After the Revelation* (2021); the last in his long series of "Tales of the Genetic Revolution," *The Elusive Shadows* (2020); and the comedy fantasy *Meat on the Bone* (2021), all published by Snuggly Books.

Contents

Introduction

This volume is a companion to the collection *Outlaws and Sorrows*, which features translations of the prose fiction produced by Charles Nodier in the first phase of his literary career, between 1800 and 1806. The introduction to that volume included a brief account of the author's biography up to that point, endeavoring to put those early works into the historical and personal context that determined their production and their content.

The introduction in question concluded with the observation that Nodier's life and career reached a crucial watershed in the year 1808, when he married Désirée Charve, shortly before the death of his father. Still under official police surveillance following his brief imprisonment in 1804, and unable to return to Paris, Nodier was forced to look for employment away from the capital that might be able to provide a secure income for his new household. In 1809 he was recommended by a friend to Sir Herbert Croft (1751-1825), an elderly English exile resident in Amiens, who had been involved all his life in various esoteric literary projects, some of which dovetailed neatly with Nodier's interest in languages, especially a project to correct the allegedly-falsified punctuation of various Greek and Latin classics, currently the works of Horace. Croft offered Nodier a position as his secretary, which included expenses for his relocation and accommodation in a village near Amiens, as well as a monthly salary, and Nodier accepted.

Croft had inherited his father's baronetcy but not his property, and he was living with another elderly English writer, Lady Mary Hamilton (1736-1821). Croft was best-known for the epistolary novel *Love and Madness* (1780), the subject-matter of which echoed one of Nodier's enduring obsessions, and Hamilton for a strange feminist utopia, *Munster Village* (1778). Nodier assisted both of them in their work; as well as aiding Croft in his classical revisions he translated *Munster Village* into French and helped Hamilton write her last novel, *Le Duc de Popoli* (1810), in French (a language she could not speak). He found the demands made on him by the eccentric couple taxing, and the promised salary slow to materialize; although Croft apparently became very fond of him, Nodier felt that he had to leave and seek other employment following the birth of his daughter Marie in 1811.

In 1812, Nodier's prospective brother-in-law, a diplomat stationed in Illyria—which had become a province of the Empire in 1809—obtained a position for him with the province's official newspaper, for which he worked for several months before the Empire lost its grip on the region and he had to return to France—an exceedingly difficult journey across war-torn Europe. His official surveillance having been lifted, he was then able to return to Paris, where he obtained employment in 1814 with the *Journal de l'Empire*, which swiftly mutated after Napoléon's defeat and abdication into the *Journal des Débats politiques et littéraires*, partly reclaiming the title under which it had been founded in 1789. Nodier was a regular contributor to the newspaper's pages until 1823, and was thus embarked on a long and somewhat precarious career as a Parisian journalist, engaged in routine political reportage and commentary, and criticism of theater and books, always politically suspect because of his past and increasingly so as the post-Imperial regime became increasingly repressive.

In 1815 Nodier published the anonymous *Histoire des sociétés secretes de l'armée* [History of the Secret Societies of the Army], a fanciful work that anticipated many other "histories" of secret societies, which became a thriving genre in France, crucial to the origin and development of many historical myths, including the substance of the French Occult revival, and to the strategies inherent in modern "conspiracy theories" and "fake news." Nodier certainly did not invent the genre, whose roots went back a long way, but his research and invention made a substantial contribution to its development.

The precise extent of Nodier's journalistic work in the troubled years following the fall of the Empire is now difficult to determine, although his regular columns in the *Journal des Débats* must have constituted the bulk of it. He never stopped investigating other opportunities, however; in 1818 he set forth on another eastward journey to Odessa, where he had been offered a teaching post, but he soon returned from what he subsequently referred to, wryly, as his "Russian campaign." In the same year, the publication of the novella *Jean Sbogar* by Gide fils marked a new departure for his fiction. Issued anonymously, the novella was markedly different from his earlier works, even though its subject matter remained, essentially, outlaws and sorrows. In the former regard it was more extreme than his earlier works, featuring an outlaw who is an actual bandit, supposedly guilty of numerous heinous crimes, although we never actually see him committing any, and the fragmentary statements that he makes—unlike most of Nodier's works, the bulk of this one consists of third-person narrative—are more than a little enigmatic. His banditry is partly explained as guerrilla resistance against Napoléon's conquering army, but that apology is half-hearted, and his small army seems mostly to be engaged in looting and highway robbery.

The fortunes of the book were a trifle mixed; initially slow to sell, it soon received a boost from an unexpected source.

Napoléon was in remote exile in Saint Helena with a small number of companions, including the Comte de Las Cases, who was keeping a journal of his exile and preparing a biography. Despite his removal from Europe, Napoléon was still the focus of intense interest in Paris and his every move—insofar as he could make any moves at all—was considered to be newsworthy. His reading material was scrupulously reported, and he read *Jean Sbogar*, taking an enthusiastic interest in it and annotating his copy, for reasons that are not entirely clear. The publicity helped the sales of the book considerably, and excited curiosity as to the identity of its author. Nodier having taken few serious precautions to hide his responsibility, it soon came out, revealed to Napoléon and to the world.

Before that happened, Nodier had already placed a second novella, *Thérèse Aubert*, with a different publisher, Ladvocat, which appeared with the by-line "by the author of *Jean Sbogar*" in 1819. The preliminary material of that book included an advertisement for a further two-volume work by the same author, entitled *Rosalba*. Although advertised as if it were already in print, it never actually appeared. A comment in the review section of the *Revue de Paris* in 1833 alleged that Nodier had been planning to write the story of Rosalba—based on a historical anecdote included in a posthumously-published collection of items by the Academician Jean-Pierre Claris de Florian (1755-1794), who died in prison during the Revolution—for a long time, but presumably he failed to deliver it. A further novella did appear from Gide fils in 1820 under the by-line "by the author of *Jean Sbogar* and *Thérèse Aubert*," along with reprints of his earlier fiction, but both *Thérèse Aubert* and *Adèle* had been written before *Jean Sbogar*—the latter probably long before—and they represented a continuation of his previous career rather than a supplement to his new beginning; three years separated the appearance of *Jean Sbogar* from the publication of what was presumably his next new novella.

The reasons for that interruption are not obvious. The likelihood is that the revelation of his identity did not work entirely to his advantage; although no longer a *proscrit* he was still politically suspect, perhaps becoming more so as the *Journal des Débats* became increasingly liberal in the political views it supported and the Bourbon regime became increasingly repressive. The publishers of Paris were not a pusillanimous crowd, though, and they probably would not have hesitated to cash in on *Jean Sbogar*'s sudden notoriety had Nodier been in a position to supply something new. The popularity of *Thérèse Aubert* and *Adèle* did not benefit very much from the publicity obtained by *Jean Sbogar*, the two stories being more similar in their tone and narrative construction to *Les Proscrits* and *Le Peintre de Saltzbourg*.

Because *Jean Sbogar* was similarly downbeat in its denouement, the two novelettes that followed it in publication are not out of keeping with its morosity. *Adèle*, in fact, sustains the relentlessly downbeat outlook of the previous novelettes in a peculiar fashion that must have seemed to many readers to be a perverse defiance of conventional expectation. Whereas the fundamental situations detailed in *Jean Sboga*r and *Thérèse Aubert* are clearly not going to end well, so that the eventual frustration of the amorous obsession at the heart of each story is the unfolding of an inevitable tragedy; the plot of *Adèle*, by contrast, is carefully constructed not only to permit but to facilitate a conventional "happy ending," whose failure to materialize must have left many readers feeling cheated as well as disappointed.

Adèle's bibliography is a trifle confused; it appears to have been planned for publication in a two-volume collection of *Romans, Nouvelles et mélanges* in 1820, the first volume of which reprinted *Les Proscrits* as "Stella; ou Les Proscrits," and selections from "Tristes." The second might have been projected to contain *Adèle* and *Le Peintre de Saltzbourg*, but *Adèle* actually appeared independently, and *Le Peintre de Saltzbourg* was added into the second edition of volume one. A new introduction added to the reprint of *Adèle* and *Le Peintre de Saltzbourg* in the 1832 edition of Nodier's *Oeuvres* confirmed that *Adèle* had been written long before *Jean Sbogar*, perhaps not long after *Le Peintre de Saltzbourg*. That suggests the possibility that, like *Le Derner chapitre de mon roman*, Nodier had begun to write *Adèle* as a commercial exercise, planning to end it in a conventional audience-flattering fashion, but that he had abandoned it—possibly when he was arrested, imprisoned and exiled from Paris—only returning to it belatedly in order to dash off a conclusion while in a different frame of mind. That is pure speculation, but it fits the pattern of Nodier's work more neatly than the hypothesis that it was written closer to its publication date and that its ending was planned from the outset.

One way or another, however, neither Gide fils nor Ladvocat issued any further fiction by Nodier to follow up *Jean Sbogar* and *Thérèse Aubert*, in spite of their continuing sales, even the second warranting a relatively prompt second edition. Nodier's next item of fiction, *Smarra, ou les demons de la nuit, songes romantiques traduit de l'esclavon par Comte Maxime Odin* (1821, signed "Ch. Nodier"), was issued by a different publisher, and represented a far more radical break with the past than *Jean Sbogar*, although it similarly owed a great deal to his sojourn in Illyria, *smarra* being the Dalmatian term for a nightmare—or, as Nodier preferred to put it, *the* nightmare. The first edition of *Smarra* was filled out by three supposed translations similarly related to his sojourn in Illyria, "Le Bey Spalatin" (tr. herein as "The Spalatin Bey"), "La Femme d'Asan" (tr. as "Asan's Wife") and "Le Luciole, idylle de Giorgi" (tr. as "The Firefly").

As a translation of *Smarra* by Ruth Berman is currently in print in the Black Coat Press collection *Trilby; The Crumb Fairy* (2015), I have not included one in the present volume, even though it would help to provide a bridge of sorts to the surreal work that began the third phase of Nodier's fiction publications in 1829, *Histoire du roi de bohême et ses sept châteaux*, which will take up the bulk of the third volume in my own series, *The Story of the King of Bohemia and His Seven Castles*. That work is also a hallucinatory fantasy, albeit of a very different stripe. I have, however, supplemented the three novellas in the present volume—which I have placed in order of their presumed composition rather than that of their publication—with the three brief items related to the author's Illyrian adventure.

If Nodier was having difficulty placing works of fiction prior to 1820 because of his reputation as a trouble-maker, it is possible that he did other unsigned work in the relevant period as well as the three novellas that were soon attributed to him. If that unsigned work included any fiction, he did not include it in his *Oeuvres*, but that does not necessarily mean that none existed. One item of initially-uncredited hackwork that did become known, however—and, indeed, notorious—was his recruitment by the director of the Théatre de la Porte-Martin to assist with the rewriting of a drama entitled *Le Vampire*, a French translation of an English play based on "The Vampyre" (1819), a novelette misattributed to Lord Byron, but actually the work of Byron's one-time private physician John Polidori.

The French play, premièred in 1820, was a huge success, and a key work in the development of Parisian theatrical melodrama. It probably helped to redirect Nodier's principal attention temporarily toward the theater, and also toward the supernatural, and that might well be why he did not make any attempt to follow up the publication of *Thérèse Aubert* and *Adèle*—at least, not immediately—with more Romantic accounts of the essential perversity of amour. He was by no means done with that aspect of his thought, though, as two of the further volumes in the current set, *The Story of the King of Bohemia and His Seven Castles* and *The Memoirs of Maxime Odin*, will demonstrate.

The year in which *Le Vampire* reached the peak of its success and notoriety, 1821, was a crucial year in Nodier's career and life. He not only published *Smarra* in that year but had his melodrama *Bertram, ou Le Pirate* produced; based on a Byronic play written in English by Charles Maturin, which cashed in on the vogue launched by *Le Vampire*. Nodier undertook a journey in the summer to Scotland with two close friends, including Baron Isidore Taylor (1789-1879), with whom he had collaborated on several theatrical enterprises as well as a handsome two-volume *Voyages pittoresques et romantiques dans l'ancienne France* (1820). The Scottish expedition supplied him with the backcloth to the folkloristic fantasy *Trilby, ou le lutin d'Argyll* (1822; tr. as *Trilby, the Goblin of Argyll*). The peak in his literary success was, however, offset by tragedy in his personal life; his wife gave birth to a son, who died before the end of the year, an incident perhaps not unconnected with the rapid furtherance of his obsession with the *fantastique*, in reverie and fiction, as a possible source of consolation for grief.

Nodier subsequently claimed that he had made a decision at that time that he would specialize in future in *contes fantastiques* and never write any other fiction, although it was undoubtedly an insincere resolution that he certainly did not keep, if he really made it at all. He is credited by many subsequent bibliographers with having made a start in an anonymous collection of anecdotal tales entitled *Infernaliana* (1822) but he probably only wrote the introduction and helped the publisher to assemble a collection of anecdotes, which borrow extensively from Dom Augustine Calmet's documentation of the vampire legendry of Eastern Europe, first published in 1746, and from Jacques Collin de Plancy's recent collection of diabolical anecdotes *Le Diable peint par lui-même* [The Devil as Depicted by Himself] (1819), which supplemented the latter's very popular *Dictionnaire infernal* (1818; augmented in later editions; tr. as *Infernal Dictionary*). Nodier presumably knew Collin, who worked as a printer and publisher in Paris in the 1820s but kept a diplomatically low profile because his mother was the sister of the Revolutionary leader Georges Danton, one of the principal instigators of the Terror—a dangerous relationship to have during the Restoration—and any projects in which they were both involved would probably have been diplomatically anonymous or pseudonymous.

In the early 1820s, Nodier formed a close friendship with the much younger Victor Hugo, with whom he had a good deal in common; Hugo's father had also been a magistrate distressed by the necessity to order executions during the revolutionary wars, and who had ordered the hanging of the guerrilla fighter Michele Pezza, branded a notorious "bandit" by the French and nick-named "Fra Diavolo." Pezza had been one of the models for Jean Sbogar, and he was later to be extravagantly featured in historical novels by Alexandre Dumas and Paul Féval. Like Nodier, Hugo had become a fervent opponent of the death penalty.

With Hugo's disciple Émile Deschamps, the poets Alphonse de Lamartine and Alfred de Vigny, and the critic Charles-Augustine Sainte-Beuve, Nodier and Hugo formed the core of a group of writers who began to hold regular meetings in 1823 and who founded the short-lived periodical *La Muse Française*, with a declared mission to revive the spirit of French Medieval Romance in a new and revitalized form. The meetings of the group became the *cénacle* that Nodier hosted at the Bibliothèque d'Arsenal when he was appointed as its librarian in January 1824.

La Muse française attracted sufficient attention to earn Nodier and Hugo invitations to the coronation of Charles X—who liked to pose as a patron of the arts and took an interest in what was already being hailed by commentators and critics as a romanticist movement, although the fervent republicanism of many of its adherents must have made him wary—and once the cénacle was established at the Arsénal it became a magnet for writers interested in attaching themselves to the flag of romanticism, as well as a few who refused any such affiliation but were lumped into it by critics and commentators whether they liked it or not. No minutes were kept of the meetings of the cénacle and there was no register of attendance; the people involved probably did not attach more importance to it than the various things they did during the rest of the week, but considered through the lens of history, it became legendary in its importance to the Movement.

The memoirs that mention the cénacle are inevitably anecdotal and rather vague, but in the first few years of its existence Théophile Gautier joined in, with his friend Gérard de Nerval, and so did Alfred de Musset, Prosper Mérimée, Alexandre Dumas, Honoré de Balzac, Jules Janin and Pierre Lacroix, who preferred to sign himself "P. L. Jacob le Bibliophile." Almost every writer associated with the French Romantic Movement probably dropped in occasionally during the early 1820s, and its core members certainly discussed their work in progress extensively, taking a keen interest in its concerns and its methodology.[1] Parallel meetings were soon being hosted by Hugo on a different day of the week, while Gautier and other younger writers formed a splinter group they dubbed "*le petit cénacle*," and allegiances shifted fairly rapidly, but all those involved, even peripherally, were well aware that it was Nodier who had started the whole thing off.

That position as host and his reputation as a pioneer probably did not stop Nodier feeling that he was still something of an

---

1 Although the lists of members cited by almost all sources consist entirely of men, women were also involved. Although the leading female contributors to nascent Romanticism who were still alive in 1824, Sophie Gay and Marceline Desbordes-Valmore, did not live in Paris, Sophie Gay is known to have visited the cénacle in order to introduce her daughter Delphine to Victor Hugo, and Nodier's daughter Marie—who attended the cénacle herself while still in her teens—includes a long list of women in her memoir of her father who were regular visitors to the Arsenal, including such writers as the Duchesse d'Abrantès, who allegedly became Balzac's mistress.

odd man out, and also rather hard-done-by in the burgeoning critical commentary that the movement accumulated. As well as being of lower social status than some of the members of the cénacle—and he was very status-conscious—Nodier was not the most prestigious member of the original group of writers; several others either had or swiftly acquired a greater literary celebrity. Insofar as the ensemble had a figurative leader, it was Victor Hugo, although Hugo retained a polite deference for Lamartine, who was twelve years his elder, having been born in 1790. Nodier, ten years older than Lamartine, might well have felt even more entitled to deference, and probably thought of himself not merely as the doyen of the Movement but as its chief theoretician and philosophical guide—but he also seems to have felt that he did not get the respect he deserved from his peers, and, paradoxical as it might seem in view of his status as the president of the cénacle, he seems to have thought of himself as an outsider therein, disdained as a mere librarian and newspaper reporter in spite of a publication record that surely ought to have been reckoned impressive by the time that *Trilby* appeared in 1822.

After the coronation of Charles X in 1825, Nodier and Hugo traveled together to Switzerland, pausing at the start of the journey to confer with Lamartine; the three of them agreed to collaborate on a travel book, and found a publisher, but they never completed it. The exact nature of the creative difficulties that sank the project are impossible to determine, but the three became increasingly distant from one another thereafter; although the cénacle at the Arsenal continued to thrive for some years and Nodier and Hugo remained close friends, its location within the Movement shifted by degrees, and no longer seemed central by 1830. Although he published a collection of *Poésies* in 1827 Nodier was never highly reputed as a poet, and his guests, many of whom thought themselves possessed of poetic genius—correctly in some instances—and certainly regarded poetry as a higher art than prose, probably felt entitled to look down on writers of prose fiction.

Nevertheless, Nodier certainly did not lack self-confidence in the mid-1820s, and although eight years passed between the publication of *Trilby* and *Histoire du roi de bohême et ses sept châteaux*, marking a substantial gap in his productivity, it seems certain that he was gestating new work in that period, and might even have written some that was delayed in publication until 1830, when the July Revolution brought a sudden thaw in the political climate and changed the perceived spectrum of opportunity considerably. That story, however, is more aptly continued in the introduction to the next volume in the series.

Like many of Nodier's early works, *Jean Sbogar* took its primary inspiration from one of the key works of German Romanticism, in this case Friderich Schiller's *sturm und drang* drama *Die Räuber* (1781; tr. as *The Robbers*), in which Karl Moor, one of two estranged brothers, is forced by the theft of his inheritance to retreat to the Bohemian forest, where he gathers a band of revolutionaries intent on promoting political anarchy by violent means, from which he is problematically deflected by his love for Amalia, which he cannot pursue because he has sworn never to desert the outlaw band following the death of his two closest associates. The work was very influential, eventually becoming the basis for four operas, but it was still little known in France in 1818. Its influence on the French Romantic Movement was profound, however, and its fundamental motif was adapted into popular fiction by Paul Féval in a sequence of feuilletons, begun with *Le Loup blanc* (1843; tr. as *The White Wolf*), which surely took some inspiration from *Jean Sbogar*.

The Romantic historian Augustin Thierry also seems to have taken some inspiration from *Die Räuber* and *Jean Sbogar* in his flamboyant reconstruction of *La Conquête d'Angleterre par les Normands* [The Norman Conquest of England] (1825), in which he recast the character of Robin Hood, featured in a number of English ballads recently repopularized by British Romantics, as an Anglo-Saxon leader of a guerrilla resistance against the invaders, providing him with a wholly invented biography markedly akin to that of Jean Sbogar, but not quite as fantastic. The modern mythology of Robin Hood, almost entirely derived from Thierry's inventions, became the precursor of an entire subgenre of popular fiction, into which Paul Féval's picaresque fictions also fed.

Thérèse Aubert and *Adèle*, being earlier works, a trifle cruder in construction, might well have seemed slightly outmoded by the time they achieved publication, and probably had little influence on later Romantic fiction by other hands, but they did represent a significant stepping-stone in Nodier's own development of his curious obsession with *amour*. His most prolific alter ego, Maxime Odin—who had been obliquely introduced in *Les Tristes* and, having been resurrected and ennobled, was credited as the translator of *Smarra*—went on to feature in a whole series of memoirs of failed romances, running eccentrically parallel to Nodier's own biography, in which the accounts of *amour* featured in *Thérèse Aubert* and *Adèle* are reiterated, sometimes with greater intensity, in accordance with the pattern of "melodramatic inflation." Curiously, *Souvenirs de jeunesse, extraits des mémoire de Maxime Odin* (1832), does not include all the stories featuring Maxime Odin, but does include a quasi-autobiographical story, "Thérèse," in which the protagonist is one Charles Nodier, who claims to have written two novelettes based on the (wholly fictitious) story told therein—presumably *Les Proscrits* and *Thérèse Aubert*, although there are other possible candidates.

Although they were published out of chronological sequence within the evolving pattern of Nodier's fiction, *Thérèse Aubert* and *Adèle* nevertheless have a significant place in its evolution, and in respect of their depiction of the ravages of amour they are by no means entirely distinct from *Jean Sbogar*. The *proscrits* they feature as protagonists are far less active, their essential impotence being taken to an extreme in *Thérèse Aubert* by the narrator's implausible masquerade—which is surely fortunate to have survived its very first hurdle, when Monsieur Aubert strokes his unshaven cheek. When Jean Sbogar is actually on stage in *Jean Sbogar*, invariably in disguise, he too takes passivity to an unusual extreme, limiting himself when forced by circumstance to take action to uttering a curious scream and an enigmatic exclamation, gestures seemingly sufficient to sow paralyzing terror among desperate ruffians.

That impotence, also taken to an extreme in "Adèle," makes it difficult to classify Nodier's protagonists as heroes, and even though Maxime Odin and later avatars were routinely required to undertake feats of physical prowess, they were never required to emulate the protagonist of the disowned *Le dernier chapitre de mon roman*, who is forced to fight a mortal duel—but even he only seeks to defend himself, killing his opponent entirely by accident. We only see the protagonist of *Thérèse Aubert* in panic-stricken retreat with a sword broken near the hilt—a circumstance to delight any believer in Freudian symbolism—and Jean Sbogar is not even given a weapon to hold when he is seen in the climactic scene running from his enemies. The allegedly-valorous past of the protagonist of "Adèle" is firmly behind him before the story opens, and even when he discovers that the love of his life has been locked in a tower by the villain he simply sits at home while her father goes to release her. Although everything in the story has been set up to support an eventual bloody confrontation with the villain, it never materializes.

In their context, the determined pacifism credited to the protagonists of the three novellas—surely implausible in the two soldiers, let alone the bandit—is a stubborn defiance of one of the cardinal features of popular romance. On the part of a writer avid to be read and appreciated, it surely warrants consideration as a puzzling psychological quirk. Squeamishness is certainly a highly significant feature of all modern fiction dealing with quasi-heroic outlaws, always shielded by the physical competence and resilience that Nodier attributes to his characters, but the total failure of the latter to demonstrate it in the stories contained herein, except in allegations made by their narrative voices, does set them somewhat apart.

With regard to their representations of the psychology and existential significance of amour, the three stories assembled herein mark a step forward from his earlier novelettes in terms of their stylistic sophistication, but it would be difficult to argue that it is a step in the direction of plausibility. In trying to represent his own brand of *romanticisme* as something distinct from Jean-Jacques Rousseau's *sensibilité*, Nodier once remarked, snidely, that Rousseau knew something about amour "by hearsay," while implying that his own accounts were based on bitter authentic experience, but that claim might be doubly suspect, not only in casting aspersions on Rousseau but perhaps overestimating drastically the extent to which Nodier's own sentimental experience, shaped in its interpretation by the fictitious model of Werther, was amenable to wide generalization—as he clearly suspected himself, expressing that doubt explicitly in the defensive "Advertisement" of *Thérèse Aubert*.

One might suspect, given the objective facts of Nodier's life, that if his fictitious accounts of ideal amour really are based in real emotional experience, they are wildly exaggerated, and if the allegations regarding Nodier's over-indulgence in opium made by Charles Weiss in the letter trying to excuse him when he was imprisoned can be taken seriously, it is possible that his descriptions of the quasi-hallucinatory nature of amorous sensations owe more to laudanum than to infatuation *per se*. Either way, however, the question of what was going on in the creative process that generated the stories, and what can be obtained by reading them, remains puzzling and interesting. One cannot help wondering, too, what Désirée Nodier made of them, if she read them, and of the fact that he kept on writing obsessively fervent accounts of a perfect love that can only end in death, prior to consummation, long after their marriage. Whatever the answer to that puzzle might be, the stories are certainly intriguing, unusual, and strangely effective, because rather than in spite of their antipathy to conventional expectation.

The three novellas translated here are all transitional works, intermediary in their philosophy, methodology and sophistication between the author's early novelettes and the more elaborate work of his final phase, but they are interesting in their own right as well as in the role of a set of stepping-stones, and "Thérèse Aubert" and "Jean Sbogar" are certainly not lacking in energy or in visionary flair. Even if that visionary flair can be credited in part to the effects of opium—and it is difficult to account for the phantasmagorical effects in the climax of *Jean Sbogar* without some such explanatory aid—it is still very remarkable, and fascinating in its paradoxicality.

Nodier could not make up his mind in later apologies whether Jean Sbogar's aphoristic philosophy, recovered by Antonia from Lothario's lost notebook, is an artifice to be denied and deplored or an honest account of feelings and fantasies that he dared not admit in polite society or cautious "non-fiction." In all probability, he was in conflict with himself regarding that matter, and attentive readers of *Jean Sbogar* could not have been unduly surprised to find the opium-dreaming protagonist of *Histoire du roi de Bohême et ses sept châteaux* (1830; tr. in *The Story of the King of Bohemia and His Seven Castles*)—the work that began the author's third burst of productivity, as *Jean Sbogar* had begun his second—representing himself as a split personality, one component of which is an anarchic mischief-maker.

The minimalist utopia in which Sbogar, prior to adopting that name, enjoys an interval of perfect happiness would surely not have been to anyone's convenience or liking, including Nodier's, but it was an image to which he returned again and again in his work, always elevating it as an ideal, albeit one no longer attainable by humans irredeemably corrupted by civilization, if it ever had been. Lothario's notebook and the long speech in which he narrates his early history to Antonia remained key passages within Nodier's oeuvre, enigmatic by virtue of their very naivety, and because of their location in the strange context of the story, *Jean Sbogar* remains an important work within his multifaceted production, without which the import of the whole is difficult to appreciate fully. We can only speculate as to exactly why the fallen Napoléon Bonaparte found the work so captivating and so meaningful, but he was not unjustified in doing so.

The translations of *Jean Sbogar* and *Thérèse Aubert* were made from copies of the text reproduced on gallica. The remaining translations were all made from copies of the texts reproduced on Google Books.

JEAN SBOGAR
AND OTHER STORIES

Adèle

Gaston de Germancé to Édouard de Millanges

Germancé, 12 April 1801

I am grateful to you, my dear Édouard, for having suggested this idea. Accustomed to sharing with you all my pains and pleasures, in drawing from your heart all my consolations and all my hopes, not believing myself to be sure of the possession of a thought or a sentiment until you were associated with it to some degree; and now, separated from you by the force of events, drawn into a new theater and into the midst of a new existence, it would cost me too much no longer to know where to deposit each of the emotions that this order of things destines for me. Fortunately, we have provided for the sadness of this solitary life by promising to make a faithful account of our days, our adventures, our projects, our secrets and sweet reveries, so that each of us, in receiving his friend's sincere journal at the end of each month, can still identify with him, as before, relive all his hours, and render all his actions present. There is no time and no distance of which this continual exchange of secrets will not abridge the interval, no absence of which it will not diminish the rigor.

We anticipated that the calm of your character, the mildness of your mores and the gravity of your mind will have assured you of simple and tranquil days, the placid uniformity of which will be troubled as little as possible by worldly storms. The exaltation of my head, the ardor of my passions, my penchant for enthusiasm—and perhaps folly, as you sometimes say—have given grounds to conjecture that my narrations will be much more varied and animated than yours. According to that calculation, you would be charged with the philosophical and rational part of our correspondence, and I would furnish you with a rather extravagant romantic journal. Don't count on that. That hypothesis was founded on the plausibility of the past; it is false, and will certainly be false in the future.

I am twenty-eight years old, Édouard, and—which is rare at that age—I have the experience of a dozen years of misfortune. I have lived rapidly, because my sensibility, which was my life, has been used up in fruitless trials and sterile affections. The calamities of the revolution, the dangers of proscription and war, the ever-renascent agitations of an uncertain and mobile life, multiple losses, keenly-felt and dolorous, have doubtless all imprinted on my organization, my character, the movement of my thoughts and the turn of my expressions something singular, unusual and bizarre: the species of exaggeration whose aberrations you criticize with so much reason; but in truth, I only needed to be returned to my own nature to find myself free of all the foreign impressions that fatigued my heart, and to reenter into the delightful repose of solitude and the circle of facile duties, in order to renew myself. You would not believe the tranquility with which I conceive that hope since I have crossed the threshold of the old paternal château again and I can run my eyes, through the window of my little bedroom, over these woods, these magnificent fields, these beautiful areas of verdure, places so familiar and so dear to my childhood!

My mother has received me with tenderness, but with a tenderness mingled with those airs of pomp and ceremony with which you are familiar, and which drive back, so to speak, into the depths of the soul, a sentiment ready to burst forth. How cruel it is, Édouard, not to be able to express what one feels for a person one loves, not to have the right to love, and to be unable to say that one loves without violating decorum. I have contained myself.

It required mustering all my manly strength to visit my father's apartment, the place where I quit him, where I received his last instructions and his last embraces, from which he followed me with such a sad and soft gaze, and where I hoped to see and embrace him again when I had paid my debt to the prince and the fatherland. What a father I have lost in him! You know that, having been able to appreciate the grandeur of his qualities, the elevation of his mind, the purity and simplicity of his mores, and the calm and religious philosophy that rendered him so superior to adversity that all unfortunate circumstances appeared to him to be subjects of triumph. God has not permitted him to assist me any longer with his advice, and to guide me any further through the reefs of life. He has left me alone on earth, and I sense that that idea, the conviction of complete abandonment that I have, is near to breaking my heart. I am quitting you momentarily in order to weep.

I have traced a plan of life that you will scarcely have expected. First of all, my intention is to see very few people, as few as possible. I want to reform myself, to remake myself entirely, and for that I need meditation and solitude.

My domestic staff is limited to Latour, whom you know, the brave Latour who was on campaign in the Vendée with me and is less a domestic than a reliable comrade, a faithful friend, whom my heart could no longer do without. His presence of mind has saved my life on two occasions, when he also distinguished himself by prodigies of valor, which attracted the amity of the officers and the esteem of the army, and which assimilated him in my eyes to the noblest, most generous and most eminent men I know. If he had desired another estate, another genre of establishment, I was, fortunately, rich enough to give it to him. He is here by choice.

As it is difficult for me to live for long without occupation; or, rather, I cannot do without contracting, from time to time, a few more or less lively tastes in order to distract myself from living, I have returned to botany, once my most pleasant study. I have recommended my destroyed herbaria and renewed my acquaintance with the rich families of vegetables, to which long neglect had rendered me almost a stranger. Is there any need to tell you what inexpressible joys those happy memories procure me, to which so many delights are linked, so many charming harmonies: the enchanting privilege of the pure and simple pleasures of adolescence, not one of which can be awakened without them all coming to attach themselves to it, and to embellish it further.

Can I rediscover, for example, the pretty forget-me-not, so beloved by Rousseau, without recalling that, in your first excursion in our countryside, we loved to collect it on the cool and shady slope of that little wood, in memory of a writer whose works we adored? The columbine is not rare in the light and sandy soils of the edges of the forests, but Lucile, whom I still mourn, loved it above all flowers. An eglantine struck by the burning rays of the midday sun or hanging from a branch broken by a storm represents the one that Fanny had given me, which desiccated and paled over my heart. A clump of sorb-trees reminds me of those that I rounded out into an arbor in Victoire's passage, and I shall never see, O prettiest of trees, your little winged leaves, so fine and light, and your large corymbs of white flowers or crimson fruits without feeling my lips and my blood burn again with the first amorous kiss that I received under your shade!

18 April

I occupy the last room in the right wing of the château, the one that overlooks the circular pond where we navigated so much in our childhood.

There is no luxury in my furniture save for two portraits—my father's and yours—a pianoforte and a few books. I have made great economies, particularly in the last genre, for I am convinced that apart from a very small number, books are only good for idlers and certain lazy minds that cannot think without a vehicle. I'll go further; the Bible is the only absolutely indispensable body of work that I know, and it seems to me that, in giving it to humans, God has supplied all the needs of their intelligence. Thus, I have conserved the usage of it by reading a chapter every evening in accordance with the situation of my heart. Just now, for example, the imagination enchanted by a thousand pastoral reveries that have lulled me in the course of my walk, my thoughts went astray under the tents of the patriarchs or among the reapers of Bethlehem, and I witnessed in idea the wedding of Ruth.

I have toned down somewhat my enthusiasm for Ossian, and even for Shakespeare. In general I have freed myself as much as I can from the influence of romantic sentiments, but without seeking a genre of illusions a thousand times more miserable in the superb vanities of philosophy that are known as positive knowledge, as if there were anything positive on earth, and as if the little that God permits us to see in his works were anything other than fodder delivered to the prideful ignorance of fallen humankind.

I cannot do without a few botanical primers, but as the collection of my species will never be very considerable, I now hold to the most ancient and simple guides. I find that the men of times past had much more beautiful and touching ideas about nature than us, and that the religious and intellectual manner of penetrating its mysteries that distinguishes our old writers is worth more than the sterile advantages that we draw from the perfection of analyses. The men of enlightened centuries resemble children who break their toys in order to discover the secret of their construction; what remains of the broken instrument but a steel spring, a fragment of glass and a little bell? As for the marvel, that has gone.

21 April

Renew myself, I said the other day! Alas, if I could only distract myself . . . or forget myself! I don't desire, and don't hope for happiness, but a durable and profound repose, a liberty without reserve. I've repeated to you frequently that I don't hate life for the things that one finds in it, which in general, attach me and retain me. I understand its illusions, and I seek them willingly. I hate life such as men have made it, like a social duty that subjugates my independence to recognized interests and conventions established without me. I hate it, like everything that is not spontaneous in the will of a sensitive, strong and intelligent creature that God has deigned to form in his image. Agree that it's frightful to think that living is not a free action, and that the soul is condemned in advance to existence—what am I saying? to immortality—without having consented to it.

The mental disposition into which I have fallen for several days has, however, procured me a pleasant emotion, an emotion all the more agreeable because it is not very familiar to me. My mother, alarmed by my melancholy, has made some effort to penetrate the reason for it and to oppose consolations and hopes to my heartache. I shivered with an involuntary joy in thinking that she loved me enough to feel sorry for me, and then I regretted bitterly having given her a subject of chagrin so ill-founded, for I would have difficulty explaining to myself what she calls my dolor. Would you believe that she has supposed that amour . . . ?

Amour! Miserable childish illusions, the frivolity of which I have recognized so many times! Amour! Oh, doubtless, I love women in their brilliant harmonies with nature, as one of the most enchanting works and one of the most seductive ornaments of creation; I love them like flowers, as I would love animate and thinking flowers that would have, in the development of their ideas and their sentiments, the grace and delicacy of roses. There are some that I distinguish more, and then I experience the need to occupy their mind or to interest their heart. If one of their gazes falls upon me, if it encounters mine, I feel, as before, my heart beating more rapidly, my eyes becoming troubled, by blood turning in my bosom or rising to my cheeks, my nerves shaken by I know not what vague and sweet mixture of shame and pleasure, anxiety and tenderness. In fact, I remember the time . . .

What man has not been prey in his turn to the errors of frivolous, credulous, unoccupied adolescence? The friction of a dress or a shawl that brushed me in passing, the movement of a feather floating over a woman's hair, the play of light scintillating on the gemstones of her comb or her clasp, the melody of an angelic voice that their air brings from afar through all the noises, the vibration of which resonates for a long time in your ear—the slightest thing suffices then to absorb all your thought, to suspend all your existence. There are instants, hours, entire days when you are distracted in spite of yourself by a charming image that appeals to you, which pursues you, which you avoid in vain, which you rediscover everywhere, the ideal perfection of which is composed of features that belong to a thousand different women, or, at the most, to an unknown woman whom you will never see. Why is it necessary to have lived for years, my dear Édouard, in order to sense the emptiness of those chimeras?

Oh my friend, be sure that there are in the world we inhabit souls punished for an ancient sin, perhaps punished in anticipation of an indispensable sin to come, souls of expiation who bear for a generation all the weight of God's vengeance, and who are condemned to the amour of the impossible, as if the supreme power, which cannot without contravening its own edict take away from them infinity in eternity, wanted to give them emptiness in the present; who have the deplorable faculty of conceiving and embracing in imagination lusts before which all earthly women are degraded and annihilated, whereas what I now understand to be love does not belong to the time and space in which my life is enclosed.

There is in me a premature appetite for a future happiness that has nothing terrestrial, nothing limited, which might one day fill the immense void of my heart and fulfill all the ambition of my desires. Great gods, what do you expect me to ask of the woman who would consent to love me? What could I expect of her, of the engagement of two beings so feeble, so transient, who only appreciate by means the least of their faculties the moment that they enjoy, and who can only respond to the most immediate of their emotions, who would be astonished by themselves every day, if every day they became their future selves? A transaction, a lease of a few years or a few months, which an unexpected circumstance, a jealousy, a chagrin or an hour of modified absence, which is altered by duration and dissolved by death, and which a mistake, a caprice or a malady might change into an aversion?

No, no . . .

Nothing finite, nothing perishable can be sufficient for the need to love that torments me. It is necessary that I wear away, you see, it is necessary that I dispose of, all the bonds that attach me to temporary affections in order to take possession of them again in the assured future life for which my life is the fatiguing preparation. In order to enjoy fully what I love and what I find in the happiness of loving and being loved I need the security of an entire eternity, and can even eternity ever be too long for love?

The love of a woman, of a mortal woman . . . what do you understand by that? A smile full of charm, the sound of a voice that disturbs and upsets the senses, the clasp of a hot hand that burns yours . . . I know that. But that hand and that heart will turn to dust, and the dust of my extinct heart will not be confounded with it, and what will live after me will remain forever foreign to the soul that has replaced mine momentarily! That isn't possible, and the amour of which we speak, Édouard, is only an invention of our vanity. Amour is not an earthly thing! It is the first conquest of the resuscitated man. Let me depart.

23 April

I was told a few days ago that we would be rendering a visit yesterday evening to Mademoiselle de Valency, the sole offspring of that illustrious family and the proprietor of the neighboring château. I had lost sight of that young person, who is no more than twenty, and who was still a child when I emigrated, but I conserved respectfully the memory of her aunt, the prioress, Madame Adélaïde, a woman of sage intelligence and high virtue, whose lessons my most tender youth appreciated, and to whom I am perhaps indebted for the foundation of piety that has, if not preserved me from many errors, at least consoled me in many disasters. I had not learned without joy that Heaven had protected her existence in the midst of the catastrophic events that had taken away all her relatives.

Eudoxie de Valency is tall and shapely in stature; her bearing is full of majesty, but a majesty without affectation. Her features have a remarkable but fixed expression, which does not appear to be devoid of study. A smile, that amiable indication of self-satisfaction, sometimes pauses on her lips, but almost invariably, nothing figures there but disdain. I searched fruitlessly and waited in vain for a movement, a gesture or an inflection in her conversation that would reveal some heartfelt thought. Even her abandon is so carefully negligent; there is so much measure in her liberty and so much circumspection in her frankness, that on seeing her you would experience the painful sentiment that is inspired by those overly exact imitations of nature that are not natural, and which are shocking by virtue of resembling it.

You do not have to wonder; her terms are chosen, her elocution ornamental and her slightest speeches brilliant with citations and quips. She knows three languages and writes poetry. When we entered, she seemed to be meditating profoundly some passage in a book open on her lectern, and on approaching I recognized the book as one of the masterpieces of our modern metaphysics—masterpieces, indeed, of the total aridity of the heart allied with all the presumption of the mind. I would immediately have given a good part of my life to be persuaded that there is no woman who reads Condillac,[1] as I

---

1 Étienne Bonnot de Condillac (1714-1780), author of *Essai sur l'origine des connaissances humaines* (1746) and other pioneering exercises in epistemology and the theory of mind influenced by the English philosopher John Locke; he was a friend of Denis Diderot and Jean-Jacques Rousseau. Nodier disapproved of his insistence that all knowledge originates in sensation.

am convinced that there is no woman who understands him, and I believe that it requires no more than that annoyance to make me quarrel irrevocably with the entire sex.

My mother remarked that Mademoiselle de Valency had changed apartment—but you will never guess the reason! Can you imagine that at the extremity of the English garden overlooked by her drawing room and dressing-room there is a waterfall, veritably not very noisy, but the dull murmur of which has something importunate. On the edge of the pond that it forms, and which then divides into little streams, sad weeping willows have been planted, and Madame de Valency has an aversion to that tree. Finally, the exposure of that entire lodgment is to the rising sun, whose first rays come every morning, in spite of all obstacles, to offend her eyelids, still charged with sleep.

I leave you to imagine that kind of impression was left on me by a woman who does not like the rising sun, nor the foliage of weeping willows, nor the sound of distant waters, and who also reads Condillac, or wants to pass for reading him.

Madame Adélaïde is confined to bed by a malady of languor that is undermining and consuming her life, and will perhaps soon steal from the world that saint's examples. I obtained an introduction to her bedroom, or, rather, into the modest cell that she has been given in the château. She was lying down but dressed, her hand deployed over her breast. A black wooden crucifix rose above her head. Close to her there was a small table covered with pious books for her own usage and surmounted by a few semi-desiccated blessed branches, which crossed over against the wall. At the noise I made as I entered, she turned toward me and immediately smiled.

"Is that you, my dear Gaston?" she said. "At my age, and after such a long absence, could I have hoped to see you again? God be praised for this new favor he has granted me? But do you believe that it is without a reason that his Providence has saved you from so many dangers? You promised to be good, generous in your penchants and moderate in your passions, and the example of good people is a treasure for the century."

I was moved to tears. Her pallor, her debility and the weakness of her voice tormented me with the idea of another absence, an imminent and eternal separation. I saw that she was striving to seem better in order to cause me less pain. I withdrew, very emotional.

I confess to you that Mademoiselle de Valency does not gain from being seen so close to such a woman. However, the judgment that I formed of the young Eudoxie after a quarter of an hour of vague conversation and insignificant rapports in a milieu of the embarrassing decorum and constraint of a first visit might well be the effect of an ill-founded prejudice. I am so ready to allow myself to be surprised by a few appearances of ridiculous sympathy or unjust antipathy; but I speak to you as I think, and people can say what they like. Eudoxie is certainly very good; I admit that she is perfectly beautiful; I doubt that one can have as much intelligence; I like to believe, with everyone else, that it is difficult to practice virtue in a more exact and more irreproachable manner—but it is a kind of intelligence and a sort of beauty that you will permit me never to love.

29 April

There are people whom the mania to appear grand causes to descend to pettiness in which it would be difficult to believe if they did not force you to witness them every day. For myself, that causes me an indignation so violent that I am not the master of containing it, and it is absolutely necessary for me to explode when something similar falls under my eyes.

My father honored one of his ancestors in particular, a simple man of law toward the end of the sixteenth century, but a writer of uncommon knowledge and erudition, who distinguished himself by very precious works on jurisprudence and the sages of remote times, and who clarified with an exquisite sagacity important but confused texts whose interpretation the most skillful had not dared to attempt. It is to be remarked, in passing, that it is to that great man that our family owes its illustriousness, and that my nobility dates from him—which does not prove that it comes from a remote era, but does prove that it does not come from an unworthy source, and that is what would be a veritable misfortune.

Hazard took me yesterday to a drawing room of the château that I had previously seen covered in family portraits, and where I recognized all the august images of my mother's ancestors, with their armories, their decorations and their ermines; but I searched in vain for what interested me the most in that genealogical decoration: the image of the respectable scholar whose vast and useful works had founded my fortune, and endowed my cradle with the heritage of a name dear to society. The memory of that painting was all the more present to me because my father had, as I said, a singular veneration for it, and always showed it preferentially to strangers whose visits we received. I could have marked with a finger the place where I had seen it, but it is decidedly empty, and I leave you to divine the cause of the suppression. I blush to inform you of it, so ridiculous and ungrateful do I find it.

When I returned to my mother's apartment I asked about the motives for such a strange change; she replied to me, alas, as I had expected, but I insisted, with a respectful firmness, that the portrait be replaced.

✳

This morning Eudoxie returned the visit that we had recently made to her. She was accompanied by a gentleman of the vicinity named Ferréol de Montbreuse. I have not yet mentioned Ferréol de Montbreuse, although everyone here talks about him. He is a man thirty-six years old at the most, but whose calm politeness, inalterable gravity and recognized severity of mores and principles would do honor to a more advanced age. I had been told about his frequentation as the most real advantage of my sojourn in Touraine, but I have not sought him out. I hold perfection in singular esteem, but it does not have for me the attraction that takes possession of the heart, which my heart needs to experience, for it does not attach itself to anything by ordinary bonds, and when it does not sense that it loves.

You are the only friend that I have received from society—nature had given me another—the only one, I say, who has reduced me to suffering and pardoning the desolating and inimitable fault of perfection; but yours has something so natural, so involuntary and so unconscious, it is so inseparable from you, that one can become accustomed to it without perceiving it, and one only arrives at suspecting it when one no longer has the liberty of indifference or the strength to forget it.

Whatever the merit of Monsieur de Montbreuse might be, it is said that he had had the good fortune of occupying for a moment the noble thoughts of Eudoxie, and two such solemn friends were worthy of being close. The dilapidation of their fortunes had impeded that establishment. It is an unfortunate thing that at the end of a revolution, families that have run the same risks, neighbors, relatives and friends struck by the same misfortune, do not imitate navigators cast by a tempest on to a desert island and do not put everything they possess in common. Did I need to remain so rich?

The news of the almost complete recovery of Madame the Prioress caused me a joy so great that I was unable to put off until tomorrow going to testify it to her. I escorted Mademoiselle de Valency back to the château with an urgency that she probably attributed to other motives.

Her aunt was sitting in a large armchair, at a place on the terrace where the rays of the sun, feebly balanced between a few tufts of lilac, spread an agreeable warmth. She wanted to get up as I approached, but I hastened to go to her in order to prevent her from doing so. We conversed gaily and for a long time about a thousand different things. She made me promise to recount my travels to her and to talk to her about my friends. I've already named you. For her part, she recommended me, with some authority, to cultivate the acquaintance of Monsieur de Montbreuse, in whom she only finds fault with an austerity a trifle rigorous for his age and his estate.

Finally, it was already late and we were still chatting, and I only perceived by the freshness of the evening air that it was time for her to go back in. She leaned on my arm on one side and on the other on the shoulder of a little girl whom she loves dearly and whose praises she never ceased repeating. She calls her a friend, her benefactress, and her angelic savior, in recognition of a few cares that she received from her during her illness, and the child is, in fact, an angel. I cannot remember having seen anything so gracious and as gentle as her features, nothing that reposes the heart more agreeably. It is one of those ravishing ensembles of harmony that are a pleasure to behold.

Do you have some idea of that? Have you never encountered those celestial faces in which can be read in advance so much peace and happiness, the supernatural expression of which fascinates the soul? I would give a great deal for you to be able to see this one.

One charming circumstance: my gaze chanced to encounter that of the angel. Then, if you had seen her beautiful eyes lowered, her long lashes timidly shading her eyelid and her complexion colored with a bright and sudden gleam! The angel blushed, and she was no longer anything but mortal, but an adorable mortal—and I was about to say adored. What folly!

This is what is said about her. She is a poor orphan whose parents abandoned her without anyone knowing the cause. Eight or ten years ago they quit the village where they lived on their labor, in order to go no one knows where. Some people even say that they finished rather miserably, but I'm talking about people who are probably poorly-informed. What is certain is that Madame the Prioress took in little Adèle, whose godmother she was, and gave her an education of sorts.

If my Adèle interests you, I will tell you more another time, although it is fundamentally only a matter of Mademoiselle de Valency's chambermaid, for I forgot to say that it is by that entitlement that Adèle lives at the château.

As I had gone in Mademoiselle de Valency's carriage, I returned on foot through the wood, which is magnificent in full vegetation. The evening was delectably serene, the sunset very pure and luminous. Enchanting illusions, which succeeded one another in my mind like the ideas of a beautiful dream, distracted my senses in the mildest fog. I don't know now why I was so happy, for nothing has changed since then in my estate, and yet . . . how difficult human beings are to explain!

The wellbeing that I savor here proves, at least, that I was not mistaken when I wrote to you that the peace of the countryside is marvelously suited to my present situation, and that I am putting all my happiness into letting my days go by obscurely here. You can see that the romantic turn of my mind and the exaltation of my ideas stem from causes quite independent of the mad passions of youth, and that is what you have never wanted to understand. I have a consciousness of myself that rarely deceives me.

※

Yesterday evening, as I finished writing, Latour entered my room with an anxious, and even slightly fearful, expression. He sat down to one side and maintained a bleak silence for some time, and then started muttering something between his teeth.

"What's the matter, my poor Latour?" I said to him. "You seem very occupied!"

"Let no one ever call me Latour, alias Coeur-de-Roi," he replied, "if it isn't Maugis, the infamous, execrable Maugis. Monsieur will remember that adventurer who presented himself as a general with fake powers, and made use of them, the coward, to deliver a considerable detachment of ours to the enemy—and who unfortunately avoided, by a prompt flight, the punishment he merited?"

"I've heard mention of that wretch, and I believe, like you, Latour, that he did indeed call himself Maugis,[1] either with the intention of disguising his veritable name or to conform with the rather bizarre practice of our officers; but what connection . . . ?"

"What connection!" he cried. "That infernal Maugis, whom I'd recognize among a thousand, and could paint at need, is none other than the honest Ferréol de Montbreuse, whom you saw yesterday, and at the peril of a million deaths I'd affirm that there is no other Maugis. Rage and malediction! It's a shame for Providence to see people like that enjoying the air and the sunlight!"

---

1 Maugis is the name of an enchanter and thief featured in several Medieval *chansons de geste*, including the well-known *Les Quatre fils Aymon*. It would have been an odd choice as a *nom de guerre* for one of the officers of the royalist army during the Vendéan insurrection.

I had great difficulty appeasing Latour's anger and making him understand that his suspicions could not be well-founded. He went out more astonished by my incredulity than satisfied by my arguments.

I had reserved to sustain today a more difficult discussion, a discussion for which what I wrote to you a few days ago might, however, have prepared you better than I was myself. My mother had asked me to go to her apartment in order to discuss serious things—very serious, in fact. It was a matter of perpetuating my name and making it illustrious by noble alliances. You understand correctly—making the name of my father illustrious!

I ought to know, I was told, that the nobility of my family on the paternal side did not respond entirely to the splendor of my fortune; and if fortune has some advantage, is it not above all that of favoring honorable establishments that raise the splendor of our own titles and transmit them more gloriously to our children? I was then made to sense modestly that it was to those sage combinations of convention that I owed my mother. I had believed that I only owed her to amour and nature.

What can I tell you? The Valencys are less rich than I am, Eudoxie is less rich than I am, but she is noble, like my mother, to whom her hand has the honor of belonging. You can guess the rest.

All that had struck me with a surprise so vivid and so dolorous that I was searching for an idea for a long time and I took even longer finding an expression. What I recall rather imperfectly of the confused words that must have escaped me in that instant of trouble and dejection is that they had for a goal, I think, soliciting a few months of delay that I wanted to give to reflection, and I doubtless added that nothing would be obtained from me otherwise, in a manner to lift all suspicion in that regard, for my mother went out launching an even more severe gaze than usual at me. It is, however, probable that she did not hope to gain anything by doing violence to my heart, since she came to accede to my request before I had found the strength to repeat it. In any case, she awaits my resolution in six weeks, and it is scarcely to be supposed that I will change it between now and then.

That is to tell you that my resolution was made at the same moment, and that it is invariable, like the principles that have directed my life thus far. No, I would not traffic my happiness, and I am certain that Eudoxie would not make me happy. I shall not buy with my repose my liberty and the delectable uncertainty of my hopes the ridiculous honor of associating my name with that of a woman I can never love. If I attach some price to my fortune and the position I hold in society, it is above all because of the independence that it gives me and the immense latitude that it leaves to my choice, for in the end . . . why should I not say it? I would a hundred times rather contract a misalliance than suffer that anyone should contract a misalliance for me. I am too proud to consent to augment the sum of my personal value by a cowardly borrowing, and to give that purchase on me to the vanity of a woman.

Rather than submit to that humiliation I would even marry Adèle! Truly, I believe so!

5 May

There are certain days, days that go by too quickly, that the hazard that Providence reserves for us when our heart, too fatigued by chagrin, needs, in order not to yield, to recover the temper of wellbeing, which alone can compensate for an eternity of abandon and misery. Yes, I shall say it: let this day be returned to me, let it recommence with all its charms and all its illusions, let it be permitted to me to live it like the first time, without anything deflecting my thought, to savor the pleasures with the same confidence, with the same abandon, and to extract the same delights again—and then let the void commence!

Near the Château de Valency, I had remarked in the wood a cool and enchanting site where pretty paths ended departing from each village, and which were distributed thereafter in the distance of the plain. That verdant vestibule of sorts, agreeably shaded by a broad vault of foliage, and carpeted by flowery grass from which the most delightful odors are exhaled, offers natural little seats on all sides as comfortable as if art had fashioned them. A short distance away, shining through the branches, one sees the polished surface of a pond of the clearest water, which encloses the wood in its detours like a vast crystal bowl, and which attracts to its banks an innumerable host of birds.

It was there that I was sitting, scrupulously counting the stamens of a dubious flower, when the sound of a light footstep and the rustle of a woman's dress turned my attention to another object. The woman was Adèle, and although there was nothing astonishing in seeing her there, I had expected, I don't know how, to encounter her.

Although Adèle is, what is more, nothing to me but an interesting but almost unknown young woman, the palpitations of my heart were multiplied violently. I shivered; I trembled; a variegated cloud of several different colors troubled my senses; a vague weakness ran through my limbs and slowed me down. Meanwhile, I had arrived close to Adèle without looking at her, or at least without seeing her, and I had offered her my arm without asking her where she was going.

When the veil that obscured my eyelids had begun to clear, to the point of allowing me to observe Adèle's features and physiognomy distinctly, I remarked that she was astonished by my proposition, and, to tell you the truth, I was also astonished that I had made it; but I repeated it in a voice that was doubtless more assured.

After a few moments of a hesitation full of grace, Adèle appeared to be yielding to an order rather than deferring to a plea, in placing her hand lightly on my arm. Then I fixed that hand forcefully, drawing tightly to my bosom the arm on which she was engaged, and I started walking precipitately in the direction that Adèle seemed to be following.

When my agitation, half-calmed, left some liberty to my mind, I perceived that Adèle's agitation was scarcely less evident than mine, not by means of her gaze, which I was still avoiding, but by the quivering of her fingers, which my right hand had seized, by virtue of I know not what involuntary movement, and was holding deployed against my heart. Nothing was more appropriate to distract both of us from that state of emotion than the question, so cold and so natural, that I had initially omitted, and I thought that a conversation necessarily less passionate and less stormy than our silence would complete rendering us a little tranquility. I therefore asked Adèle where she was going, and Adèle replied to me, with a delicate smile devoid of malignity, that it was a great secret.

That mystery did not cause me any anxiety. I had already forgotten it when the last sound of Adèle's words had not finished agitating the air, and had not reached as far as me. I searched my imagination, as you can well believe, for some new diversion that might deceive her and deceive me with regard to what I was experiencing. I sensed simultaneously the desire and the dread of being divined. I was so happy to be beside her, and so impatient to be alone in order to think about everything there was to say to her.

After a few minutes of silence, I repeated my question, for want of anything better. This time Adèle consented to tell me that she was taking to a neighboring hamlet the petty aid that the good Prioress sent there every day to an ill family. I should have suspected it, but I was so occupied with other things.

I shall pass rapidly this evening over that journey of an hour, a charming hour that ought to have been a century and might have been only a minute. I shall neglect the details because I would lose everything in describing them; because they would be devoid of warmth under my pen and they are burning in my heart; because there is in all this a flower of sensuality that escapes the imperfect faculties that humans have received in order to express and comprehend; because I believe that would be limiting my happiness by limiting the wave of my memories; and because, in this narrative where everything relates to Adèle, there are nevertheless circumstances that are not Adèle, and it is firmly decided that Adèle will have all my thoughts today . . . all the thoughts of my life.

6 May

Decorum prescribes that I ought at least to see Eudoxie. My heart draws me toward her aunt. I have seen them. I have also seen Adèle. What am I saying, alas? I have only seen Adèle.

Yes, my Édouard, it would be superfluous, it would be unworthy of me to dissimulate from you the sentiment that dominates me, which fills and absorbs my existence. Inferno and paradise! Who would have thought that at twenty-eight, a very simple young woman, very good and almost devoid of splendor, would subjugate me, as in the time of the weakness and ignorance of my heart? Who could express what I am feeling of ecstasy and delirium merely at the memory of seeing her, merely at the sound of her name? It already requires no more than that. I was drifting in such a pure atmosphere of wellbeing, my breast was lifted by a joy so perfect and so new . . . for everything has become new for this soul that is awakening once again from the debris of my life to love and to suffer . . .

To suffer . . . I know how such a passion can cause shame and woe to fall upon me. I am not blind to this strange aberration of my imagination, or, rather, to the pitiless contrariety of my fortune that is pushing me toward what I ought to flee, and plunging me all the more deeply into the abyss of my resolutions because its menacing obscurity leaves me less hope of returning. I curse the folly of my projects, the incredible weakness of my reason, which the slightest illusion dazzles, over which the slightest caprice triumphs; I am indignant at myself, and yet I am abandoning myself to the penchant that is drawing me without trying to resist it.

There is more. If I knew a power that might be capable of liberating me conclusively, of effacing from my bosom even the trace of a memory, I would not have the strength to invoke it. Everything that other men would find in it of the vile and the hateful would be precisely what would attach me to it by knots difficult to break, and I need to tell you that this sentiment has acquired such authority in my heart that the advice and pleas of amity would only redouble its prevalence.

Édouard, my dear Édouard, you in whom Heaven has given me a brother, a guide and a protector in the midst of the storms of youth, you who have been for such a long time the light of my intelligence and the brake of my passions, don't abandon me in this state of perplexity.

It's not for you that I've said that.

Oh my friend, what will result from the violence of so many contrary thoughts, which bring me a new torment every minute? Who can enable me to triumph over the image that follows me everywhere? What will banish her from my memory, which she occupies without division with her large dark eyes, so noble and so touching, her lips, so voluptuously beautiful, the air of amour and bounty that floats over her face, and her slightly slow speech, the frank melody of which penetrates me?

8 May

What will prevent me from searching elsewhere for independence and savoring, in a profound forgetfulness, under some shelter impenetrable to all the research of men, the happiness that society refuses me? What am I doing here, and who would perceive my absence in this whirlwind of cold strangers continually distracted by the interests of their fortune and their pride? Have I not fulfilled the duties to my fatherland that my name prescribed? Does the limit of my obligations extend beyond the sacrifice of my life, risked a hundred times in battles? I shall go away, for I have thought of it often. I shall oppose to all their decorum and all the puerile vanities of their etiquette the silence and obscurity of my own etiquette.

An epoch arrives in which the soul finally needs to take possession of itself and to collect itself in imposing meditations, far from the chaos of social affairs—very far—on the peak of a mountain that rips the clouds and commands immense plains and shoreless seas. It seems to me that the creator, in producing his universe so accomplished in beauty, in casting such a marvelous magnificence over the works of his hands and making their riches contrast in such a humiliating manner with the misery of our sentiments, wanted to reveal to us by means of a sensible object of comparison the emptiness of all the pleasures that place us outside of him and all the judgments that we found on the vain opinion of the multitude. I sometimes transport myself in idea to that day when, still young but already outlawed, I attained for the first time the high summits of the Jura.

When you have followed over the highest of its plateaux the sinuosities of a severe and savage route that is prolonged over the flanks of the Dôle; when, at the extremity of that taciturn promenade, where you are accompanied, at the most, by the cry of an old eagle frightened for its chicks, which is astonished to hear beneath its crags the long-forgotten sound of a human voice, when it seems that the earth is about to lack beneath your feet and that with your extended arm you are about to touch the solid azure of the firmament . . . at that place, a spectacle is suddenly manifest so devoid of vulgarity that it enables you to comprehend at the same instant the necessity of a divine will in the mystery of creation. You believe that the spirit of the earth is lifting the curtain that separates from a magical world this world of mud and stone, and that it is introducing you into a region of miracles. I would like to describe that for you, but with what colors?

Can you imagine that at the extremity of the woods of Lavatay there is, on the last crest of the mountain, a poor house that appears from a distance to be lost in the backcloth of the clouds, and which is known as "the chalet of the sickles" because the paths that once descended from it over the escarpment of the abyss curbed back on themselves like a reaper's sickle. Today, when slavery and toil have made sumptuous roads of them for the corrupting exchanges of commerce and the invasions of war, the sickles develop in a less menacing manner in the depths of the precipice, and the chamois, surprised that a servile hand has dared to embellish its dwelling, no longer hazards itself in those human ways. It remains motionless at the most salient corner of a steeply-carved rock and sadly contemplates the sky, the sole desert that civilization has left it.

All the parts of the scene that present themselves together to your gaze, preoccupy your thoughts so powerfully at first that it takes you a long time to put your sensations in order and to distinguish the details: at your feet, where the Jura and France finish, a lake that, in its immensity, presents the aspect of a sea; on its shores, the romantic vistas of the land of Vaux, the agrarian landscapes of the Valais and the harsh solitudes of the Savoy; on your horizon, a chain equally vast, that of the Alps, the innumerable cupolas of which are grouped over the entire demi-circumference of the sky, diverse in form, character, physiognomy and colors, but all affecting in the fires of the sun the gleam of various metals. Some are as resplendent as polished silver, others, in accordance with the effect of the shadows projected over their contours, as dull as vulgar lead or as brilliant as burnished steel, with blue and violet reflections; some are so dazzling, when the light of the setting sun inundates them entirely, that one might take them for masses of iron whitening in a furnace.

That day, for example, the sun set with so much magnificence and in a sky so pure! The vapors of the lake, aspired by the dusk, suspended in its radiance, were balanced over the waters like a light crepe tinted the softest pink, rising gradually from the feet of the traveler all the way to the summit of the mountains, and deploying before him, on the horizon, a flaming curtain that spread the magic of its light over all the objects; and then, having become denser and more obscure, finally crowned the whole of the magnificent spectacle with a crimson and gold awning, the splendor of which only paled with the rising of the nocturnal stars.

And those immense, inhabited mountains, unknown for the most part, do not hide a place of refuge to which I can take with me, to hide from insolent curiosity and hypocritical censure the secret of my happiness and my life? I shall not be the master of relegating and exiling my future there? I shall die bound by the odious chain that they have imposed on me without making an effort to break it? Édouard, let no one flatter themselves as to that. I would rather break all chains at once.

Take pity on my misfortune!

✳

I have not told you that the conversation of the other day had touched on the question of misalliances, with regard to that fool de Sabligny, who had just ended his romantic career by marrying a dancer. I seized that text with a warmth and abundance of ideas for which I was indebted more to certain circumstances of my particular situation than to the richness of the subject.

I sustained that there was nothing unforgivable or anti-social, in the full force of the word, but moral misalliances, and that they were extremely difficult, because it is rare that beautiful souls do not accost their counterparts, as Shakespeare says, or that they are abused for long enough by exterior impostures to arrive at the moment of forming such a solemn bond without having had the good fortune of being undeceived; that moreover, what is called misalliance, in the general acceptance of the word, which relates solely to differences in status, can only shock the most absurd and the most revolting of prejudices, which attribute to a determinate class, to an infinitely circumscribed order of citizens, special—or, to put it better, exclusive—faculties; that, as I did not know anyone who would push temerity to the point of advancing that virtue is proved by titles or acquired by privileges, I could not see why one should forbid a sensitive and delicate man the right to seek anywhere that virtue is found a happiness that virtue alone can provide; that it was a atrocity, by dint of being ridiculous, to condemn an interesting individual endowed with all the qualities and all the graces, to the despair of never belonging to the beloved object because that unfortunate, heaped with the most precious advantages of nature and education, is deprived by hazard of an advantage that only depends on hazard and has no connection with any others, even in society; that if great talents imprint those who are ornamented thereby with an incontestable character of nobility in the eyes of the century and posterity, the private exercise of the duties most difficult to practice of religion and morality, a title less ostentatious in the favor of society, is no less commendable to the esteem and respect of good minds; and that, in consequence, I would never permit myself to criticize an alliance of the kind under discussion if I were able to recognize therein the fortunate harmony of mores and characters that is the sole reliable gauge of the happiness of households and the prosperity of families.

It is probable that those arguments, the weak side of which I am well aware, appeared totally unworthy of response to Monsieur de Montbreuse, for he contented himself with looking at me severely without speaking to me, and I noticed that he turned then toward Eudoxie, with a knowing expression pierced by I know not what mixture of bitterness and scorn.

Eudoxie herself, whose ideas I had shocked too overtly, did not seem to take sufficient account of my arguments to deign to refute them in an orderly manner; she scarcely let escape a few trite commonplaces to which the grace of her elocution and the finesse or her irony lent no more charm than solidity.

Adèle listened to me with emotion, for her cheeks were very animated, and I tried in vain to meet her eyes.

Madame Adélaïde had smiled at first, and then her physiognomy had taken on a graver character, and, I tremble to think, an expression sadder than usual. She reacted mildly to my speech, reproaching me in an affectionate manner for the ardor that I brought to the discussion and the enthusiasm with which I embraced the most extraordinary, and often the most catastrophic, ideas. She complained of the facility that men of this generation have in seizing and propagating sophisms, the consequences of which they did not appreciate and which tend to denature successively all the true relationships of things.

While granting that there were nobly felt verities in what I had just said, she recommended me to reflect on the origin and effects of those moral conventions, so respectable, moreover, by virtue of the authority they had exercised over our ancestors, and the almost religious consideration that they had received from the centuries, the definitive judgment of which is, in the final analysis, all of social reason. She added, in a tone of modest resignation, and not of imperious conviction, that the duty of a good citizen is to submit to established institutions without argument, and that, since the imperfection of human beings renders them essential tributaries of certain errors sanctioned by necessity or by time, the interest of the human species prescribes to sage and righteous hearts the duty of adapting their reason to common deference.

It is possible that that is true. But how can I cede the point, while I recognize the weakness of demarcation that the hazard of birth has traced between a few families and the great family of human beings; that circumstance so foreign to my will, which has submitted me to a particular order of habits and obligations; which has restricted, compressed and limited the independence of my heart; which has forbidden me the simplest and happiest of affections; which separates me from Adèle and happiness?

Separated! Barbaric prejudice, I submit you to the indignation of strong and sensitive souls!

Separated! Me, who would traverse the globe for a kiss from her lips!

Separated! Come, come to Gaston's heart, poor orphan whom men reject! Come with confidence; and I swear by the innocence and candor of your angelic soul that all the powers of Hell will not succeed in separating us!

❋

Never have I been more assiduous in the little wood than the last few days, and never has my herbarium increased so slowly. That greatly astonishes Latour, who takes the same interest in my herbarium as in all my pleasures, but to whom I only confide them by exception. That will not astonish you, who will recall quite distinctly that Adèle passes through the little wood every day at a certain hour, and who does not believe me capable of pleasing myself anywhere else than in the place where I expect to find her. You have also remarked that my letter is at a considerable distance from the previous one, and you have doubtless concluded therefrom that only the abundance of sensations and events could have distracted me for several days from the most pleasurable of my occupations.

All that is in conformity with the truth, my dear Édouard, and yet there is nothing new in my life to tell you, for my amour is not new for you and all my life is therein.

I have only given you imperfect information on Adèle's origin, collected from vague popular rumor. Madame Adélaïde had told me a little more, but not enough to satisfy my curiosity, which I feared, in any case, to reveal too overtly. Finally, the other day, I asked Adèle while I was conducting her from the wood to the hamlet; I sought the information with all the precaution that the broaching of such a delicate question required, and as the story might not be without interest even to people completely indifferent to everything that interests me, I want to enable you to hear it from Adèle's own mouth, as I heard it. Pardon me if, with the simplicity of her words, I have not had the good fortune to conserve their natural grace, and the effusion of sentiment, so facile and so touching, that lent them the most engaging charm. There are things that one despairs of expressing.

"My father," Adèle told me, "was born in Valency, of a family of rich laborers. His name was Jacques Evrard, and as he announced an intelligence and manners above the common, his parents resolved to give him an honorable intelligence that might enable him to enter into a worldly career more brilliant than the one they had followed. His progress responded to all their hopes, but in vain. Multiple misfortunes that happened at that time to my grandfather, several bad years in succession, which exhausted his harvests without replacing them, two fires that successively consumed his barn and his house, and finally the loss of a considerable lawsuit on which everything else depended, changed his fortune into poverty. It was impossible to give any consequence to the projects that had been formed for my father; they were renounced, and, more unfortunate than if he had never emerged from his condition, he enlisted, in despair.

"The regiment that he joined was then garrisoned at Saumur. In that epoch my father was still very young, with a pleasant appearance that was found to be distinguished and a bravery proof against anything; and he combined with that a host of agreeable talents that open to those who posses them access to any society. Esteemed by his colonel and cherished by his officers, he had already been promoted twice with a rapidity unusual in the service, but without it resulting in the slightest complaint from his comrades, who rendered justice sincerely to his advantages. In sum, he had few superiors who were not accustomed to regard him in advance as their equal.

"Hazard enabled a demoiselle of the town, who belonged to a noble family, to remark him on several occasions and, without being aware of her penchant, she made seeing him a habit so pleasant that her heart could no longer do without it. She soon sensed that the need in question was amour, but it was too late to remedy it; at least, she believed so, and my father believed the same. What can I tell you, Monsieur Gaston; that was the error of which I was the fruit.

"My mother could not dissimulate her fault from her parents, but, although they were tender and good, they were too proud to suffer that Jacques Evrard repair it. They contented themselves with taking the necessary precautions to hide my birth from everyone and sent my nurse to a distant village, where I was baptized under the auspices of Madame the Prioress.

"You will divine that the refuge was not given to me without reason, and that my mother was pleased to think that I would grow up under the eyes of a father attentive to all my needs. The term of his service having been complete for some time, he sacrificed without difficulty his hopes of advancement to the pleasure of no longer quitting me and to seeing a resemblance gradually develop in my features to a person who was so dear to him. His tenderness went much further. Would he have been happy if he had not dared to name me his daughter? The nurse who had been given to me, the young and unfortunate victim of a deceptive inclination, passed for my mother and for his wife. Only Madame Adélaïde knew the secret, and bore an ardent compassion to his chagrins.

"It is thus that I was brought up, and my childhood was not without pleasures. The amity of my good godmother, the attentive and truly maternal caress of the nurse, whom I believed had even more sacred titles to my gratitude, and above all the affection of my excellent father, embellished everything. When he returned from the fields, I sometimes felt him bathing me with tears, but I was not troubled by that, thinking that he was weeping with joy.

"Meanwhile, my veritable mother had not withdrawn her heart from us. She wrote frequently to my father, and made him party to her regrets, and even her hopes. It happened that, in the third or fourth year of the revolution, her father left her alone in Saumur in order to go to serve the king in his army in the Vendée, and she desired to profit from the liberty that she enjoyed to see me, for it was already some years since she had lost her mother. It was a fine day for our little family, the one when the unexpected news of that journey reached us.

"Although I was too young to understand things clearly, my father did his best to enable me to comprehend, and we departed, after brief preparations, which he did not think sufficiently abridged. Finally, I was returned to the person from whom I had received the light of day, and I told her about the tenderness that another had stolen from her for such a long time, without taking it away from her entirely. My mother was not afflicted, and saw me with pleasure combining the duties of gratitude with those of nature. I was very happy and much loved; why was it necessary that it lasted for such a short time . . . ?

"My father had conceived a project worthy of such a noble soul, and my mother had approved it. The civil troubles, which had reached their highest point, opened a facile career to men of resolution, and he had not despaired of acquiring, under the eyes of my grandfather such titles to glory that no one would believe it a derogation to approve his marriage. That is why he left us, taking away the hope of soon seeing us again and never quitting us thereafter.

"During his absence, my mother placed me in a pension where she often came to see me. I was taken for an orphan of her relatives and I was treated with the same care as if my veritable relationship with her had been known. When we were alone we talked about my father and wept together for a long time. After a few months I perceived that she had other chagrins that she was not revealing to me, but I limited myself to being afflicted in secret without knowing what they were, and I didn't interrogate her. Finally, one day she stopped coming; the week and the month went by. I asked everyone about her, but no one responded. I sensed that there was no longer any happiness for me and that I was waiting in vain for my mother.

"This is what had happened. My father's hopes had been realized. Actions of the greatest splendor had distinguished him to his generals, and he had just been promoted to the rank of division chief."

"That's true!" I exclaimed, interrupting Adèle at that point in her story. "He was known as Marcus Evrard."

"That was his *nom de guerre*, so I'm told," said Adèle.

"Yes," I continued. "The moment is present to me as if it were yesterday. The general, surrounded by a host of enemies, is near to succumbing; his horse has been killed under him and he has been dragged down in its fall and seriously wounded. He is only opposing futile resistance to the forces that are overwhelming him. Suddenly, Captain Evrard pierces the crowd, which is astonished by his temerity; he snatches the unconscious and bloodied general from the hands disputing the honor of striking him, and returns to our ranks under a hail of bullets that do not reach him. The rank of division chief was, in fact, the price of his courage, but he disappeared a few days later, and the entire army was convinced that he had perished in an ambush."

"I can explain that event," said Adèle, resuming the story of her parents where she had left it. "As soon as he had received before the army the new title under which he ought to be recognized, less proud of that distinction than delighted to be able to make it serve the success of his amour, he ran to throw himself at the feet of my grandfather and confide to him his fault, his repentance and his desires. Imagine the contentment that succeeded in his soul so many anxieties and dolors, by which he had been overwhelmed for several years, when he saw that my mother was accorded to him as a wife. But it was not enough for him to experience; he needed to share it. Saumur was not far from the general quarters of the army. Two days of truce gave him time to escape in the first disguise that came to hand and fly to my mother's arms. The first moment was entirely given to the pleasure of seeing one another again, the second to anxiety and terror. Saumur belongs to the republicans, and my father is an outlaw.

"I have not told you the secret of the somber sadness that I had remarked in my mother the last time she had visited the school. A young gentleman, who had just quit the royal flag under the appearance of I know not what interior service, and who had obtained for my grandfather a rather vague recommendation for his family, had not feared to testify for my mother sentiments that she could only share once. That stranger's passion was all the more importunate because everything prejudiced her against him and particular information armed her in his regard with a mistrust that, even in a perfectly free heart, would never have been compatible with amour. However, her respect for that sacred recommendation, and above all her natural timidity, further augmented by the ascendancy of a wild and impetuous character, had constrained her, in a way, to support his pursuits patiently and dissimulate a part of the antipathy he inspired in her.

"As for him, convinced that he had a beloved rival, he neglected nothing to discover some circumstance that could confirm his suspicions, and hazard served his jealousy in the most catastrophic manner, by guiding him to my mother's house at the very moment when she was receiving the last adieux and the last embraces of her husband.

"Nothing can give an idea of the anger and recklessness of that furious individual at the sight of the man who had stolen from him a heart over which he had promised to reign; he filled the house with his threats and his cries, and did not hesitate to provoke my father, whose patience, already fatigued, could not tolerate that final mark of audacity. They went out, as animated as one another, and went after a short interval to a place appropriate to conclude their argument, while my tearful mother waited for her life or death to be determined by that frightful contest.

"Scarcely were they in presence than my father threw his coat on the ground, inconsiderately uncovering his breast. The noble heart of the Vendéans, the sole decoration, as you know, of that pious army, struck the eyes of his adversary, and the latter, seizing with a ferocious joy the opportunity to doom an enemy without paying with his courage, uttered a clamor, the noise of which brought a dozen brigands, who had doubtless been posted in that place to second him in some other cowardice. 'Arrest him!' he cried. 'He's a royalist officer, an enemy of the republic!' My father fought in vain against the wretches, who surrounded him, pressed him, disarmed him and dragged him to a dungeon.

"Meanwhile, my mother had been counting the hours impatiently without receiving any consoling news, and had delivered herself to all the bitterness of her dread, less terrible than the truth, when a confused tumult that went up in the street, the roll of a drum interrupted at intervals and the dull rumor of an armed troop . . . Suffer, Monsieur Gaston, that I weep freely before you; it would cost me too much to contain my dolor . . .

"She listens, she runs, she runs down the stairs, she traverses the square, she parts the crowd, she arrives at the detachment, looks, utters a scream and falls. 'Angélique, my Angélique, come round! Be worthy of your father and your friend. Live for Adèle and for my memory . . . !' He speaks without being heard. The kisses that he deposits on her eyelids do not revive her. She does not feel his tears.

"Already, they have been separated; the drum falls silent, the escort stops. My mother comes round; her eyes open wildly, scanning everything surrounding her . . . She does not recall very well . . . but the explosion strikes her ears, and sentiment abandons her again. My father is dead!

"Three months had passed after that day when someone came to fetch me from the pension to take me to my mother. She was detained in a house of reclusion and I was led to her in the midst of bayonets. My heart will never forget the sorrow and fear by which it was suddenly penetrated when, through that frightful apparatus, behind those hideous men whose mere gaze made me shiver, lying on a little black straw, I recognized my mother, pale, disfigured, livid and dying.

"I threw myself into her arms, weeping with all my strength, asking her why she had been put in prison and why she was being treated thus. She told me without weeping, but her eyes were red and hollow; she told me what I have just told you, and that I no longer had any resource in the world than my godmother's pity, to whom she had sent everything of which she could dispose, for me, and to whom she had obtained that I would be returned permanently.

"Finally, in an extinct voice which she extracted from her breast with great effort, she said 'My daughter, my poor Adèle, my unique amour, may God enable you to prosper . . . and that one day, the husband that he will give you in his bounty . . . do you hear, my daughter,' she cried raising her head and adopting a grave and lugubrious tone that still resounds in my ears, 'that that husband destined to avenge your parents will satisfy the blood of your murdered father with the blood of Maugis!'"

At that name, I felt all my limbs quiver, and Adèle, who attributed my agitation to another cause, continued her story is these terms:

"I did not want to quit my mother in the state in which I saw her and I remained sitting on her straw until the hour came to close the cells. Then one of the warders pulled me away brutally from that place and told me brusquely that I could not sleep there. My mother was asleep; her complexion was highly-colored and her respiration rapid. I feared troubling her repose by embracing her, and I contented myself with imprinting my lips on a corner of my dress. After that, I was taken to the concierge's lodge, where I was permitted to sleep with his children; but I could not sleep all night because of my chagrin and some noise that was made inside the prison.

"I had scarcely heard the bolts withdrawn and the doors grating on their hinges than I ran to my mother's room. I went in, I searched, I called out, I enquired; she was no longer there. Her body, I was told, had been taken away at an early hour. I was not to embrace my mother again."

Thus concluded, my dear Édouard, the story of Adèle's parents; and often, during her narration, my tears had mingled with hers. Regarding the aftermath of that conversation, the new ideas that had been born within me, I shall open my heart to you sincerely: I shall soon talk to you with the unreserved abandon of our fraternal amity. Today, I shall deliver you to your own sensation. Oh, my dear Édouard, you will understand it . . . there is a holocaust that I owe to virtue, to honor and amour. What beneficent delator will show me this Maugis?

19 May

It was time to relieve my heart of the burden by which it was charged. The days became long at the behest of my impatience. What consideration stops me, I said to myself, and since all my happiness is in her, what can prevent me from assuring it, if she loves me? However, I confess it to you, it seems that I forget my resolutions every time I find an opportunity to accomplish them, and I had delayed thus far speaking to her about what I feel. This is the event that served me.

There is a new romance whose hero has touched me, either because his situation has some of those rapports with mine that make us identify involuntarily with an unknown person, or because he resembles somewhat the man I would have liked to be if I had composed my life.[1] It is not that I approve greatly

---

1 It is not obvious what this "new romance"—new, that is, in May 1801—might be.

of romantic characters, especially in well organized societies, where they are almost always out of place by virtue of their foolish exaggeration or their stupid ingenuousness, but there are times when the caprice of the most bizarre imagination is worth more than everything that one is summoned to see around one, and to compensate for all the sad realities of the world.

To get to the point, as the judgment that I formed of that imaginary hero had furnished the brilliant Eudoxie with an inexhaustible subject of persiflage, the title of the romance was exciting Adèle's curiosity more and more every day; and, although convinced that there is nothing more pernicious for a young woman whose sensibility is beginning to develop than reading a work of that species; although very far from calculating the effect that it might produce on a new and tender soul—a lax and odious combination the mere idea of which revolts me—I have not been able to refuse to let her have the book, so much power does the slightest of her desires have over my will.

Today, I was astonished that Adèle was slightly belated in her little journey through the wood, and I was marching back and forth with long strides in all directions in the path to Valency when I saw her advancing with a preoccupied expression, her head inclined and the volume in her hand. As soon as she perceived me she returned it to me with a sad smile and walked beside me without speaking.

"Well," I said to her, "What do you think of that insensate, that madman, whose name alone revolts Mademoiselle Eudoxie? Does he seem so hateful to you?"

She did not reply, but a few tears were still rolling in her eyes and her hand was trembling in mine.

"Oh, good Adèle," I cried, "fortunate the heart that will be understood by your heart! A thousand times fortunate the man that you will love!"

And that hand, of which I had taken possession, my lips pressed recklessly.

"What are you doing, Gaston! Monsieur Gaston, what are you doing, for the love of Heaven? Leave me be," she continued, in an altered voice. "You know very well that I am Adèle Evrard!"

My breast was inflated, my head confused, I was choking.

"Adèle, my sister, my wife. My beloved, the unique object of all my thoughts, the unique charm of my existence, the affection, the hope that remains to me, that is what you are for Gaston."

And my tears, such delectable tears, streamed down my cheeks!

As I sensed myself tottering, I sat down on one of the natural benches that surrounded, as I have said, the little arbor where the principal paths of the wood met, and I put my head in my hands.

After a short time, I looked up, and I saw Adèle standing, but turned in the opposite direction, sorting out a small bouquet of flowers, I went to her and I put my arm gently around her neck, without daring to say anything.

"Look," she said, "look at these beautiful flowers I've picked; I'd like to know the name of this one."

It was the charming flower knows as the *Silvia*, because it only likes wild places in the shadow of forests.[1] I suddenly remembered, and I repeated, the charming strophe of the German poet:

"It's Silvia, the fresh Silvia, the sweet anemone of the woods. There is no floret, O Silvia, that can rival you in grace and beauty when you swing your five-part white and rose crown in the breath of the air. All the pomp of the other flowerers,

---

1 *Silvia* is an obsolete Latin name once attributed to the wood anemone nowadays classified as *Anemone nemorosa*. John Ruskin used it, among others, in England.

even the passion-flower itself, not excepting the rose, will never equal your modest beauty. Your curved stem is the emblem of melancholy, the mobility of your floating calyx expresses the agitation of a young heart. May Heaven, O most amiable of flowers, multiply forever around you the softness of moist grass, the coolness of new shade and the breath of new zephyrs! It's Silvia, fresh Silvia, the flower of solitude and spring, the sweet anemone of the woods."

Adèle had already forgotten her bouquet. It was about to fall from her hand, and I took possession of it in order to attach it over my heart.

She said to me, softly: "Gaston, I shall not come back again."

Our walk was tranquil, however. What is singular is that the conversation was as vague between us as that of two strangers, and there was not one of those indifferent words that did not reach my heart burning. Things that would not have seemed worthy of attention in any other circumstance made such a flattering impression on me! What a charm that is, which animates and embellishes everything and shines on light a light of apotheosis and divinity! The senses themselves, abused by the intoxication of the soul, only dream of perfumes, light and celestial melodies. It is the ideal of a paradise.

I can hear the long cry of prejudice repeating in my ear that she is the illegitimate daughter of Jacques Evrard. That, Gaston, is your lover!

Yes, she is the illegitimate daughter of Jacques Evrard, and that is, my Adèle, the most precious of your titles. The more unfortunate you are, the more delight I will find in filling your future with a happiness devoid of vicissitudes. Illegitimate! Amour, constancy, glory, the very confession of your grandfather, are they not legitimate? Could that cold and serious ceremony called marriage have certified your birth any better than the last kiss that your parents gave you in the face of God, the people and the executioners, than the sacrament of blood that unites them in eternity?

The daughter of Jacques Evrard! Laborer or soldier, no man has surpassed that one in nobility; and if nobility is the price of rare actions, is not the man who transmits it to his descendants more noble than those who receive it from him? To be born noble is the work of hazard; to become so by courage is the highest fortune of heroism. A commoner, they say! You do not know, children smitten with ridiculous baubles, that nobility dates from great political revolutions, that it is born, grows old and is renewed with empires.

Veritable nobility, as it is understood in monarchies, is to make a king or to be immolated with him. It only shines around a throne that is rising or a throne that is falling. The warriors who carry a sovereign on the pavis, the warriors who die with his race, those are the nobles. I only recognize titles those that have been sealed with the sword or sanctioned by the scaffold. The rest are only plebeians illustrated by letters-patent.

What, in any case, does the present state of society matter? When one order of things has ended, it is not nobles who remain but heroes. One no longer asks now about the father of Coriolanus or of Spartacus.

Do I need, after all, to accumulate so many arguments to justify what I have invariably resolved? Is it not sufficient for me and for all those who love me, that this action is the only one that can enable me to enjoy a pure felicity? Shall I yield to the dread of the imbecile rumors of the titled populace? Shall I lack the strength to brave the criticism of those sterile hearts desiccated by egotism and pride, the derision of some haughty woman and the scorn of a few miserable parvenus?

It is settled in my heart, Édouard; I shall be free!

It will be necessary to avoid, to flee the society whose esteem people seek so ardently, and which lavishes it or steals it in accordance with such strange and uncertain rules. So much the better. I have always aspired to circumscribe my life, to enclose it within the circle of a few affections, only to give to conventions and common habitudes what it is impossible to withhold from them. I shall endeavor to be me.

Come now to break around my retreat, as at the foot of an unbreakable rock, all the storms of society and vanish, without reaching my heart, insensate murmurs of hated and prejudice! Let them inspire me with pity, those unfortunates tormented by the need to live in everything that surrounds them, who march hastily in the midst of the crowd, putting aside with difficulty whatever opposes their passage, elbowing aside the weak or trampling them underfoot, elbowed aside by the strong or crawling before them, ever ready to sacrifice human victims to their prejudices, as barbarians do to their gods.

These last few days have had the freshness of one of those consoling dreams that one dreads to see finish, and when I think that its enchantment has already lasted for several weeks and I descend into my heart to make sure that it is not one of its customary illusions, a host of terrible presentiments suddenly accumulate around my thought, and I discover within me a vague but infallible consciousness of some great misfortune to come.

I have heard people who say, in deploring the death of a friend, that death only wants the fortunate, and that it is a very cruel thing to be struck down in the midst of one's youth and one's pleasure, at the very moment when everything commences to smile upon us and flatter us. It is, however, then that it is necessary to die, before the curtain has fallen on our chimeras, when the enchantment still endures, and what we enjoy that is temporary has not changed into irreparable regrets. I have often felt myself seized by a joy so powerful that all my overwhelmed senses sought to collect it in order to savor the possession of that fugitive present and fix it momentarily. It seems to me that I would like to die in that state.

Can you conceive how bitter and terrible is the death of an unfortunate abandoned by everyone, disappointed by existence, frightened by annihilation, repelling, in order to die more calmly, some sweet memory, the contrast of which would add to the horror of his agony, rendering the last sigh between cold arms, upon a breast that does not palpitate?

I would like to die; I would like to be dead today.

She was there, against me, leaning over my bosom, weeping with emotion. "Yes," I said to her, "before God and before men I attest that I will have no other wife!"

"Stop!" she cried. "Gaston is not a perjurer, but he is attesting before God something that nothing can render possible!"

"What obstacle is there?"

"Me! Gaston cannot be the husband of Adèle. Gaston is not a man of the people, obscure and poor, the husband—the only husband—appropriate to my estate and my indigence."

"I will be the husband of Adèle," I said. "That reparation is in the order of Providence. I shall acquit society's debt."

I have said it, Édouard, and sworn it in honor; it is necessary that the design be accomplished.

We were so preoccupied that dusk almost surprised us in the wood. As I quit my Adèle I wanted, I dared, to press her again in my arms. One of hers pushed me away feebly; the other, perhaps, encouraged me. A dazzle like that produced by the light of a meteor suddenly troubled my sight; me head inclined and my mouth—what can I tell you?—encountered her mouth. Incomparable voluptuousness! It is a kiss from Adèle, the imprint, the sweet imprint of her lips that reposes on my lips! Oh, I shall conserve it there entire, inalterable! It will never be effaced! Perish the day when I profane it, that precious seal of amour, in the kisses of another woman when an inanimate, insensible mouth steals from me the moist flower of your kiss! Annihilate my soul before I commit that sacrilege!

How difficult the weight of my sensations is to support! I sometimes regret my past dolors! Who would have believed that happiness requires so much strength?

Never have I lived so rapidly; never have I been obsessed by more cares. A single day of my life assembles as many tumultuous sentiments, dreads, hopes, enjoyments and torments, projects and irresolutions, as all the rest of my youth. One cannot do better than compare this state to that of a fever victim whose imagination, wandering in an unknown world and pursued by confused reminiscences, passes at hazard objects in objects, assembles under the same point of view the most bizarre contrasts, the most disparate images, and loses its self in those transitions, without a motive and without a goal, as incapable of judging his sensations as of choosing them. If, from time to time, I dare to count on some repose, the minute that follows disabuses me, and I am like a soul in pain, balanced by malign spirits between Heaven and Hell.

I have accompanied my mother to the Château de Valency, where we were to find the usual society, including Monsieur de Montbreuse, whose assiduities perhaps have something remarkable. It was natural that the conversation should fall on the subject most appropriate to interest him in that proud circle, the vanity of all society; and I was not astonished to see him renewing the eternal thesis of our moral superiority. But after having posed in principle that it was only among us that those delicate ideas are found of honor and the elevation of character and sentiments that are the fruit of an education appropriate to our political destination, the "romantic" edifice of the false virtue of the common man were beaten in the breach and reduced pitilessly to a simple spirit of emulation of which we still had the honor of being the vehicle—a dissertation that, I believe, would not have extracted me from a meditation entirely foreign to all that was happening there if, with regard to the inalienable baseness of the pariahs of Europe and the little confidence it is necessary to have in the mores of the people, he had not cited . . .

Great gods! My revolted blood still boils at that idea . . .

It was a matter of the young woman raised with so much care under the eyes of Mademoiselle Eudoxie, who would have blindly guaranteed her innocence . . . it was a matter of Adèle!

At that name, I no longer knew myself and, in a tone of voice that perhaps marked more anger that curiosity, I asked what crime the child had committed.

"Almost nothing," said Eudoxie. "One of those things for which your sentimental philanthropy surely reserves all its indulgence; one of those secret and contemplative passions that have such a fine effect in dramas and romances; a noble and tender affection for I know not what rustic of the next hamlet, to whom she renders innocent visits every day, which will end God knows how! You see that it is not worth the trouble of mentioning; but you will nevertheless find it good that I sequester her and expel her, while waiting until your eloquent declamations have entirely disabused me of certain miserable prejudices that I have the weakness to hold."

"That's too much sarcasm," I responded, "in an affair such as this, in which it is a matter of nothing less than ruining forever and irreproachable young woman; but it is not for me to justify her, and I have no doubt that Madame the Prioress will make the sacrifice of her modesty in such a precious interest. She knows the reason that takes Adèle to the hamlet every day, and irony has found without being aware of it the just expression when it qualifies as innocent the officious voyage of charity."

Madame the Prioress was present and I was astonished that she had not yet interrupted me. Imagine my dolorous surprise when I perceived, on raising my eyes toward her, that hers were moist with tears, and that she was gazing at me anxiously, as if to penetrate my intention, and divine what I meant.

"What, Madame!" I said. "It was not on your order, it was not on your part?"

A negative sign . . . it would have cost her too much to condemn her more positively! A gesture accompanied by a sigh was all that I obtained from her.

I confess that I had not expected that blow, and it was necessary for me to leave to hide my despair and my confusion.

I plunged into the wood without knowing where I ought to go but impatient to be distant from the place I had quit and to remain alone with myself, fortunate at that moment if I had been able also to isolate myself from my memories and an act of will would have sufficed to efface the entire past.

Finally, either because hazard had determined it or because I had headed for that goal without taking account of my design, I found myself near the hamlet to which I was accustomed to accompany Adèle and I recognized the miserable cottage that I had seen her enter so many times. It was so easy for me to obtain precise information there, and I had such a great need to be undeceived—or convinced, for my soul had no more energy for woe than uncertainty. My life and my honor were engaged to such an extent in that mystery that I had no hesitation in entering the home of those poor folk, and I had not even thought about the fright that my appearance, in the disorder I was in, would cause them.

The family was gathered in a rather large room, but in which everything announced indigence. An old man with a respectable face was lying in a corner, on an old bed-frame filed with straw, receiving a beverage from a very old woman, who turned her head while wiping away a tear. A young girl of ten or twelve had quit her spinning-wheel in order to readjust over the legs of the invalid a piece of worn tapestry that served as a coverlet. Two or three little children, strangers to that scene, were playing on the threshold of the door in the rays of the setting sun with a gaiety so full of frankness and insouciance that it squeezed my heart.

I sat down on the end of a broken bench and tried to collect my ideas in order to discover what I had to say; but as much as I had been impatient to be informed during the course of the minutes that had gone before, I feared then an enlightenment that might destroy all my illusions at once. I would have liked not to have come.

You could guess, if necessary, my first question. I asked the good woman whether she did not have a son. It seemed to me that I would feel the blow she was about to deal me less by letting it penetrate gradually and storing my dolor.

"Alas," she replied, "we only have one, who is a great subject of chagrin to us. God has given him a terrible affliction. He fell very ill at the age of eighteen and he can no longer work. The physicians have renounced his cure completely," she added, weeping, "for his sadness has been increasing for some time, and it's said that it's a sign that the illness is getting worse. I also have a daughter who was married, but our son-in-law was killed in the army when he was about to be promoted to sergeant, and she died six months ago. The children you see are theirs."

The children had gathered behind me.

"It's very unfortunate," I said to her, "to be struck thus in the family, but at least you're not without aid. I believe that this village belongs to Monsieur de Montbreuse, and that the château is also his. He's a sensitive and benevolent man who does not leave the poor in need."

The old woman said nothing to that, but she looked at me with astonishment, and without mentioning Montbreuse she praised ardently the generous souls who assisted her. The name of Madame the Prioress and that of Adèle, narrowly united in her gratitude, were confounded several times on her lips, in a manner to convince me of her sincerity.

After having left the little money that my purse contained in that sad dwelling of indigence, I went out slightly reassured, but still very uncertain and very unhappy.

Some distance from the house, on the edge of the wood, I saw a tall man whose face announced some thirty years, pale, distraught, his head inclined and his arms dangling, his shoulders covered with long black hair. On looking at him more closely I remarked in his haggard eyes an air of grim melancholy that allowed me to recognize him as the son of the unfortunates that I had just visited.

"Well, my friend," I said to him, "are you feeling better now?"

"Oh," he replied, "I believe that I'll be better when the trees grow their leaves again and the meadows are green again, as in the past; but I believe that this time, there won't be a spring. The sun is wan and cold, the flowers are all blooming palely, and all that can be heard in the fields are little winter birds whistling in the bushes. Once there was a soft wind, so agreeable when dusk came, and I never felt it so much blowing in my hair. Now there are breezes that dry out everything, and the noise frightens me when they make the dead branches creak. If I could only see a spring again like those of my youth, it seems to me that I'd be cured, but I believe there won't be any more of them."

I tried to talk to him about Adèle, but he interrupted me, placing his finger over his mouth as if to engage me to silence

"It's necessary not to name her aloud," she said, "for fear that they might remember her. The angels only pass over the earth momentarily. They're never seen to grow old. God sometimes sends them to console the poor and the sick, but he recalls them so soon! When they die, it's with a smile of joy, because they love to return. If by chance you encounter them, take care not to lose sight of them for a moment, for it would be finished forever."

As he finished speaking, he knelt down on a block of stone and started to pray in a low voice. I drew away without him noticing, reflecting on everything I had experienced that day and still uncertain as to what it remained for me to do, but already persuaded of Adèle's innocence.

As I went back into the Château de Valency I perceived her walking slowly in the vestibule toward the staircase that leads up to her room. I ran to her and, seizing her abruptly by the arm, without saying a word, I drew her into the drawing room where everyone was still gathered.

Quite indifferent to what anyone might think of that indiscretion, I cried, as I introduced her: "Speak, Mademoiselle, justify yourself with regard to the suspicions raised against your character. It is, in fact, to bear aid that you go to the hamlet of Bois every day, and I have just assured myself of that, but tell us how it comes about that the aid in question, given in the name of Madame le Prioress, was denied by her, and what species of secret is hidden under these appearances."

Then I let myself fall on to a chair, and I covered my eyes with one of my hands, impatient to know what she was about to respond and trembling to hear it.

In the meantime, she precipitated herself to Madame the Prioress's knees, moistening them with her tears. "Forgive me," she said, "for having dared to make use of your name. It was your benefits that I was distributing, since everything that I possess comes from you; but, touched by the misfortunes of a poor family, and seeing your savings already exhausted by the liberalities you spread in the village, I had recourse to mine in order also to have the pleasure of doing good. Would I not have been unjust to collect all the fruit of it, and rob you of gratitude that is due to you alone? What could I do for the unfortunate if you had not done everything for me?"

What a burden that scene lifted from my bosom! Everyone was moved and nonplussed. My mother, Monsieur de Montbreuse and Eudoxie herself retained a respectful silence. Such is the empire of innocence and goodness. There was not one of those superb souls that was not involuntarily humiliated before that young woman, so scorned a little while ago. As for Madame Adélaïde, she had raised Adèle up, and, in no condition to express her delight other than by tears, she was sobbing and pressing her to her heart, while Adèle, utterly confused, hid her modest blush and her touching emotion in her arms.

With what bitterness I would have been able to restitute the bloody ironies with which I had just been heaped, if I had wanted to seize that advantage, but I was able to content my just indignation—or, rather, I limited myself to expressing it by means of a rigorous silence. Montbreuse, in whom I would like to see a good man, but whom an exaggerated austerity of principles, perhaps fortified by some natural pride, too often renders skeptical of virtue, testified to me however by a hand-shake that he was content with me.

Finally, my mother, after a few polite remarks, asked for her carriage, and I accompanied her. The trouble of her manner, the embarrassment and constraint of her position and a comment escaped by chance had given my reason to think that the time had come to tell her what it was necessary for her to know sooner or later.

I talked to her about Eudoxie and I said firmly that she would not be my wife. Either because I had judged my mother's dispositions well or because the tone in which I made her party to my resolution imposed on her, she did not insist as much as I had expected, and everything promises that my choice will no longer be forced.

An indispensable business matter summons me to the city. My mother's own fortune depends on a lawsuit that will be judged in a few days and she has charged me with its pursuit. Personal interests would never have taken me away from here in these circumstances, and I know not what terror of which I am not the master . . . the superstitious idea to which I sometimes abandon myself would really move you to pity.

The city inspires me with such disgust that I have quit it as soon as possible in order to resume my solitary life. Other sentiments contributed to precipitate my return. I was in haste to see Adèle again and to provide for the means of no longer being separated from her. A man's days go by so rapidly that only a quite inexplicable insouciance can distract us from the care of embellishing them.

My mother's lawsuit was very bad, which did not prevent her losing it by a unanimous vote, with the result that she is ruined in her properties. At least mine remain to her, and I have made her a facile homage of them. She can dispose of them henceforth without responsibility and without obstacle, and if that is a sacrifice there are certainly sacrifices that are pleasures. What need have I of a superfluity of opulence? I am rich in simple tastes and moderate desires. A comfortable domain that brings in a little more than the necessary, gardens that are not vast but well-ordered; a little wood where I can indulge my reveries; a very modest little house, which will not prevent it being elegant; and around me a beautiful nature, a picturesque variety of sites and solitudes, fecund fields that nourish their inhabitants; and if possible, no poverty that I cannot relieve—what more is necessary for happiness? My imagination is not irrelevant to that design. I was rich enough to choose and that is the choice I made. Add to that perspective a wife like Adèle, a friend like Édouard—or, rather, my Adèle and my Édouard themselves, for there is only them for my heart—and you make my retreat an enchanted place, the Eden for which I still hope!

I forgot to tell you that the adverse party of my mother is one of her distant relatives, the old Comte de Séligni, who served with such distinction under our flags. That truly venerable man showed an almost paternal interest in me of which I feel proud. He told me that if my mother had not been deceived by the lawyers who were advising her he would have spared her the greater part of the damage she had sustained, but that the event had not changed his views and that he had decided to see her, either to offer her satisfying accommodations or to retighten the knots that the effects of the quarrel had loosened a long time ago. He even added that I might well not be a stranger to the plan that he would propose, but that the final clause was subordinate to certain information that he had to obtain in a village in the neighborhood.

We have therefore made the journey together, chatting warmly about our feats of arms, the battles in which we encountered one another, the vices of our military organization and the reasons that rendered the war in which we were actors so disastrously futile. Monsieur de Séligni argued those matters with just and accurate good sense, and his opinions have singularly rectified mine on a number of matters about which I shall have occasion to discuss with you one day.

As we posed Eudoxie's château I launched myself to the carriage window in order to search with my eyes Adèle's little window at the corner of the building. I was annoyed that she was not there, as I thought that she might have been informed of my passage. She was not there, and I shall not see her this evening, for we arrived at dusk. The cares that have retained me were, in any case, too urgent to permit me an hour of absence and yet it only required one glimpse of her to dissipate the terrors that pursued me in spite of myself as soon as I was away from her. My God, abridge this night!

9 June

Édouard, it is finished for me! All my illusions are destroyed; my heart has been cruelly scourged . . .

I no longer require, Édouard, anything but a grave in which to sleep eternally; for it is the slumber of annihilation that I implore. Heaven spare me the cruel benefit of an immortality that would eternalize my dolor and my humiliation!

This is what I have learned at the Château de Valency . . . why can I not write it coldly? I know remedies for everything.

Adèle has deceived me; so I am told, at least. Unfortunate that I am, it's impossible to doubt it—but you would also search for reasons not to believe it. She secretly adored one of Montbreuse's domestics, a vile, ignoble, odious man that I had never remarked. Is it not surprising that their intelligence escaped me, whose heart is alarmed so easily? Would she have betrayed me if I had loved her with less confidence, less abandon? She loved me, though . . . alas, she did not tell me so; but it would be frightful to spare my tenderness at that price.

The coldest souls were abused like mine. Montbreuse says that he did not expect it. Celestial candor of virtue, you are a chimera, then!

The domestic asked for his wages; the next day they left in order to be married elsewhere; I am grateful to her for that attention; it is all that she has done for me.

It appears, to begin with, that nothing is more false than all that I have told you. I would give my life to be persuaded that that is untrue. To believe her innocent; it would be so sweet to die with that idea!

She has departed without telling anyone; she was too ashamed; she has not even seen her godmother, who is weeping for her. I am not weeping; indignation does not weep; I would weep for her if she were dead.

It is five days since they were seen departing. There was no one in the village who did not see them; I have just sent Latour there; he was told that she had been recognized; she was wearing a veil but it was not lowered, the children followed them with their eyes as far as the wood.

It seems to me that vengeance would soothe me, but what vengeance can a man like me take? A man like me! Malediction! Perhaps that is what she dreaded. She has thrown herself into the arms of her equal in order to escape a man like me!

What have I done to merit this outrage? Oh, if she knew what it cost to be abandoned, to search around one for the person one loves and no longer to find them! What favor I would have owed her if, with the blow of a dagger delivered from behind—that cowardly assassination has nothing too reckless for the hand of a woman—she had deigned to prevent the torments that are devouring me!

If she saw for a moment, if the least of my dolors was known to her, she would be forced to admit that the most pitiless hatred . . .

A calm, silent night, beautiful and enchanted for the fortunate! My repose alone destroyed in that immense harmony! I alone am doomed, neglected, forgotten by God, who has withdrawn his Providence from me!

✳

Everything concurs in sharpening and envenoming my despair. It is frightful to see circumstances that we would not have dared to foresee or desire, circumstances that would have granted our prayers, succeed and multiply around us when everything is forbidden to us, when nothing remains of the happiness that was assured to us but a regret.

Can you imagine that Monsieur de Seligni is the father of the unfortunate woman from whom Adèle received the light of day. There is nothing more exact than the story that she told me. The marriage of Evrard and Angélique was concluded, and without the infamous perfidy of Maugis, that family would have lived happily. Scarcely had he recovered his wealth than the comte had believed that he could do nothing more agreeable to the manes of his children than to report to their daughter the tenderness that he had had for them and to consecrate the rights of his heiress by means of a solemn adoption. He had come to take her back from the hands to which she had been confided and to restitute to her the advantages of her birth and her fortune and repair by the force of amour the troubles of her childhood.

Finally, he had thought that my mother would not hesitate to approve under those conditions of my marriage to Adèle. She had, in fact, consented to it and I was summoned by her this evening to be informed on that new project. The comte was also there, and with what unexpected blow did I not strike that good old man when, my heart and eyes full of tears, suffocated by shame and dolor, I cried to him while embracing his knees: "Renounce, renounce a design that the ingrate has disavowed, a hope that she has deceived! Adèle is no longer worthy of her father or her lover! She has married another."

There is no expression that can give an idea of the bitterness of heart with which I repeated the details that I gave you yesterday. It seemed to me that I was not pronouncing a word in which my sentence of death was not resounding, and how many times I could have desire that my bosom would burst in order to spare me the horror of that humiliating revelation.

Her father—what a redness rose over that venerable forehead—confounded his tears with mine and sobbed in my arms.

"Gaston," he said to me, after a long silence, "I have only lost Adèle. You will be my son none the less. The ties that I had on earth are broken. It is you alone, Gaston, who attach me to it. Promise me not to abandon your old father, and suffer that he die close to you."

I fell at his feet and I asked for his benediction.

My mother was moved. She embraced me. I had suspected for a long time that her sensibility, damaged by the commerce of the narrow minds that surrounded her, might be reborn to the mild emotions of nature. I found once again in her kiss all the soul of a mother, and that discovery would have caused me a great deal of joy if I had still been able to feel any.

Why has Adèle quit us, when we would have been so happy?

I know, Édouard, why she quit us. It was not me that she loved.

Me, for whom Adèle was everything; me, who would have given my life several times over to spare her the slightest pain—it is me that she has sacrificed so unworthily. It was not me that she loved.

12 June

Obstacles that one might have believed to be invincible, by which even the imagination was alarmed—the distance of ranks to cross, Eudoxie's hand to refuse, opinion to brave, my mother's pride to overcome or her malediction to suffer—what future could be more sinister and more menacing?

Everything was smoothed over, and, more unfortunate than before, I would have ransomed with all my blood shed drop by drop one of those instants of anguish that I was unable to appreciate.

I would like to see you there again as I had seen you, to press you and enlace you in my arms, to brush with my mouth one of the tresses of your hair. I would like merely to hear the sound of your dress floating against the bushes, the sound of your footsteps imprinted on the dry leaves, as at the corner of the path when that sound announced your approach to me.

Alas, I would like my error to be returned to me, I would like still to believe in your love, and not to have been undeceived.

If at least my reason could go astray . . . people in delirium are subject to such bizarre illusions. Perhaps I would see you.

Latour has just come into my room. He believes that he has seen Adèle's lover, the man who, it is said, made her leave here. That wretch evaded his gaze and escaped his questions by flight. Latour, whom I have informed of everything concerning Adèle, persists in doubting her treason. Why can I not doubt it too?

There are certain moments when I think, however, that I can disentangle . . . what am I saying, and what is my blindness? I am like a traveler by night who loses his footing on the brink of a frightful abyss and who clings on to anything that he can seize: a feeble bush, a tuft of grass, the sprig of a creeper; the most mobile and most uncertain point of support is sufficient to reconcile him with hope; but soon, everything escapes at the same time and he disappears forever.

Come to me, Édouard, I shall no longer fatigue you with my chagrins; a day, an hour, a few minutes, have changed everything; I am happy forever; only your presence is lacking to my felicity.

But how can I tell you all that without anticipating events? These recent instants are so full of events and emotions.

Since Adèle's departure I had prescribed myself the facile duty of succeeding her in the distribution of her aid to the invalids of the hamlet; I liked that employment, Édouard; those good people had seen her, and only spoke of her tenderly; I talked about her with them.

Yesterday was the anniversary of a very dolorous day; I went to renew, at my father's grave, the ceremony of mourning that, absent and condemned, I had been unable to witness the first time. Latour had to replace me with regard to our paupers; he came back early, in great agitation. On the way he had encountered the little girl from the cottage, who was coming in great haste to ask for Monsieur de Séligni and me on behalf of Monsieur de Montbreuse, who was dying.

I don't know whether I have told you that, a few days ago, Montbreuse had appeared to withdraw entirely from society and that he had virtually imprisoned himself in the abandoned château that he possesses near here, although it is scarcely appropriate to lodge the local birds of prey, of which its old towers are the ordinary rendezvous. His absence was covered, however, by the pretext of hunting.

Yesterday, while trying to cross a ditch on the side of which he had supported the butt of his rifle, the unfortunate Montbreuse had triggered the shot and the entire charge had traversed his breast. A valet and a few peasants had transported him to the house of the epileptic and his parents.

As I was still far from returning, Monsieur de Séligni did not lose a moment in going to see the dying man. Montbreuse expired; but the exclamation of the alarmed Monsieur de Séligni, who proffered involuntarily the name of Maugis on recognizing him, reawaked him momentarily from the slumber of death.

"Maugis," he said, moving his head effortfully, "may God forgive me! Can he forgive him, alas?"

Then he was without movement and without respiration for some time, but the cares he received for Monsieur de Séligni and the people of the house having reanimated him again for an instant, he seemed pressed by the need of an important revelation. Inarticulate sounds succeeded one another, embossed on his lips.

"Adèle," he said.

"I know," said Monsieur de Séligni, trying to spare him the difficulty of unnecessary explanation.

Adèle," said Montbreuse, "Angélique's daughter . . ."

"I know."

"Adèle the most virtuous, the most perfect of creatures . . ."

"What!"

"Adèle, innocent, worthy of you, worthy of him . . . she is . . ."

Maugis died without finishing.

I will spare you the anguish of that night. Montbreuse's domestic, whom Latour had been on the point of surprising, informed of his master's death, came to my home this morning; he told me everything, confessed everything. Montbreuse had contrived that infernal treason, in the apparent interests of Eudoxie, who was probably uninformed of his secret designs; she had been able to believe, and must in consequence have tried to prove to Adèle, that it was a great evil to suffer and to authorize my amour, that my happiness depended on being distanced from her and forgetting her—for they thought that I could forget her—and that everything prescribed, in sum, entering a religious retreat until further notice, where she could live sheltered from my pursuits.

Even Madame the Prioress had approved of the plan and had indicated the house where they wanted to hide her from me. But such were not the views of Maugis, who had adored Adèle for a long time, and who only took an active part in that intrigue in order to obtain one victim more. Some distance from the village the carriage changed direction and took Adèle to the château by a roundabout path; the night was dark and no one perceived it.

It is there that Adèle is captive, under a triple key of which the domestic is the sole depositary, for Montbreuse, faithful to his hypocrisy, still affected only to communicate with Adèle by means of passionate messages, and it was only today that he was to present himself to her eyes for the first time. At the news of that visit, Adèle cried: "Let the monster not appear or expect to find me dead!" The man repeated that just now.

You can see, Édouard, whether I shall be happy, and whether Adèle is worthy of me. She had only consented to it out of deference to her godmother, whose tenderness and good intentions she could only mistake by virtue of a devotion for me that would have calumniated her. Forget, forget my unworthy suspicions!

Do not be astonished that I am taking the time to write to you before she is returned to me. What could I do to distract my impatience from the happiness for which it is waiting? It is necessary, before she is returned to me, that I occupy myself with her, and there was her father, whose touching beneficence I had to respect. It was for Monsieur de Ségini to release her from her prison. Imagine the slowness with which the moments have gone by this evening!

But I shall not seal my letter. A carriage is entering the avenue! Inexpressible happiness. Adèle, my father, my friend! Come right away . . .

Come, Édouard, come to me.

*

Latour to Monsieur Édouard de Millanges

The same day.

Yes, Monsieur, come, don't lose a minute, my poor master has need of you. He wrote to you about his happiness. He did not know . . .

I accompanied Monsieur de Séligni to the château. We went up the stairs of the part of the building where Mademoiselle Evrard was imprisoned. We arrived at the top floor. Scarcely had the key turned in the lock that she uttered a cry of fright.

"Adèle! Adèle!" said Monsieur de Séligni, beside himself.

We go in. The room is empty. An idea strikes me. The window was open, and I run to it. What scene, Monsieur Édouard! The unfortunate woman had thought that she heard Maugis.

She had said that she would die if he presented himself before her.

No resources, not a breath of life! Poor father! And him, above all! Imagine his despair!

Come, come, Monsieur Édouard. You alone might be able . . .

But what a noise!

Can it be . . . ?

Oh, omnipotent God, what have we done to attract your wrath to this degree?

Alas, Monsieur Édouard, don't come!

Thérèse Aubert

Advertisement

The manuscript of this novelette was found in one of those houses that served as prisons in a certain epoch and which have since been rendered to their original destination. It was hidden, without any other precaution, underneath a paving stone, with the consequence that, time and damp having damaged several pages, several lacunae remained that the editor has been obliged to fill. That is the only part that he has had in the work, for he has made no correction of the style in the places where it was only necessary to make an erasure in order to improve it. He thought that the inspirations of a sensitive and unhappy young man had a character that it was not permissible to alter under the pretext that they were not always well served by expression. He has respected even slight incorrections, out of regard for the sentiments, even though the sentiments that the author has tried to describe are not of a very general interest. The unfortunate fellow had only been acquainted with a genre of emotions that few people have experienced profoundly, the memory of which, rejected by a sage man, importunes a cold man, revolts a corrupt man and is, at the most, conserved by certain passionate souls which have made the error or had the misfortune of not finding anything better. If one were sure of having encountered all those who understand us, doubtless one would not write, but why write, if not to search for them?

There is one reproach that the editor of a work of this sort ought to condemn in advance: that of presenting the reader with scenes that are too somber, of awakening in his heart sentiments that are too painful. It is necessary to admit that this sad distraction is only entirely suitable for a small number of chagrined minds for whom it is a need to sympathize with the pains of others in moments of relaxation when they can savor the forgetfulness of their own dolors, and it is to them that this novelette is addressed. As for the writers who are ambitious for that species of success, I suppose that they have not always been masters of the choice.

Thérèse Aubert

My name is Adolphe de S***. I was born in Strasbourg on the nineteenth of January 1777, to a noble family of which I was the last scion. I lost my father in the emigration. My mother perished in a house of detention for the suspect; I have no brother or sister, or any relatives of my name. I have been seventeen years old for a few days, and nothing suggests that that short existence can be prolonged. I shall explain the reason for that later, although my position no longer interests anyone. So, it is not for the world that I am writing these lines; it is for myself, myself alone; it is to occupy and to use up the sad and desperate intervals of leisure, which are fortunately very brief. It is to open a more facile path to the sentiments that oppress me, in order to soothe my heart, if memory is a relief, or to finish breaking it.

I had accompanied my father at thirteen; I lost him at sixteen. I returned to Strasbourg, bringing back for all wealth his last adieu, his last advice, the example of his devotion, his courage, his personal virtues and I know not what emulation of misfortune that relieves the soul. I looked for my mother; even her grave was unknown. Our property was no longer ours. Our relatives were vagabond or dead. Our old friends would have dreaded to recognize me, and there was probably no longer any among them who would have loved me. I had so much to lament!

I had had for a professor of Greek a monk named Père Schneider and for a music master a virtuoso named Monsieur Edelmann. Both had embraced the party of the revolution violently; I asked after them anyway, because I had seen them honor the amity of my father and their pity was my last resource.

The former had just been tied to the stake of the scaffold by a popular movement; I passed through the square of arms; I recognized him, pale, disfigured and bloody. The public clamor accused him of the most odious sins; but he had been my master, perhaps he had loved me; I would have run to him if I had not dreaded that my affection might charge him with one crime more. I wept bitterly, hiding my face,

Monsieur Edelmann had been arrested the same day. A few months later, I was told, they fell in Paris under the terrible scythe of the revolution, which does not spare its children.

My last assignat[1] had been exchanged for a little bread. It was very cold, the day was advanced and I did not know where to retire. I remembered that in a nearby small town I had spent a few days of my childhood in the house of the pretty hostess of ****. My gratitude, alas, dared not name her. As she was known for her attachment to what were called "the aristocrats," it was in her house that my father and I had slept on the night before our emigration.

I employed in that journey all the strength that remained to me. I arrived in the dead of night. I went precipitately to Madame T***'s cabinet and I threw myself, or rather fell, at her feet, for I could no longer sustain myself.

"In the name of charity," I said to her, "a little wine to revive your poor little Adolphe and a little straw on which to repose. I'll die if I have to spend another night in the snow."

She embraced me and wept; and how her tears embellished her! Then she recommended me to be prudent and took me to

---

1 Assignats were a species of paper money issued by the National Government and the Directoire, initially backed by the property confiscated from the Church and the aristocracy.

a room apart, in which there were three beds. I was only told in advance that I had nothing to fear from my neighbors. They were companions in misfortune, but I did not know them then.

I had scarcely finished my meager meal than all my senses were bound by slumber. When I opened my eyes again it was daylight.

My comrades embraced me as a brother; my father's name was not unknown to them. Our sentiments were the same, our fortune and our destiny were common; they offered me in addition something more than consolations; they spoke of great dangers to run, of some glory to merit. They wanted to change my fate, and I was already eager to share theirs, whatever it might be. Amity must be a delectable sentiment in all epochs and all conditions of life, but between young friends crushed by noble misfortunes it is almost a religion.

One of those messieurs was between eighteen and twenty years old. He was a young man with an affable but serious countenance, full of calm and resolution, energy and presence of mind. His name was Forestier and I believe that he was the son of a shoemaker in Saumur or Chollet, I don't know which. The other, the Chevalier de Mondyon, who had the greatest deference for him, was two or three years younger. Although he was the same age as me, at the most, he was much more developed than me. My short stature, my blue eyes, the ardent color of my curly hair and the freshness of my complexion, which I obtained from my mother and which is characteristic of our Alsatian women, gave me, to my great regret, something feminine and timid, which had often exposed me in my passage to the suspicions and the mockery of badly brought-up travelers.

"In truth," said Mondyon," in a tone of expressive gaiety that never abandoned him, "we'll scarcely be able to persuade the general that this new comrade is not a young woman in disguise."

"I'll disabuse him of that error," I replied, "on the first battle-field where there is blood to shed for the service of the king."

Forestier smiled and shook my hand, firmly. Mondyon, who feared having mortified me, threw his arms around my neck.

Those two officers were to show themselves with the greatest brilliance in the first affairs in the Vendée. Their intelligence, their zeal, their proven courage and their very youth, which repelled in their regard even the suspicion of an important and perhaps mission had made them preferred to the brave Larochejacquelein[1] to be sent to the princes of the house of Bourbon. They arrived at their army at the moment when it was occupied in establishing communications with France that might save it, and they had the generous temerity to request that new employment, more fertile in dangerous hazards than a hundred battles.

The most important part of their instructions had already been fulfilled, and the most fortunate success—an unexpected success, the results of which will probably not be lost for the generation to come—had crowned their enterprises. It only remained, in order for them to retake through France the road to the Vendée, for them to receive the passports that had been promised to them by one of the chiefs of the party of the interior.

Those papers arrived a few days later; the bonds of our amity had continued to tighten in the intimacy of our solitude. We swore that death alone would separate us from one another. The good Madame T*** procured us volunteers' uniforms, furnished us with a few provisions for our journey, and made us promise to come back to see her one day, if we escaped the almost inevitable perils that menaced us. I did not doubt it; the first risks of life do not astonish the soul, they embolden it.

---

1 Henri du Vergier, Comte de La Rochejacqeulein (1772-1794) was the youngest general in the makeshift royalist army during the Vendéan insurrection.

Everything is vast, as unlimited as the future and hope, for a man whom hope has not yet deceived, who has not yet seen at close range the enchanting future that has not yet been stripped of all its illusions, reduced to all its miseries, as poor and empty as a void.

Everything succeeded as we wished; we arrived under the white flag, not without obstacles but without accidents, and we were then able to deem ourselves fortunate, if it is good fortune to escape the present evil that would strike our hearts full of sweet sentiments and agreeable illusions, in order to fall with a withered heart, desiccated by dolor, under the empire of despair and death.

I am passing over these events rapidly. Although they remind me of names dear to my gratitude and my amity, I sense that the recitation is fatiguing me. I can no longer explain the interest that one attaches to the futile conservation of a painful existence, the care that one takes to retain it, the vain dissipations of the heart in which one is pleased to consume one's days. I feel that there are really only a few hours in life, a few fugitive moments; that when they have passed, irreparably passed, everything is injurious in the images of those times that will never return. It is not only bitterness, but disgust; it is something that renders memory burdensome, and which causes one to desire the imbecilic apathy of the brute, which does not feel, or forgets rapidly.

The same reason will render impossible the detailed narration of the military events of which I was the witness. I understand that those reminiscences, so indifferent in the host of trivia that wear away our years, have a certain charm for a fortunate soul served by its organization or its destiny, which has experienced nothing very intense. But I am not writing a story. I am in haste to escape from these sterile details that constrain and oppress my heart. I need another atmosphere, another horizon, where my thoughts can expand freely and commence to participate in the immensity that opens before me. Let it suffice for me to say that five or six noteworthy actions had earned me, in spite of my extreme youth, the esteem of the royal army, the confidence of my chiefs and the command of a company a few weeks after the disaster of Le Mans.[1]

I had received several wounds in anterior affairs; some had not closed entirely; the fatigue of the previous days was still weighing upon me. To complete my misfortunes, I lost my horse to a gunshot and my sword had broken near the hilt at the beginning of the battle. It is necessary to have seen the disorder of the army, the tumult and confusion of the people; it is necessary to have witnessed that catastrophic day, to form any idea of it. The bravest of our soldiers were wandering at random in the streets, trying unsuccessfully to rally and augmenting the horror of our situation with their uncertain movements, their cries of terror and rage, and all their pointless efforts.

Finally, I succeeded in assembling a few of them around me, at the bottom of a steep street whose top was occupied by a contingent of republicans, who were trying to barricade it with all the debris that came to hand. I threw myself forward adeptly, encouraging my little troop by voice and gesture; the enemy broke away and seemed disposed to leave the position to us, but as they abandoned it they shoved toward us with a violence augmented by the rapidity of the slope, a number of their gun-carriages that were obstructing their passage. One of the poles struck me in the stomach and knocked me down, dying, on to a heap of corpses, where I spent the night without any other sentiment than a confused perception of pain.

The freshness of the morning developed that impression and rendered it more distinct; my ideas recovered a little order

1 By the time that the remnants of the royalist counter-revolutionary army were cornered in Le Mans in December 1793 it had lost more than half of its original strength of 80,000 men and was in dire straits, although the survivors did manage to regroup after the republicans took the town, and eked out the massacre that followed.

and clarity; I came round; dawn had broken. I heard a vague rumor, which drew away and approached by turns, which left me time to recognize a few sounds and distinguish a few words. They were accompanied by the click of bayonets colliding in the march. They were evidently republicans; I thought that they were exploring all the quarters in search of those of us who had hidden, or to count the dead.

There was not one house that was not closed with the utmost care, but among the objects that had been used to barricade the street I remarked a ladder. I set it up against a wall. I arrived on the roof at the moment when a discharge of rifle fire broke the last rung under my feet; I was not hit but I was not saved. I passed from that roof to another, and, always pursued and always in evidence, I reached the street corner before the soldiers, who had reloaded their weapons and had been slowed down by that operation.

At the corner I found myself next to a window whose poorly-attached shutter ceded at the first effort, and I fell with a jump into the middle of a room, the appearance of which announced the dwelling of a pauper. A young woman uttered a scream; she was in bed.

"Have no fear," I said to her. "Save a poor brigand and God will recompense you."

As I spoke I had thrown myself on to her bed and turned over me a part of her blanket. My hat had remained with the corpses; I had stuck the stump of my sword through my belt; my hair, which was very long and attached by a knot over my head, partly covered my face.

The soldiers came in, approached the bed, looked under it, searched the room and came back to us. I closed my eyes and hid my face, blackened by fire and soiled by the dust of the battle, under the sheet.

"It's all right," said one of them. "I know this one; it's Jeannette."

"The blonde is her younger sister," said the other. "The brigand isn't here."

The door finally closed behind them; it was just in time for my companion, whose teeth were chattering in terror.

There was not a moment to lose to avoid their return; I was already standing behind the curtain that separated the foot of Jeannette's bed from the interior of the room. A few words rapidly exchanged with my protectress was sufficient to determine her to sacrifice one of her two sets of clothing to me, and in spite of the novelty of my disguise, it only cost me a few minutes. My costume was simple but neat; my hair was put up again, with little art, under a bonnet that Jeanette would have placed better, but all the outfits of that day could reflect the disorder and terror of the day before. Finally, the bronze of my features was no more disparate with my garments; the sun burns the skin like cannon-smoke,

After having made sure, with a single glance at a fragment of a mirror suspended on the wall, that it was not impossible for me to give the illusion to the soldiers, even if they had seen me in the battle, I hastened to wrap up my iron-gray jacket, with the heart and epaulette that decorated it, my pistols, my dagger and the rest of my equipment in the red handkerchief that had served me as a sash a moment before; I passed it over my arm.

I approached Jeannette's bed and forced her to receive a few gold coins, which were exactly half my petty fortune, which her hand rejected. Then I imprinted on her cheeks and forehead a kiss of gratitude more expressive than any words.

I arrived at the foot of the staircase just as the soldiers pursuing me completed their fruitless search. They paid no heed to me.

I did not know the town. I walked at hazard, searching for an exit in the direction in which it seemed to me that my comrades must have gone. Finally, I perceived open country, and believed myself near to liberty when a soldier lowered the barrel of his rifle in front of me and forced me to take two steps back.

"Halt there, young woman," he said. "No one passes without making themselves known. Come into the office."

I obeyed.

The "office" was a vast depot, where a host of moaning women and weeping children—some of whom had been separated from their mothers in the turmoil of the retreat, perhaps forever—was already gathered. They were waiting there in a horrible anxiety, until it pleased the victors to decide their fate.

"Are you a brigandess too?" said a man with a ferocious physiognomy, whose heart doubtless swelled with joy on seeing one victim more fall into his power.

"No," I said.

"Where is your passport?"

"I don't have one. I'm the daughter of the miller of P***, who died defending the republic against the brigands, and as we're a numerous and poor family, I came to Le Mans seeking to go into service here. I arrived in the midst of yesterday's events, and I was trying to go back where I came from. That's all."

"Of the miller of P***," said my interrogator. "That's possible. Take her to President Aubert, he said, turning round. "He's from that village, and if she isn't lying to us, he'll recognize her."

The president was at the far end of the room. He had his back turned. Tricolor plumes were floating over his hat; a tricolor ribbon descended in a saltire over his shoulders. He was speaking actively, and, it seemed to me, violently. I had a sentiment of imminent death.

My heart constricted momentarily; my brow was moist with sweat; I let my packet slip and it was about to escape me when I pulled myself together. At the worst, it was only a matter of dying, and what interest, what affection, could reattach me to life? I heard with sufficient calmness the man who was conducting me repeat the lie that I had just invented; or rather, if I experienced any emotion, it only came from the shame of having lied in order to redeem my life, for which the sovereign judge would soon hold me to account.

President Aubert had repeated the same words in an emotional and anxious voice. He turned toward me abruptly and fixed me with a sad gaze, the expression of which I shall never forget. That state of uncertainty did not last long. His physiognomy, which was noble and tender but bore the imprint of habitual worry, cleared rapidly. He smiled mildly and touched me on the cheek with the back of his hand, saying to me affectionately: "So it's you, poor Antoinette. You must have been very frightened."

With what transport of gratitude and joy I would have pressed my lips to that hand if I had been able to do it without dooming my benefactor. He must have read in my gaze a part of what I was experiencing. For myself, I acquired at the same moment singular and new ideas. I conceived, for the first time, that there is no nuance of opinion, however absolute one supposes it to be, that excludes humanity and justice entirely. I criticized myself internally for the excessively general severity of certain sentiments that I had previously made on the faith of the prejudices and passions of others. I promised myself to consult before anything else, in my future conduct, the general rules of benevolence and pity before abandoning myself to the unjust impression of party hatreds.

While I was making those reflections, Monsieur Aubert had written and sealed a short note. He gave it to me.

"I thought," he said, "that since you're disposed to go into service, it's more convenient if you enter into it with my daughter, who is elsewhere. The death of her mother has left in her heart and mine a void that only a tender intimacy can fill. Her grandmother is infirm and ill. So much isolation makes me anxious for her happiness, and I've proposed for some time to give her a companion of her own age. You have the education, the mores and the recommendation of an honest name. My Thérèse will receive you and love you as a sister. Perhaps you know that we are living, since the war, on our little farm at Sancy, near the Sarthe. As you can't know the way, and your age and sex need protection in a journey of four leagues, this worthy man will take you. He has the necessary authority to pass the obstacle."

My eyes were lowered. I trembled to allow what was happening within me to be read in my physiognomy. When I chanced to look in the direction of the president he had resumed his conversation and did not appear to be occupied with anything else.

May the protection of God be attached to you for all the days that remain to you, I said in the depths of my heart. *May it extend over your family and all those you love. And if it is not given to you to enjoy on earth, in these times of corruption and cruelty, all the happiness that you merit, may celestial bounty measure it in another life, an eternal life, on the prayers that I make for you!*

I departed with my guide. I experienced some embarrassment in regard to the conversation that I would have to sustain with him, in a region where I did not know the people or the places, in which the slightest awkwardness might betray my imposture and put in salvation in doubt again, but I did not take long to perceive that the man did not enjoy the confidence of Monsieur Aubert without reason. A few words of general benevolence, which did not announce the design of an application, but made me understand that it would be without danger, finished rendering me a perfect tranquility.

Gradually, moreover, we gathered around us poor peasants whom fear of the armies had driven from their hearths and were in haste to return to them with their children in their arms. The inconsequential speech of those good folk informed me of a part of what it was necessary for me to know. They confirmed me in the idea I had formed of the previous day and its consequences; they demonstrated the impossibility of rejoining the debris of the royalist troops, and the pointlessness of that step, which would only serve, in the case of success, to embarrass their retreat with one more outlaw. They enabled me to appreciate the good fortune of finding a refuge for a few days, while awaiting a better opportunity to reunite with my unfortunate comrades, and most of all the good fortune of being in the house of Monsieur Aubert, whose generous character was increasingly developed in my eyes by a few circumstances.

It resulted from all that I heard, as from all that I had initially presumed, that Monsieur Aubert, engaged in the first movements of the revolution by irreflection or enthusiasm, had continued to follow its march by reason and by virtue, in order at least to obtain some advantage from the just influence of a righteous and sensitive soul upon the blind multitude, and to make use of what remained to him of the fugitive popularity that is only faithful to excess, in order to help and save a few unfortunates. I had not taken account until then of that genre of devotion and courage in the number of those who were able to honor humanity, but I was only the more disposed to appreciate it. I even supposed that it was perhaps less rare than one might imagine at first; that there were in the ranks of the malevolent many who only remained confused with them by virtue of the excess of a sublime abnegation, and that, attributing a great part to error and weakness, there were probably very few evil men, in the absolute sense of the word.

Those ideas reposed my heart; they softened the sentiment of my life, they cast a charm over all the impressions that I received from external objects, and the instinct of wellbeing that caused my breast to palpate was further augmented by the sight of the little farm at Sancy. My eyes had never settled on a more agreeable scene. Alas, even today I find a sort of pleasure in recalling it, as if my existence were going back to the day when I perceived it for the first time, and everything that has happened since was still in the future.

Sancy is only composed of three or four houses, among which Monsieur Aubert's is distinguished by its four white chimneys and the extent of its gardens. One arrives there by a tortuous path traced for a single person on the side of an arid but extremely picturesque hill, the surface of which is strewn with rocks that affect the most bizarre forms. A few bushes of brambles, holly and juniper, and mosses of different colors are the only vegetation that can be observed there for most of the year, but in spring it redeems its customary poverty with a quite extraordinary luxury. It is charged with violets, yellow primroses and a countless quantity of those pretty anemones whose inclined stems like obscure places in the cool shade of damp rocks. That ephemeral adornment disappears in the first ardors of the May sun.

At the summit of the mountain, on a little esplanade of verdure from where the eye wanders in the distance over delightful plains, a stone cross rose up, which someone had already broken but which they had not been able to fell. It was sustained between stones to which its base was linked by strong iron bands, although it was inclined to the point that it appeared from below to be suspended over the slope of the precipice, and it added to the singularity of that savage aspect the impression of a miraculous ruin.

A pretty stream, which runs between two rows of willows, and goes to join the Sarthe a quarter of a league further on, bathes the foot of that hill, which it embraces entirely, and whose murmur alone animates its mute solitude. Beyond it, cheerful fields are deployed, cut at intervals with an infinite grace by little wooded hills or by solitary clumps of trees that design islets of verdure against the backcloth of the landscape. The eye wandering between their rustic but harmonious contours is pleased to discover from time to time the brilliant silvery track of the stream, or sections of the river, which, continually intercepted by new objects, only offers the appearance of a few sparse lakes deliberately placed in the scene in order to augment its variety. Their shores, dotted with hamlets, announced the mild prosperity of which the sentiment awakens so agreeably in the heart of a fond traveler at the sight of a group of small white houses surrounded by fruit trees: a consolatory spectacle that makes him forget momentarily the hideous poverty and cruel opulence of cities.

When I arrived in Sancy, the season was well advanced, and a few features of that scene, altered by the first influences of winter, lacked the perfection of the whole, but I reassembled them thereafter around the first idea that I had formed of it, which caused me a kind of ecstasy. In fact, I had never experienced until then a profound impression of pleasure at the sight of nature; it had sometimes astonished me, but it had not yet delighted me. My strongly dilated heart had never felt as if it were imprisoned in my bosom, as if tormented by the need to launch itself out of me in order to embrace creation; and yet that enjoyment, so new for it, did not fill the immense desires that it had just conceived. It took possession without any obstacle of all the infinity that it was beginning to discover, but in folding back upon itself it was astonished to find itself still so empty, and only to bring back from its conquests an insatiable curiosity and unknown anxieties. It wondered whether that was all that was given to it, and it palpitated with an indefinable impatience that was full of cares and charms. My throat tightened, my eyelids moistened with tears, there was an unknown murmur in my ears and a mobile and deceptive gleam dazzled my eyes.

For more than a year I had been living in the midst of the distractions of war, occupied with continual cares, surrounded by ever-renewed perils. I attributed the singular state in which I found myself to the effect of solitude, but I did not understand that disorders could be produced in my imagination and my organs that approached delirium. That uncertainty followed me all the way to the farm, where it sought to cease.

My conductor introduced me into Thérèse's room and I gave her the letter from her father. At the moment when she looked at me, my heart filled. The universe was complete.

Thérèse was a little less than sixteen years old. She was not the most beautiful of women, but she was the only woman who had made me comprehend the happiness of loving and being loved; for I understood immediately, not without astonishment that a sentiment so powerful and tyrannical, which absorbed all the faculties of my life so completely, had required so little to subjugate them. I have often wondered since whether it is the same for other men, but I have not been able to find out from them.

The impression was as sudden as thought, as sudden as the gaze that Thérèse directed at me, which was animated by such a touching benevolence that the sight of the heaven opening would not have rejoiced my soul with such a vivid and pure sensuality. I say *her gaze* because I do not know any other expression to depict the emanation of a soft fire that escapes between the eyelashes of a beloved woman, contact with which overturns the heart and causes the blood to turn in all the arteries.

Thérèse's eyelids had not entirely lowered over her father's letter when I already knew that my destiny belonged to her forever. I dared to look at her then, because she was no longer looking at me, and I was so feeble in my happiness that I almost doubted the moment when she would finish reading. I did not feel the strength to support at such a short distance two emotions, the first of which had sufficed to inundate my senses with an intoxicating felicity.

The benefits of existence seemed to me to be poorly divided; I would have liked to distribute the excess of my sentiments and my illusions throughout all the years that remained to me to live, or I would have liked to accumulate them to the point of overwhelming me, and for my heart, broken by delight, to be annihilated in its joy. The later idea prevailed, and I commenced to nourish myself on the contemplation of her features; I strove to engrave them indelibly in my memory, to appropriate all of them, in such a manner that no eventuality could deprive me of them in future, and that, if it were reserved for me to die a death so accomplished in mildness, that image identified with my last thought would occupy it alone during all of eternity.

Thérèse was short in stature, but one only perceived that by comparison, because nature had never given forms more gracious or proportions more remarkable in their elegance and harmony. Her black hair, which was bound up with simplicity on the top of her head, uncovered a forehead whiter than ivory; only two curls were rounded to either side as if to heighten its brightness. She did not have a complexion animated by color, but the slightest keen impression gave birth to it, and that fugitive charm was all the more enchanting for it. The result of that was a character of beauty made no less for the soul than for the eyes.

That advantage, which in other women is only a sign of youth and health, appeared in Thérèse to be a particular privilege of sentiment. At first glance one found her charming, but one did not know to what point she was worthy of being loved as long as one had not seen her blush with a mild emotion. The same facility of sensation and expression embellished all the parts of her physiognomy with the indefinable attraction that one senses better than one can describe, and which is renewed so rapid that even the attentive eye of amour cannot always grasp it. It was sometimes the transport of a gaiety so frank and so ingenuous, the expression of the facile happiness of a child content with very little, but it was more often an indeterminate sadness that did not seem to be nourished by a real object, and which went astray in thoughts foreign to the places, times and circumstances in which it became manifest. It is possible that melancholy is not in all sensitive beings the effect of memories of past troubles. Why should it not sometimes be an involuntary disposition of the heart to try the troubles that threaten it, and an advice to prepare for them?

Her neck was extremely agile and ceded almost continually to the weight of her head, which then inclined over one of her shoulders with an abandon full of grace. That habit was probably a fault, but a fault whose charm no perfection could replace so intimately was it linked with tender and delicate ideas.

In any case, those are only reminiscences, and not a portrait. I wanted to talk about her, and not to substitute for the vivid image that she left in my heart, and which no human effort would be able to pass into the mind and heart of others an imperfect sketch that loses its color and is extinguished under my pen. Oh, it was not thus that I saw her; or, rather, I never saw her distinctly enough to attempt to depict her. There was a luminous veil over her features that hid all its details from me, and even now I can only recall her face in the blur of the dazzling vapor with which it was enveloped.

My first approach had inspired in Thérèse an affectionate but familiar interest. She had smiled at me with a frank cordiality that revealed all the bounty of her heart. As she read, her dispositions, without entirely changing their nature, took on another character. An embarrassment, which augmented at every line, developed in her face. Timidity appeared to hinder the effusion of soul that the letter inspired in her. Her bosom palpitated; her cheeks were vividly colored. It was visible that she was trying to retain tears that were ready to spring from her eyes.

When she had finished, she came toward me, took me by the hand expressively, threw her father's letter in the fire after applying her lips to it, and, putting her finger over her mouth, she looked at me in a knowing fashion.

"Mademoiselle," she said to me, "count on all cares . . ." She looked at me again, and, remarking my emotion, she put one of her arms around my neck. "If amity can compensate your pains," she continued, "or if, at least, it can soften them, you will not be entirely unfortunate."

My cheeks were moistened by tears of gratitude, my heart deceived its trouble by delivering itself without reserve to that sentiment. I felt my knees buckling; my lips attached themselves to her hand, an unknown fire escaped from it and spread through all my veins. All my emotions were as new to me as if I were making the first trial of air, light and life.

I tried to speak; I stammered a few confused words like a man in a dream.

Finally, she let herself fall into my arms, saying to me: "Oh, if you knew how I love you already . . ."

She loved me; she had said so.

"Tell me your name," she continued, "or the one that you want to be given."

That question and that language reminded me that I was passing for a woman, and all the illusion of my happiness vanished. My life with Thérèse would be no more than a role, and that role was the only one appropriate to me in the home of my benefactor's daughter. My heart profited somewhat, in any case, from her mistake, and I enjoyed the idea that she might retain a tender memory of me if I did not correct it.

"My name is Antoinette," I replied, blushing, and I yielded to a movement that drew me toward her. We walked arm in arm to the bedroom of her grandmother, who was sitting beside the fire on a chaise longue with a lectern. A book of hours was open in front of her and occupying all her attention.

Thérèse advanced quietly in order not to startle her, and when she was beside her she put her arms around her neck and put her hands over her eyes.

"That's naughty, mischievous child," old Madame Aubert said to her. "Do you think I wouldn't recognize you, even if I were blind—and I soon will be, for my eyes are getting weaker every day; but I shall never confuse your pretty little hand with another's."

As she said that she embraced her.

Thérèse turned to me with an anxious expression. I thought I divined that she regretted having given birth in her grandmother's mind to a thought that might sadden her: that old age was weakening her eyesight and that she might soon lose it. In any case, that impression had been very brief. Madame Aubert had just perceived me. Thérèse drew nearer to her and spoke to her in a quiet voice, with a great deal of charm. In the meantime, Madame Aubert raised her eyes to the heavens, looked at me tenderly, took Thérèse's hand, sought mine, and wept. I bent my knee and knelt down. I heard her bless me, and her benediction did not alarm me, for I found that I had the strength to render myself worthy of it.

I shall not depict my situation during the first weeks that I spent with Thérèse. It had something so embarrassing that I could scarcely conceive that I had the strength to maintain it for so long if I did not recall how much I feared that it might cease. There was a kind of intoxication that troubled all my faculties, the best effect of which was often to suspend their usage. Crushed by the weight of the emotions that succeeded one another continually, which multiplied in my heart, I sometimes yielded to a prostration that was not without charm, and which I found myself glad to maintain. However, a painful idea came continually to interrupt that kind of slumber into which I liked to plunge myself. Thérèse and her generous father were deceived. I was not what I appeared to be, and I was nourishing a passion that both of them might disavow one day.

That idea became all the more insupportable to me, it must be said, because the misery of our sentiments mingles with what they have of the most elevated, and I consented with difficulty to being loved for someone else, hiding under a woman's clothing the tenderness that it would be necessary to renounce one day, deceiving a heart that was giving me everything and to which I was only offering an ideal object, a vain phantom whose appearance was about to vanish and be stolen from her by a separation worse than death; for it is less cruel to lose a person one loves by death than to be disillusioned by them.

I decided, therefore, to tell Thérèse everything—but the weakness of my soul stopped me. I dreaded that in ceasing to love Antoinette, who would no longer exist for her, she would cease to love Adolphe, whom she had never known. I persuaded myself, I don't know why, that the innocent caresses that I owed to my disguise would be the last happiness of my life, and that as soon as I had confessed my secret I would be doomed forever. Caught between the need to be loved by Thérèse and the more imperious need not to deceive either Thérèse's amity or her father's confidence, however, I felt that I ought not to hesitate. I searched for an opportunity—or rather, I awaited one tremulously. It did not take long to present itself.

Thérèse had a friend who lived half a league from the farm in an agreeably situated little château that was visible from the mountain of the cross, the orchards of which, in an amphitheater, were crowned by a platform planted with cherry trees. At the bottom extended a pretty garden bathed by the stream that came a little further on, through a hollow valley shaded by young beech trees, to irrigate the slopes of Sancy. A path, profoundly sunk in a narrow gorge, snaked between two hills that were not very high but extended over a long distance. The sight was only distracted there by a small number of scattered houses, almost all deserted because of the war; an abandoned mill under a waterfall; the remains of a burned cottage that still allowed the perception, between sections of blackened wall, the vestiges of the domestic hearth around which so many pleasant evenings had been spent and, finally, a few pyramidal huts built of lava, where the poor people who came to extract the stone from nearby quarries came to rest after their labor.

That path became our customary walk, because Thérèse's friend was ordinarily encountered half way. Her name was Henriette de F*** and she was noble; but, although the misfortune of circumstances had augmented rather than weakened in her the sentiment of birth and pride of character, it was impossible to find in the commerce of life a simpler soul as devoid of all pretention. Her age was slightly more advanced than ours. Her name, her education and her manners seemed to give her some advantage, which she always sought to lose, and became a burden to her as soon as it was remarked.

She had a kind of coquetry that must be rare. She only made expenses in order to be simpler. She was, in addition, so natural in her sentiments, so frank in her abandon, that one became accustomed right away to being loved by her, and it was understandable that she was loved by Thérèse. Thérèse's amity was her greatest charm in my eyes, but I sensed that a man who had never seen Thérèse might be happy with the amour of Henriette.

Not as pretty as Thérèse, she was nevertheless very good, although her physiognomy lacked wholeness and harmony. Never have features so melancholy been animated by such an extraordinary expression of joy. It is true that the expression in question was very fleeting, but it was so frequent that it would have passed for habitual without the contrast that it produced. Her gaze, sparkling with gaiety, was suddenly obscured and became fixed and somber, her laughter, emitted at short intervals, giving way to silence and the bleakest immobility: a strange alternative of exaltation and dejection rendered the idea of that joy importunate and painful. One divined, I don't know why, that behind the temporary illusion that she produced, there was a hidden woe.

One day . . . the first influences of spring were beginning to make themselves felt in the country; little white flowers fashioned in delicate cups that almost escaped the sight were blooming between the stones by which the path is bordered; the sweet odor of violets revealed their presence under the bushes, and the air, warmed by the rays of the renascent sun, was populated by crowds of insects that only appeared momentarily before dying, but which spread through the scene the movement of life. Our hearts were open to the pleasant impressions of that season of renewal and happiness when we perceived Henriette.

For the first time, her physiognomy was immobile; she looked at us, and sighed; she did not laugh, as usual, at the first object that struck her imagination, so easy to excite; even our conversation did not occupy her. She seemed to be living and thinking elsewhere. That situation soon became embarrassing for all of us; Thérèse's heart, in particular, broke under the weight of such a novel constraint. She did not resist for long; her eyes moistened with tears, and her arm thrown around Henriette's shoulder she asked: "You have a chagrin?"

"Oh, a great deal," replied Henriette, also weeping, "but you wouldn't understand."

"What!" said Thérèse. "Is there one of your chagrins that I can't understand?"

This time, Henriette smiled bitterly. "I believe so, if you aren't loved."

"Can you ask that? Am I not loved by those who love me? Am I not loved by my father? My poor mother, oh my God, was I not loved by her? And my other mother, am I happier anywhere than with her? But you, ingrate, I don't love you, do I? That's how you judge me! Antoinette wouldn't treat me so cruelly. She knows that I love her."

"That's all?" said Henriette, coldly.

"That's all!" continued Thérèse, with a hint of astonishment. "Oh, I know," she cried, in the tone of a singular reminiscence that only returned by chance to her mind. "You mean another sentiment, amour, don't you? Do you know what amour is, tell me, pray?"

Henriette shook her head.

"What does it matter, anyway?" said Thérèse. "I've always been convinced that the passionate depictions that are made of it in books and ballads are only an inconsequential abuse of the known privilege of poets. I know very well that whoever the husband will be that my father will give me, or permit me to choose, I won't love him any better than you . . . or you," she added, turning toward me and attaching a more intense gaze to me."

"You promise me?" I said to her.

"Yes, I promise you."

I took her hand and I covered it by turns with my mouth and my eyes in order not to allow her to receive my disturbance. I already had a right over her heart that could no longer be disputed, and Adolphe was commencing to participate in Antoinette's good fortune.

"Fortunate in thinking thus," said Henriette, "there is no need today for you to know more; and the sentiment that you do not know, may you only ever know its sweetness! Now, this is what you are asking. I have lost my father, as you know, but I have a brother on whom I depend, and who takes a keener interest in my happiness than his own, for he had assumed in my regard the tenderness as well as the duties of a father. A long time ago, based on the advantageous testimonies rendered to him of one of our relatives, he formed the project of uniting me with him, supposing that that arrangement would suit me. The events of the war delayed the accomplishment of his design without causing him to forget it, and even without entirely contradicting his opinion. My cousin was my age, at the most;

he had commenced a brilliant career honorably and it could only be advantageous for him to pursue it for some years before our marriage.

"For my part, my desires did not hasten the moment of that union; I had never seen my cousin, my heart was free and, like yours, my dear Thérèse, it did not believe itself capable of ever experiencing a sentiment more intense than amity, if it is necessary to tell you, at the moment when the will of a husband, the sole arbiter of my life to come, might remove me from my happy solitude, from our dear woods, our rendezvous and our games. However, I could not avoid a keen curiosity when, after the catastrophe of Le Mans, my brother, having arrived precipitately at the château, announced to us that we would see the same evening a young officer escaped as if by a miracle from that day's disasters, who was the Chevalier de Mondyon."

"The Chevalier de Mondyon!" I exclaimed.

"Well, yes," said Thérèse. "There's nothing extraordinary in that."

"It's the name of my cousin," said Henriette, who had not even noticed my astonishment. He finally arrived, and I would try in vain to depict for you the impression that the sight of him made on me. I felt that my entire existence was about to depend on the one that I made on him. It surpassed my hopes. The knots that convention had formed were tightened by the truest sympathy. One single anxiety—but a frightful one—troubled the charm of those moments of happiness. Perhaps it augmented their price, in giving them an intoxication that amour doubtless lacks when it is savored in security, with nothing to fear from men and the future. Mondyon was pursued; every witness to his presence might be an informer; every instant of our excessively rapid felicity might be the last, every day that of his arrest and his death. I urged him myself to hasten his departure and to rejoin the errant army corps."

"So organized army corps still exist?" I asked her.

"So he was assured," replied Henriette, looking at me with surprise.

"And where are they, I beg you to tell me?"

"In truth, Antoinette," Thérèse interjected, "I don't know why you're asking these questions. What has become of your cousin, Henriette?"

"You can imagine that my brother did not neglect anything to procure us positive information regarding the situation of the Vendéans, and the means of rejoining them. Finally, the day before yesterday, he brought us the news that while effecting their retreat they had dispersed the republicans at a few points nearby, and that there was one where the passage remained free."

"Do you know that point?" I exclaimed.

"That was the chevalier's question. There was not a moment to lose. They mounted up and departed, after brief adieux that I trembled, alas, to prolong, for a minute's delay might leave the enemy the time to rob them of that last hope of salvation. My presentiment was not ill-founded, since the domestic who accompanied them that far only escaped with difficulty in coming back between the republican columns that have retaken possession of the entire region and closed all the issues."

"Possession of the entire region," I murmured between my teeth, "but there was a passage, and Mondyon was at the château, and Adolphe did not know it!"

"That's singular," said Henriette. "He regretted that Adolphe of whom you speak. He named him frequently, and sometimes hoped to rediscover him. Do you know him?"

"Very well."

"Very well," said Thérèse, "and you're blushing—and you're trembling like Henriette when she mentioned her cousin. I knew you were keeping secrets from me . . ."

I smiled at her mistake, and the conversation changed its object thereafter. When we arrived at Henriette's home, night was beginning to fall and we did not stop. We returned to the farm, hastening our pace, in order that our overly long absence would not worry Madame Aubert. Both preoccupied by our conversation with Henriette, we walked without talking.

My blood was seething at the thought that Mondyon had been so close to us, that he had been living in a house that I went into every day, and it was there that he had found an opportunity to rejoin the army—an opportunity that might never be presented to me, to whom it was all the more necessary because my position in regard to Thérèse alarmed my heart with the shame of a fraud and the dread of an ingratitude.

In the disorder into which that idea threw me, I had hastened my pace so much that Thérèse could no longer keep up with me. We had already gone through the gate that opened between Monsieur Aubert's gardens and the country, but we were still some way from the house. At the entrance to a small garden that Thérèse cultivated for her pleasure, she let herself fall on to a large stone that had been placed there in the form of a seat, and around which she took pleasure in maintaining the wild plants and parasitic mosses that grew among the rocks of the mountain.

I stopped, and I observed that she was exhausted.

"You're only thinking about that Adolphe," she said to me, reproachfully. "Since we quit Henriette, I've seen that you're no longer taking any notice of me."

"Dear Thérèse," I cried, "how unjust you are, and how little you should suspect me of preferring to you that Adolphe, whose name I let slip, if I could enable you to know him! What am I saying? Is it not necessary that you finally know him, that you love him for himself, and that you at least pardon him for having loved him for so long as another."

"There's something in this that I don't understand," said Thérèse, "something that astonishes and frightens me. Don't leave me in this uncertainty; it's more painful than a real chagrin."

"Thérèse, you don't know how all my happiness depends on a single word. I might lose everything or gain everything, for my entire life is in your love, which you might perhaps take away from me. However, the word that might decide my fate irrevocably . . . and yours . . . it is my duty to say to you; and if I die of your anger or your indifference, at least I shall die worthy of your esteem."

"Go on."

"I am not Antoinette, I am Adolphe."

And I fell at her knees, seizing her hands—which escaped from mine. She uttered a loud scream and fled.

Needless to say, that confession changed our relationship instantly. From that moment on, Thérèse no longer looked at me except with an anxious eye, as if she dreaded finding in me an enemy and as if she mistrusted the sentiments that I might have inspired in her. The expression of her features, so naïve and so familiar, had become serious and even somber. Often, when my eyes encountered hers, and when they forced them, so to speak, to remain fixed on me by virtue of the ascendancy that a strongly felt amour exercises upon the person who inspires it, the cloud of dolor that obscured them caused me a sort of regret and dread.

I found myself glad to occupy her life, and even to give birth in her heart the idea of the storms that mine was experiencing, but the thought that loving me might cause her distress sometimes broke my soul, which had no strength against Thérèse's chagrins. My dangers had never caused me as much anxiety as my happiness. I desired strongly that Thérèse should be moved, but trembled that she might suffer. So I carefully avoided, or at least believed that I was avoiding, anything that might remind her of our reciprocal situation, and what I had said to her about my love.

While burning with impatience to be alone with her, I was glad if a third person came to intervene in our walks, but, as soon that stranger had arrived I desired that they would go away, even though I was determined to say nothing to Thérèse and to preserve her repose. When we remained together, her reserve augmented and she drew away subtly, in such a manner as no longer to touch me, so that only happened by mistake, in a moment of distraction or in making an involuntary movement. Then she withdrew even further away and her attitude became even more anxious.

For myself, as I could only count on those hazards occurring rarely, I made a study of multiplying them, because they were my only happiness. With what attention I watched her eyes for the slightest of her desires, in order to anticipate it, in order to surprise the slightest of her gestures in order to make it concur with a fortunate awkwardness that brought my hand close to her hand, my foot close to her foot, and my mouth close to her shoulder or her neck. How many times, under the pretext of presenting her with a flower from her garden, or returning an item of needlework that she had dropped, I shivered on touching her tremulous fingers, the light impression of which awakened in all my veins an inexpressible sentiment of pleasure.

Between her bedroom and her grandmother's there was a narrow corridor that she traveled continually, and where I never failed to stop as soon as I could presume that she was about to do so, because there was so little space for two persons that it was impossible for her to pass me by without brushing me. As she approached I gathered all the strength of my heart to support the sensuality of that rapid and delectable friction. That hazard appeared to me to be a favor, because I thought that she would have been able to avoid it or go another way, and it was, in my view, inconceivable that a similar emotion could not be communicated in some measure to the person who engendered it. I had a sort of certainty that a woman by whom he is hated does not produce the same effect on a man that she touches in passing, whatever amour he has for her, or that she would not touch him in the same way.

I had also noticed that her voice was no longer the same when she spoke to me, and I was so convinced that amour, which has so many mysteries, even had an accent and a melody of its own, that she never addressed me in order to say the most indifferent things without me trembling with joy, as if those trivia had a meaning other than the one she attached to them, as if I had agreed a key with her that could explain her language.

That state of things was so unnatural, that secret so easy to penetrate, that even my disguise did not reassure me, and her obligatory testimonies of amity for Antoinette gave me as much anxiety as if they were addressed to Adolphe. Furthermore, they caused me jealousy, and I was no less tormented by her attentions before others than I was afflicted by her coldness when we were alone. I needed to be loved less, or more. My position was false everywhere; I was Adolphe for Thérèse when we were observed, because then she only found danger in letting me see what she was experiencing; when we found ourselves together, I was no longer him. That idea was so painful that when it oppressed me, I would sometimes have preferred a complete indifference—but more frequently, I preferred to suffer.

In all the places where I liked to hide my chagrin, there was none that I preferred to Thérèse's garden, and in Thérèse's garden, none that I preferred to the rock on which she had been sitting when I made her the confession that had distanced her from me. As she had perceived that, she did not go there as frequently, for fear of encountering me there, or else she affected to take a long detour around it and to go and walk further away in a solitary path, where I would only perceive her at intervals between the clumps of trees and the orchards.

That had lasted for several weeks, and I was lying on the bench, as usual, my head covered by my hands, which I was inundating with tears, when I felt a woman's fingers imposed on my neck, gently but with a sort of authority as if she wanted to instruct me not to look at her, because she had things to say to me, the confession of which embarrassed her. I recognized Thérèse easily and I remained motionless, sobbing, because I was weeping when she came.

She commenced and paused several times in a phrase that she had just begun, and then she told me in an emotional and tremulous voice that we were about to be separated. Her father, who had never ceased to take me for a young woman, thought he had found a means of enabling me to rejoin my relatives, or the army to which they were attached and that I ought to have followed with them. He flattered himself that he could in any case, shield me from pursuit and persecution. He was waiting for me in Le Mans, and a letter transmitted by a reliable man— the one who had guided me to Sancy—had brought the news.

After that, Thérèse thought she owed me consolations; she expected my despair, and when, unable to sustain myself, I let my head fall upon the rock, she enveloped me with her arms and called me by my name, Adolphe.

"Adolphe!" I said to her. "Oh my God, am I at least Adolphe for you?"

"Adolphe, my Adolphe," she replied.

"Adolphe!" I cried, snatching away the headband that attached my hair. "Thérèse's Adolphe? Be careful, for that word is an irrevocable bond, an engagement for all of life."

"All of life!"

"You love me, then?"

She looked at me with a bewildered expression. Her lips were pale and trembling; her entire physiognomy had changed.

"Yes, I love you!" said Thérèse.

I thought I might die, and that it would be sweet to have died then. However, her father's intention was a law. The next day, everything was ready for my departure, and our adieux had been the most beautiful moment of my life, because she had promised to accompany me as far as the crest of the mountain.

We went up the path of the Cross, above which we had agreed to quit one another, because she had been complaining of a slight illness for two days and I feared that she might be fatigued; but the weather was so mild, the air so serene, nature so brilliant with verdure and flowers that I could not oppose allowing her to continue her walk as far as a picturesque spot shaded by trees of various species, which we had often visited together.

At the summit of a rising and rather difficult route that led to old walls ruined centuries before, which divided there into multiple paths through thickets cut at hazard, whose confused compartments formed a labyrinth of sorts, and which ended between clumps of trees at a lateral path, there was a small resting place under a few eglantine bushes, where we had often stopped before she knew me as Adolphe, and where were had sometimes spent very pleasant moments chatting about everything that interested her: her father, her mother, the past and the future. The place was covered, as I said, by wild roses, the first flowers of which we had promised ourselves to pick, and to which we came from time to time in order to observe their development, me for her and her for me, because we were rivals in impatience to bring one another the first tributes of the new season.

Since the clarification that I had been obliged to give Thérèse, we no longer took those walks, and it was already some time since we had seen the ridge of the rose-bushes. When Thérèse arrived there she gave evidence of some disturbance and took a step back. I understood her astonishment—or, rather, her fear—and at first I was likewise ready to yield to it. However, I took her hand and led her to the place where she was accustomed to sit down, over which the hedge hung down in long garlands.

I stopped there, and as I remarked that she hesitated I said: "The eglantines have bloomed, as you see. I was the one who saw them first."

"First!" she said.

I knew full well that our situation had changed, but that word reminded me of it in an almost dolorous manner; we were about to quit one another, and it was cruel on her part to reproach me for the happiness I had stolen from her confidence. My physiognomy must have expressed that sentiment, for she said to me, smiling: "Since it's you who saw them, give me one of those eglantines; I shall keep it as long as I live."

I picked a few eglantines and I came to sit down beside her. I spread them over her knees, on her handkerchief, and in her hair. She took one, looked at it for a long time, then looked at me with a somber expression, and pulled off the petals absent-mindedly. I gave her another, but I collected the petals that had fallen under her fingers and as I picked them up I applied them to her lips; I took them back thereafter and bore them to mine, still moist on the side that her lips had touched. For a few minutes I enjoyed that artifice without her perceiving it, but as soon as she noticed it she became alarmed. She disputed with me the petal that I had stolen and refused the one that I presented to her.

"What!" I said. "When we're about to be separated for God knows how many days, months or years, you won't permit your Adolphe, whom you might never see again, to seek the impression of your mouth on the debris of an eglantine! Oh, I believe, in truth, that my heart is as innocent as yours, but I don't understand anything of human ideas if there is a crime between us when a kiss from Thérèse's mouth is transported to Adolphe's by a rose petal. In any case, believe me, I shall tell your father that, and I'm sure of telling him without blushing. One day . . . if I don't die in the war, you'll grant me sweeter kisses . . ."

"I'd like to believe you," she said, "but it's possible that that is bad today, and even probable, since I'm so ill at ease that I'm trembling and I'm afraid. I'll be more tranquil if I don't already have something for which to reproach myself."

"And do you believe," I said, "that my heart is any more placid? It's doubtless the effect of the unknown sentiment about which Henriette spoke to us two months ago, and which we're experiencing like her. Anyway, Henriette knows how to love! She wouldn't refuse Mondyon the pleasure of attaching his mouth to a little flower that she had pressed against hers."

"And me," said Thérèse, "I don't love you?"

She put a rose petal over my lips and put it between her teeth. I moved closer to her. I looked at her, and I turned away from her, because my heart was breaking, and I conceived I know not what idea, one of those bizarre presentiments that obfuscate the mind in a fever and in slumber: the persuasion that all my happiness would be brief and that I would only kiss Thérèse once.

Her complexion was animated in an extraordinary manner; her hand was hot and tremulous at the same time. I would have liked to take account of my condition. I knew nothing, but the thought of death did not frighten me as it ought to frighten people. It seemed to me that it would be very good.

In the meantime, the domestics who had accompanied us had reached the bottom of the avenue; it was time to go. Only one petal remained on the last eglantine that I had given her. I detached it, pressed it firmly to her mouth, and stuck it to mine, pulling Thérèse forcefully to my bosom. I don't know how I succeeded in retaining her there. That petal, there was nothing but that petal . . .

My sight was obscured, my breast swelled, I lost my respiration, consciousness and the sentiment of life; and when I came round, I was alone.

I hastened to reach the lateral path, because I remembered that there was a place from which the path of the Cross was visible and I hoped to see Thérèse there as she passed by. Either because chance had served my desire or because Thérèse, animated by the same thought, had stopped in that short interval of the hill, which seemed from a distance to be framed between a clump of trees and a mass of rocks, I saw her standing still and turned in my direction; I thought so, at least, and I convinced myself foolishly that my last adieu could reach her; my mouth stammered a word; I said "Adieu" as if she could hear me, and when she had passed on, I accused her in my heart of having quit me too quickly, when so many things still remained for me to explain, across the distance that separated us. If she had at least sat down, so that I could continue looking at her . . .

For myself, I had not turned my gaze away for a moment from the little space that I had seen her cross like a shadow. It seemed to me to be impossible that she had not felt the need to come back to me, as I felt that to return to her, and I still believed that she would come back momentarily, with the sole intention of recognizing the place where we had just been together.

The day was not far advanced; that place was not far from Sancy; she could, she ought to come back; there were, in any case, so many enchantments for my heart in that point of view; all of that area she had explored, she had occupied at different moments; all the contours of the mountain her footsteps had followed. Those trees had covered her with their shade, those rocks had been brushed by her garments; even the sky, which formed the backcloth to the scene in which she had appeared to me, was unalloyed in its purity. There was not a cloud, not a wisp of vapor, that had not dissipated with her; there was the sky, the light, the air that she had touched . . .

My life is marked by so few fortunate epochs that that one, in its unspeakable sadness, still fills my heart with a sentiment of pure felicity. I hoped; my hand had just quit her hand; I could feel the gentle warmth of the imprint of her fingers, which had been linked with mine. I could see the regular and smooth arc that crowned her eyes, the mild gaze that escaped them, and I inflamed that gaze with the fires of an amour similar to the one that I was experiencing.

One day I had stolen a lock of her hair; but, miserly with the pleasure of pressing it to my lips I had wrapped it in the folds of a ribbon that she had given me and which I carried next to my heart. In the movement that I made to search for the ribbon, I saw the petal of a shredded rose fall on to the sand where I was sitting. I gazed at it; I recognized it; I would not have mistaken it after a thousand years, but I sensed that it was still hot.

As I drew away from Sancy I thought I could feel the bonds of my life relaxing, breaking one after another, and that there was no longer anything that could attach me to it.

The world that I had found so narrow for my heart a short while before had become a limitless desert in which, with the exception of a single point, I perceived nothing anywhere but solitude and a void; and I was astonished that the point in question, at which all my desires, all my hopes and all the strength of my soul had taken refuge, I was forced to quit in order to obey a few unfortunate conventions established, unknown to me, between people. I turned my gaze toward it; I fixed my thoughts upon it; I cursed the duties that subjugated me to the fatal obligation to draw away from it, perhaps forever; and who knew with what motive, useless to my happiness and that of others, society presented it to me like bait in order to deprive me of the advantages of my destiny?

Society! How bitterly I conceived that it was possible to hate it, and that the excess of those violent souls who were preparing its dissolution without knowing it, might well be nothing more than the explosion of the sentiments of the natural man, repressed for so many centuries! How ambitious I was sometimes to assist in the accomplishment of their deadly mission! Could society be good, when it was what was separating me from Thérèse, preventing me from seizing her by the right of force and amour and carrying her away in my arms, palpitating with a mixture of terror and joy, to the depths of some hospitable valley favored by a temperate sky, refreshed by pure springs and shaded by fruit trees of all seasons?

My father had spoken to me about the beautiful landscapes of the New World, where he had tried his arms, and my blood boiled when I thought that I might have been born there beside her, to live there as her brother, her friend, her lover and her husband, in the midst of the wealth that a savage and liberal nature lavished upon its inhabitants, and that I might have accomplished there without trouble the years that were reserved for me, exempt from all the tributes imposed on civilized man by the caprice of propriety, the routine of customs or the tyranny of laws.

What did the future fate of States matter to me, an orphan, henceforth devoid of a family and a name, and the success, or lack of it, of the convulsive struggle that was exhausting in doubtless impotent efforts the last faculties of a generation consecrated to all misfortunes? It was foreign to me. What imperious necessity was making me run again to the hazards of a futile and bloody war, and forcing me to reenter a career in which I could not leave a single footprint without distancing myself more irrevocably from the lonely living being who was truly necessary to my life, and who had consecrated hers to me? Did I even know whether the incredible sacrifice of all interests, of all sentiments, of existence entire, whether the thousand times more painful sacrifice of the existence of an angel whose happiness depended on me, would defend me one day from the magnificent disdain of the nobles of the court, from the ingratitude and rejection of their masters; whether it would not become a title of reproach against the unfortunates who shared my fate, and whether history, sold to a triumphant party, would not dare to pursue us even in the tomb with the name of brigands, the barbaric irony of the victor?

I shivered at that prospect, and then I smiled, for the motives that opposed my resolution were precisely those that ought to found and affirm them. Never does a noble heart engage so far in an enterprise in which it has nothing to gain as when there is everything to lose. One does not detach oneself from one's habitudes, affections and pretentions to happiness or renown, if it is only a matter of dying.

In general—and I am revealing here all the secrets of my soul—when I have experienced a few feeble hesitations, like those I have just recounted, they have only lasted a moment, and I flatter myself that it will only require a moment to expiate them.

When I arrived near Le Mans, the day had not entirely ended. However, as I went toward the home of my protector, and I had to avoid compromising him, I was not the master of all my steps. My life alone depended on me; I had to take every precaution for the sake of others. I resolved to wait for nightfall to introduce myself into the town. A short distance away I had remarked a small area of verdure covered at intervals by a few disorderly plants, the short and trodden grass of which scarcely covered the ground because the local young women often came there to dance on the fine evenings of the year. I stopped there on a circular bank adapted to the trunk of an old elm, turning toward the part of the horizon where the farm of Sancy was.

The evening mists that were accumulating in the west were beginning to extend in my direction, and I was pleased to see those clouds, colored by the last fires of the day, rolling, flattening out, dividing into wisps, sheets and webs, suspended at first from the gilded vault of the occident like pink curtains and then developing slowly into coppery, violet or black-tinted shadows before disappearing in the obscurity of the night. Their rapid passage and their varied forms seemed to multiply, by as many messages, Thérèse's last adieu. Each of those clouds had passed over her head; she had seen them; she was still gazing at them; perhaps the same idea was occupying her, and my eyes might be attached to the same place as hers on the confused figure that was vanishing between us and carrying away our last gaze. Was I sure of ever seeing again a cloud that she had seen?

As the weather was fine, the young women did not fail to arrive at their evening rendezvous and to form their customary dances around the old elm where I had chanced to sit down, singing in chorus the verses of their round, which astonished me by their simplicity and grace, because exile and the war had deprived me too soon of those innocent joys of childhood. I understood the pleasure of them, however, and I regretted, with my eyes moistened by tears, not having lived in a time and in a state where it was permissible to be happy so easily.

Amour was mingled with those pleasures, for there were a few young men of my age with each group, who disputed at every refrain the inappreciable favor of a preferential kiss. I cannot recall very clearly the words of those songs, but it seemed to me that they would never vibrate in my ear without my heart quivering, so many charming things did they reveal to me. However, that was nothing in itself; or, rather, it would be impossible to express to those who have not felt the same thing.

If I remember rightly, there was a beauty who fell asleep by the edge of a spring, and her father and her fiancé were searching for her. There were daughters of a king expelled from their palace who woke up in the forest on the day of a battle, and said more prayers for their suitors than for the crown. There were the regrets of shepherdesses who were afflicted at no longer going to the woods because the laurels had been cut, and who were looking forward to the season that would bring back their dances and their amours.

I found myself enclosed in the circle of the games; I had been retained there at first by the curiosity of a new sensation, and then by the satisfaction of a fatigued soul able to relax in mild emotions, and finally by an interest of a singular species that would have absorbed all my other sentiments if I had not known Sancy. Several times the name of Jeannette, the name attached to a young person whose candor, frank gaiety, air of wellbeing and contentment reposed thought agreeably, had struck my ear and echoed all the way to my heart. At first I was placed alongside her; I gazed at her, I compared our heights and our garments, and I wondered whether she was Jeannette, but at the moment when I believed that my conjectures were confirmed, she disappeared, as if by design, into the crowd.

Eventually the combinations of a new game brought me close to her, and the rule of that game prescribed me to tell her a secret. I took possession of her hand, raised it to my bosom, attached my eyes to hers in such a manner as to force her to sustain my gaze momentarily, I let a tress of my hair fall back as it was in the disorder of my flight, and I leaned over her shoulder in order only to be heard by her.

"Jeannette," I said to her, "God will recompense you because you took pity on a poor brigand."

She uttered a cry and, trembling at my imprudence and hers, she disguised her alarm under some pretext or other, after which she rejoined her companions.

It was very late when I went into the town, and the obscurity favored my designs. I arrived easily enough at Monsieur Aubert's house, because Thérèse had indicated it to me very carefully, and the old domestic who opened the door to me recognized me immediately for having seen me several times at the farm when he was sent there by his master. I was struck by his sadness and dejection, and I had no difficulty perceiving, by the lamplight illuminating his face, that recent tears had moistened his eyelids.

He did not proffer a word while the door was open, but as soon as he had allowed it to fall back on its hinges, he hastened to put down the lamp that was flickering in his trembling hand, fell into a chair, dissolved in tears and told me that Monsieur Aubert had been arrested.

"Arrested!" I cried.

"Two days ago."

"Why?"

"Does one know why one is taken to prison, and from prison to the scaffold?" he said to me, shaking his head. "But it had to happen sooner or later," he continued. "He was too honest a man for these people, and for a long time I thought to myself that they would end up killing him for not being as wicked as them."

"They shan't kill him, or I shall die beside him!"

"Antoinette!" said the old man, astonished

What was I in fact, and how could I try to liberate my generous liberator in my turn without completely dooming him?

It was necessary, however, to attempt anything, and in order to succeed in something it was necessary to communicate with him. That was not easy. An entire week passed before obtaining anything, because Monsieur Aubert was being held in secret, and the permission finally granted to our pleas only regarded Dominique. At the same time, Monsieur Aubert's correspondence was handed to him, already opened by the warden of the prison. There were two letters from Sancy, posterior to my departure.

I spent the day waiting in an inconceivable anxiety, not because I had glimpsed the slightest possibility of saving Monsieur Aubert by a hazardous act of violence, or because the state of things was so desperate for him that there only remained, of all my hypotheses, the certainty of his doom, but because an indefinable sentiment rendered Dominique's return increasingly necessary, as if my life depended on what he would have to say to me.

When he returned, I sought impatiently to read in his eyes whether there was any new circumstance that might justify my fears. He seemed tranquil to me, but his tranquility did not reassure me at all. Finally, he sat down and took from a fold of his garments a letter addressed to Antoinette, of which I took possession in haste. It was conceived in these terms:

Dear child, when I wrote to Thérèse to send you to Le Mans I believed that I was sure that I would be able to return you to your family before long. You know how my fate has changed, and the interest that you have taken in it is known to me. My sole misfortune now is not being able to put an end to yours. I am not in any personal danger; or, rather, I have a certainty so positive of incessantly escaping all dangers that if I recommend you to destroy my letter, it is in view of not compromising your secrets and your existence. Mine has become useless to the unfortunate, and if it were to end in consequence of a judgment, the confiscation would deprive my family of its last resources. It is for that reason that I have resolved to be free and that I have contrived the means. I swear to you that everything will succeed for that to my satisfaction. In the state that the recent event will have left you I can see nothing better for you to do than to return to Sancy. I engage you to do that in your own interest, because that house will remain your refuge for as long as you require a refuge. Later, in addition, my daughter can devote her happiness to the liaison that she has contracted with you and find in your amity and your protection the price of the feeble services of her father. She has need of you today. They have written to me twice that she is ill, that she is very ill, and I fear that they might still be dissimulating from me the extent to which my Thérèse's life is compromised. Go to Sancy, then, dear Antoinette; it is her father who begs you to do so; and above all, do not talk about my captivity, either before my old mother or before my poor Thérèse. I repeat to you that it is not worth the trouble. My captivity will end.

Jules Aubert

That letter caused me intense alarm regarding Thérèse's fate. It only reassured me feebly regarding that of Monsieur Aubert, whose resources and hopes I did not understand. Dominique's permission gave him the right to enter the prison every day; I resolved to wait until the next day. That day, Dominque came back early, after an absence so short that it barely gave me time for impatience and anxiety. He was radiant with joy.

"Our master is no longer in prison," he said, when he had taken the time to assemble his ideas and gathered the strength to make himself heard.

"He's no longer in prison!" I cried. "But where is he? Do you know?"

Dominique looked at me with an embarrassed expression.

"I don't know anything, in truth, but what I'm certain of is that Monsieur Aubert is no longer in the prison where I saw him and that he hasn't been transferred to another. I made sure of that myself, and elsewhere. The concierge replied to me, moreover, in a somber tone of voice and with a frightful expression, like that of an assassin who has lost track of his victim before finishing him off. He said to me abruptly: 'He's no longer here.'

"'Is he is another house?' I retorted.

"'No,' he replied, and slammed the door on me.

"As true as God is God," Dominique continued. "I protest to you that our master is saved."

I reread Monsieur Aubert's letter. There was something vague about it that frightened me at first, but I found that it might lend itself to that explanation. While I was reflecting on that, the rumor of the escape of several prisoners reached us, and confirmed me in that idea. I had therefore, no more to do than fulfill the intentions of my benefactor and satisfy the need of my soul, which was tormented by the most cruel anguish as soon as I imagined Thérèse ill, perhaps dying, and appealing in vain for her father and me. I embraced Dominique and departed.

Although I was returning to Thérèse, and a few days before I could not have imagined any greater happiness, and although I loved her more than ever, I marched penetrated by sadness, and as slowly as if I had never had to see her again. I had never found myself so weak and so at odds with the world. There was a kind of dolorous cloud before my eyes, which obscured even the sweet memories of my life. The uncertainty I was in regarding the eventual fate of Monsieur Aubert, the doubt he had left me regarding the veritable condition of Thérèse, the dread of finding her in a dangerous situation, even the annoyance of the costume that hid my sex, which was beginning to disguise it poorly and becoming a burden to my impatience and my courage, and finally, I know not what need to die, which is perhaps in all men the presentiment of misfortunes about to end, all acted at the same time on my imagination and on my heart. It seemed to me that I would always arrive too soon where I was going, and that it would be better not to arrive.

I sat down above the mountain of the Cross in order to gaze at the house. Nothing had changed. There was no troubling movement there. The cultivators were at their ordinary labors. The air was calm and mild, and one imagines that if one had real motives for suffering, all nature ought to take taking part therein. I was contemplating with an involuntary fear, therefore, the hamlet that had seen me so happy, and I was trembling to return to it.

At that moment I heard a noise behind me in the wood. I turned round to see where it was coming from. It was a woman, who was still distant, but whom I recognized through a strange disorder of her physiognomy as Henriette de F***. At first I thought I was dreaming; her hair was scattered, her dress torn and her feet bare; she was climbing with the agility of a phantom on the sharp points of rocks, singing the refrains of ballads and laughing excessively.

A man was following her at a distance, his eyes attentive to all her movements, his expression afflicted and pensive; I also recognized him as one of her domestics. He had perceived me at the same time—or rather he had perceived Antoinette, for that was all I was to him. He put his hand to his forehead with a movement of the head that expressed the sharpest dolor, to make me understand that Henriette was mad.

I got up and ran to her; her wide eyes arrested on me fixedly. She remained standing on the rock on to the point of which she had just launched herself, manifesting by her immobile and irreflective attitude the desire to remember something. The laughter that flew from her mouth continually was not entirely effaced, but her eyelids were soon moistened by abundant tears, and that contrast had something horrible about it. As I saw her at closer range I remarked more clearly the disarray of her features and the bizarrerie of her garments. She was wearing a red kerchief as a sash, like our officers; her long brown hair, which was falling to either side in front of her, was sewn with marigolds, and the dark violet flowers known, I believe, as columbines. Her arms, tanned by the sun, emerged bare from the short sleeves of her black dress; they were already thin and withered, as if death had touched them.

"You don't know, Antoinette," she said to me, "those people have killed Mondyon. Killed, killed . . ."

"Mondyon is dead!" I cried. "Can it be true?"

She struck the pose of a man taking aim at another. "Not like that," she said. Then she raised her hand and let it fall along her neck with a frightful burst of laughter. I did not understand the gesture very well; she clarified my doubt by repeating it. The domestic who was following her inclined his head affirmatively.

Mondyon! My poor Mondyon! I searched for a sword, but I was wearing a dress, the clothing of a woman.

Henriette was no longer present to my thought, but she was occupied even less with Antoinette and everything that remained of the world. When I raised my eyes to the place where I had seen her she was already far away. She had resumed the monotonous refrain of her song and was leaping from rock to rock to the summit of the mountain. I collapsed on the one that she had just quit, on which her feet had left traces of blood.

"Mondyon is dead!" I said, biting the earth. "My father is dead! My unfortunate mother, who I scarcely embraced, died before her time, dead in a dungeon . . . Everything that I have loved, consecrated to the scaffold . . . sacrificed to the absurd reveries of a few fanatics . . . and I'm wearing a woman's clothes! Oh, Adolphe, you have a woman's clothes, and yet you don't lack the garments and weapons of a man; all that is at your disposal, and you're wearing a woman's clothes, and you think you enjoy your strength and your reason! Oh, poor creature, that woman, deprived of reason, who has just spoken to you, would be scornful of you if she knew that a soldier is hidden under the clothes of the farm servant; Henriette is a thousand times more of a man than you; if she had, like you, a piece of iron that could give death, she would avenge Mondyon, and would not weep uselessly over misfortunes that, in your place, she would have had to share.

"Very well," I said, getting up, "Thérèse is ill; her father, who has the most sacred authority over me, wanted me to go to her.

I shall see her; I shall serve her; I shall make sure that she has no more need of my presence and I shall quit her tomorrow, and I shall go to die too. Thérèse is all my happiness, but honor is everything before her. What right do I have to love when they are dead? Great gods! Would she deign to support the gaze of a feeble and unworthy creature who has survived his friends, who dares to attest their memory, and who has not redeemed their blood!"

I stopped and I hugged myself with my own arms as if my father were enveloping me with his. I said to myself, with an authority that did not come from me, which belonged to a power superior to my will: "Adolphe, go and die!"

The weight that was crushing me diminished; my heart expanded as it must have done at the first sensuality of life; I sensed that I was acting upon the weakness of my soul with an irresistible force, and that idea penetrated me with an as-yet-unknown joy. I repeated, in a loud voice: "Adolphe, go and die!"

And I responded: "I will go."

I arrived at Sancy without meeting anyone; or, rather, I avoided a few children who were guarding their flocks on the slope of the hill, and who could have told me what was happening. The door was open, the domestics were not there.

Thérèse was lying in the second room; there were many people there: domestics, friends, neighbors and physicians around her bed. I entered as quietly as possible, but I remarked that they were talking. I advanced without precaution, as far as the place where she ought to be able to see me. She did not see me, however; I did not understand precisely why.

A girl leaned over her and said to her with a singular expression: "Antoinette has arrived!"

I observed a movement and I heard a muted cry, a veiled cry, which did not remind me distinctly of Thérèse's voice. She raised herself up on her bed, and asked: "Where is she?"

It was not Thérèse as I had seen her; her complexion was animated by an extraordinary brightness, which contrasted with the livid pallor of her forehead. Her eyes were turned toward me, but I did not find her gaze. I thought of the smallpox that I must have had shortly after my birth, according to what my mother had told me, and the effects of which I did not know. Confirmed in that idea by a word that escaped one of the persons who was there, I was struck by the thought that smallpox is sometimes fatal, and that Thérèse had a mortal illness; that was the affair of a moment, but that moment used up my life to such an extent that I felt that even happiness could not prolong it.

"Oh, don't come any closer," said Thérèse. "Don't come any closer if you haven't had smallpox!"

"I've had smallpox," I told her, leaning on her bed, because I had difficulty sustaining myself, and covering with tears and kisses the hand that she had just abandoned to me. "I've had smallpox."

I was not completely sure of that, and how I wished to be sure of the contrary, in order to hope to suffer from the same disease and to run the same dangers.

Thérèse had pressed my hand; she had lifted it to her mouth. I had kissed her too. She had pushed me away slightly. Her lips were dry and hot.

When I had rested and calmed the trouble in my soul, I noticed that there was no longer anyone with us, and that Thérèse had covered her face with her sheet. I understood, or thought I understood, her intention. I revolted against the idea that she did not think me worthy of looking at her and loving her in the ugliness of her malady.

"You no longer love your Adolphe," I said to her, in a low voice, "since you no longer want to see him."

"Adolphe," she said, in an even lower voice. "Remember that you're naming yourself . . ."

"They've gone," I continued. "There's no longer anyone but you and your Adolphe, whom you no longer want to see."

She squeezed my hand, raised her head, and let it fall back under the sheet, which covered her like a shroud.

That thought displeased me. I tried to snatch it away; she retained it.

"That I don't want to see," she murmured, with a sob that broke my heart. "Say that I can no longer see him, and that I'll never see him again. Thérèse is nothing for Adolphe but a specter, the head of a skeleton that rolls in a cemetery. She no longer has eyes!"

"Shut up," I said to her, drawing her to me. "Your poor mind is wandering; it's weakened and troubled by your illness. If it weren't abusing you, you wouldn't deceive me so cruelly."

She threw back the sheet and turned toward me as if she were looking at me. I could not see her eyes, but I had never seen the effects of smallpox and had only formed a vague idea of it.

"It's a common accident," I told her, "which only lasts as long as the malady, and ought not to frighten you."

She smiled, seized my fingers, bore them toward the orbits of her eyes and placed them in their profundities. They were empty. I shuddered voluntarily, for I would have liked to hide what I was feeling, but my hands were engaged in hers; she pressed them swiftly, and then abandoned them, as if she wanted to return my liberty. I divined that, seized her hands again and retained them forcefully. I was weeping bitterly.

"Thérèse," I said, "those who love like you are fortunate. What supple and facile bonds they have! You would have abandoned blind Adolphe?" She tried to interrupt me, but I continued. "Adolphe whom you collected, whom you nourished, whom you saved—I no longer dare say, alas, whom you loved—you would have abandoned for one misfortune more? Your pity would have gone that far and no further! A gunshot might have taken away my eyes, and Adolphe would then have had no one who loved him, who would guide him, who would receive for him the alms of charity? It's thus that you loved me, thus that you love! Oh, I hope that you're not blind, but if you were. I would cease to see you myself and live for you! Tell me, how could I quit you without dying? The blind man has a dog that precedes him, which serves him, which solicits for him with its attitude and its gaze the charity of passers-by, a dog by whom he is loved; and what one expects of a brute, you will not request of the heart that you have chosen! No, Thérèse, you have no need of eyes while Adolphe has them to watch over you; and as for him, if he needed to be seen by you, by you alone, forever, you would pardon him for the vanities of amour; but there, in your heart, can you not still see him?"

"Oh, forever, forever," said Thérèse. "Oh, I can see you better. I have never seen you so clearly; I can even see the crease in your forehead, the movement of your eyebrow, the little scar on your upper lip, and I shall see that for much longer than other women; but why bind yourself to a cadaver?

"I'm causing you pain," she went on. "Oh, I know my Adolphe well, and I would not renounce him on earth if I did not know where to find him again! But I shall find him again one day in order never to be separated from him.

"You would have done well," she continued, passing her fingers through my hair, "you could live and love; it's in the order of things; but your eternity belongs to me alone. Then I shall have, and forever, my beauty, my youth and my eyes."

As she said that she covered with her hand the place where they had been.

I had lost the strength to respond to her. I succumbed under the weight of my dolor. It seems to me that the tears with which I wet her hand should have spoken for me, but might they not have been taken for those of pity, an ordinary and comfortable pity, like that which other men have for their fellows, and which does not engage the life of the person who experiences it? Her hand, in any case, was so pale and so cold; she might be insensible to my tears.

I felt that I lacked a language, that the signs lost for her eyes, the action of my hand perhaps lost for her hand, which was scarcely responding, that of my speech, sustained by vulgar exclamations, the cold oaths that lovers make in order to deceive, surely could not reach her heart. I would have liked to open mine, and that her eyes, momentarily restored, might be able to assure her that I was not deceiving her.

Oh, I conceived in that idea an inexpressibly sensual desire to die! In that impotence to make myself understood, I tore her sheet with my teeth, I stifled my sobs therein, I dried my eyes by compressing them forcefully in order to stop the tears by which they were inundated. I desired to lose them.

"Do you want me to tear out," I said to her, "these eyes that displease you, in order that we might parade our infirmity together from town to town, at the mercy of Heaven and human sympathy? Tell me, do you want me to be blind, for me to destroy with two thrusts of a dagger this feeble and unfortunate advantage that excessively unjust nature has given me over you? Then people will say: *there are two lovers, the mistress who has lost her eyes by smallpox, and the lover who blinded himself in order to resemble his mistress; they go through the world faithful and happy, for their happiness consists of loving one another.* They will say that, have no doubt, and take pity on our misery!"

"I understand you," she replied. "What you are saying there, I have experienced so many times in my heart, before thinking that I would become so unfortunate, when I imagined that it would be for me to protect, to sustain and to embellish your life. But perhaps they are the illusions of insensate youth, for which the entire future is in a moment of intoxication and aberration. You will always be everything for me, whatever happens, because my heart will never have the fatal privilege of being able to change. I will love you all my life as I have loved you, because I will see you all my life as I have seen you, and no new impression can any longer reach me through these extinct eyes, because my life will be entirely composed of memories of the past, and it will no longer have a present. But are you, so young and so long condemned to be the unique thought of a poor imperfect girl, infirm and disfigured, very sure of never experiencing lassitude and disgust?

"You're annoyed," she continued, smiling. "Oh, you're a skillful man, full of experience and reason, who knows all of life already, as if he had lived several times! Don't torment that seventeen-year-old lover with the idea that there are no eternal sentiments, and that the constraint of a repulsive obligation might fatigue at length a soul that even happiness would have bored. Listen! Don't promise me so much. I'm very demanding, though; I love a great deal, and it's natural to demand a great deal from the person one loves. Promise me—this engagement can be kept—to conserve your amity for me as long as you live; promise me, when you love someone else, not to tell me so, for I want to love everything that you love, and I sense that I wouldn't be able to love her. Consent, too, to let me live where you live, and if I ever become something of a burden, promise to act in such a way that I won't divine it. That's a lot of sacrifices, but I understand them, and I expect them of you. I disengage you in advance of any other oath."

I tried to speak; she sought my mouth with her hand and covered it firmly. I got up, desperate. I marched back and forth in the room with a kind of fury, I saw that she was anxious, I came back. I touched her.

"Thérèse," I said to her, "let's put an end to these frightful debates. You're speaking as a woman, and you're killing your friend. Do you know that it would cost no more to end it? It's to eternity that you're appealing? Well then, let's go into eternity, and if your soul revolts against death, well, I'll take charge of everything. Don't shiver like that. God won't reject us. There are strong actions that are above the capacity and judgments of men, but which God appreciates, and which will find before him the grace that the despicable wisdom of the vulgar has refused them. Since our existence on this earth is lost, annihilated forever, and you can comprehend no other means of ameliorating it than transactions that would humiliate both of us, that is a sign that God is content, and that he is recalling us to him. Don't be persuaded, Thérèse, that his sovereign bounty might heap with so many evils two innocent souls that he has formed with predilection, if he did not want to indicate to us that the time for us to return has come. Have no fear, Thérèse. If I find enough strength within me for what I conceive, it's because that strength is given to me; it's because it was marked in the decrees of Heaven that we would die together, and that I would bear you in my arms to our divine father before taking possession of you for eternity."

"Adolphe!" she cried, with a sound of voice that announced terror; and she raised herself up effortfully, her arm extended toward me. I drew nearer in order to sustain her. She was trembling. Her breast was swollen and heaving. She perceived that I was nearby and fell back, shivering.

"Do as you like with my life," she said to me. "Dispose of the last days that God has granted to me, if you wish, but don't talk to me like that. Remember that I'm ill, and that you're frightening me."

I thought that my recklessness might indeed aggravate her malaise. "I frighten you, Thérèse! Adolphe frightens you? Oh, rather die a thousand times than disquiet your heart with the slightest trouble! What am I saying? Rather die alone and lose you forever. I shall only do myself what you want, and if you mistrust my constancy too much to be happy on the faith of my promises, if it's necessary to test my life to reassure you, I'll consent to follow you, to watch you from afar, to keep my eyes fixed on every move you make, my thoughts attentive to all your thoughts; I won't weary you with the obstinacy of a sentiment in which you don't have the strength to believe; I'll only talk to you about it when you can no longer fear those illusions of youth and passions that inspire so much mistrust in you. I'll wait, in order to say *here I am*, until time and despair have used up my days and turned my hair white. Then I'll come back close to you, devoted to your happiness as today, and I'll prove to you, by dying at your feet of the pleasure of hearing you say once more that you love me, that you were cruelly mistaken about my heart."

In the meantime, I bathed her hands with my tears. She no longer pushed me away.

"I want that," she said. "I'll believe in all that you've promised me. I'll believe it for as long as you wish. If it's an illusion, it's worth life entire. I'd be mad to reject it. Yes, I believe that you love me, Adolphe, that you love me as I am and that you'll always love me. Doesn't one find lovers who don't survive their mistress? A sentiment that can survive death can certainly resist misfortune."

She engaged her arms with mine. She was pressed against my breast. I feared discomfiting her, because she was in pain everywhere. I drew away weakly, leaving my mouth close enough to hers to aspire her breath, and as that position was difficult to maintain for long without excessive fatigue, I leaned my upper body on the bed, and little by little, I lay down entirely without her perceiving it. That idea caused me a horrible constriction of the heart. I experienced an inexpressible mixture of dolor and intoxication in thinking that I was lying with Thérèse, with blind and dying Thérèse; I compared that to the felicities that I had promised myself, and I perceived profoundly that a man's life cannot embrace all of his destiny. I was sure that mine lacked a great deal, but that it would not finish here, and that God had only given me for my torture a soul that desired happiness and which understood eternity.

Since I had been able to take account of my actions, I had never neglected to pray. Night had fallen. It was known that I would watch over Thérèse; a lamp had been brought, and the night's remedies. I wanted to collect myself in order to pray, and I had an instant of anxiety because I was lying next to a woman; my heart beat violently and rejected that idea was a profanation.

O God, I said within myself, *you can read my soul and you know whether it is unworthy of you.* That rendered me a singular calm, which changed into confidence all the alarm that the first sentiment of that appearance of sin had inspired. I placed myself closer to Thérèse. Her feet were icy; I warmed them with my hands.

Her slumber was unquiet, and the slightest tremor of her limbs did not escape me. I was at least more in range to help her. She often turned her head sharply, uttering little cries and articulating two or three confused syllables.

My right arm was engaged under her neck for several hours. At first I had sensed a slight malaise there, and then a numbness, and I had ended up not feeling anything. It was an apprenticeship of death, and death is such a little thing. If it had been able to gain me thus entirely, if I had been able to cease to be, without ceasing to be bound forever to Thérèse's body, even annihilation would not have frightened me at that price.

When I perceived that she was waking up by degrees I drew away gently, so that she would not know that I had been so close to her and that her innocent soul would not be alarmed.

"Is that you?" she said to me.

"Yes," I replied, kissing her.

"Is it daylight?" she said,

I had not expected that question; it cut through me.

"Not entirely," I replied, with a trouble whose origin she divined.

"I want you," she said, "to strive to sustain that idea, and to correct my errors with as much sang-froid as if they didn't remind you of a time that is past and will never return. When I woke up, I almost yielded to that impression. I couldn't see you, but you touched me; it was you, really you, and I forgot the other thought like something foreign to my life. Among God's creatures there are many that feel and do not see, but we don't pity their misfortune because we regard it as natural to their species. A being deprived of the advantage of sight, who can see by means of the eyes of a fellow being, who loves her and cares for her, we ought to judge infinitely favored on earth. What does it matter, in fact, if I cannot see, if you, who are the stronger and greater part of my life, can see to guide us and to enable us both to live?"

I perceived by that exaltation of sentiment and language that she was animated by fever. I pressed my lips to her fingers in order to testify that I was obtaining pleasure in hearing her, and that what she was saying was in perfect accord with my thoughts.

"Amour is a strange commerce," she continued, "in which the one who gives the most is always the more favored. Admire the graces that fortune has given you! Between the two of us you will be everything and I shall be nothing, absolutely nothing!"

"You're mistaken," I told her, affecting to enter, in order to please her, into the dreams of her imagination, "for you will always be the thought that animates both of us, and I shall only be the body that obeys it."

That idea made her smile

"That," she said, "is worthy of your heart. There will be a soul and a body; but the soul will still be you, for I sense that all of mine has passed into you, and that outside of you I no longer have one. God forgive me, my friend, but only he can give us back to one another as we are. It appears that it is finished here, and that he is keeping us, as you said yesterday, for the future life. I had a strange dream about that last night."

She remarked that I was listening; she laughed. "You don't have much confidence in dreams, do you?"

I pressed her fingers again, which were interlaced with mine. "Can you imagine," she said, "that I found myself again such as I was when you saw me for the first time. I was invited to a fine feast with Henriette"—I had not told her about Henriette—"and there were two officers with us. I imagine that it was a wedding feast. One of the officers was you. I saw with astonishment that your physiognomy was animated by a martial and terrible expression, without losing the mildness for which I loved you, for you still had the tenderness of your gaze and the timidity of your smile, and I rejoiced in having touched a heart so modest and so proud. The other officer must have been Mondyon. I saw him much as you had depicted him to me, cheerful, mutinous, sulky and reckless, but worthy of being loved by my Adolphe. We were as madly joyful as poor young people who believe themselves to be happy and who believe that happiness is something durable. Suddenly I looked up at Henriette, because she was singing. I was surprised and frightened; she was so pale, so ill, so sadly dressed. Oh, if you had seen her like that! Seized by dolor, I turned to you. Mondyon and you had staring, immobile, extinct eyes. You resembled those images molded of plaster or wax, which only lack the movement of life to give them the illusion of it. You weren't alive, because you weren't looking at me, or didn't seem to see me, and that was a hideous thing to consider, because your heads no longer seemed to belong to your bodies, and were only attached to them by I know not what bloody threads."

After having told me that, Thérèse was extremely dejected. I sought in vain to dissipate the ideas that were tormenting her, because I was pursued by them myself, but I tried to make her believe that I was tranquil, although my voice was altered and trembling.

Finally, daylight had come. Thérèse had asked for a confessor, and I desired that she talk to a man who would have authority over her soul, in the hope that the result might be a little consolation for her. A noise that I heard outside told me that he had arrived. I informed Thérèse and placed myself next to the door.

The priest went past me without looking at me. He was a man of short stature and common physiognomy, who was twenty-six years old at the most, but his hair was already thin and white. There was a singular expression in his features, of courage beginning to be worn away by dolor, of patience ceding under the weight of everyday suffering, of bodily strength about to lack the devotion of the soul, which can only be sustained for a moment longer by favor of the enthusiasm of virtue or the sentiment of faith that is known nowadays as fanaticism. He walked with scant assurance, supporting himself on the woodwork, and only appeared to have been in inhabited places for just long enough to take the help of his ministry thereinto. His clothing did not announce the sacerdocy of the outlawed religion; it was a mixture of various garments that indicates a costume foreign to its wearer, which is only owed to charity. I passed the threshold of the room and I stopped outside. All that reached me from the interior was a dull and confused rumor, but I liked hearing it, because at least it proved the existence of two persons.

The other domestics were on their knees before me; the grandmother had had her chaise longue wheeled into the middle of them, and as she could not kneel because her legs were feeble and immobile, she was leaning on her crossed hands, imploring the assistance of God with tears and sobs. I fainted; I followed the door jamb against which I was leaning with my hand, and when I was on my knees I retained myself forcefully by sticking my face to it and digging my fingers into the inequalities in the moldings.

I had the sentiment that the thought of God paused momentarily over the farm of Sancy, and that my soul was in his presence. I would have liked to say a prayer; I don't know what secret inspiration told me that it would not be granted, and that the day was not a day of promises but a day of sacrifices.

I was only able to get up when the priest emerged. He was wiping away a tear.

After having taken a few steps, he suddenly stopped and named Antoinette; I presented myself.

"Mademoiselle is asking for you," he said, looking at me fixedly with an expression that was sad and austere at first, but gradually clarified. Then he drew nearer to me swiftly, pressed my hand between his, and gave me his benediction. Everyone looked on with astonishment, for I was the only one who understood. I thought I divined that the benediction and the handshake of the holy priest were only an adjournment of an imminent rendezvous, in a world where we were awaited.

That thought gave me a little strength, because the appearances of death embellished for me everything that I had lost, and everything that remained to me to lose in life.

I went into Thérèse's bedroom with a steady step; I believed, however, that I would find her alive, and I was astonished by her immobility. A slight movement of her head, which has lifted on her pillow, and was animated by a vivid color, although the traces of her malady no longer appeared there, convinced me to draw nearer. She summoned m me in a low voice; I fell to my knees beside her, and I took her hand, which fell from her bed, in order to apply it to my lips.

It was extraordinarily cold; I tried in vain to warm it with my breath; even the ardor of my mouth could not recall life to it.

Thérèse appealed to me again, trying to raise her voice.

"I'm here!" I cried. "Can't you hear me?"

She seemed astonished. "I can hear you very well," she said, "but I can't feel you."

I got up and put my face very close to hers, to the point of brushing her with my breath.

"Like that," she said, "I'm more sure that you're with me. You can even kiss me once as your sister and your wife. I was given permission just now, and I was told that he was not irritated against our amour, since you've returned."

I kissed her.

"Good," she said. "This isn't a sin; it won't do the harm of the eglantine kiss."

"Oh, my Thérèse," I said, "That time, it's me who was guilty."

"Refrain from thinking that," she interjected swiftly. "For as yet, it's only me who has redeemed it."

I perceived that her voice was embarrassed, that her breast was rising and falling more frequently, that her respiration was becoming short and dolorous.

"Don't talk like that," I said. "You're fatigued and you're in pain. I have no need to hear your thoughts. As they succeed one another in your heart, they reach mine."

She turned toward me, smiling. I leaned my head very gently on her shoulder and I glued my lips to her neck. She shivered against me.

"Are you suffering greatly?" I asked her.

"On the contrary," she replied, "I feel better."

She shivered again, and her head fell entirely upon mine. I don't know what I experienced; I couldn't take account of anything; but I sensed that she gripped my hair with her teeth, and at the same moment my heart froze and my blood congealed in my veins.

When I came round I was on my bed; I only had a purely physical idea of my existence, the impression of a sharp pain in the place where an instant before I had felt Thérèse's teeth clench. I put my hand to it. My hair had been severed at that place. Thérèse was dead.

I had never tested my courage on that supposition. It had not presented itself to my mind. I was astonished to be alive, and even more astonished to be calm.

I got up. I picked up the kerchief that contained my Vendéan garments; I put it over my arm, as when I had arrived at Sancy, and I walked at a firm pace toward the door of the house. It was necessary to pass before Thérèse's, which was ajar. There were people all around it who were weeping and praying. Inside, a little light was visible.

My first thought was to go in and die there, but that aberration only lasted a moment. The presence of a young man hidden for six months in female attire in Thérèse's house might injure her memory, and the name of that man would have doomed Thérèse's family if he were recognized as an outlaw. In any case, the suicide of which I had not yet thought would be a great crime before God, and the crime might forbid me the only hope that remains to a Christian in his misfortunes, that of seeing again in another world the cherished individuals that he had lost. That idea made me shudder because it presented itself to my mind for the first time, and I had been ready, in yielding to my first impulse, to sacrifice my entire future and to lose Thérèse for eternity, for not having the strength to survive her for a few days in time.

While I was making those reflections, I crossed the last door of the farm, pursued by the cries and groans that rose up from inside.

"Oh, my daughter, my beautiful Thérèse, my beloved," cried the grandmother "I shall never see you again, never . . . !" Her voice was stifled by sobs.

Why never? I said in my heart. *Oh, as for me, I shall see you soon, soon; I shall see you forever, forever . . . !* And that conviction rendered me some strength, because all my faculties were absorbed in it. My senses confirmed it, enveloped as they still were in the darkness of life. I followed with my eyes a brilliant phantom that was summoning me in its wake. I heard a loud voice resounding, which repeated to me: "Soon, soon, forever, forever . . ." And when I wondered whether it might be deceiving me, it responded to me with multiple cries, like a voice in anger.

That resembled a commencement of delirium, and I invoked as a supreme happiness an uninterrupted delirium that would deliver me without return to memories of the past.

The sun was setting; I climbed the path of the Cross; when I was at the top of the mountain there was not enough daylight for the house still to be distinguished, but its four white chimneys stood out in the increasing obscurity of the night, and presented an image of a funereal monument. I turned in that direction, and searched for a long sequence of rocky banks that I had sometimes remarked, which projected in a ledge over the precipice. I lay down in that place, with my eyes fixed in the line on which Thérèse's body must lie, and I prayed to God with a vivid abundance of heart that I might fall into it as I slept. I did not weep, however.

I had not slept the previous night; my senses yielded to an invincible collapse; I abandoned myself to it; but the slumber I savored was not that of repose. It was a succession of tumultuous and fantastic thoughts, painful and hideous dreams. I imagine that, if Providence grants any relaxation to the torture of the damned, it is thus that they must sleep.

Sometimes I persuaded myself that appearances had been deceptive in regard to Thérèse's death, and that she was not really dead but was ill and dying, and yet that consoled me. I made an effort to wake up in order to run and rejoin her, but scarcely had I succeeded than the horrible verity gripped my heart again.

"She's dead," I cried, and I fell back into my torpor for want of sufficient strength to maintain my dolor in all its power. An instant later, lightning flashes brushed my eyelids, I heard a noise like that of thunder, and I saw Thérèse, who was flying on wings of flame; but she turned away from me and I woke up calling to her; it was thus that I spent the night.

When the sun had risen I sat on the rock and I gazed at Sancy. A little more than an hour later I perceived some movement and I thought I distinguished three or four men emerging from the farm, who were carrying something. Then I got up, because I understood that it was all over. I headed toward a remote spot in the nearby forest; I took off Antoinette's clothes there; I put on my uniform again, and I followed at random the first road that was offered to me.

I marched for several hours without encountering anyone or without exciting any other sentiment than surprise. Finally, having arrived at the gates of a town whose name I don't know, I was arrested by soldiers and brought to prison. A week has passed since then. I shall be judged tomorrow.

Jean Sbogar

I

Alas, what is this life that never lacks afflictions and
miseries, in which everything is full of traps and enemies?
For the cup of dolor is no sooner drained than it is filled
again; and an enemy is no sooner vanquished than others
present themselves to fight in his stead.
(*The Imitation of Christ*)

A little beyond the port of Trieste, advancing over the shores of
the sea in the direction of the verdant bay of Pirano, one finds a
small hermitage, long since abandoned, which was once under
the invocation of Saint André, and which has conserved the
name. The strand, which shrinks incessantly toward that place,
where it seems to terminate between the foot of the mountain
and the waves of the Adriatic, seems to gain in beauty as it loses
in extent; an almost impenetrable thicket of fig-trees and wild
vines, the foliage of which the fresh vapors of the gulf maintain
in a state of perpetual verdure and youth, surrounds that house
of meditation and mystery on all sides.

When dusk dies away and the surface of the sea, lightly
rippled by the serene nocturnal breeze, commences to balance
the tremulous image of the stars, it is impossible to express all
the enchantments there are in the silence and repose of that

solitude. One can scarcely distinguish there, because of the continuity that renders it similar to an eternal sigh, the soft sound of the waters dying on the sand; rarely, a torch running along the horizon with the invisible hull of a fishing boat leaves a wake of light over the waves, which extends or diminishes in accordance with the agitation of the sea; it soon disappears behind a sandbank, and everything reenters obscurity.

In that beautiful place, the senses, completely unoccupied, do not trouble the thoughts of the soul with any distraction; it takes possession of space and time freely there, as if they had already ceased to enclose it in the narrow limits of life; and a man arriving at the hermitage of Saint André, whose heart full of storms only opens any longer to tumultuous and violent sentiments, sometimes understands the happiness of a profound calm that nothing threatens and nothing alters.

Near there in 1806 stood a manor house of simple but elegant architecture, which disappeared during the recent wars. The inhabitants called it the Casa Monteleone, the Italianized name of a French émigré who had died a short while before, leaving an immense fortune that he had acquired in commerce. His two daughters still lived there. Monsieur Alberti, a simple businessman, his son-in-law and associate, had been carried away by the plague in Salonika. A few months later, Monsieur de Montyon lost his wife, the mother of his second daughter; Madame Alberti was from another marriage. Naturally borne to sadness, he had abandoned himself without reserve after the latter misfortune. A somber melancholy consumed him slowly between his two children, whose caresses could not console him. What remained of his happiness only reminded him bitterly of what he had lost.

A smile only returned to his lips as death approached; when he sensed that his heart was about to freeze, his troubled brow cleared momentarily; he grasped the hands of his two daughters, bore them to his lips, pronounced the names Lucile and Antonia, and died.

Madame Alberti was thirty-two years old. She was a sensible woman, but her sensibility was mild and a little grave, not susceptible to outbursts and transports. She had suffered a great deal, and none of the painful impressions of her life had been entirely effaced from her soul, but she conserved her memories without nourishing them deliberately. She did not make an occupation of her dolor, and she did not reject the sentiments that reattached by a few connections those whose dearest bonds had been broken. She did not pride herself on the courage of her resignation; they were instinctive. A mobile imagination, easily straying over a host of diverse objects, rendered her more appropriate to receive distractions, and even to seek them.

Long a unique daughter and the sole object of her family's cares, she had had a brilliant education, but the habitude of ceding to events without resistance had often rendered futile the usage of her judgment; her manner of appreciating things owed less to reasoning than to imagination. No one was less exalted, and yet no one was less romantic, but that was the fault of ignorance of the world. In sum, the past had been so severe that she could no longer aspire to a very happy state, but her organization also forbade her an absolute unhappiness.

When she had lost her father she regarded Antonia as her daughter. She had no children, and Antonia had just reached her seventeenth year. Madame Alberti promised to watch over her wellbeing; that was her first thought, and it softened the bitterness of the others. Madame Alberti had never been able to understand disgust for life, as long as she sensed the possibility of being useful and of still being loved.

Antonia's mother had succumbed to a malady of the lungs; Antonia appeared to be attained by the same affliction; she seemed only to have obtained, in a womb already inhabited by death, a fragile and imperfect existence. She was tall, however, and as developed as one ordinarily is at her age; but there was an abandon in the slim and svelte figure that was announced with weakness. Her head, of a gracious expression and full of charms, was tilted slightly over her shoulder; her bright blonde hair was put up negligently. Her complexion, dazzlingly white, was scarcely animated by a light nuance of the softest incarnadine. Her slightly veiled gaze, which a natural organic fault rendered timid and anxious, became vaguely sad in seeking distant objects, and gave the impression of a habitual state of languor and suffering. She was not suffering, but she lived imperfectly, and with a species of effort.

Accustomed since childhood to the most vivid emotions, that dolorous apprenticeship had not blunted her sensibility and had not rendered her less accessible to less profound emotions; on the contrary, she was subject to them all with the same force. It seemed that her heart only had one manner of feeling, because it still had only one sentiment, and everything it experienced reminded it of the same dolors, the loss of her mother and her father, so the slightest circumstance reawakened in her that deadly faculty of associating herself with the pain of others. Anything that could permit her imagination that liaison of ideas extracted tears from her or struck her with a sudden shudder.

That tremor was so frequent that physicians had regarded it as a malady. Antonia, who knew that it ceased to exist with its cause, did not share their anxiety, but she had soon concluded, from that circumstance and a few others, that there was something particular in her organization. From one consequence to another she came to think that she was, up to a point, disgraced by nature. That conviction augmented her timidity, and above all her penchant for solitude, to the point of alarming Madame Alberti, who was easily alarmed, as all those are who love.

Their ordinary walk was along the edge of the gulf, as far as the first large building announcing the entrance to Trieste.

From there, the eyes extended over the sea, and, at intervals, over a few more or less distant points, which escaped the sight of Antonia but which Madame Alberti rendered present to her, in a way, by describing them to her. There were few days when she did not talk to her about the great memories that populate that poetic country, of the Argonauts, who had visited it, Japix,[1] who had given his name to its inhabitants, and Diomedes and Antenor, who had given them their laws.

"In making the tour of the horizon, and after having scanned that dark blue line that stands out from the paler blue of the sky," she said to her, "can you distinguish a tower whose summit reflects the sun's rays? It's that of the powerful Aquileia, one of the ancient rulers of the world. Only a few ruins of it remain. Not far from there runs a river, which my father showed me in my childhood, the Timave, of which Virgil sang. The chain of mountains that crowns Trieste rises almost sheerly above its walls, which develops to our right from the hamlet of Opschina over an incalculable extent, serves as a refuge for a host of peoples celebrated in history or interesting in their mores. There live the brave Tyroleans whose agrarian genius, courage and loyalty you still love; here the amiable peasants of the Frioul, whose pastoral dances and joyful songs have become European.

"Returning toward us, you ought to remark, a little higher up than the last masts of the port, above the roofs of the Lazaret, a part of the mountain that is much darker than the others, which dominates it considerably, and the gigantic and tenebrous appearance of which inspires respect and terror;

---

1 Nodier had quoted this name in the same form before in an article on the city he called Laybach (Ljubljana, now the capital of Slovenia) in volume 7 of the *Annales générales des science physiques* (1820), signed "Charles Naudier" as that of the "legislator" of the city; it is his version of the name of Iapyx, a favorite of Apollo credited in Virgil's *Aeneid* with the founding of Apulia in southern Italy, and his application of it to the environs of Trieste is idiosyncratic.

that's the Cap di Duino. The castle that occupies the summit, the crenellations of which I can see from here, is said to have been constructed in the time of an ancient invasion by barbarians; the people still call it Attila's palace. During the civil wars in Italy, Dante, exiled from Florence, sought a refuge there. It's claimed that that sinister abode inspired him with the plan for his poem, and that it was there that he undertook to depict the Inferno. Since then it has been inhabited in turn by party leaders and by thieves. In this century, when everything is discolored, I fear that it has fallen to the share of some peaceful castellan who will depopulate its formidable towers of demons in order to make dovecots."

Such was usually the subject of Madame Alberti's conversations with her sister, in whom she was seeking gradually to inspire the desire to see new objects, in the hope of producing a favorable diversion in her habitual ideas; but Antonia's character had insufficient tenacity to follow the impulsion of a curious desire for long. She was too weak, and mistrusted herself too much, to dare to conceive a project outside her estate, and as her depression appeared natural to her, she did not think of emerging from it. It required something more than a simple motive of curiosity to determine her to do so. The tomb of her parents was all that she knew of the world, and she did not suppose that there was anything for which to search beyond it.

"But Bretagne is our homeland," Madame Alberti said to her.

"It isn't there're that they died," replied Antonia, embracing her, "and their memory does not live there."

II

There are redoubtable men whom the desire to see blood
keeps them awake during the long winter nights, and who
would cut the throat of a young bride in order to have her
pearl necklace.

Condola.[1]

Istria, successively occupied and abandoned by the armies
of different nations, was enjoying one of those moments of
stormy liberty that a weak people savor between two conquests.
The laws had not yet resumed their force, and suspended justice even seemed to respect those crimes that a revolution can
render fortunate. In great political anxieties there is a security
of sorts attached to the banner of scoundrels; it can become
that of the State and the world, and even men who believe
themselves to be virtuous respect it by virtue of prudence.

The multiplicity of irregular troops, levied in the name of national independence almost unknown to kings, had familiarized
the citizens with those armed bands, which descended at any
moment from the mountains, and spread out from there along
the rim of the gulf. Almost all of them were animated by the most
generous sentiments and conducted by the purest devotion, but
behind them formed the refuse of those violent men for whom
political disorders were merely a pretext, a league redoubtable to
all governments and disavowed by all. A determined enemy of
social forces, it tended overtly to the destruction of all established
institutions. It proclaimed liberty and happiness, but it marched
accompanied by conflagration, pillage and murder. Ten smoking
villages already attested the horrible progress of the Brothers of
the Common Wealth. It was thus that the sanguinary troop of
Jean Sbogar was named at first, before putting itself above all
propriety and violating all laws.

---

1 This attribution is enigmatic, perhaps fictitious.

The brigands had appeared at Santa Croce, at Opschina, at Materia; it was said that they had now even occupied the castle of Duino, and that it was from the foot of that promontory that they threw themselves, under cover of darkness, like hungry wolves, upon all the shores of the gulf, to which they brought desolation and terror. The frightened people soon rushed to take refuge in Trieste. The Casa Monteleone, above all, was far from being a safe haven. A rumor spread that Jean Sbogar himself had been seen wandering under the walls of the manor in the middle of the night.

Renown gave him colossal and terrible forms. It was claimed that fearful battalions had recoiled at the mere sight of him; so he was not a simple Istrian or Croatian peasant like the majority of the adventurers who accompanied him. The vulgar made him the grandson of the famous brigand Sociviska,[1] and men of the world said that he was descended from Scanderbeg, the Pyrrhus of modern Illyria.[2] Simple folk, ever amorous of marvels, ornamented his history with the most singular and the most various episodes, but people were in accord in admitting that he was intrepid and pitiless. In a short time his name had acquired the credit of a tradition of remote times, and in the colorful language of the people, in whom all ideas of grandeur and power are united with that of advanced age, he was called

---

1 Stanislas Sociviska was the captain of a troop of bandits *circa* 1770, who was said to have obtained protection from the Austrian emperor Josef II because of his exploits in plundering the ever-intrusive Ottoman Turks. He and his followers are described in contemporary accounts as Morlachs, members of a distinct ethnic population living in the mountains of the regions, who were treated as pariahs, like the Romani, and were reputedly savage. There is a long ethnographic account of them in Alberto Fortis' *Viaggio in Dalmazia* (1774; tr. as *Voyages in Dalmatia*), which Nodier employed extensively in constructing the present novel and other works.

2 Scanderbeg, a corruption of Iskander Bey, was the name under which the rebel leader Gjergj Kastrioti (1405-1468) became legendary following his insurrection in what is now northern Albania against the rule of the Ottoman Turks.

Old Sbogar, although no one knew how many years had passed over his head, and none of his companions who had fallen into the hands of the law had been able to give the slightest description of him.

Madame Alberti, whom an imagination easy to stir disposed to welcome extraordinary ideas, and who had been occupied with Jean Sbogar since the moment when the man's name had struck her ear for the first time, did not take long to feel the necessity to quit the Casa Monteleone for Trieste, but she hid her motives from Antonia, whose sensibility she feared. The latter had also heard mention of the Brothers of the Common Wealth and their captain; she had wept over the crimes of which they rendered themselves culpable when the stories reached her, but that impression left few traces in her mind because she did not understand wicked people; it seemed that she avoided thinking about them in order not to be forced to hate them. That sentiment surpassed the measure of her strength.

The position of Trieste has something melancholy about it that constricts the heart, if the imagination is not distracted by the magnificence of its most beautiful constructions, the richness of its most cheerful fields. It is on the other side of an arid rock embraced by the sea, but human efforts have not given birth there to the most precious gifts of nature. Squeezed between the immense sea and the inaccessible heights, it offers the image of a prison, but art, the vanquisher of the soil, has made a delightful abode of it. Its buildings, which extend in an amphitheater from the port to a third of the elevation of the mountain, beyond which develop, by degrees, orchards of an inexpressible grace, pretty woods of chestnut trees, figs, pomegranates, myrtles and jasmines, which embalm the air, and above all that, the austere summits of the Illyrian Alps remind travelers traversing the gulf of the ingenious invention of the Corinthian arch; it is a basket of bouquets, as fresh as the spring, which reposes under a rock. In that ravishing but limited solitude, nothing has been neglected to multiply agreeable sensations.

Nature has given Trieste a little forest of green oaks, which has become a place of delights; it is known in the local language as the *Farnedo*, or the Boscage. Never have the rustic divinities whose favorite land is the fortunate shores of the Adriatic lavished more seductive beauties in such a narrow space. The Boscage even joins with all its charms that of solitude, for the inhabitant of Trieste, occupied in distant speculations, needs a point of view as vast and indecisive as hope. Standing on the extremity of a cape, his telescope fixed on the horizon, his pleasure is to seek a distant city, and from the Farnedo one can only perceive the sea.

Madame Alberti often took Antonia there, because from there alone she found the tableau of a world foreign to the one in which her pupil had lived thus far, capable of exciting in her young imagination a desire for new sensations. For a vivid soul, the Farnedo is a thousand leagues from cities, and Madame Alberti was trying to develop in Antonia the instinct of immensity that attenuates local impressions and renders them less durable or less dangerous. She already had enough experience of life to know that being happy is only being distracted.

The fête of the Boscage of oaks had, in addition, the most piquant charm for Madame Alberti. Brought up like a man of whom one wants to make into an educated man, she knew the poets and had often dreamed of the dances of Arcadia and Sicily which have so much charm in their verses. She was reminded of them, save for the costume, on seeing an Istrian shepherd in his light, loose garment charged with knots and ribbons, under his broad hat charged with bouquets of flowers, lifting up in passing and replacing on the grass the young woman who escapes him, her head veiled, without having been recognized, and who loses herself in another group, in the midst of companions similar to herself. Often, a voice suddenly rises among

162

the dancers, that of an adventurer from the Apennines singing a few strophes of Ariosto or Tasso, the death of Isabella or that of Sophronia; and in that nation, which enjoys all its emotions and is proud of all its errors, the illusions of a poet are authorities that demand tears.

One day, as Antonia went into the midst of one of those assemblies with her sister, she was stopped by the sound of an instrument that she did not know; she approached and saw an old man who was running a crude bow regularly over a kind of guitar garnished with a single string of horsehair, drawing therefrom a hoarse and monotonous sound well matched to his grave and cadenced voice. He was singing Slavonian verses about the misfortune of Dalmatians exiled from their homeland by poverty, improvising laments for the native soil; on the beauties of the countryside of fortunate Marcasca, ancient Trao, Curzole of the dark shade; of Cherso and Isserom where Medea dispersed the torn limbs of Absyrthe; of the beautiful Epidaure covered in oleanders; and of Salone, which Diocletian preferred to the empire of the world.

At his voice, spectators crowded around, moved at first, then softened and transported, sobbing; for in the tender and mobile organization of the Istrian, all sympathies become personal emotions and all sentiments passions. A few uttered shrill cries, others brought their wives and children closer to them; there were some who kissed the sand and crushed it between their teeth, as if someone had tried to snatch them from their homeland too.

Surprised, Antonia advanced slowly toward the old man, and on looking at him more closely she perceived that he was blind, like Homer. She sought his hand in order to deposit a pierced silver coin there, because she knew that that gift was precious to poor Morlachs, who ornamented the hair of their young women with them.

The old poet seized her by the arm and smiled, because he perceived that she was a young woman. Then, immediately changing style and subject, he began celebrating the pleasures of Amour and the graces of youth. He was no longer accompanying himself on the guzla, but he accentuated his verses with far more vehemence, and assembled all the strength he had, like a man whose reason is disturbed by intoxication or violent passion; he struck the ground with his feet, drawing Antonia toward him eagerly, almost frightened.

"Flowering, flowering," he cried, "in the perfumed boscage of Pirano, and among the grapes of Trieste that smell like roses, even the jasmine, which is the ornament of our bushes, perishes and delivers its little flower to the air before it opens, when the wind has cast its seed in the poisoned planes of Narente. It is thus that you will dry out, if ever you grow, young plant, in the forests submissive to the domination of Jean Sbogar."

III

The hills hear the sound of that terrible voice, and their
black rocks and bushes tremble. Warned by dreams of
the danger, the people run through the heather and light
the signals of alarm,
Ossian.

Antonia returned to the city slowly, leaning on her sister, but silent and pensive. The name of the brigand gave rise in her heart for the first time to a sentiment of dread for herself and a vague anxiety for her future. She had thought about the fate of the unfortunates who fell into his hands, without ever supposing that that destiny might be hers, but the language of the old Morlach improviser, as if inspired, had struck her with terror, by making her understand the possibility of that frightful misfortune, among the various accidents by which life is menaced. That idea was, however, so denuded of reason, the danger so remote from all plausibility, that Antonia, who had no secrets from Madame Alberti, dared not confide the subject of her disturbance to her. She drew nearer to her and pressed herself against her with a frisson that was only augmented by the progress of the night, the silence and the solitude, the ever more frightening rumor that emerged from time to time from the depths of the woods.

Madame Alberti sought to rid her thought of the sentiment that appeared to be filling it, but as she did not know what might have excited it, hazard made her choose the subject of conversation most appropriate to maintain it.

"What a dire renown this Jean Sbogar has!" she said. "How dolorous it is to capture the attention of men at that price!"

"Who knows, however," said Antonia, "whether it might not be the insensate desire to capture their attention that has produced so many aberrations and so many crimes? In any case," she added, perhaps with the secret intention of reassuring herself, "there is doubtless much exaggeration in what is said about him. I'm inclined to believe that we calumniate a little these men who are called villains, and the idea that I have of God's bounty is difficult to conciliate with such horrible depravity."

"The benevolence of your heart is deceiving you," Madame Alberti replied. "It's true that absolute evil offends the just idea that we form of the extreme goodness of the Creator and the perfection of his works, but he has certainly deemed it necessary to their harmony, since he has placed it in everything that has emerged from his hands alongside the good and the beautiful. Why would he not have thrown into society terrible and devouring souls, which only conceive thoughts of death, just as he has unleashed into deserts the frightful tigers and panthers that drink the blood of animals without ever slaking their thirst?

"Although he is the principle of all good, he wanted to permit evil in the moral order; but has he not given hideous forms to certain species in the physical order, although he is the principle of all beauty, and had clad his works in so many attractions when he wished? Have you not remarked that it pleased him to attach the repulsive seal of the most disgusting ugliness to the most malevolent and dangerous species?

"Do you remember that species of vulture as white as snow that one of my father's correspondents brought from Malta? Its form had nothing disagreeable; there was nothing purer and more elegant than its plumage; when one sees it from behind on one of those stones scattered in the cemeteries where it makes its abode, one desires to approach it and examine it in detail; but if it turns around, hopping on its thin legs and fixes you with its eye full of bloody fire, surrounded by a broad cadaverous pellicle, like a spectral mask, you shudder with horror and disgust. Under the most flattering appearances, I am convinced that it is the same with the wicked, and that one finds in them, at the first glance, the distinct sign of reprobation that God has attached to them in creating them for crime."

"In that case," said Antonia, pretending to smile, "your imagination does not lend very seductive charms to the leader of the Brothers of the Common Wealth; you must have a strange idea of the beauty of Jean Sbogar."

Madame Alberti, who imagined with an extreme facility the objects by which her thought was struck, and who had immediately composed the ideal type of the most ferocious of bandits, was about to respond to her sister when the sound of precipitate footsteps was heard behind them at a bend in the path,

Night had fallen completely and all the strollers had gone back into the houses distributed at intervals about the amphitheater. The two sisters stopped, trembling, painfully prejudiced by the somber images that had just passed through their minds. They listened, motionless, holding their breath.

A soft, melodious voice—one of those voices that has the privilege of enchanting cares and transporting the soul into a calmer region, into a more perfect life—caused their disturbance to be succeeded by an agreeable emotion.

It was a young man; one could tell that by the delicacy and freshness of his voice. He was enveloped in a short Venetian cloak, coiffed with a tiled hat with a floating plume, and he passed above the path—or, rather, flew from rock to rock like a nocturnal phantom—repeating the refrain of the blind old man:

". . . If ever you grow, young plant, in the forests submissive to the domination of Jean Sbogar, of the cruel Jean Sbogar . . ."

Having reached a higher rock, where his paleness stood out against the obscure contour of the mountain, he remained standing, and suddenly interrupted his refrain. Then, after a moment of silence, he uttered from the place where he had stopped a cry so savage, so dolorous, so formidable and so plaintive at the same time that it did not seem to proceed from a human throat; and at the same instant, that wild howl, similar to that of a hyena that has lost her young, was repeated from twenty different points in the forest; then the stranger disappeared, resuming his ballad.

Antonia was not entirely reassured until they had reentered the city, and she had often promised herself on returning, not to quit the Farnedo so late again. On subsequent reflection, she condemned her terrors and found natural explanations for everything that had frightened her; but her weakness and timidity did not take long to prevail over the efforts of her reason. For want of external exercise, her sensibility was increasingly attached to frightening chimeras; she lost herself in a limitless blur and composed within herself an unquiet sentiment of the world, which her isolation, her suspicion and her distance from all numerous societies rendered more irritable every day.

Sometimes, that disorder in her ideas, which produced fear, went as far as a kind of aberration that caused her shame and alarm.

Madame Alberti had noticed that, with an extreme dolor; but, faithful to her system of distraction, she always promised herself to furnish enough diversion to her mind, until a fortunate and legitimate affection could give as much to her heart. That was the last, and also the most agreeable and most specious, of her hopes. It is, in fact, necessary not to despair for those who are not loved; their existence has a complement to receive, and a complement that often makes the destiny of the rest of their life.

IV

Then strange, unexpected and portentous figures appeared;
and it was impossible to say whether they were men or
demons, or whether such frenzy was the effect of sleeping
awake, or of waking slumber.
De Lancry.[1]

The walks in the Farnedo had not been discontinued, but Madame Alberti took care to commence them at an early hour and to return to Trieste before dusk. The season was torrid, and the shade of the oaks scarcely entertained enough coolness to temper the ardors of the sun when the wind from Africa blew over the gulf.

Enormous yellow clouds, dull and yet dazzling, gather in a part of the sky, with something like avalanches of fire rolling and falling from their gigantic summits, extending, flattening out and settling. A dull noise accompanies them, ceasing when

---

1 The witchfinder Pierre de Lancre, author of *Tableau de l'inconstance des mauvais anges et démons* (1613).

they stop; then nature entire remains enchained by terror, like an animal menaced by destruction, which takes on the appearance of death in order to escape it. Not a single leaf quivers, not an insect buzzes in the motionless grass. If one turns one's eyes toward the place where the sun ought to be, one sees, floating in an oblique column of luminous atoms, the impalpable dust that the sirocco has lifted from the desert, the origin of which can be recognized by its brick-red hue. No movement, however, is perceptible, except for that of a kite describing its circular course in the height of the firmament, marking its prey from afar in the sand, weighed down by that redoubtable atmosphere.

No voice can be heard, except the shrill and plaintive cries of carnivorous animals, which, filled with ferocious instinct and believing it to be the last day of the world, are coming to claim the debris of created beings that has been promised to them. Even humans, in spite of their mental power, cede to that force, against which they have never tried their faculties. Their noble foreheads incline toward the ground, their limbs weaken and give way beneath them; devoid of courage and energy, they fall and wait, in an invincible languor, waiting for milder air to reanimate them, render movement to their minds, warmth to their blood and life to nature.

Madame Alberti often rested with Antonia under a clump of trees in a pretty place from which a part of Trieste is visible, all the way to the Greek church, and where the ground is covered by short fresh grass that invites slumber. Antonia, whose delicate organs could not resist the impression of the sirocco, had fallen asleep, and her sister was walking a short distance away, making her a garland of little blue veronicas, in the fashion of the young women of Istria, who weave them with a great deal of artistry. As a few were lacking in order to complete it she had marched in various directions outside the area where Antonia was reposing when she perceived that she had emerged from it, and that the efforts she had made to return to it had drawn her further away.

At first she was amused by her error, as if by an inconsequential accident, but then she became slightly anxious, and her anxiety, which rendered her stride more precipitate, also rendered it more uncertain. Finally, anxiety had given way to a more painful sentiment, but which ought to cede to reflection. There was a sure means of finding Antonia, which was to shout loudly. But a cry would have troubled her repose, and not without danger for that keen and sensitive organization, which the slightest unexpected emotion always offended. What was more natural, on the other hand, than thinking that when Antonia awoke, she would call out to her sister before being frightened by her absence? At that idea, Madame Alberti, reassured, sat down and continued her garland.

In the meantime, Antonia had, in fact, woken up. A slight sound that she heard in the foliage facing her had interrupted her slumber and her eyelid had half-lifted under the arm that enveloped her head. Through the curls of her hair, which covered a part of her face, she had perceived, but in a manner that the weakness of her sight rendered vaguer and more alarming, two men who were looking at her attentively. One of them, as if veiled by a large plume that hung down over his face, was leaning on the other, who was kneeling at his feet, his legs crossed beneath him, in the attitude of Ragusans at repose.

Seized by dread, Antonia closed her eyes again and held her breath, in order not to allow the agitation that she was experiencing to be detected by the movement of her bosom.

"That's her," said one of the unknown men. "That's the daughter of the Casa Monteleone, who has fixed the fate of my life."

"Master," replied the other, "you said as much of the daughter of the bey of the mountains, all of whose people we killed, and the favorite slave of that dog of a Turk who made us pay so dear for the fortress of Czetim. By Saint Nicolas, if we had wanted to do as much to reduce Walachia, you'd be a hospodar now, and we wouldn't have any need . . ."

"Shut up, Ziska," said the one who had spoken first. "Your ridiculous exclamations will wake her up, and I'd be deprived of the joy of seeing her, which I might not have again. Take care not to agitate the air that is circulating around her, for I'll punish you in your old father, who is weeping so bitterly at having engendered you. You're laughing, Ziska . . . agree, however, that my Antonia is beautiful . . ."

"Not bad," said Ziska, "but not enough to effeminate a man's heart and stop a troop of brave men in a forest of pleasure where there's no water to drink. Master," he continued, getting to his feet, "where do you want me to take that child?"

Antonia trembled, and involuntarily, her arm fell back over her breast.

"Wretch!" said Ziska's master, in a dull voice. "Who asked you for your execrable services? Do you know that that young woman is my wife before God, and that I have sworn that no mortal hand will ever detach a single floret from her virginal crown—not even mine! No, I shall never have a common bed with her on earth . . . what am I saying? Oh, if I knew that my lips would one day profane those innocent lips, which have only ever parted to the chaste kisses of a father, I would burn them with a red-hot iron. Our youth was cradled in violent and grim ideas, but that young woman is sacred for my amour, and I shall watch over the least of her hairs. My soul is attached to her, floating above her, you see, and it is following her through this brief life, in the midst of all the ambushes of men and destiny, without her perceiving me for a moment. That is my conquest of eternity, and since I have lost my existence, since it is forbidden to make a gentle and noble creature like that share it, I shall take possession of her for the entire future. I swear by the slumber that she is savoring now that her final slumber will unite us, and that she will sleep beside me until the earth is renewed."

Antonia's disturbance had not ceased to increase, but it was beginning to be mingled with curiosity and interest. She wanted to look, but her weak sight served her poorly; she raised her head slightly, but the strangers were going away. She lifted it entirely and fixed her eyes on the place where she had heard them; only one of them was still visible, sliding through the bushes bent double; he was hideous.

The strangers had scarcely disappeared when Madame Alberti, alerted by some noise, arrived at the oak at the foot of which Antonia had been asleep. She listened to her story without believing it. Antonia had given her too much evidence of the weakness of her reason for her to suspect that there was anything in what she recounted but a vision or the illusion of a dream; but as the same idea inspired her with a remarkable tenderness, her sister mistook the nature of her emotion; she attributed to the compassion that a great peril excites the pity to which a mental aberration gives birth. She delivered herself with abandon to the ideas she had conceived, and that habitual preoccupation took on, as much as it could, the character of a mania.

"What, you poor thing!" cried Madame Alberti, finally. "By whom are you persuaded that you are loved? By one of the lieutenants of Jean Sbogar, God forgive me!"

"Of Jean Sbogar?" said Antonia, recoiling as if she had stepped on a viper. "That's probable!"

It was impossible, after that, to return to the Farnedo. Antonia hardly ever left the house, and only when her calmer mind had not been troubled by one of those terrors whose object passed for imaginary; she went alone to respire the cool evening breeze over the port. Sometimes, she stopped under the walls of the Saint Charles palace, and she sought to discover from there the castle of Duino about which her father and her sister had spoken to her so frequently.

Having arrived at the môle that approached it, she advanced mechanically along the causeway, as far as the place where it was terminated but a little raised mound surmounted on the seaward side by a narrow bench, which could only accommodate one person comfortably. That solitude, placed between and inhabited city and the deserted sea, pleased her imagination and did not frighten her. After a nebulous day she loved to watch the sensible flux of the gulf, when its slate-colored face is abruptly broken at intervals, and the foaming banks precipitate themselves over one another toward the shore, which the waves mount, and then whiten and fall back under the next wave, which envelops it and draws it away into a more distant wave; while the gulls rise to the limit of vision, and fall back, circling, like a shepherd's crook escaped from his hand, skimming the water, lifting it with a wing, or seeming to run over its surface.

One evening, when she had stayed there longer than usual, retained by the charm of the night, which had never had a purer serenity, illuminated by a resplendent moon, she took pleasure in seeing the light of that placid star extend from the height of the mountains in silvery sheets, washed with a light blue tint, and marry the earth, the sea and the sky, inundated by its immobile clarity. The silence of the coast, only interrupted from time to time by the signals of the coastguards, allowed the shiver of the water that came to die in front of Antonia to be heard, and the beating of a little boat attached to the end of the môle, which the waves pushed against the foot of the causeway at regular intervals.

Her thought, plunged in a vague infinity, like the element offered to her eyes, had lost sight of the world, when a sudden impression of fear rendered all her alarms. That sensation, as rapid as lightning, determined by an inexplicable liaison of ideas, was the memory of what had happened in her last excursion to the Farnedo: the incomprehensible apparition of the man who had arrogated an absolute power over her life. Such is the empire of the imagination that she immediately represented that scene to herself, and after a moment, all her senses, equally troubled, surrendered to the most complete illusion. She still believed that she could see and hear.

A bright light, departing from Duino, and followed by a dull explosion, destroyed the illusion, but the impression subsisted. Antonia's heart was beating violently; cold sweat ran over her brow; her anxious gaze sought right and left an object that she dreaded to see; her ear listened in the silence, impatient with its desolating continuity. She would have liked to be distracted from that object-less terror by a reasonable cause for dread.

By force of attention, she believed that she discerned some-one talking in a low voice nearby; she got up and sat down again; her legs were trembling. The voices gained a little more force, but they came closer. She believed that she recognized the accent of the Ragusan who had proposed abducting her in the forest: *Where do you want me to take that young woman?* At the same instant it seemed to her that almost the same words were pronounced. She had difficulty convincing herself that her senses had not been deceived by a dream. She leaned forward in order to hear better; the words had not finished, or they were repeated; they struck her ear distinctly.

"Rather die!" replied a louder voice, which was even closer to her. She judged that she was only separated from the man who was speaking by the narrow corner that the wall projected over the causeway; a little more, and she would have felt the air agitated by his breath. She moved rapidly to the other extrem-ity of the bench, and during that movement she saw two men leap into the little boat, which drew away, impelled by oars.

The moon was hidden behind pearl-gray clouds, which were torn here and there into thick flakes. One of its rays fell upon the hull and illuminated a white plume abandoned to the winds, which shaded the hat of one of the travelers. Antonia could no longer distinguish anything.

In haste to return to the city, she ran along the causeway in two or three minutes, and passed like a shadow alongside the sentry, who was leaning on his blunderbuss.

"God protect you, Signora," he said. "It's late for young women."

"I thought I was alone on the môle," she said

"You were alone there," said the soldier, "for an hour, no living soul has approached it, unless it was the demon or Jean Sbogar."

"Heaven preserve us from Jean Sbogar!" cried Antonia.

"May God hear you," said the soldier, making the sign of the cross.

At the same instant, a cannon resounded for a second time in the direction of Duino.

Antonia's new story was not welcomed with any more confidence than the first. It was only too visible that the obliging and dolorous attention that people pretended to accord to it had nothing in common with the interest of conviction. Struck by that idea, she insisted with a noble calm that astonished Madame Alberti, but could not persuade her. Antonia, left alone, covered her eyes with her hands and reflected on her situation with a profound bitterness.

The opinion she had formed, since childhood, of the singularity of her organization and the state of disgrace in which nature had caused her to be born, confirmed by the sentiment that she excited around her, was fixed in her mind, and developed to the highest degree the extreme disposition to suspicion and dread that formed the basis of her character. Her weakness was a species of mental illness, which would not have been difficult to cure with the cares and protections of which Madame Alberti was capable, but the latter saw it as something else, and her prejudice had been augmented in that regard by all the efforts that she had made to vanquish it.

Antonia was her unique thought, the amour and goal of her life. To lose that girl cherished by death, or to see her stolen from the projects that she had founded upon her by an incurable mental aberration was very nearly the same thing, and when she had reason to fear the latter misfortune she had everything ready to persuade herself that it was impossible.

In the deadly error of her tenderness, she firmly rejected the suspicion that obsessed it, because it would have killed her; there was too much danger in looking it in the face and discussing it coldly—in taking account of it, in sum—for her to dare to attempt it. She had succeeded in distracting herself from it, but not in chasing it away. Her imagination, vivid and absolute in all the ideas that it formed of things, and which was attached by an involuntary and invincible preference to those that were the most painful to believe, almost never modified the aspect under which she had seen them once.

The two sisters regarded one another therefore, with a mutual tenderness originating in one from an excess of timidity and in the other from an excess of solicitude which rendered them equally unhappy.

V

Oh, my God, you will not confound the innocent with the guilty in the rigors of your justice! Strike, strike this head long condemned; it is owed to your judgments; but spare that woman and that child, alone amidst of the difficult and perilous ways of the world! Is there not among those pure intelligences, the first work of your hands, some benevolent angel favorable to innocence and weakness, who deigns to attach himself to their footsteps in the form of a pilgrim, in order to preserve them from the tempests of the sea and turn away from their hearts the sharp steel of brigands?
Traveler's prayer.

In that epoch, very important affairs that their father had left behind to be regulated in Venice required the presence of Madame Alberti. She regarded that circumstance as the most fortunate that could arrive in Antonia's condition, and convinced herself again that the unfortunate impressions that had altered her judgment, and which appeared to depend on the influence of places and memories, would finally yield to a complete change of habitude and way of life. The great fortune that they enjoyed permitted them to procure, in that opulent and magnificent city, all the pleasures that luxury and the arts gather there from all parts of the world; and that new species of emotion, which addresses itself more to the imagination than to sensibility, would offer infinitely less danger for an irritable soul than those resulting from the contemplation of the natural beauties of the world, the imposing grandeur of which over-whelms thought.

The journey to Venice was therefore resolved, and Antonia had never received any news with more joy. Trieste had become for her a magical palace where, incessantly observed by invis-ible spies, she lived at the mercy of an unknown tyrant, the absolute master of her liberty and her life, who had considered several times abducting her from the midst of her relatives in order to transport her into a new world, of which she could not form an idea without shivering, and who might be on the eve of accomplishing that fatal resolution, if Providence did not remove her from his sight.

The hope of seeing herself liberated from that subject of terror acted upon her promptly, and rendered her in a few days the freshness and grace of youth that anxiety had withered some time ago. The smile reappeared on her lips, serenity on her brow; a more expansive confidence and a milder abandon reigned in her speech, and Madame Alberti, delighted that the mere approach of the departure produced effects so appropriate to justify her conjectures, neglected nothing to hasten it further. The lack of security of the public roads, however, required that it be put off until a fixed day that would bring together all the travelers heading toward the same point, in order for them to serve reciprocally as an escort.

Madame Alberti's carriage was at the rendezvous on the ninth, on the sandy platform of Opschina, from which the eye embraces the gulf in the distance, and the irregular dunes with which its long circumference bristles. Antonia and her sister were accompanied by an almoner, a businessman, an old domestic of confidence and two women. One place remained vacant in the interior. The day was already advanced because the *bora*, which had blown in the morning, had caused one of those storms to be feared that are never braved with impunity on the elevated coasts of Istria, from which they lift the heaviest charges, which they roll into the depths of abysms.

The caravan was sufficiently numerous for there to be no reasonable fear of brigands to be conceived, even if it were surprised by the most obscure night; they were due to spend the night in Montefalcone, which is a few leagues from there on the poetic banks of the Timave.

The evening was suddenly embellished, the air was fresh and pure, the sky cloudless. The carriages made their way in a slow convoy along the steep and rugged slopes of the mountains of Trieste, through vast thickets strewn with rocks, which raise their sharp and forbidding crests here and there in a short and arid moss. The sole verdure to be seen is that of the lustrous leaves of holly, and a few brambles trailing their thorny arms over the sand. At the foot of the coast a group of houses was perceptible, of the saddest aspect, the roofs of which, charged with enormous stones, attested to the ravages of the bora by the often-useless obstacles that are multiplied against it in all the places where it is accustomed to be unleashed. That was the hamlet of Sestiana, populated by mariners and fishermen.

While the horses were relieved of the long effort they had opposed to the weight precipitated upon them in a slippery and steep road, the aged innkeeper of Sestiana appeared at the window of Madame Alberti's carriage and asked them in the name of Christian charity, to accept as far as Montefalcone a poor traveler exhausted by fatigue who was unable to continue his route. It was a young monk from the Armenian convent of the Venice Lagoons, who was returning from a mission, and whose mild and honest face had inspired him with the keenest interest.

That plea was one of those that Madame Alberti and her sister never refused, whatever reason they had for doing so. The door opened, and the Armenian, sustained by the old man who had presented himself, set foot on the steps of the carriage, after having stammered a few words of thanks, had lifted himself painfully toward the place destined for him. His hand, as white and soft as that of a young woman, fell by mistake on Madame Alberti's hand, but he withdrew it precipitately; and, recognizing that the carriage was almost entirely occupied by women, he pulled the wide brim of his round hat down over his face before it had been perceived.

Soon afterwards, they set forth again. Night had fallen completely by then.

The interval between Sestiana and Duino is filled by a light strand of fine and mobile sand, which fled in all directions under the wheels, and in which the vehicle, lifted up and sinking by turns, seemed agitated by an undulating movement similar to that of waves. One circumstance that augments that illusion in the faint and deceptive light of the evening stars is the brilliant color of the silvery arena and the vague extent of the horizon, which, less circumscribed than it is during the day, is prolonged very uncertainly in the darkness, and presents to the eyes and image of a vast sea. It seems then that the horses have descended into a vast ford and are running through an area inundated by the water of mountain streams.

Antonia, who occupied one of the corners of the carriage, had raised the glass on her side, and was enjoying that illusion, while respiring the cold but energetic night air. The difficulty of the progress of the horses over the fugitive and profound soil that continually slipped away beneath their hooves had slowed them down greatly, and the slightest exterior agitation was noticeable. Several times, Antonia, who was only too disposed to seize upon all subjects of anxiety, had thought she had seen shadows of a singular form gliding in the indecisive space that extended before her, and, troubled, she had held her breath while trying to determine whether the movement might be accompanied by some sound, which would indubitably be the case if it were anything other than a simple error of sight.

Suddenly, the postillion, who might have been experiencing something similar, or who feared yielding to sleep, started to intone a Dalmatian pismé, a kind of ballad that is not without charm when the ear is accustomed to it, but which astonishes by its extraordinary and savage character when one is hearing it for the first time, and the modulations of which are so bizarre that only the inhabitants of the country possess the secret of them.

The song is extremely simple, however, for it is only composed of a single motif repeated infinitely, in accordance with the custom of primitive peoples, and two or three sounds, at the most, which return in the same order; what is incomprehensible is the very species of these sounds, which do not appear to proceed from a human voice, and which an artifice analogous to the French street performers known as ventriloquists, but which is natural to Illyrian singers, changes the expression, the volume and the seeming place of origin continually. It is a successive and rapid imitation of the shrillest of sounds, especially those of the inhabitant of deserted places collected in the middle of nights in the rumor of the wind, the whistling of tempests, the howls of frightened animals, in the concert of plaints that emerges from solitary forests at the commencement of a storm, when everything in nature takes on a voice in order to moan, all the way to the branch that the wind has broken, without detaching it entirely from the tree to which it belongs, and which is swinging and shrieking, suspended by a residuum of bark.

Sometimes the full and sonorous voice resounds without any obstacle around the listeners; sometimes one could believe that it is resonating under a vault, and sometimes the air lifts it above the clouds and scatters it in the sky, where it imprints it with a charm that has never been savored in human melodies. However, that aerial music does not have the calm purity so appropriate to repose the soul that we attribute to those of angels, even when it approaches most closely; on the contrary, it is severe to the human heart, because the thought it awakens is full of tumultuous memories, passionate sentiments, anxieties and regrets; but it attaches, it draws and subjugates the attention, which cannot free itself from its empire. It recalls the redoubtable and soft harmonies of marine divinities that spellbind voyagers and draw their ship toward inevitable reefs.

The stranger endowed with a vivid imagination who has once heard, while sitting on the shores of Dalmatia, a young Morlach woman exhaling her evening song and delivering to the winds accents that no art could have taught her, which no instrument will ever imitate, and which no words can describe, has been able to comprehend the marvel of the sirens of the *Odyssey*, and he has excused, smiling, the mistake of Ulysses.

Antonia, by virtue of a penchant common to all feeble souls who launch themselves voluntarily beyond the bounds of nature, because they need to be protected, and above all to be loved—for them it is perhaps the same thing—enjoyed more than anyone else the mysterious effects that double the aspect of life, and which give a new world to intelligence. She did not believe in the existence of the intermediary beings that play such a great role in the superstitions of her native land and her adoptive country—those tenebrous giants that reign over high mountains where they are sometimes seen seated on a cloud, armed with an enormous pine; the sylphs lighter than air who have their palace in the calyx of a little flower, which the zephyr carries away in passing; the nocturnal spirits that guard treasures hidden under a rock inverted on its apex or which wander around in order to drive away thieves, leaving in their passage an inconstant flame that rises and falls, is extinguished only to be reborn, disappear and be reborn again—but she loved those illusions, and the Morlach song, which she had often heard with pleasure, renewed them all at once. She was listening to it, therefore, with a keen and unalloyed interest when a singular movement of the carriage, which stopped suddenly and swayed, came to interrupt her reverie.

The horses had taken a step back, and the Morlach song expired in the postillion's mouth.

"The carriages that were preceding us have drawn ahead," he said, "while the monk was climbing into this one, and if I'm not mistaken, the road has been cut by brigands."

"What is he saying?" cried Madame Alberti, launching herself toward the door.

"That we've stopped," said Antonia, who had just fallen back into the corner of the carriage, shivering with terror.

"Stopped!" repeated Madame Alberti and the travelers.

"Stopped! Murdered! Doomed!" continued the postillion. "It's them; it's Jean Sbogar's troop; and there's the execrable castle of Duino, which will be the tomb of us all."

"By Saint Nicolas of Ragusa!" said the Armenian monk, in a profound and terrible tone. "Better that the ground should crumble under our feet."

As he finished that speech he had launched himself into the midst of the brigands. The ferocious cry that had frightened Antonia in the Farnedo was heard at the same moment, and a thousand horrible voices roared in repeating it. The door had closed again behind the missionary; the blinds were lowered, the horses remained motionless; a mortal silence reigned in the carriage; nothing any longer arrived from outside but a dull sound that gradually drew further away when, at the redoubled whistle of the whip, the horses departed against at a fast gallop, impatiently, as if that warning had destroyed the action of a magic spell upon them.

They did not stop until they had caught up with the other travelers.

"What about the Armenian?" Antonia had been crying for some time, leaning out of the window. "That generous, brave man who devoted himself for us . . . my God, my God! Have we abandoned him to the murderers? That would be a horrible action!"

"Horrible," repeated Madame Alberti, swiftly.

"Don't worry, my good ladies," replied the postillion, who had descended from his seat and had recovered all his security. "That monk has nothing to fear from the assassins; they can do nothing against him; and, in order that you know it, it was him who ordered me to chase my horses when I did it, and who rendered me the strength and the voice for that. Also, did you notice with what impetuosity they launched forth? As for him, I saw him at close range, I swear to you, for the brigands touched me, and he threw himself between them and me, so terrible that some of them fell down with fear, and all the others took flight without even looking back. A minute later he was alone, and he was there, standing with his hand raised, with commanding air. 'Get away' he shouted to me, with a voice so imposing that my blood would have frozen in my veins if it had announced anger, but it was a protective voice, the voice in which he usually speaks to the matelots . . ."

"To the matelots?" said Madame Alberti. "Do you know that Armenian, then?"

"Do I know him?" said the postillion. "Did he not name himself when he cried *By Saint Nicolas of Ragusa?* Who is the saint who tests voyagers and recompenses them? And what other saint disperses with a word, a gesture, a gaze, an army of bandits who have blades in their hands and rage in their hearts, who are in search of danger, gold and blood? I ask you!"

The postillion fell silent, gazing at the sky, which seemed to be traversed by a sudden light. The cannon growled at Duino.

VI

Some call him the Great Mogul, others the Prophet Elia.
He is an extraordinary man who is found everywhere,
who is known to no one, and whom no one wishes to harm.
Lévis.[1]

That explanation was not sufficient for everyone. Madame Alberti conceived several others and collected them by turns. Antonia saw nothing distinct in the events, but she found everything therein necessary to maintain somber and thoughtful ideas. It was in that disposition of mind that she continued her voyage in the midst of the enchanted landscapes that remained for her to traverse.

The next day she saw the cheerful Gorizia, rich in flowers and fruits, the aspect of which charms from afar the eyes of travelers newly emerged from the infecund sands of the Istria coast. Antique memories awaken so naturally on that hill cherished by nature, which are conserved with such facility that one could believe oneself still living under the poetic empire of mythology. Beauties stroll there under arbors dedicated to

---

1 Pierre Marc Gaston de Lévis (1764-1830), the émigré son of a Maréchal de France, who published several works of imaginative fiction before concentrating on political essays.

the Graces, hunters assemble there in the boscage of Diana; it is from there that they descend to go to surprise their prey in the fields that border the Isonzo, the most elegant of the rivers of Italy and Greece, the sky blue waves of which, as pure as the firmament they reflect, and whose brilliance they have no need to borrow, flow profoundly encased between two mountains of silver sand. When it is veiled by clouds, the inhabitant of Gorizia rediscovers its azure on the limpid surface of the Isonzo.

A day later, she perceived the delectable canals of the Brenta, bordered by rich palaces, and the modest village of Mestre, which serves as a point of communication between a part of Europe and a city to which Europe can show nothing equal, the superb Venice, whose very existence is a phenomenon.

Day had scarcely dawned when the boat that was to take Madame Alberti, Antonia and the people accompanying them entered marine waters from the Brenta. The little craft glided gently over the motionless surface alongside the stakes that guided the navigator. To her right, Madame Alberti perceived a white house of a very simple construction in the midst of the islets with which that part of the lagoon is strewn. She was told that it was the Armenian Catholic convent, and Antonia shivered, without being able to explain her emotion.

Finally, Venice commenced to stand out on the horizon, like a dark silhouette, with its domes, its edifices and a forest of ships' masts; then it brightened, developed and opened out before the boat, which circled for a long time through boats of every size before entering the particular canal on which the Palazzo Monteleone was situated, of which Madame Alberti had made the acquisition shortly before.

One painful circumstance delayed their arrival. The canal was charged with gondolas following a funeral procession; it was that of a young woman, for the gondola bearing the coffin was draped in white and decorated with roses of the same color. Two torches were burning at each extremity, and their light, eclipsed by that of the rising sun, seemed to be nothing more than blue-tinted smoke. There was only one oarsman. A priest, standing in the prow of the gondola, but turned in the direction of the bier with a silver cross in his hands, was murmuring the prayers for the dead in a low voice. Facing him, a young man clad in black, kneeling at the head of the coffin, was weeping bitterly; the sound of his stifled sobs had a heart-rending quality; he was probably the brother of the deceased. His grief was so intense and so profoundly felt that if it had been exalted by another sentiment, it would have been mortal. A lover would not have wept.

That encounter of bad augury moved Antonia's sensibility easily, but the first remarkable object made her forget the superstitious thought that it had suggested to her. She was with her sister, without any reasonable motive of future dread, surrounded, on the contrary, by all the probabilities of a comfortable life of unalterable tranquility—of happiness, in sum, if there is any for tender souls who sympathize with all the sufferings of society and require little to summon them to feel something similar. She paused at that perspective; for the first time she enjoyed the sentiment of a pure security; she judged that she was happy; she conceived the possibility of always being so, and, in truth she had never been more so.

The common people in every country are fond of the extraordinary and subject to being impassioned by persons and things, but in Venice more than anywhere else the faculty extends of creating gods, temporary objects of an enthusiasm whose reaction is often fatal for those who have excited it. There was no question at that time of anything but a young stranger who had acquired that brilliant and fugitive favor without anyone knowing how, for he had not allowed any such pretention to be divined. The genius, courage and generosity of Lothario was the subject of all conversations; his name was in all mouths.

During the short journey from Mestre to Venice, it had been brought into the conversation of the mariners twenty times.

After having explored her new dwelling, while sustaining Antonia, to whom the habit of delicate health rendered the support on an arm necessary even when she was not suffering. Madame Alberti conducted her to one of the principal rooms of the apartment and they sat down side by side. The aged steward presented himself to welcome them and remained standing, awaiting their orders.

"We're content," Madame Alberti told him. "Everything responds to what I expected of your cares, honest Matteo, and I can judge by these beginnings that no one in Venice will be better served."

"No, not even Signor Lothario," replied the old man, inclining his bald head and twisting his black silk *goura* in his hands.

Antonia burst out laughing. "And who, great God, is Signor Lothario? I've heard no other name since we arrived."

"That's true," said Madame Alberti, recapitulating her ideas with her usual precipitation. "Who is Signor Lothario? Tell us, my dear Matteo, what it is necessary to think of that man, whose reputation has become proverbial in Venice before having crossed the gulf."

"Mesdames," replied Matteo, "I'm not much more instructed myself, although I ceded to custom in making use of that name, which has such credit in a country where even bandits are respected. That might appear exaggerated, but nothing is truer; and Signor Lothario inspires a respect so universal that it has sometimes happened that naming him has caused the stiletto to fall from an assassin's hand and the rumor—merely the rumor—of his approach has calmed a revolt, dissipated a furious mob and rendered tranquility to Venice. However, he is a young man, scarcely redoubtable I assure you, for everyone is in accord in saying that in society he has the mildness and timidity of a child. I have only seen him once, at a distance, but in contemplating his physiognomy I experienced a shock that made me believe everything that is thought about him. Since that time I have sought in vain to see him again. He had left the city."

"He is no longer in Venice!" exclaimed Antonia.

"He has been absent for nearly a year, contrary to his custom," said Matteo, "for it is rare for two or three months to pass without him returning."

"This is not his ordinary residence, then?" said Madame Alberti.

"No, certainly not," Matteo continued, "but for a long time—a very long time—he was coming almost every month to spend a few days, sometimes more, sometimes less, hardly ever longer than a week or two. This time, his long absence would have caused the fear that he had abandoned Venice entirely if there had not been other examples, but people recall that he once disappeared for several years."

"Several years?" said Antonia. "You can't think so, Matteo; you told us just now, if I understood you rightly, that he was a very young man."

"Very young, in truth," replied Matteo. "At least, he appears to be. I have not said the contrary, but I am speaking in accordance with the singular ideas of the people, which do not merit your attention, my illustrious ladies, and I blush myself . . ."

"Continue, continue, Matteo," said Madame Alberti, vehemently. "This interests us greatly, isn't that true, Antonia? Sit down, Matteo, and do not forget anything, absolutely anything, of what concerns Lothario."

Madame Alberti was, in fact, keenly interested, and her mind, rapid in grasping all the aspects of things, had run far ahead of Matteo's narration in romantic and marvelous conjectures, which she was eager to see verified. Antonia had a sensibility no less vivid; it was, on the contrary, more irritable more avid for emotions, but she feared them because her weakness always exposed her to yielding to them. When Matteo had begun to excite Madame Alberti's curiosity with the vague and bizarre circumstances of his story she had pressed herself against her sister with a frisson of anxiety and fear, the impression of which she tried to cover with a smile.

"What I know about Signor Lothario," said Matteo, gravely, having sat down in order to obey Madame Alberti, "is only known to me, as I have told you, illustrious ladies, by way of public rumor. He is a young man with the most handsome face, who appears in Venice from time to time with the retinue of a prince, but who only seems, however, to have sought the habitation of a great city in order to find an opportunity to spread the most abundant liberalities among the poor, for he does not frequent society very much and almost nothing is known of his habits and familiar amities either with men or women. He sometimes visits an unfortunate family in order to bring them succor.

"Passionate about the arts, which he cultivates successfully, he sometimes seeks the conversation and the advice of those who exercise them. Outside of those relations, which he limits with an extraordinary care, he lives almost solitary in Venice. He has not entered any particular house ten times, and he does not correspond with anyone; no one has ever entered far enough into his intimacy to know the name of his family or the place of his origin, or to form a reliable conjecture on the mystery of his birth. It's true that he has many servants, but they are all foreigners, because he changes them every time he travels, and does not even procure in Venice those who are to serve him while he resides here.

"His relations outside his household give no more light. Since he has been known, the post has never brought him a letter, and the bankers have never furnished him with a sequin. The revolutions of States do not change his position in the slightest; in stormy times he does not go away any more than usual, and when travelers are submitted to formalities of precaution, his papers are always signed by the governing authorities under the simple name of Lothario, which a similar circumstance would render suspect if it were not known that the host of good deeds attributed to him have recommended him to the powerful men of all epochs and all parties.

"It would be difficult, in any case, to disturb him in Venice, where he is, for an immense class, an object of gratitude, affection and, so to speak, worship. The proscription of Lothario, if there were ever reason to think of it, might be the signal for a revolution; but he does not give the impression of believing it, for he obliges the unfortunate class without caressing it. His severe and slightly arrogant attitude, so it is said, separates him from them by an obstacle that he is the sole master of removing, which he would not obliterate without overturning the Venetian States, if he had decided to do so. The distance that he has left between himself and the people does not revolt anyone, because they sense that nature itself has marked its limits, and that it separates him even more manifestly from people who appear to approach his condition.

"In fact, it is from them that he distances himself furthest, and if Signor Lothario is seen to descend from the heights of his character in favor of someone, it is never for an aristocrat; it is for an invalid that needs his support, a lost child, or an epileptic the sight of whom repels passers-by. That does not prevent him from frequenting public meetings and great societies in which men can appear, and even shine, without communicating immediately with anyone. He is easily remarked there, since it is said that Venice has no artist and virtuoso comparable to him, but, far from using those advantages, it is said that he fears exhibiting them, and only allows them to be perceived with regret; and it is at a moment when they might procure him agreeable acquaintances or great establishments that he flees

Venice, as if to avoid the glamour of a public and exposed life, which might steal him from himself and the secrecy with which he likes to envelop himself.

"Ambition has no effect on him; even amour has never stopped him, although there are no women on earth more seductive than those of Venice. Once, he seemed to be occupied with a noble young woman, who, for her part, had testified to an ardent passion for him, but an extraordinary misfortune put an end to the relationship that the public supposed to exist between them. It was at the moment of Lothario's departure; after having resided in Venice for a little longer than usual, although that sentiment, if it existed, could not retain him here. Two or three days before his departure, she disappeared, and her body was only found a long time afterwards, on the sandbank where the Armenian convent has since been established."

"That's incomprehensible," said Antonia, with a profoundly concentrated expression.

"No, Mademoiselle," Matteo replied, following his thought, which was perhaps not the same as Antonia's. "The movement of the waters driven back by the sea brings in that direction the greater part of the debris that floats in our canals. As the lady had a hot head, and details that I have forgotten announced that her death had been violent, it was attributed to despair rather than an accident; I even believe that a letter in her handwriting, which was found subsequently, and in which she explained her design, justified that supposition."

"Be careful, Matteo," said Madame Alberti. "You commenced by telling us that Lothario was young."

"Twenty-five or twenty-six at the most," replied Matteo, "but he is very blond and delicate to see, although more adroit and more robust than the most strongly constituted men, and it is possible . . ."

"It is not possible," she continued, forcefully, "that he had been absent for several years, since he had become known in

Venice; that is what you have not explained to us. Think, also, that the story of the young woman found dead on the isle of the Armenians must be anterior, in your terms, to the epoch when the Armenians came to establish themselves there,[1] in which case . . ."

"I don't know any more," said Matteo, with a sort of confusion, "and I have only told these ladies what I have heard Venetians of an advanced age say, who sustain that they once saw Lothario as he is today, but who suppose that he has been absent for no less than fifty years, and you sense the extravagance of that idea. Furthermore, it's quite natural to believe, given Signor Lothario's way of life, that he has a strong interest in hiding what he really is, in order to understand the care he doubtless takes to favor, and even to give birth, to rumors that must increase the uncertainty of opinion in his regard. So it is necessary to admit that there are none so strange and so ridiculous that they do not have at least the credit of being repeated, for some time, by people who have the reputation of being sensate. You can judge that by the most plausible of all, which is that the mysterious stranger has the secret of the philosopher's stone; and in truth, it is difficult to see any other way of explaining the magnificent existence and regal expenditure of an unknown man who is not known to undertake any commerce or industry, to own the smallest property or to have the slightest business dealings of any kind.

"Three years ago, in the epoch of his first voyage since the long absence about which those people talk, jealous individuals irritated by his prodigious success, all the more so because he attached scant importance to it himself and the most ordinary mark of attention that could be obtained from him was disdain, spread the most outrageous fable regarding him. I scarcely dare

---

1 San Lazzaro degli Armeni, the Benedictine monastery of the Armenian Mekhitarists, situated on a small island in the Venetian lagoon, was established in 1717. Byron visited it in 1816.

to repeat it, and could not do so without danger anywhere but here. People went so far as to say that he was the agent of a troop of forgers hidden in the grottos of the Tyrol or some forest in Croatia. That error did not endure for long, for Signor Lothario spreads gold in such profusion that it is easy to verify its authenticity and its fabrication. It was evident that there is none better in all the States of Venice, and since then, if fables have been invented in his account they have at least ceased to be insulting and atrocious.

"What he really is, I do not know," Matteo said, rising from his seat, "but I can repeat that it depends almost entirely on him to be anything he wishes in Venice, if he comes back."

"He will come back," said Madame Alberti, embracing that idea with the romantic susceptibility that she adopted too frequently for penetration; it was her only fault.

VII

> You will see me once again in this form, and that day
> will be the last.
> Shakespeare.[1]

That conversation had not left very profound traces in Antonia's mind. As the name of Lothario recurred frequently in the circles into which her sister had introduced her, it scarcely struck her ears without reminding her vaguely of the bizarre and singular ideas with which Matteo had entertained them, but it was only a fleeting sensation, to which she would have blushed to deliver herself. In trying to take account at first of the impression that the story had made on her, she was afflicted not to be able to

---

1 The original of this back-translated quote is not easily identifiable, but printed French versions of Shakespeare's plays were often exceedingly free translations.

make a reliable judgment of Lothario, but it was not in her character to go astray for long in futile conjectures on things that touched her so lightly. The weakness of her constitution and the habitual depression of her organs forced her to circumscribe her sensations, and the more powerful they were around her the less she was capable of extending them to unknown objects.

One day, however, the rumor ran around Venice that Lothario had arrived, and that rumor, soon confirmed by the hectic joy of an enthusiastic populace, reached Antonia rapidly. The same day she was due to accompany Madame Alberti, into a society composed in large measure of strangers attracted to Venice by the pleasures of the carnival, who met from time to time in order to make music.

Scarcely had they entered than a lackey announced Signor Lothario. A sudden frisson of astonishment and pleasure ran through the assembly, gripping Madame Alberti in particular, who was easily preoccupied by any extraordinary idea. She took that moment for a fortunate presentiment, and as all her thoughts related to Antonia, she squeezed her hand abruptly, without knowing exactly what that demonstration might signify.

Antonia was affected differently; her heart was constricted by a sort of fear, because she assembled around the name of Lothario some of the disquieting and terrible circumstances that had struck her in the old steward's discourse. She even hesitated for some time to look at him, but she saw him then distinctly, because he was not far away from her, and appeared to look at her when he perceived her. At the same moment, he had turned his gaze away, but without fixing it only any other object. Leaning on the edge of an antique marble vase laden with flowers, he gave the impression of taking part in a conversation of scant importance in order to dispense with directing his attention elsewhere.

At the sight of him Antonia was seized by an emotion that she had never experienced before, which did not resemble any familiar sentiment. It was not fear, nor did it correspond to the idea that she had formed of the initial disturbances of amour; it was something vague, indecisive and obscure, which had something of reminiscence, dreaming or a fit of fever. Her breast palpitated violently, her limbs lost their suppleness, her vision was troubled, and an indefinable languor enchained her fascinated organs.

She tried in vain to break the spell; its efforts were augmented. She had heard mention of the invincible numbness of a frightened voyager gone astray in the forests of America frozen by the gaze of a boa, and the vertigo that surprises a shepherd in pursuit of his goats at the extremity of one of the gigantic ridges of the Alps, who, suddenly dazzled by the circular movement that his imagination lends, like a magic mirror, to the abysms that surround him, precipitates himself into their horrible depths, incapable of resisting the power that revolts him but draws him. She felt something similar, and just as difficult to explain, something tender and odious, which astonished, repelled and summoned her, and which overwhelmed her heart. She trembled.

That tremor, which was rather ordinary in her, did not frighten Madame Alberti, but she urged Antonia to leave and Antonia desired that. She made an effort to stand up, felt weak, sat down again and smiled at Madame Alberti, who regarded the smile as a consent to stay.

Lothario had not changed place. He was dressed in the French style, with an elegant simplicity. Nothing announced the slightest research in his costume and his adornment, except for two small emeralds suspended from his ears, and which, under the thick curls of the blond hair by which his visage was shaded, gave him a singular and savage aspect. That ornament had ceased a long time before to be fashionable in the Venetian States, as in almost all of civilized Europe.

Lothario was not conventionally handsome, but his face had an extraordinary charm. His wide mouth, his narrow and pale lips, which allowed the sight of dazzlingly white teeth, the disdainful and sometimes grim habitude of his expression was repellent at first glance, but his gaze, full of tenderness and power, force and generosity, imposed respect and amour, especially when one saw a certain soft gleam escaping from it, which embellished all his features. His high and pure forehead also had something strange about it, a deep crease that age had not produced, which marked the trace of a troublesome and frequent thought.

In general, his physiognomy was serious and somber, but no one had more facility in effacing a disagreeable prejudice. It was sufficient for him to raise an eyebrow and to allow the celestial fire by which his eyes were animated to descend. For observers, that gaze had something indescribable, which derived from an organization superior to human. For the vulgar it was, according to the occasion, caressant or imperious; one sensed that it could be terrible.

Antonia had a certain strength on the piano, but her timidity almost always prevented her from developing her knowledge before a numerous society. There is a kind of modesty, which was hers, that consists of continually dissimulating one's faculties in order not to wound mediocre individuals, who are found in the majority everywhere, and perhaps also not to displease the minority who judge by means of an appearance of prejudice. She had never consented to play a piece of music in public except by condescension to invitations that she attributed to simple politeness, and which she was sure of satisfying without involving in that feeble effort of propriety all the resources of her talent. She had even observed that the testimonies of obliged satisfaction that greeted her complaisance were no fewer when she had rendered a passage simply, only following mechanical rules of execution, than when she found herself directed by a sudden and fortunate inspiration that satisfied her internally.

She sat down at the piano calmly enough, therefore, when she was summoned, and was letting her fingers run over the keyboard with her usual indifference, when her eyes, distracted by the reflection in a mirror placed in front of her, were struck by a strange and terrible illusion.

Lothario had approached her seat and, as the seat was mounted on the platform where the instrument was placed, only his pale and motionless head emerged above Antonia's red cashmere. The disorderly hair of the mysterious young man, the bleak fixity of his sad and severe eyes, the painful contemplation in which he appeared to be plunged, and the convulsive movement of the bizarre and tortuous crease that misfortune had doubtless engraved on his forehead, all concurred to give that aspect something frightening

Surprised, nonplussed and alarmed, Antonia, moving her gaze successively from the lectern to the mirror and from the mirror to the lectern, soon lost sight of the confused notes and the audience that surrounded her. Involuntarily substituting the sentiment by which she was gripped for that which she had to depict, she improvised by means of an extraordinary transition, but which must have passed for a singular play of her imagination rather than what it really was: an expression of terror so true that everyone shivered.

She threw herself into Madame Alberti's arms, who took her back to her place amid a rumor of applause mingled with surprise and anxiety.

After having followed her with his eyes to the place where she stopped, Lothario approached a harp, and a universal movement of curiosity and pleasure succeeded the one that had just troubled the assembly momentarily. Even Antonia, reassured and distracted by a new impression, expressed the keenest impatience to hear Lothario, and as he appeared to dread that her condition was insufficiently tranquil for her to take part in the rest of the evening's pleasures, she felt obliged to testify to him with her gaze that her indisposition had ceased.

That mark of interest on Lothario's part had touched her vividly, but one would have thought that Lothario, more sensible still to the slight demonstration he had just received of it, had changed existence while Antonia was looking at him. His brow had cleared, his eyes were shining with a bizarre gleam; a smile in which a residue of tenderness and a commencement of joy were visible embellished his severe mouth. Passing his left hand through the broad waves of his hair in search of a motif or a memory, and seizing the strings of the harp lightly with the other, in such a manner as only to impart a vague vibration to them, her drew by way of a prelude the fugitive but enchanting sounds that resemble a concert of spirits, and he seemed to throw them without effort and abandon them to the atmosphere.

"Woe betide you," he murmured. "Woe betide you, if ever you grow in the forests that are submissive to the domination of Jean Sbogar!

"This, he continued," is the famous ballad of the anemone, so well known in Zara, and the most recent production of Morlach poetry."

Antonia, sharply stirred by the choice of that song and the sound of Lothario's voice, drew closer to Madame Alberti, who was very preoccupied beside her. She too recalled that harmonious voice and the place where she had heard it, but thought it might be the result of a fortuitous resemblance. Dalmatian song is too simple, too uniform, too deprived of ornamentation for it not to be easy to be mistaken with regard to two analogous voices.

Finally, after a moment of reflection, Lothario rendered his ballad in its entirety, continuing to accompany it with the aerial harmonies that the harp produced under his fingers, the religious melody of which was mingled with his song in the most imposing manner. Having reached the old Morlach's refrain, he put into it a tone of pity so dolorous that all hearts were softened, most of all that of Antonia, who attached to that idea a memory of anxiety and fear. Lothario's ballad had finished a long time ago when its final words, and the redoubtable name of Jean Sbogar, were still resounding in her thoughts.

VIII

> Dream, innocent creatures in the gentle slumber that holds you entranced; you shall soon, alas, have sad late nights and cruel insomnias.
>
> Milton

Among the number of the suppositions that succeeded one another in Madame Alberti's mind after that evening, there was one that offered enough plausibility to strike vulgar imaginations, but which did not lack the romantic aspect that she usually sought in her combinations. The rest of her conjectures were so ill-founded that she did not take long to cling to that one, which suited her all the more because it flattered the most agreeable and the most dominant of her sentiments, her love for Antonia.

The establishment of her cherished sister occupied her incessantly; she was determined to neglect nothing in order to ensure her happiness, and to subordinate all other proprieties to that sole interest. Antonia's immense heritage, and the one that Madame Alberti would leave her one day, were made to excite the cupidity of a host of suitors, and Madame Alberti did not want her sister's life to depend on a vile man for whom amour would be a speculation and marriage a bargain. It was in accordance with the sentiments that she promised herself to see blooming within her that she had resolved to dispose of her hand, almost sure that Antonia's hand, directed by the judgment and experience of a second mother, could not be mistaken.

Already, several young men of great fortune or distinguished birth had entered the lists in vain. None of them had succeeded in fixing the attention of her sister, and Madame Alberti, attentive to looking out for the slightest sensations of that ingenuous and uncomplicated soul, had never surprised a secret there. The first sight of Lothario, on the contrary, had produced a profound impression on her, the only possible explanation for the singular scene of the piano. Lothario had appeared to be no less emotional, no less troubled and no less penetrated by a powerful affection himself, and the idea that such a man, so renowned for the brilliance of his mind, the variety of his talents, the tenderness and generosity of his character, the grandeur of his manners and the purity of his mores might become Antonia's husband was for Madame Alberti the sweetest of illusions.

What was this Lothario, however, and how could such serious relations be linked with an unknown who was obstinate, so everyone said, in surrounding himself with the most suspect mystery? That problem only worried Madame Alberti momentarily. In a short time she had found explanations for everything and had had the art or the good luck to attach them all to her first thought with sufficient appearance of verity that even Antonia, who did not always see things with the same eyes, had no objection or response.

It is true that Antonia's heart was beginning to be interested in that hypothesis and to wish that it might be a reality, not because she felt for Lothario the movement of sympathy that indicates a need to love, the indefinable attraction that causes one to cease to be oneself in order to live the existence of another; what she experienced did not have that character yet; it was more the traction of a submissive soul, the resignation of weakness that only asks to be protected, the voluntary dependence of a timid and sensitive creature toward one that imposes confidence and respect. Thus had Lothario appeared to her, and the young man's first glance had arrested upon her with so much empire that it seemed to her that from that moment on he had acquired rights over her destiny.

I have not yet said what Madame Alberti's supposition was. She thought, reasonably enough, that in retrenching from Lothario's history what popular rumor had added of the ridiculous and the absurd, it was probable that his condition and his fortune were all that his education and his magnificence announced; that if he had reasons for hiding his name and his rank, they could only be temporary; that the disguise in question had nothing alarming for Antonia's amour, which was not under any alliance; and that the desire to strike her attention, to draw nearer to her an interest her heart by considerations independent of those that determine the majority of marriages was probably the principal object of the mysterious appearances with which Lothario had wanted to envelop himself; that the most extraordinary, the most inexplicable of the facts that were reported about him were doubtless only lies insinuated to Antonia's servants by interested individuals with the intention of increasing the uncertainty in which they wanted to retain her.

That last conjecture was not devoid of evidence, for it was impossible to dissimulate that Lothario had played a large part in the latest events of Antonia's life. On due reflection, he was the young man who had passed close to her when returning from the Farnedo singing the Morlach refrain, and that young man has not been in Trieste without design. The apparitions that had alarmed Antonia so often, and which had inspired so much anxiety in Madame Alberti when she regarded them as the illusions of a sick mind, might have proceeded from the same cause. If she had exaggerated or changed a few circumstances, that is the prerogative of weak souls who have everything to fear and tender souls that never believe themselves to be interested enough.

Finally, the event at Duino had not been explained. How could brigands, animated to pillage and murder, have yielded merely at the appearance of a young Armenian monk if that man, redoubtable by virtue of his valor and perhaps his renown, had not imposed an invincible terror upon them by launching himself out of the carriage where Madame Albani had accorded him a place? No doubt, he had knocked some of them down before dispersing them, and then, indecisive in the darkness, on a road that he had never traveled, he had found it impossible to rejoin his traveling companions.

Who could that monk have been, armed in violation of the statutes of his order and who had devoted himself with so much courage and self-disregard to the salvation of a few strangers, if not a disguised lover who wanted to save Antonia or to die for her? If the postillion's pious vision had been, as there was no way to doubt, the error of a man of the people entirely deprived of enlightenment, what other explanation could be substituted for Madame Alberti's?

Dubious and incomprehensible things still remained, but it would be astonishing if there were not, in the life of a man who seeks to multiply uncertainties and mysteries around him and who has all the necessary skill to prepare, plan and make use of the means he employs in that design. Lothario loved and adored Antonia and all his actions announced, in addition, a man so judicious and so enlightened that it was impossible to attribute the apparent bizarrerie of some of his steps to mental aberration. He had his reasons, and why seek them ahead of time? What was important for Madame Alberti was to know Lothario better, to make sure by a more habitual frequentation of the perfection of character that general opinion attributed to him, and to see declared before her eyes the sentiments that she had only suspected thus far.

Lothario did not flee general gatherings where everyone was a tributary to his talent. He avoided private societies to which it was necessary to take confidence or affection, and it was very rare, as Matteo had observed, that he consented to appear more than once. However, he seized eagerly, when it was presented to him, the opportunity to see Madame Alberti and her sister at home; and that singularity, promptly remarked by everyone, rid Antonia of many annoying pretentions. A visit from Lothario had the appearance of a step, and a step on the part of Lothario excluded even men who could rival him in regard to certain advantages, because he conserved advantages over them that are never mistaken by the vulgar and even by the imagination of women besotted by the glamour and rumor of a serious soul, an imposing character and a hidden life.

We have seen that the impression that Antonia experienced at the sight of Lothario did not resemble those that announce the birth of a first amour in ordinary hearts. One circumstance quite indifferent in itself, the effect of which had not been entirely destroyed however—the singular illusion of the mirror in which Lothario had appeared to her—had mingled with it a sort of trouble and indefinable terror.

The interest she took in Lothario, the penchant that drew her toward him, was nevertheless no less powerful for having less mildness. It bore an imprint of fatality that surprised and sometimes frightened Antonia, but from which she did not attempt to defend herself, since Madame Alberti approved of the sentiment and even found a certain pleasure in nourishing it. She was astonished, however, that amour was so different from the idea that she had formed of it, based on the tender and passionate depictions of romancers and poets. She only saw it as yet as an austere and menacing chain that enveloped her with inflexible bonds, the weight of which she strove in vain to shake off.

However, when Lothario, distracted for her sake from his somber reveries, deigned to devote himself momentarily, in a natural manner full of grace, to simple conversations of familiar amity; when the supercilious pride and dolorous mental tension that gave his physiognomy such a majestic and sad dignity, gave way to a mild abandon; when a smile blossomed on the mouth that had lost the habitude of it for such a long time and rendered his severe features a frank and pure serenity, Antonia, transported by a joy that she had never known, understood something of the happiness of loving a being similar to oneself, and being loved without division; it was still Lothario who gave birth to that, but it was Lothario stripped of something strange and redoubtable that alarmed her tenderness.

It is true that those instants were rare, but Antonia enjoyed them with so much intoxication that she had reached the point of no longer desiring any other felicity, and she was then so scantly able to dissimulate what she experienced that Lothario could not mistake it for long. It is true that the first time he made the observation, it was evident that it was not without bitterness for him; his brow darkened, his breast swelled, he put his hand over his eyes forcefully, and he left. After that he smiled even more rarely, and when it happened, he hastened to turn an anxious and chagrined gaze toward Antonia.

His amour for her was no longer a secret. It was sensed that all his thoughts, all his speech and all his actions related to her, that she was the unique idea and sole goal of his life. Madame Alberti had no doubt of it, and Antonia said it sometimes to herself, in a surge of pride that she had difficulty repressing; but Lothario's amour, which was marked with a particular seal, like the entire existence of that inconceivable man, had nothing in common with the sentiment that bears the same name in society; it was a grave and reflective affection, with demonstrations and transports that were hardly satisfactory, and was gathered within itself with an excessive reserve as soon as it could dread being extended too far.

The fire of his gaze often betrayed it, but in the ineffable expression of chaste and mild sentiment that soon filled the fit of temporary fever, Lothario no longer appeared to be a lover. One might have thought him a father to whom only one daughter remains, a single daughter, and who has concentrated in her all the affections that he had once permitted himself to divide between other children. He reveled then in his passion for Antonia, in something more powerful and greater than amour: a dominant determination of protection so benevolent and tutelary that it could not be depicted otherwise than that of the angel of light who stands sentry over virtue and escorts it from the cradle to the grave.

There was also the kind of ascendancy that he exercised over the young woman, and that could not be compared to anything in the order of purely human relations. The tender and slightly superstitious imagination of Antonia had not forgotten that idea in the host of hypotheses that the incomprehensible existence of Lothario caused her to conceive and reject by turns, but she enjoyed it herself and with Madame Alberti as an inconsequential illusion. In their intimacy, Lothario was called Antonia's Angel.

IX

Alas, the sweetest prospect that can flatter my heart is
annihilation. Oh, not to be deceived, the unique hope
that remains to me. It seems to me that I would now
dare to beg my judge to annihilate me; it seems that
I would now find him disposed to grant my wish. Then,
O rapturous thought, I would no longer be! I would fall
back into the inviolable calm of non-existence, effaced
and retrenched from the number of beings, forgotten by
all creatures, angels and God himself. Omnipotent God,
here I am; deign to render me to the chaos from which
you extracted me!
Klopstock.

One day, at sunset, Antonia had gone into the church of San Marco to pray. The last rays of twilight were expiring through the stained glass widows under the great arches of the dome, and gradually being extinguished in the corners of the distant chapels. One could scarcely see a few dying reflections of the most apparent mosaics shining in the vaults and on the walls. From there the increasing shadows descended, ever more thickly, along the mighty columns of the nave, and fended up inundating with a profound and immobile obscurity the unequal surface of the paving stones, furrowed like the sea that surrounds them, which often comes as far as the holy line to reconquer its empire from the usurpations of man.

A few paces away from her she perceived a kneeling man whose attitude announced that he was very preoccupied. At the same instant, one of the clerics of the church came to deposit a lamp before a miraculous image suspended in that place, and the flame, agitated by the movement of his stride, spread a faint and transient light around him, which was sufficient for Antonia to recognize Lothario. He got up hastily and he was about to disappear when Antonia found herself in front of him on the parvis.

She seized his arm, and walked for some time without speaking to him; then, with an effusion full of tenderness, she said: "Well, Lothario, what anxiety is tormenting you? Do you blush to be a Christian, and is that belief so unworthy of a strong soul that one dare not admit it before one's friends? As for me, the greatest of my chagrins, I can assure you, was doubting your faith, and I feel relieved of a mortal pain now that I am sure that we recognize the same God and that we await the same future."

"Alas, what are you saying, dear Antonia?" Lothario replied. "Why did my evil destiny have to lead to this explanation? However, I cannot avoid it; it would be too frightful to abuse a soul like yours.

"The man, perhaps poorly organized, who does not believe in the religion into which he is born; who, more unfortunate still, does not understand either the great intelligence that governs the world or the immortal life of the soul, is more worthy of pity than horror; but if he hid his incredulity under pious practices, if he only worshiped what society worships in order to deceive society, if his superb reason disavowed the homage that he rendered to public reverence at the very moment that he prostrated himself with the faithful, that man would be a monster of hypocrisy, the most perfidious and the most odious of creatures. Rather see my heart in all its infirmity and all its misery.

"Balanced since childhood between the need and the impossibility of belief, devoured by the thirst for another life and the impatience to raise myself to it, but pursued by the conviction of annihilation, like a fury attached to my existence, I have long, often and everywhere sought the God that my despair implores, in churches, in temples, in mosques, in the schools of philosophers and priests, in nature entire, which show him to me and refuse him to me. When the night, already advanced, permits me to penetrate under these vaults, and to humiliate myself without being seen on the steps of this sanctuary, I come here to beg God to communicate with me. My voice begs him, my heart appeals to him, and nothing responds to me.

"More frequently, because then I am surer of not deceiving a witness by misinterpreted demonstrations, it is in the heart of the woods, on the sand of the shore, or lying in a boat abandoned at sea that I invoke that Heavenly light, the gentle influence of which would cure all my woes. How many times, and with what fervor, O Heaven, I have prostrated myself before this immense creation, asking it for its author! How many times I have shed tears of rage, while, descending again into my heart, I have found nothing but doubt, ignorance and death!

"Antonia, you are trembling to hear me. Forgive me, pity me, and be reassured. The blindness of a wretch disavowed by Heaven, proves nothing against the faith of a simple soul. Believe, Antonia! Your God exists, your soul is immortal, your religion is true. But that God has divided his graces and his punishments with the far-sighted intelligence that reigns in all his works. He has given the prescience of immortality to the pure souls for whom immortality is made. To the souls he has devoted in advance to annihilation, he has only shown annihilation."

"Annihilation!" exclaimed Antonia. "Can you think so, Lothario? Oh, my friend, your soul is not devoted to annihilation! You will believe if only for a moment, a single moment; but the instant will arrive when immortality will be sensed by Lothario's reason, as by his heart! If Lothario's soul were mortal, omnipotent God, if Lothario's soul were to end, what would be the purpose of creation entire?

"Oh, as for me," she continued, more calmly, "I sense firmly that I shall live, that I shall not finish, that I shall possess everything that has been so dear to me, in a future without vicissitudes: my father, my mother, my good sister . . . and I know that all the dolors of the most difficult life, all the proofs to which Providence might submit a frail creature in this brief passage from birth to death, will never reduce me to absolute despair, because eternity remains to me in order to love and to be loved."

"To love, Antonia!" said Lothario. "What man is worthy to be loved by you?"

He finished those words as he entered Madame Alberti's drawing room; she smiled at him with a significant expression. Lothario smiled too, but it was not the enchanting smile that a fortunate distraction sometimes stole from him; it was a bitter and dolorous smile that seemed foreign to his visage.

Antonia was beginning to find an explanation for Lothario's profound sadness. She could imagine how that unfortunate man, disinherited from the mildest favor of Providence, of the happiness of knowing God and loving him, cast upon the earth like a voyager without a goal, might furnish that futile career with impatience and aspire momentarily to emerge from it forever. It appeared, too, that he was alone in the world, for he never spoke about his parents. If he had once had a mother, he would doubtless have named her. For a man who was not bound by any other sentiment, the immense void in which his soul was plunged could not fail to be frightening and terrible, and Antonia, who had never supposed that a creature could fall into that excess of misery and solitude, did not contemplate it without fear.

She reflected above all, with an extreme constriction of the heart, on Lothario's idea that there was, for certain beings reproved by God, a predestination of annihilation that made their misfortune in this world from the conviction of not reviving in another. She thought for the first time about that terrible annihilation, about the profound, immeasurable horror of that eternal separation; she put herself in the place of the unfortunate who only saw in life a succession of partial deaths that ended in a complete death, and in the most delightful affections nothing but the fugitive effusion of two hearts of ash; she imagined the terror of the husband who clutches his beloved wife in his arms, when he comes to think that after a few years, perhaps a few days, all the centuries will be between them, and that each moment of the present flowing by is an advance payment given to the endless future; and in that dolorous meditation she experienced the same sentiment as a poor and feeble child gone astray in the woods, who, from error to error and detour to detour, has arrived without any means of recognizing his track and retracing his steps, on the steep slope of a precipice.

Absorbed in those reflections, as if by a painful dream, she had risen from her seat, while Madame Alberti and Lothario gazed at her in silence, and she had gone to her room. Scarcely had she arrived there than her heart, freed of all exterior constraint, submitted without resistance to the oppression that was overwhelming it, and savored the liberty of suffering with a sort of sensuality.

Until then the passions had exercised little empire over her, and even the love for Lothario that Madame Alberti loved to see developing in her had not been manifested by the storms that accompany exalted sentiments, which augment the action of life, and which enable all the faculties to reach their highest degree of power. She had realized that she loved Lothario, and that persuasion, full of sweetness and abandon had cost nothing to her happiness; but the thought of annihilation and damnation, the damnation and annihilation of Lothario, excited in her heart the most tumultuous ideas and filled it with confusion and terror.

What, she said, *beyond this life so rapidly elapsed . . . nothing! No longer anything for him! And it's him who thinks so! And it's him who says so! It's him who threatens us with never seeing one another again in the places where people see one another again in order never to quit one another!*

Annihilation! What, then, is annihilation? And what is eternity, if Lothario is not in it?

While she was trying to take account of that thought, she had, without being aware of it, drawn nearer to her crucifix, and her hand was supported on one of the arms of the cross. She raised her eyes and fell to her knees.

"My God, my God!" she cried. "You to whom space and eternity belong, you who can do anything and who loves so much, have you done nothing for Lothario?"

As she pronounced those words, Antonia felt faint, but she was recalled to herself by the impression of a hand sustaining her, that of Madame Alberti, who had quit Lothario in order to follow her, in the fear that she might be ill.

"Be tranquil, poor Antonia," Madame Alberti said to her. "Your ancestors have given princes to the Orient, and your fortune is counted in millions. You will be Lothario's wife, even if he is the son of a king."

"What does it matter?" responded Antonia with a wild expression. "What does it to matter, if he is not resuscitated?"

Madame Alberti, who could not grasp the meaning of those words, shook her head sadly, like a person reluctantly confirmed in a desolating conviction that she has rejected in vain for a long time.

"Unfortunate child," she said, pressing her in her arms and sprinkling her with her tears, "how much harm you are doing your sister! Oh, if Heaven reserves that misfortune for you, may I at least die before witnessing it!"

X

One is disillusioned without having enjoyed. Desires still remain, but one no longer has illusions. The imagination is rich, abundant and marvelous; existence poor, dry and disenchanted.
One lives with a full heart in an empty world,
and without having used anything,
one is disabused of everything.
Chateaubriand.

The intimacy of Lothario had become a need for Antonia, whom the hope of bringing his heart back to the faith inflamed with a zeal full of tenderness, and who already loved him ardently before having admitted that she loved him. She was no less precious to Madame Alberti, who, increasingly anxious about the fate of a young woman devoid of support, who entered into society with a debilitated organism, unsteady health and an extreme disposition to suffer dolorously all strong impressions, could only conceive the possibility of ensuring her some happiness by enabling her to find it in a powerfully felt affection, one protection more against the frictions of life.

She saw a great advantage in aiding soon the almost maternal affection that she had for her sister with the help of a sentiment even more tender and more far-sighted, such as Antonia had doubtless inspired in Lothario, although, by virtue of a singularity difficult to define, he avoided reporting what he so evidently experienced to any particular person. One might have thought that he had formed in a more elevated world an admirable type of perfection, of whom the figure and character of Antonia only enabled him to retrace the memory, and that he had arrested his gaze on her with an attention so sharp and so tender because her features awakened a reminiscence whose object was not on earth. That circumstance had maintained in their relationship a kind of painful mystery, which was a burden to everyone, but which time alone could clarify.

In any case, Antonia found herself happy enough with the amity of a man like Lothario, and her soul, timid and suspicious, which understood another happiness very well, dared not desire it. Her life was embellished by the idea that she occupied Lothario's life, and that she had taken in the thought of that extraordinary man a place that perhaps no one shared with her.

As for Lothario, his melancholy was augmented every day, and augmented above all by that which seemed appropriate to dissipate it. Often, in shaking the hand of Madame Alberti, while reposing his gaze on Antonia's soft smile, he had talked about his departure with a stifled sigh, and his eyelids had been moistened by tears.

The melancholy disposition of mind that was common to them both distanced them from public places and the noisy pleasures to which the Venetians deliver themselves for the greater part of the year. Their time was ordinarily spent in excursions over the lagoons, to the isles that are strewn there, or to the pretty villages of Terra Firma that border the elegant banks of the Brenta. However, of all the places they loved to revisit there was none that offered them more charms than a narrow and elongated isle that the inhabitants of Venice call the Lido, where the shore, because it effectively terminates the lagoons in the direction of the open sea, is like their limit. Nature seems to have imprinted on that place a particular character of sadness and solemnity, which only excites grave and pensive ideas

On the coast where it has a view of Venice, the Lido is covered with gardens, pretty orchards, and simple but picturesque little houses. On the fine feast days of the year it is the rendezvous of the people, who come to relax from the week's fatigues with games and country dances. From there, Venice develops to the eyes in all its magnificence; the canal, covered with gondolas, presents in its vast extent the image of an immense river, which bathes the foot of the doge's palace and the steps of San Marco. A bitter thought clutches the heart when one distinguishes beneath its majestic domes the walls blackened by the times of the state inquisition, and when one tries to count privately the innumerable victims of an anxious and jealous tyranny that the dungeons have devoured.

While climbing toward the crest of the Lido, one is attracted by the aspect of an oak-wood that occupies all of the highest part, which extends in a curtain of verdure above the landscape, or divides here and there into cool and shady clumps. One would think, at first, that the place in question, favorable to sensuality, encloses no mysteries other than those of pleasure, but it is consecrated to the mysteries of death. A large number of scattered tombs, charged with singular characters, unintelligible for the majority of strollers, seems to announce the last abode of a people effaced from the earth, who have not left other monuments.

That imposing idea, which is combined and confounded with the sentiment of the brevity of life and that of the antiquity of time, has something vaster and more austere than the one engendered by the mortuary stone of a man we have known alive; but it is an error. One has only taken a few steps when an encounter with a whiter stone ornamented in a more modern manner, often still strewn with flowers that are scarcely faded, deposited there by conjugal amour or filial piety in mourning, dissipates that illusion. Those unknown letters are borrowed from the language of a nation to which God has promised that it will never end, and which lives separated from people with whom it does not even have the right to mingle its dust. It is the Jewish cemetery.

On descending the side opposite to Venice, the trees suddenly become rarer; the dusty and withered grass only appears at intervals; the vegetation disappears entirely and the feet sink into a light, mobile, silvery sand, which coats all of that side of the Lido and ends at the open sea. Here the view changes completely, or, rather, the eye, wandering over a boundless area, seeks in vain those forests of superb bell-towers, those dazzling domes, those sumptuous monuments, those elegantly decorated buildings, those agile gondolas, which, a moment before, occupied it with so many brilliant and flattering distractions. There is no reef, no sandbank on which to repose the gaze in that vague extent. It is no longer the flat and opaque surface of the tranquil canals, which is often only wrinkled by the light oar of a gondolier, and which embellish with their even course streets in which every house is a palace worthy of kings. It is the turbulent waves of the independent sea, which do not receive human law, and which bathe indifferently opulent cities or sterile and deserted strands.

That genre of ideas was very serious in nature for Antonia's timid soul, but she gradually familiarized herself with the most somber scenes and images because she knew that Lothario took pleasure in them, and that he only savored with mildness and plenitude the charm of a meditative conversation in the most rural solitudes. Hostile to forms of society that constrained and repressed the expansion of his ardent sensibility, he was only veritably himself when the circle of society was crossed and, alone with nature and amity, he could give free rein to the impetuosity of his thoughts, often bizarre, always energetic and frank, sometimes as grandiose and savage as the desert that inspired them.

It was then above all that Lothario appeared to be something more than human. It was when, free of the conventions that shrink humanity, he seemed to take possession of a separate creation and respire, unburdened by social institutions, in a place that they had not penetrated. Leaning against an uncultivated tree, on ground that the footsteps of travelers had never trodden, he recalled something of the beauty of Adam after his fault.

Several times, Antonia had considered him in that situation on in the upper reaches of the Lido, where the Israelite cemetery was. From there, while he bore his gaze alternately toward Venice and toward the sea, his physiognomy, so mobile animated and expressive, depicted what was happening within him with as much clarity and precision as speech.

Legible in his gaze was the painful connection that his mind made between those tombs, intermediate between a tumultuous society and the eternal monotony of the seas, and the term of human life, perhaps also placed between a purposeless agitation and an endless inaction. His sight was arrested dolorously at the ultimate limits of the horizon on the side of the gulf, as if it were seeking to push them back further and find beyond them some evidence against annihilation.

One day, penetrated by that idea as if he had communicated it to her, Antonia launched herself toward him from the mound on which she was sitting, and, seizing his hand with all the force of which she was capable, she pointed with her finger at the indecisive line where the last wave mingled with the first cloud and cried: "God! God is there!"

Lothario, less surprised than touched by having been understood, hugged her to his breast.

"God might be lacking in all of nature," he replied, "and be found in Antonia's heart."

Madame Alberti, a witness to all their conversation, took less interest in those that turned toward such great objects of meditation, because she believed without effort, with a naïve faith, and had never supposed that one could put in doubt the only ideas on which human happiness and hope repose. A few circumstances had given her reason to believe that Lothario's religious ideas were not in accord with Antonia's, but she was far from thinking that the discord extended to fundamental principles of belief, and that small lack of harmony between two hearts that she wanted to unite only worried her very slightly. Perfect as Lothario might be, she sensed that he might be mistaken, but she was sure that someone as perfect as Lothario could not be mistaken forever.

XI

I grind my teeth when I see the injustices that are committed,
and how poor wretches are persecuted in the name of justice
and the law.
Goethe.

One day, when their excursion ended later than usual, at an hour when the obscurity that was beginning to extend over the sea no longer allowed Venice to be distinguished except by the scattered lights of its buildings, in the silence where all of nature reposed, and in which the ears easily seized the slightest sounds, Antonia's was suddenly struck by an extraordinary cry, which was not, however, new for her, and which made her shudder. She remembered having heard it in the Farnedo on the day when she had encountered an old Morlach poet, and after that in the vicinity of the castle of Duino, when the

Armenian monk had launched himself into the midst of the brigands and had dispersed them before him.

She drew nearer to her sister with an involuntary movement and searched with her gaze for Lothario, who was standing in the prow of the gondola. Shortly thereafter the cry was renewed, but it came from a much closer point, and at the same instant the gondola experienced a violent shock, as if it had collided with another.

Lothario was no longer there. Antonia uttered a scream and stood up precipitately, calling to him. The gondola remained motionless. A loud noise that came from the side fixed her attention and changed her fear into curiosity. She distinguished quite clearly, in that confused rumor, Lothario's voice, speaking with authority in the middle of a group of men assembled in an open boat.

It only required a moment to understand that the men were disguised sbires taking a prisoner to Venice, who were complaining that someone had caused them to lose their prey. In fact, indignant at the violence that was being done to the poor fellow, and only seeing in the rigorous treatment that he was experiencing an odious abuse of force, Lothario had leapt into the boat and freed the stranger, precipitating him into the sea, from which he could reach a nearby shore by swimming.

At first, the sbires burst forth in reproaches and menaces, for the prisoner was very important; they even had reason to think that he was an emissary of Jean Sbogar, and they expected a high price for his capture; but they reentered into a respectful silence when they recognized Lothario, whose mysterious influence served as a brake, in those times of crisis, on all the excesses of power. After addressing a few scornful words to them, he dropped a handful of sequins into their midst and climbed back placidly into the gondola, where his return put an end to Antonia's anxieties.

At the moment when they entered the canal, the singular cry that had attracted Lothario's attention a little while before was heard again at the point of the Giudecca, Antonia presumed that the man who Lothario had just snatched from the hands of the sbires had come ashore at the point and that he was giving notice of it to his liberator, to inform him that he had not received a futile benefit. Lothario appeared to experience a sharp surge of joy, and that sentiment was communicated to Antonia's heart, which, through the vague dread that still occupied it, enjoyed the perfection of Lothario's soul, which she had always seen ready to revolt against injustice and devote itself in favor of misfortune.

She understood that an invincible impetuosity of sentiments sometimes exposed him to the risk of dangerous excesses, but she supposed that one could never criticize faults so noble in their motivation.

Madame Alberti rarely received society, because she had re-marked that that kind of distraction, which generally consists of an exchange of reciprocally importunate politenesses, did not suit Antonia, whose tastes directed her in all things. That day, however, unusually, she was expecting a rather numerous company, which arrived almost at the same time as her. Already, the rumor of the singular incident that had just occurred had spread through the crowds in the Piazza San Marco, and popu-lar opinion, always favorable to Lothario, had presented his conduct in the most brilliant light.

The Venetian people, who are in appearance the most supple of all and the easiest to subjugate, so submissive, so humble and so mild toward their masters, are perhaps the most jealous of all of their liberty; in moments of public torment, when indecisive power passes from hand to hand at the mercy of hazard, they attach themselves enthusiastically to anything that appears to guarantee their independence, or to defend it in the absence in institutions. The slightest affliction of the security of individuals worries and offends their umbrageous irritability, and they are less inclined to see, in the most legitimate actions of the authority, measures taken in order to maintain security than measures that might one day destroy it.

The name of Jean Sbogar had reached Venice as that of a dangerous and redoubtable man, but it had never caused alarm there, because his troop, too few in number to attempt violence against a great city, only brought the ravages for which renown reproached him into a few mainland villages, which were as foreign to the inhabitants of the lagoons as if they were separated by immense seas. An emissary of Jean Sbogar was therefore not an enemy of Venice, and Lothario's action was generally seen as one of those impulses of energetic generosity that appeared so natural to his character, which had already won him the affection of the inferior classes and the esteem of everyone.

In Madame Alberti's circle the conversation turned naturally to that subject in spite of the visible embarrassment of Lothario, whose modesty could not support the slightest eulogy without impatience, and nothing announced that the inexhaustible thesis, in the style of Venetian politeness, would finally conclude to the satisfaction of the man who was its object, when Antonia, tormented by the malaise that his physiognomy expressed, hastened to seize upon a less favorable aspect of the event in order to relieve Lothario of the weight of an importunate admiration.

"What if, however," she said, smiling, "Signor Lothario was mistaken regarding the object of his generous devotion? What if the bad opinion that he has of the sbires was in default this time, if he had combined with the misfortune of impeding the action of the law and opposing a resistance to it that is always reprehensible, that of sparing from due punishment one of those culpable individuals that no class of society praises, of returning to the fearful word one of those monsters who only mark their days with crimes? What if he had freed one of the accomplices of Jean Sbogar . . . or, and I shudder at the thought, Jean Sbogar himself?"

"Jean Sbogar!" Lothario interjected, in a tone of anxiety and surprise. "But who could think," he continued, "that Jean Sbogar, or even one of his men, would have dared to throw himself into the heart of Venice, without a goal, without a known interest—for it isn't in a great city that bandits can openly carry out brigandage and murder? That artifice of the sbires is too gross!"

"It's absurd!" cried Madame Alberti. "One can imagine that an outlaw of an elevated order, the chief of a generous party, might introduce himself into a city where his judgment has been delivered, where he is consecrated to death and the scaffold awaits him; even if that attempt would not serve to his cause, how many sentiments might determine it! But what sentiment, what passion could determine a wretched leader of thieves, whose heart has only ever beaten faster at the hope of booty, to execute such a reckless enterprise? It doubtless isn't amour! Fortunate or unfortunate in his designs, always sure of inspiring the same scorn, from what woman could he obtain regard, except for those for whom one would be ashamed to undertake anything? Could anyone understand the lover of Jean Sbogar?"

"That would indeed be singular," said Lothario.

"Furthermore," Madame Alberti continued, "who even knows whether that man exists, whether his name is not the password of a gang as despicable as the others, but adroit enough to elevate its baseness by means of the brilliance of some renown?"

"On that point, Madame," said a man of advanced age, who had listened to Madame Alberti attentively while she was speaking and had marked the intention several times to respond to her, "your doubts are ill-founded. Jean Sbogar really exists, and is not entirely unknown to me."

The circle tightened, with the exception of Lothario, who continued to lend a rather cold attention to the conversation, as was his custom—at the most, that demanded by politeness in a conversation whose subject is equally indifferent to everyone.

"I am Dalmatian," the stranger continued, "born in Spalato."

"In Spalato!" said Lothario, drawing nearer. "I know that country well."

"It was in the vicinity of that city that Jean Sbogar was born," said the old man, "at least if I can believe the testimony that has reached me, for that name is not his. He took it when he quit his family, which is one of the most noble and the most illustrious in our province, and he is descended in a direct line from a prince of Albania. I cannot tell you what determined that step, but, while almost a child, he passed into the service of the Turks, where he promptly acquired a great military reputation. Events having been unfavorable to his party, he was obliged to flee in order to escape proscription. It is said that he returned to Dalmatia, where he found himself disinherited. Accustomed to a turbulent life and tormented, it appears, by somber and violent passions, he seized the first opportunity that came along to attach himself to a state of permanent revolution. If he had found himself in one of those fortunate positions where activity and genius lead to anything, he might perhaps have acquired an honorable reputation. For want of the perils that bring glory, he embraced those that only bring scorn and the scaffold. He is an individual greatly to be pitied!"

"You have seen him? You have seen Jean Sbogar?" said Antonia.

"I often held him in my arms when he was a child," replied the old man. "He was then a mild and tender soul, with such noble and beautiful features."

"He was handsome?" exclaimed Madame Alberti.

"Why not?" murmured Lothario. "A beautiful physiognomy is the expression of a beautiful soul; and how many beautiful souls have been altered, embittered and sometimes degraded by misfortune! How many children were the pride of their mothers, who have become the rejects or the terror of society! Satan, on the eve of his fall, was the most beautiful of the angels. But," he continued, raising his voice, "have you known him older?"

"Until the age of ten or twelve," said the old Dalmatian, "when he had become pensive and solitary for some time. I have always thought since that I would recognize him if I ever encountered him."

"God preserve you," said Lothario, "from encountering him on the assassins' bench. That moment would be equally frightful for you and for him . . . for him, who would be reminded of the memories of a youth whose promise he has belied, and which are perhaps his greatest torture now!"

"In truth, Lothario," said Antonia, "you are too disposed to sense similar impressions in others. Do you not think that, in Jean Sbogar, they have been necessarily alienated by the effect of his habits, and that his base and withered soul no longer comprehends them, even if it is true, as it is said, that it has ever been able to comprehend them?"

Lothario smiled tenderly at Antonia; then, turning to the other persons making up the society, and addressing himself most particularly to the old man who had spoken, he shook his head and said: "How unfortunate the culpable individual is on earth, since he is detested by such souls, without him retaining before them the pretext to justify himself or to soften the rigor of their judgment! He only appears to them to be a monster placed entirely outside nature by the ferocious bizarrerie of destiny, and who has nothing human about him. He has only been cast out of the ranks of the living in order to frighten them and to die. That unfortunate has not had parents. He has not counted his friends. His heart has never beaten with a profound sentiment of sadness at the sight of an unfortunate like himself. His eyes devoid of tears have closed to slumber alongside the misery that is awake and weeping.

"Great God! That such a supposition might trouble for me the order, already so sad, of human society! Oh, I would rather believe in the error of a false judgment, in the bitterness of a wounded heart, in the reaction of a noble but pitiless vanity, in revolt against everything that offends it, which had opened a path of blood among men in order to make them aware of his passage and to leave a mark thereof."

"I have thought that," said Antonia, moved, drawing nearer to Lothario and placing a hand on his shoulder.

"Antonia's thought," he continued, "is always a revelation of Heaven. For myself, I have understood, I have often sensed the bitterness with which the miseries of society could sicken an energetic soul; I can conceive the ravages that even the passion for good might sometimes produce in an ardent and inconsiderate heart. There are men turbulent by calculation, tempestuous by virtue of interest, whose hypocritical exaltation never surprises either my intelligence or my pity, but so long as I find honesty in a reckless, extravagant or ferocious action I am ready to serve as a second the man who has committed it, even if the law has already condemned him."

Antonia took away her hand with a sort of fear. Lothario seized it.

"The man has belonged to two very different estates," he said, "but he has carried into the second a few memories of the first; and every time that a great political commotion causes the balance of society to tip in the direction of his natural estate, he precipitates himself into it with an incredible ardor, because that is the tendency of his organization, which always brings him back with an irresistible authority to the enjoyment of the most complete liberty that he can procure. That sentiment might be frightful in its results; it is almost always absurd in its combinations, but it arises from the nature of the man, and is in itself noble and touching. It is something else in an exhausted society like those among which we live, and where all power, divided for a few moments between equally precarious institutions that only have the right of the time or only that, as yet, of audacity, threatens to fall at any moment from the hands of temerity into those of depravity, and to become the share of the most despicable.

"What! When a people has arrived at that point; when, snatched from its ancient mores and its ancient laws by an invincible force, uncertain of its existence, it puts its cowardly agony to sleep in the hands of hypocritical tricksters who caress it in order to inherit its last spoils; when society, so close to its ruination, no longer reposes, among the wicked, on anything but their interests, and among honest men on a few moral rules that are on the brink of ceasing to exist, it is forbidden to a strong man who finds in himself, and in the impulsion that he is capable of giving to others, a guarantee—the sole guarantee—of the rights of the entire species . . . it is forbidden to him to assemble all his faculties against the ascendancy of the destruction, against the progress of death!

"I know full well that the man in question does not raise the standard of ordinary societies. Ordinary societies reject him, for he speaks to them in a language that they do not understand, and which it is forbidden for them to understand. In order to serve them he must separate himself from them, and the war that he declares upon them is the first warning of the independence that they will find one day under his auspices, when the hand that maintains those States has withdrawn entirely. Then those despicable brigands, the object of the disgust and the horror of nations, will become their arbiters, and their scaffolds will be changed into altars.

"This is not a paradox," Lothario continued, "it is an induction drawn from the history of peoples, supported by the example of all the centuries, which sees a very natural effect of the order of things in the spirit of renewal that is manifest at the end of a civilization, and kills it in order to rejuvenate it. For, in sum, nations are only rejuvenated thus, if it is necessary to believe experience. You believe in Providence, and you dare to criticize its means! When a volcano purifies the earth by covering the countryside with smoking lava, you say that it is an act of God, and you do not believe that God has given a particular mission to those men of blood and terror who wear away and break the springs of the social estate in order to re-commence it!

"Seek in your memory for the founders of societies, and you will see that those men are brigands like those you con-demn! What, I ask you, were the likes of Theseus, Pirithous, and Romulus, who marked the passage from the barbaric ages to the heroic ages over which they presided, and Hercules him-self, whose name has remained in veneration among the weak because the strong never had a more redoubtable enemy, whose wrath was only addressed to kings and gods? Priests consecrated the memory of his labors and awarded him an apotheosis, al-though he was a bastard, a thief, a murderer and a suicide. I have seen, in my voyage to Athens, the mountain on which Mars was put on trial for murder."

While Lothario was speaking, Antonia had sat down, and was gazing at him with an indefinable sentiment. Madame Alberti did not take such a keen interest in his discourse, but she enjoyed it as a singular and new idea, and such was the empire over her of those ideas that he often made her forget how opposed they were to the sentiments that she had received from her education, or which her own reason had inspired.

The character of Lothario, known in any case for its rather grim independence and a pronounced penchant for opinions that did not bear the seal of the power and the even more shameful approval of the multitude, lent a piquant and sin-gular interest to his expressions; his position in society was such that people could only see in his most bizarre and most hazardous ideas a caprice of his imagination. That impression was so general when he spoke that it was rare for anyone to try to contradict him. It was known that he was subject to the effusion of his heart and the abandon of his impulses. No one asked him to account for them.

That speech had been finished for a long time, and Lothario, absorbed, was no longer taking part in the indifferent conversation, a cold exchange of insignificant remarks, that had succeeded it. His head supported by his hand, he attached a somber gaze to Antonia, who had changed her place without perceiving it in order to draw closer to him, and who appeared to be struck by a dolorous thought.

"Lothario," she said to him in a low voice, extending her hand to him, "your amour for the weak and the unfortunate sometimes leads you to say things of which you would no longer approve after reflection. Mistrust an enthusiasm that might, in certain circumstances, be fatal to your happiness, and the happiness of those who love you."

"Of those who love me!" Lothario exclaimed. "Oh, if I had been loved! If I could be! If the world had known me; if the gaze of a woman worthy of my heart had fallen upon my heart before misfortune had scourged it . . . ! What a strange supposition . . . !"

Antonia had drawn even closer, in order to isolate Lothario or to hear him better. Her hand had crossed his.

"Yes," Lothario said, "if a woman destined for me had permitted my wretched life a sentiment resembling amour; if a being who resembled Antonia, even remotely, like a shadow of the reality, had taken me under her protection and her pity then . . . if I had been able to breathe without profanation the air agitated by the pleats of her dress or the waves of her hair . . . if my lips had dared to say: Antonia, I love you . . ."

The company was flowing away. Tremulously, Antonia had ceased to understand her position. She remained motionless, and Madame Alberti had come back in, but Lothario had changed nothing in his language. He repeated his final phrase with a more sober expression, and drew Madame Alberti toward her sister with a dolorous exclamation.

"What are you doing?" he said. "What are you making of Lothario? Do you know Lothario, or rather than unknown, that man of hazard who has no name? And you, the sister of that child, do you know that I love her, and that my amour is fatal?"

Antonia smiled bitterly. That association of ideas did not make itself felt to her mind, but she saw it as a bad omen.

Madame Alberti was not astonished. For her, those expressions were only those of an exalted amour, such as Lothario ought to feel, and of which she had often made the image. She pressed Lothario's hand, gazing at him in an affectionate manner in order to testify to him that it only depended on him to be happy, and that he would not find any obstacle to his desires in the only person who could still exercise some empire over her sister's resolutions.

Antonia's sentiments, encouraged by that confession, were manifest with more abandon. She depicted them with a gaze, the first gaze of her eyes that amour had animated.

"Woe betide me!" said Lothario, in a stifled voice, and he disappeared.

The sound of an oar striking the canal troubled the bleak silence that had followed his departure. Antonia ran to the window. The moon illuminated with one of its rays Lothario's floating plume; he was clad that day in the Venetian manner.

The aspect of the sky, the movement of the air, the hour, the moment or perhaps some other circumstance reminded Antonia of the appearance of the unknown brigand she had seen departing from the Saint-Charles môle.

Her heart only yielded momentarily to that fearful memory. Whatever the secret motive was for Lothario's disturbance, he had said that he loved her, and his tenderness would protect her against all perils.

XII

Ah, delightful country! If there is any abode appropriate to
soothe slightly the pains of a desolate heart, to bandage the
profound wounds made by the darts of chagrin and recall
the first illusions of life, it will doubtless be you that offers
it! Your enchanting aspect, your solitary woods, and your
pure and balsamic air have the power to calm
every kind of sorrow . . . except despair.
Charlotte Smith.[1]

Madame Alberti spent the night and a part of the following day
seeking interpretations of Lothario's mysterious speech. She
did not find any that changed her dispositions in the slightest.
A birth perhaps obscure, a fortune perhaps deranged by excessive prodigalities, great political or private misfortunes which
kept him forever distant from his homeland—such were the
various suppositions on which her imagination arrested, and
none of them gave birth to the idea of a fundamental obstacle
to Antonia's happiness. Even the resistance of Lothario was
explicable by sentiments so delicate and so honorable that she
did not hesitate over the means to triumph over them.

After a few moments of conversation with Antonia, she au-
thorized her to dispose of her hand in favor of Lothario, and to
give him the news herself, convinced that his generous scruples
would not resist amour. Antonia, more fearful and threatened
by dark sentiments of which she had conserved the habitude
since childhood of never savoring the felicity of which images

---

1 Charlotte Smith (1749-1806) was a poet most famous for her quintessen-
tially Romantic sonnets, who also wrote sentimental Gothic melodramas,
but her work attracted considerable disapproval in Britain because of its
fervent support for the French Revolution.

were presented to her, waited with a more anxious impatience for the day to pass. It seemed to her that Lothario would not come back, that she had seen him for the last time.

He did come back, however.

His sad and fatigued physiognomy announced painful meditations. His complexion was leaden. His eyes had lost the ordinary mildness of their expression; they depicted the anxious and turbulent vagueness of a sick imagination. He sat down next to Antonia and looked at her fixedly; Madame Alberti was occupied some distance away, deliberately keeping out of their conversation.

That situation was rather difficult for Antonia's timid and weak organization. She tried to smile, but a tear rolled in her eyes. Her heart was beating with great violence. Sometimes she turned away from Lothario, and was then astonished, in turning back to him, to find him in the motionless and sinister contemplation in which she had left him. She tried to articulate a few words, but only stammered confused sounds, and Lothario did not ask what she was trying to say. The attention with which he was covering her with his gaze gave the impression of a spell and a nocturnal vision.

Finally, she succeeded in breaking a part of that charm by saying: "You're unhappy, then, Lothario?"

That question was linked, by an imperceptible relationship, to their last conversation, but it was more an expression of a dolorous sentiment that resulted from what she had experienced then than a prepared transition to what she had promised to say.

Lothario did not reply.

"However," she continued, "you would be too cruel to those who love you . . ."

"Those who love me!" said Lothario, covering his head with his hands. "Always those who love me! My evil angel has informed you there of a magic phrase that sickens my soul."

"I came back to it deliberately," Antonia replied, "because I know no absolute misfortune for the man who is loved, and such is your destiny, Lothario, that a great many affections have deceived your tenderness, that many felicities have escaped your hopes, but never until now, my friend, have you found beside you more of the precious compensation that redeems a sensitive heart from all dolors. You know, Lothario, that you are loved."

Lothario resumed gazing at Antonia, but the character of his physiognomy had changed completely. Nothing was evident therein but a mixture of anxious joy, astonishment and terror, which did not belong to his features.

"Lothario," she went on, "I do not know your family, nor your rank, nor your fortune, and it is of little importance for me to know all that; but I have been told that the hand of Antonia, whose heart you desire to occupy, does not have to disdain anyone for any of those reasons; and Antonia, free in her choice, will only settle it on you."

"On me!" cried Lothario, with a kind of fury.

Madame Alberti drew nearer.

"On me! And it's you, it's Antonia, who heaps me with a derision so bitter!"

"Lothario," said Antonia, in a tone of cold dignity. "Either you are scornful of Antonia, or you have not understood her."

"Scornful of Antonia! What does this language signify? What are you talking about? Of a marriage, if I'm not mistaken, and it's you . . ."

Antonia leaned on her sister. She was weeping.

"My daughter," said Madame Alberti, "respect his secrets. He would not reject you unless an invincible obstacle, perhaps another bond . . ."

Lothario interrupted her.

"Oh, don't believe that. Born to love Antonia, and only to love her, I have not engaged my liberty in any other affection.

And if her hand could be the prize of amour—or of courage—it is to me, I swear, that it would belong; but by what right and under what conditions! Under what conditions, great God, and what man would dare to propose it! Vengeance of Heaven, how redoubtable you are! Listen to me, have you not heard tell—have you not spoken, only a little while ago, of a man who calls himself . . . Lothario . . . that must be his name! And do you know in what palace, in what domains, Lothario would present his wife to his vassals?"

Antonia sat down. A mortal frisson chilled her limbs. Horrible glimmers appeared in her mind, which revolted against them. She sought to penetrate that impenetrable mystery, but all that she could distinguish was that it was profound and frightful.

Lothario drew away and approached her by turns. Sometimes his features bore the imprint of delirium, sometimes they appeared to relax and decompose under an irresistible force. For some time he was pensive and dejected.

Suddenly, his face cleared, his eyes were animated; a sudden idea that reconciliated him with hope burst forth in his physiognomy. He fell at Antonia's knees, and, pressing her hands and Madame Alberti's with transport and bathing them with tears, he said: "What if, however, I were the world for her and for you?"

"The world?" replied Antonia.

"Her and you!" continued Madame Alberti. "All my life was in that thought."

"It would be true!" cried Lothario, as if overwhelmed by the weight of a happiness that he had never foreseen. "It would be true, and I would be able to commence with you a new existence. To carry my name and my destiny into the midst of men—I could! But it's necessary . . . how would I dare submit that which I love . . . As my fatal star wishes! It's far from here, far from cities, in a country where you would enjoy, uselessly, the splendor of a great name and a great fortune, but to which, henceforth, I could consecrate my entire life . . . Oh let me repose for a moment under the sentiments that oppress me!"

Lothario maintained silence for a few minutes; then he got up and, resuming his discourse more calmly, he expressed himself thus:

"While still very young, I already sensed bitterly the evils of society, which have always revolted my soul, which have sometimes drawn it into the excesses for which Antonia reproached me yesterday, and which I have expiated only too painfully. By instinct rather than by reason I fled cities and the men who inhabited them, for I hated them, without knowing how much I would hate them one day. The mountains of Carniola, the forests of Croatia and the wild strands almost uninhabited by the poor Dalmatians fixed my unique course by turns. I did not stay long in the places where the empire of society had extended; always recoiling before a progress that offended the independence of my heart, I no longer hoped for anything but to escape from it entirely.

"There is a point in those countries, the common limit of modern civilization and an ancient civilization that has left profound traces, corruption and slavery: it is as if Montenegro is placed in the confines of two worlds, and I know not what vague tradition had given me reason to believe that it participated in neither of them. It is a European oasis, isolated by inaccessible rocks and by particular mores that contact with other peoples has not corrupted. I knew the Montenegrin language. I had conversed with some of them when needs that never increased and never changed in nature had brought them by chance into our towns. I had formed a pleasant idea of those savages, which had sufficed for so many centuries, and who had been able to conserve their independence for several centuries by carefully forbidding their approach.

"In fact, their situation is such that no interest and no ambition can summon to their deserts that troop of brigands avid to invade land in order to exploit it. Only the curious and scholars have sometimes attempted to access those solitudes, and they have found the death there that they were about to bring, for the presence of social humans is mortal to a free people who enjoy the purity of their natural sentiments. It was therefore difficult to penetrate it, but I succeeded, by courtesy of garments similar to theirs and the habitude of their language. It was not, in any case, the people for which I had gone in search; it was an independent land where the voice had never resounded of a human power founded on any other rights than paternity.

"I had measured my needs, those of an adolescent with an ardent head, who believes that he will always be self-sufficient because, in a moment of bitter intoxication, he believes that he has sensed that all affections are insufficient for his heart, and that God has made him the only one of his species. All that was necessary for my ambition was a cabin against the rigorous colds of winter, a fruit tree and a spring.

"I wandered for a long time solely in the tracks of wild beasts, through the varied groups of the Clementine Mountains, fleeing the smoke of the houses of men, in which a sentiment that the Montenegrins felt reciprocally made me see an enemy everywhere.

"I shall not describe for you the strong impressions that I received from that great and imposing nature, which has never been subjugated, and the benefits of which suffice for a population fortunately sparse enough to be dispensed of soliciting them. I shall not tell you with what joy I plundered a nourishing root from the soil, without fear of offending the cupidity of an avaricious farmer or deceiving the hope of a family of famished laborers and hearing the fatal phrase resonate that always reminds me, like one of your writers, of the usurpation of the earth: *This is my field.*

"One day, finally . . . how can I express the inexplicable mixture of sentiments that succeeded one another within me? . . . the sun was setting in the most beautiful season of the year, setting at the extremity of an immense valley shaded in all parts by woods of fig-trees, pomegranates and oleanders, and covered at intervals by little isolated houses surrounded by the most beautiful and flourishing cultures. It was a scene that belonged to society, it is true, but the society of the first age.

"In no time and in no place had the habitation of cultivators flattered my gaze with a more agreeable aspect. Never had my imagination dreamed of prosperity for the abode of villagers. I conceived then the relationships full of charm of humans loved by humans, and useful to their happiness without being necessary to them, in an agricultural tribe. I regretted not having lived at the moment when civilization had only reached that point, or had not been admitted to enjoy it among the people who savored its peace.

"Soon, I shuddered in thinking, and recalling, that the laws of such a society must be terrible, and that the stranger who soiled their territory could only expect death. My blood boiled with indignation against myself at the instant when it would have frozen with terror in the veins of another. 'Oh, woe betide the profane individual,' I exclaimed, 'who would bring the vices and false sciences of Europe here, if I had a mother, a sister or a mistress here! He would pay dearly for the insult he had made to the air I respire by poisoning it with his breath.'

"A Montenegrin had heard me, for I had expressed myself in his language. 'Such are also our laws,' he said, taking my hand, 'and those who descend like you into our valleys from the heights of Montenegro, the external barriers of which are almost insurmountable to foreigners, are not always admitted to live among the Meredite shepherds. The difference in our mores, in any case, separates us sufficiently, since you are hunters and warriors and have difficulty in consenting to share the mild habitudes and tranquil life of our pastors. In order not to hinder the natural liberty of humans, however, by abusing the power that we exercise over our children, we sometimes permit the exchange of those whom their inclination summons to defend our mountains against those among you whose simpler tastes make them ambitious for the peaceful labor of our fields; and that free commerce of people and sentiments maintains our relationships with our neighbors in spite of the difference of our mores. Thus, for centuries, the Montenegrin warriors have enveloped our mountains with a formidable girdle of men and have protected these fields, which nourish them in their turn when nature refuses to provide for their needs, which rarely happens.

"'You are probably one of the children of our brothers, and all this wide expense,' he continued, indicating an isolated corner of the valley delightful in its aspect and already covered with the hopes of a rich crop, 'belongs to you, whoever you are. If you choose a wife among our daughters; if she gives you children, and your domain is insufficient for you, we will increase it in proportion to your needs, save for rendering proportionately to nature that of which you can deprive yourself if your family is extended into our mountains; for among other peoples the prosperity of families and villages is judged by the extent of cultures, but among us it is measured by the extent of lands that remain fallow and which precocious needs, indications of an excessively numerous population, have not rendered the exploitation necessary. From the moment that you become a Meredite pastor you are free, and there does not exist between you and us any other obligatory bond but that of mutual aid and hospitality, on the rare occasions when some unexpected event renders them necessary. If you have present needs, go and take possession of your domain; otherwise, have recourse to us and you will lack nothing of what nature accords to the desires of a simple man.'

"As he finished speaking, he prepared to quit me, but an insupportable idea corrupted my happiness and rendered me incapable of enjoying it. My life might be endangered by making myself known, but something more imperious than the interest of my life forbade me to receive from the hospitable bounty of those mountain folk a benefit that was not destined for me.

"'My brother,' I said to him, 'you are abused by appearances. I was born far from the Clementine Mountains; I sought liberty here. Everything proves to me that I would have found here the sole wealth that I desire on earth: the free enjoyment of the air, the sky and my heart; but this paradise that you are offering me belongs to a man more fortunate than me. I am a stranger in this woodland, whom you have the right to punish.'

"The Morlach looked at me. 'Young man,' he said, after a moment of silence, 'one cannot be mistaken at your age, but at your age is one very certain of not deceiving oneself? May you be disabused of the world you are quitting, and be so forever. Reassure yourself, in any case. Young, like you, and then a stranger to Montenegro like you, I came here to seek a refuge, and the same benevolence welcomed me among these pastors, by whom I feared being rejected. Go,' he continued, with a sort of authority, 'take possession of the lands I have shown you. They do not belong to any man in particular, but to the first comer, and we are not at the point of being obliged to repress an embarrassing excess of population. A hundred families occupy here a territory that would be sufficient for a people. The children of your children can increase here without being a burden to their neighbors and without suffering the aspect of their poverty. Adieu,' he said to me. 'Labor, pray, and enjoy the peace of your heart.'

"I remained alone, glad of the sentiment of my liberty and the master of a fertile soil that only demanded a little labor, the facility and success of which always changed it into pleasure. My wild domain was irrigated by the waters of an abundant stream that, swelled from time to time by storms, fell in a cascade from the summit of my rocks and came from afar to bathe orchards too rich for my needs, but the fruits of which attracted innumerable families of migrating birds. I enjoyed with delight the pleasure of equipping those temporary guests of my gardens against the unexpected vicissitudes of the seasons; happy when I saved a bee suddenly seized by the mortal action of cold and brought it back, warmed by my breath, to the hollow of a solitary rock where it was accustomed to find shelter.

"I lived thus for two years without communicating with anyone. I was eighteen years old then, and the habit of an agrarian life had developed my strength in a manner that astonished me.

"I was happy, I repeat, happy because I was free, because I was sure of being, and I know nothing more appropriate to fill the human heart with delightful emotions than that thought, which it enjoys so rarely. How everything enchanted me, how everything put me outside myself in the contemplation of nature! Often, however, I was tormented by an inconceivable need to be loved, and the desolate persuasion that no woman of my choice would come into those deserts to associate herself with my fate. I experienced then that the most tender sentiment can change into fury in a passionate heart.

"I heaped the world that possessed that unknown treasure with all the hatred that I would have borne against a fortunate rival. I dreamed with chagrin, with a jealous anger, about the young women dazzled by fashionable clothes and the flatteries of a few effeminate adorers who had allowed a disdainful gaze to fall upon me because of my obscurity or my excessive youth. I sensed with a sort of rage that it would be pleasant to strip them one day of the prejudices of their vanity by shedding blood before their eyes or frightening them with the glare of a conflagration . . . forgive, Antonia, the delirium of a foolish youth abandoned to his passions.

"I searched deliberately for the bears of the mountain in order to attack them with a spear, the only weapon with which I was provided, and I regretted that those women were not obliged to come and seek refuge, quivering with terror, under the protection of my arm, for I saw them everywhere. I did not frequent the other Meredite shepherds, who almost never frequented one another, but I was known to them by virtue of the courage and great physical strength that hazard had sometimes enabled me to display before their eyes.

"The bizarrerie of my appearance, the absolute isolation in which I lived, from which no circumstance had made me emerge, and, above all, what was reported about my vigor and my audacity had acquired me the popular credit that savages accord to the extraordinary like civilized men.

"One day, the Clementine Mountains were invested by foreign troops. A few adventurous detachments came to die there. They were sustained by an army that did not attempt to follow them, but which threatened our solitudes for some time. The woods of the inferior plateau that I inhabited were almost accessible. What would the cupidity of neighboring peoples come to seek there? But many of my brothers of the exterior were dead; we rose up in order to replace them. The hazard of battle rendered me a prisoner of our enemies in spite of my resolution; I had done everything in order to die but I lost consciousness along with blood and was taken away. That would take a long time to recount, and it would be futile.

"What my life has become since is another mystery that it is perhaps necessary to explain. But how many times the memory of that inviolable and delightful refuge, which I had acquired in a new society, outside the powers and laws of the earth, has made my breast palpitate! How many times I would have quit everything in order to retake possession of it, if the ascendancy of an invincible sentiment had not retained me!"

"For how long?" said Antonia.

"Since I have seen you," said Lothario, coldly. "And if my heart, less reckless in its sentiments, had attached itself to some woman isolated like me in the milieu of society, who could have understood and envied the happiness of my woods . . . that was the dream of youth."

"It seems to me, Lothario," said Madame Alberti, "that you create chimeras in order to combat them. I have not examined, I have not attempted to fathom the strange secret that made you renounce so soon all the advantages that your fortunate qualities gave you reason to expect in society, but my existence is linked unconditionally to the existence of my sister, and I know already that she is ready to submit to the savage caprices of your philosophy, unless it pleases you to return to a way of life more worthy of her and of you. She alone has the right to disavow me."

"Let us go to the Clementine Mountains," said Antonia, throwing herself into her sister's arms.

"To the Clementine Mountains!" exclaimed Lothario. "Antonia would have come there! She would have followed me there, and the privation of such a happiness will not suffice for my eternal punishment!"

The door opened to the ordinary visits.

A mass of ice fell upon Antonia's heart. Lothario approached her gently, covering his transports with a cold and polite appearance.

"To the Clemetine Mountains!" he repeated, in a low voice. "Antonia would have come?"

Antonia sought her sister's gaze. "Anywhere," she said, indicating her. "Anywhere, with her, and with Lothario."

"Let me dream," he said, "of the happiness that is reserved for me, or that which I have lost. I am not calm enough to see my future distinctly. Tomorrow . . . or never!"

Lothario had left in the greatest trouble; Antonia's heart was no more tranquil. Her anxiety had become a frightful perplexity.

Two hours later, Matteo came in, and presented a letter to Antonia, who handed it to Madame Alberti. They were alone. The note was drafted in these terms:

> *Never, Antonia, never! Do not blame me; forget me. After having wept momentarily, I renounce everything, to the only happiness that my miserable heart has ever understood. I am going to seek the death that has spared me for too long. Oh, my Antonia, if the world in which you believe can open one day to the voice of repentance; if, among the children of God, there are none who are disinherited in advance, I shall see you again. To see you again! Never, alas! Never, Antonia!*
>
> *Lothario.*

Madame Alberti had read those lines in a tremulous voice without daring to raise her eyes toward her sister. When she looked at Antonia, she was frightened by her pallor and her immobility. A terrible blow had just been delivered to that feeble heart, and Madame Alberti understood that the blow was irreparable.

Lothario's departure was known in Venice the same day, and, as usual, it gave birth to a host of various conjectures, all stranger than one another.

When Antonia was in a state to reflect, she saw nothing but a frightful enigma, the key to which she could not seek without feeling her heart fail and her reason go astray. Only once, she thought momentarily that she might be able to grasp the mystery.

Since the day when Lothario had said his final adieu to Antonia, *tomorrow or never*, Madame Alberti had avoided allowing her to return to that apartment, which only reminded her of cruel thoughts and mortal regrets. She had succeeded in introducing herself into it without witnesses, and she was gazing, pensively, at the place where he had quit her, when she perceived, underneath the chair on which she had been sitting, a little notebook bound in Russian leather, garnished with a steel clasp whose spring was broken.

She picked it up, and, thinking that it might contain the explanation that she needed, and that perhaps Lothario had not dropped it there without design, she opened it hastily and scanned its pages rapidly with her gaze. It only contained a dozen scattered leaves, sometimes traced in pencil, sometimes with a pen, in accordance with the circumstances in which the ideas had presented themselves to Lothario's imagination.

Two or three of the lines were written in blood.

There was little connection between them, but almost all were inspired by the fatal spirit of paradox, by the savage and exalted misanthropy that dominated his discourses.

Too preoccupied by the sentiments that filled her heart fully to grasp their meaning and to see anything there except what they offered of the most remarkable: singular images, visionary thoughts and surges of somber energy, but nothing that could dissipate her doubts or fix them, Antonia closed Lothario's notebook and hid it in her bosom, without showing it to Madame Alberti.

XIII

Do not seek to understand why the innocent moan, while
crime is clad in the robe of honor. Only the day of vengeance,
the day of eternal retribution can unveil the secret of the
judge and the victim.

Hervey.[1]

LOTHARIO'S NOTES

Mount Taurus raised its brow above all the hills; one of them
said to it: I am only a hill, but I contain a volcano.

Society—which is to say, a handful of patricians and augurs—
and, on the other hand, the human race entire in its swaddling-
clothes and apron-strings . . .

The legislators of the eighteenth century resembled the archi-
tects of Lycerus,[2] who carried into the air the materials of a
palace, but did not pay any heed to the foundations.

Exhausted peoples demand to be governed. Depraved peoples
need to be subjugated. Liberty is a generous aliment that only
befits a healthy and robust adolescence.

When politics has become a science of words, all is lost. There
is something in the world viler than the slave of a tyrant; it is
the dupe of a sophist.

It is inconceivable that men murder one another for their rights,

---

1 James Hervey (1714-1758), author of *Meditations Among the Tombs*
(1746), a key work of "graveyard poetry" that had a powerful influence on
William Blake
2 A character in an anonymous fictitious life of Aesop reproduced in many
editions of his fables, from the sixteenth century onwards.

and that so-called human rights are only mystical words interpreted by advocates. Why do people never talk about the first of human rights, the right to a portion of the earth determined by the proportion of the individual to the territory?

What is the law that bears the emblems and the name of equality on its frontispiece? Is it agrarian law? No, it is the contract of sale of a nation delivered to the rich by seditious schemers who want to become rich.

A man flatters the people. He promises to serve them. He has acquired power. It is believed that he will demand the sharing of wealth. That is not what happens. He acquires wealth and associates himself with the tyrants for the people's share.

The sacred word of the Hebrews is gold. There is a manner of pronouncing it in the ear of the judges of the earth that causes your enemy to fall stone dead.

Lycurgus thought something strange, which is that theft was the sole institution that could maintain social equilibrium.

Are you not weary, young man, of harvesting the gardens of Tantalus? Open your eyes to the evils of humankind; look. The gulf of Curtius[1] is still open, and it is necessary that many precipitate themselves into it for the salvation of the world.

Alms are a partial restitution made to the amiable. The beggar makes concessions; let us plead.

---

1 Marcus Curtius, a legendary Roman whose story is told by Livy and is mentioned briefly by Virgil. After an earthquake opened a pit in the Forum in the fourth century B.C. an augur opined that the gods required as a sacrifice the city's most precious possession; Curtius declared that it could only be Roman courage, and by way of a demonstration, rode his horse into the gulf, which closed upon him.

Take a man from the depths of the woods and show him society; he will soon be as corrupt and despicable as you, but he will never understand the impassive tribunal that coldly sends a beggar to the gallows for having decimated the banquet of a millionaire.

It is a difficult question to decide as to whether the more hideous thing in social life is crime or the law, whether the crueler is the criminal or the judge, the crime or the punishment. Opinions are divided.

Killing a man in the paroxysm of a passion is understandable. Having him killed by someone else in a public place, in the calm of a serious meditation and under the pretext of an honorable ministry is incomprehensible.

A frightening thing to think is that equality, which is the object of all our wishes and all our revelations, is really only found in two human conditions: slavery and death.

To see people struggling around an idea like ants for a wisp of straw is enough to make one die of confusion. At least a wisp of straw is something; an idea is nothing.

The theft of the poor from the rich, if one goes back to the origin of things, is only, in the final analysis, a reparation—which is to say, the just and reciprocal displacement of a coin or a morsel of bread returning from the hands of the thief to the hands of the victim of theft.

The highest level of liberty that can be achieved in a nation advised of its sovereignty is the right to choose a slavery to one's taste.

There is a great obstacle to the liberation of cities; it is cities.

Show me a city, a beehive or an anthill and I will show you slavery; only the lion and the eagle are kings, because they are solitary.

Malevolence is a social disease. The natural man is no more malevolent than any other brute. The civilized man excites horror or pity. Count the stories of a house and remember the parable of Babel.

If I had the social contract at my disposal, I would not change anything therein. I would tear it up.

The fruit of the tree of the knowledge of good and evil is society. The first time that man wrapped himself in a girdle of foliage, he dressed in slavery and death.

There are two directly opposed instincts in a simple man: the instinct of conservation for himself and what proceeds from him, and the instinct of destruction for everything that is taught to him and commanded of him. Society is therefore false.

All the works of God are accomplished in their destination and in their purpose. If society had entered into the purpose of creation, the skylark would never lead its chicks into a field of ripe wheat ready for the harvest.

There are few men whose heart does not quiver with indignation and dolor at the sight of a proud lion strangled in an iron cage, humbly licking the bloody hand of the butcher that nourishes it. What ought a man to think who looks at a man?

To render political inequality less outrageous, almost all the peoples who have not reposed it on moral advantages have at least attached its origin to generous memories or sacred traditions. No legislation has yet been found sufficiently depraved to confess in its institutions the aristocracy of money. When we get there it will be necessary to live well, because everything will end.

It is very humiliating for the species that nowhere in human society are slaves in a minority. What is necessary, therefore, is to exchange a bad place for a good one, when one has strength and number.

Nothing is easier than persuading a man that he depends on another, by virtue of a mysterious right founded on an unknown entitlement. But how can he be made to understand the truth, that his dependence results purely and simply from the inequality of an ancient division of the soil, which has not changed its form or its extent, and which can be put into litigation any day.

The beehive does not belong to the drone, but the flowers of the field belong to all the insects of the air. The only inviolable property of the individual is his industry.

Is it true that the majority of the sovereigns of Europe are occupied in land registry? So be it.

Instituting monarchies today is a great pity. I would not be surprised to find the cell of a hermit half-hidden in the ashes of a crater, but I would not advise a king to build his throne on that foundation.

To draw Nimrod's bow for the last time is not a rare marvel, Napoléon! Ten others have done it before you. No one has broken it as yet.

Our firework displays end with a spray that would eclipse the midday sun. The night, which belongs to thieves, is more profound thereafter. The tomorrow of a *great nation* is the night of a firework display.

If you succeed in your projects, they say, it is to recommence tomorrow. The great evil of recommencing tomorrow! We are so comfortable today.

When one has ceased to live primarily in the heart of another, one is really dead. Nothing is any longer lacking but the appearance.

A society that kills a man is convinced that it is doing justice. What an immense and sublime retributive justice is that of a man who could kill society!

Two crimes for which I am pitiless: doing harm to someone who cannot defend himself, and stealing from someone in need. Torture and malediction to the wretch who steals a blind man's dog!

The savage of the Southern Seas who trades a woman for an ax has not made a bad bargain. Where is the country where one cannot get a woman with an ax?

There are in the depths of a man three errors or three mysteries that determine him to live: God, love and liberty. It will soon be two thousand years that society would no longer have existed if a few Galilean beggars had not made a religion with that. How many speculators do you know who would invest a sequin for life on the probable duration of the latter institution?

I would like someone to show me in history a monarchy that was not founded by a thief.

When nations arrive in their final phase, there is no longer any but a single rallying cry: *everything belongs to everyone*. And on the day when the standard bearing that device is moistened by a child's tears, I shall tear it down to make a shroud.

The history of ancient peoples is not difficult to recount; the history of peoples to come is not difficult to foresee. Fathers, old men, sages, priests, soldiers, kings. And afterwards . . . perhaps the people.

There are only three ways linking one's memory to that of the temple of Delphi. It is necessary to build it, consecrate it or set fire to it.

Give me a force that dares to adopt the name of law and I will show you a theft that will adopt the name of property.

Liberty is not such a rare treasure; it is in the hands of all the strong and the purses of all the rich.

You are the master of my money and I am the master of your life. That does not belong either to you or to me. Render it, and I will leave.

A thousand fortunes for one thought! A thousand thoughts for one sentiment! A thousand sentiments for one action! A thousand sublime actions for one hatred—and the world, the future and eternity thrown in!

The founder of a new sect, poor fellow! The illuminator of an old morality, poor fellow! A legislator, poor fellow! A conqueror, what poverty!

If there is a good society in the world, it is one where everything is divided, giving a premium to the strongest. When cunning and treason get involved, legislation arrives.

I no longer know any métier of discredit but one, that of God.

I am sometimes asked whether I like children. I think so. They are not yet men.

All the voices of the earth once announced that great Pan was dead. That was the emancipation of slaves. When you hear it for a second time, it will be the emancipation of the poor; and then the usurpation of the world will recommence.

Of all governments, the one that revolts my heart the least is the despotism of the Orient, in which the debasement of the people is at least explained by superstition. I understand a tyrant who descends from prophets and is allied with the stars. In Tibet he is invisible, immortal and sacred. That is good, but he ought never to be indifferent. Tyranny and slavery are two states that imply two species. The vilest of human beings are the slaves who recognize tyrants made in their image.

One has many thanks to render to one's star when one can quit men without being obliged to do them harm and declare oneself their enemy.

What difference is there between a crime and a heroic action, between a torture and an apotheosis? The place, the time and the despicable opinion of a stupid crowd that does not know the true names of things and applies randomly those whose usage it has learned.

Scourges are in the order of nature; laws are not.

There was an idea less appropriate to the Divinity, as I conceive it, but which had something consoling for the man who gives infirmities to the gods. I like that Apollo is banished, that Ceres suffers hunger in the home of Stellion's mother, that Venus is wounded by Diomedes, that the cradle of Hercules is surrounded by snakes, like that of genius, and that he dies devoured by the shirt of Nessus, which he has bequeathed to his successors.

If my heart could acquire faith . . . if I had to invent a god, I would like him to be born on the floor of a cowshed, that he only escape assassins in the arms of a poor artisan who passed for his father; that his childhood be spent in poverty and in exile; that he be outlawed all his life, scorned by the great, unknown to kings, persecuted by priests, denied by his friends, betrayed by one of his disciples, abandoned by the most upright of his judges, delivered to execution in preference to the worst of scoundrels, whipped with rods, crowned with thorns, insulted by the executioners and that he perish between two thieves, one of whom would follow him to Heaven.

Omnipotent God, have pity on me!

XIV

I am the one who conducts to the abode of groans, I am
the one who conducts into eternal pain, I am the one who
conducts in the midst of the reproved population of rebels.
All hope abandon, ye who enter here.
Dante.

Since Lothario's departure, Antonia's melancholy had made rapid progress. She had fallen into a depression all the more frightening because she either seemed not to know, or to have forgotten, its cause. Her sadness had nothing determinate; it was a vague malaise, from which she could be extracted by means of a vivid distraction, but into which she fell back more rapidly than she had emerged. She sometimes smiled, and sometimes without motive; then her gaiety became painful to behold, because the expression of her physiognomy seemed not to be in accord with the state of her heart.

Never had she sought solitary excursions with more care. Almost all the places she frequented reminded her of Lothario, but she never named him. She avoided conversations in which his memory was mingled; one might have thought that she was trying to persuade herself that he had not existed for her, and that he was nothing in her life but the illusion of a dream or a fit of delirium. On the contrary, she thought often about her father and her mother, whom she had not named for a long time, and she talked about them, contrary to custom, without shedding tears, as if she had only been separated from them by a short interval, and would soon rejoin them.

Madame Alberti regarded that circumstance as something fortunate in Antonia's situation. She thought that her memories would be destroyed more easily by others, and that it would be easier to forget the contrarieties of a sentiment of which she was still far from understanding all the power beside her parents' tomb. She therefore resolved to take Antonia back to Trieste, and Antonia received that proposition with a testimony of cold satisfaction, the only one that her bleak features and fixed eyes were capable of manifesting imperfectly.

Furthermore, Madame Alberti had not renounced all hope for her. She was convinced, on the contrary—and there was, in truth, nothing more probable—that Lothario's strange procedure was only a further effect of the bizarrerie of his character or the embarrassment of his position, and that he would not take long to return to Antonia's feet to reclaim the rights that she had given him to a happiness that seemed to surpass all his hopes.

It was possible that the reasons that rendered the singular system with which he enveloped his actions necessary prevented him from forming a bond that, by fixing his existence completely, would submit him too closely and in too much detail to the curiosity of others, and would extract him from the vagueness of conjectures, the uncertainties of which were doubtless useful to him.

In the present condition of Europe, how many eminent men had been forced, like Lothario, to hide their names in twenty different countries and to avoid, like him, the most profound affections and the sweetest of the duties of nature, in order to conserve their security, and above all, not to compromise that of persons who were dear to them?

Such was evidently Lothario's situation, but it was necessary that it would change some day. It would have been absurd to seek any other explanation for his conduct. One could even think that if he feared, for good reasons, prolonging his sojourn in a great capital where he was already well known, he would not fail to head in the direction of Trieste when he had learned that Antonia had returned there.

Those suppositions had a great deal of plausibility, and Antonia did not reject them; but she made no response, and gazed at her sister with a mistrustful eye when the question was raised; then she threw herself into her arms.

The affairs that had summoned them to Venice no longer retained them, and they departed in a boat that would return them to Trieste via the lagoons. That manner of traveling had appeared to them to be preferable to any other because it was necessary for them to avoid the roads infested by Jean Sbogar's troop, most of all the dangerous passage where they had nearly become his prisoners.

The channels of the lagoons offer little interest to travelers. Traced by nature between deserted and arid portions of land that the sea invaded and abandoned by turns, and which could only offer refuge to errant flocks of wading birds, nothing varies or animates their sad monotony. They present nothing to the gaze anywhere but sterile strands or forests of reeds, from which a heron surprised in its slumber by the sound of mariners and passages sometimes rises with a long cry.

The pensive Antonia had not yet been distracted by any circumstance worthy of occupying her when night fell and lent all objects a calmer and milder character. The sky was strewn with brilliant stars, but the moon was refusing its light. Nothing could any longer be distinguished outside the boat, and the alternating swing of the oarsmen was scarcely perceptible. Nothing could be heard but the cadenced fall of their oars and the hiss of the water divided by the prow.

Suddenly, the man placed at the tiller broke the silence of nature by singing, in a voice that was not without charm, a few strophes of Tasso that depicted in harmonious lines the delights of solitude for two equally smitten lovers. His tones, which nothing reflected in the immensity of the atmosphere and the sky, and which extended without obstacle over the smooth surface of the sea, enabled the soul to participate in the enjoyment of the infinity in which they went to die. Antonia listened to them with a sentiment whose mildness astonished her, which she would not have thought herself able to savor only a moment before. She did not know to what to attribute the confidence that filled her heart and calmed all its storms. It was not the vivid and tumultuous illusion of initial hopes, it was the reposed enjoyment of a pure future. It seemed to her that the tutelary intelligences that watch over the last moments of innocence, and which come to open the abode of eternal repose, ought to manifest their presence thus.

Madame Alberti experienced the same emotion. Her hand was united with Antonia's; they were leaning toward one another and their hearts were beating with a gentle and regular moment. Plunged in a languor that the extreme tranquility of the air and the almost insensible undulation of the water contributed to maintain, they went to sleep embracing one another.

Their repose had not lasted long when a rifle shot, fired a short distance away, troubled Antonia's sleep. Madam Alberti was still leaning against her, but she did not speak. Antonia thought at first that she had had a dream, but the immobility of the boat, the silence of the oars and a few strange words that she heard in the confused conversation of the frightened mariners undeceived her. She tried to wake her sister, without being able to succeed. She tried to stand up, and felt her arm seized by a cold and muscular hand.

"It's another woman," said a voice. "Jean won't be content."

At those words, her hair stood on end, a cold sweat inundated her limbs, and she lost consciousness.

She only came round at the sound of the wheels of a vehicle that was carrying her, under which the resonant planks of a drawbridge were trembling and creaking dully.

She was alone.

Having recovered from the first access of astonishment that gives unexpected misfortunes the appearance of a dream, Antonia did not take long to comprehend that one. It was beyond doubt that it was bandits posted on the sea shore who had stopped the boat, and those bandits could only belong to Jean Sbogar's troop.

Brought down from the vehicle and sustained by two men whose bizarre costume and ferocious physiognomy filled her with fear every time the lights scattered under the vaults illuminated them, she went through the vast galleries, immense stairways and Gothic halls of a castle, confirming more and more the horrible idea that she was a prisoner in Duino.

Having arrived in a chamber that seemed to be destined for her, where her frightful escort liberated her momentarily, she ran to an open window, and saw nothing before her but the sea. A distant light, which appeared to be that of the lighthouse of Aquileia, shone alone in the midst of the nocturnal stars. She no longer doubted her fate, and fell into an armchair, heartbroken.

"Duino!" she exclaimed. "Jean Sbogar! But what have they done with my sister?"

Only the sonorous vaults responded to her voice. The last word she had pronounced expired in their depths like a faint voice fading away.

Antonia got up, fearfully, repeating: "My sister . . . !" in the tone of a person afflicted by a painful dream seeking to wake up.

The illusion of the echo was renewed, more sinister still. It resembled the last groan of a violent death. The unfortunate Antonia, almost incapable of sustaining herself, leaned against one of the large pillars of the entrance door, under a lantern that spread all its light over her. She embraced the cold column tremulously, sticking her face to it, partly covered by her loose hair, and felt herself buckling under the weight of her terror.

A few men grouped in the corridor appeared to be gazing at her from a distance, but the weakness of her eyesight only allowed her to distinguish, in the shadow in which they were hidden, the movement of their plumes, and she was not entirely sure of not being mistaken when a terrible scream struck her ear.

One of the men had fled, naming her.

The night was far advanced when Antonia ceded for the second time to her cruel emotions. It was only a few hours later that someone succeeded in bringing her entirely back to consciousness.

She was astonished, on looking around, by the delicacy of the cares of which she was the object. She had been transported into a more comfortable and more ornate chamber. There were no women in the castle, but she was served by children with agreeable faces.

Only one of the brigands solicited, toward the end of the day, permission to be introduced to her proximity in order to carry out orders with which his captain had charged him. He was a very young man whose physiognomy, sad but mild and modest, would have inspired confidence and interest in any other place. He had come to tell Antonia that her boat had been attacked by the most unfortunate of mistakes; that nothing of what she possessed would be stolen from her; that she was free herself at Duino and had not ceased to be; that everything was disposed for her journey and that it only depended on her to hasten or delay it, in accordance with the demands of her health; and that finally, while waiting, she could command as a sovereign everyone who lived in the castle.

"But what about my sister?" cried Antonia.

"Your sister Madame," the young man replied, lowering his eyes, "cannot be returned to you. That is the sole reservation we are obliged to put on our obedience, and even that condition is not imposed by a force that depends on us."

"And who has been able to impose it?" Antonia demanded, sharply. "Who can prevent me being reunited with my sister, who has been arrested, abducted and brought here with me? Oh, I don't want any of the advantages or reparations that you offer me if I can't share them with her."

"Madame," said the young man, bowing, "I have not received any other instructions." And he withdrew without waiting for further protests.

Madame Alberti's name was still wandering over the lips of the bewildered Antonia; it was not heard.

The perplexity in which she remained plunged is easier to comprehend than to describe. She began to hope that the event would not have the frightful consequences that it had caused her to dread, but she could not divine the motives that they might have for keeping her apart from her sister, and that new mystery was an abyss in which her mind went astray. Everything persuaded her, moreover, that she had not been deceived by false promises. The sun had set several hours before but her doors remained open. The people employed in serving her had retired of their own accord, to leave her an entire liberty, indicating the part of her apartment that they were going to occupy and where they would await her orders. Finally, no soldier appeared in the vast extent of the corridors, which had been illuminated as if to offer her a passage at any moment when she made the resolution to leave.

Reassured by all that she observed, she did not hesitate to engage in the gallery that ended at her room and to follow its detours as far as the main stairway of the castle. She descended without obstacle, passed through the vestibule and the courtyards with the same facility and reached the drawbridge without encountering anyone. It was lowered at her approach, as if a magical power had interpreted Antonia's desire and had hastened to obey it.

Scarcely had she left it behind when she perceived a traveling carriage ready to depart, guarded by domestics. She even thought that she recognized that it was laden with the baggage that had been brought with her from the boat, and the urgency of the postillion, as she approached, gave her reason to believe that she was awaited. She enquired, however, about the destination of the carriage.

"Apparently for Trieste," replied one of the domestics, "but for any place that Signora Antonia de Monteleone pleases."

"That's me," said Antonia.

"We did not doubt it," said the postillion. "There are no other women in this castle, and we are ready to obey you."

"There is another woman in this castle!" cried Antonia. "My sister is in this castle . . . Have you not been told that I am to be accompanied by my sister?"

"Mention has only been made of the signora," he said, shaking his head, "And there is no appearance that her sister can emerge from the castle if it is not the intention of the proprietor. But perhaps Madame does not know the proprietor of the Castle of Duino. Captive for such a short time . . ."

"Pardon me," Antonia replied, "but I know where I am. It is, however, incomprehensible to me that my sister is not here."

The drawbridge was lowered again. The castle was only guarded by the watchmen on the towers. Antonia darted her gaze into the interior, and thought that her sister was a prisoner there.

"I'll stay," she said, in a firm voice. "I won't leave without her, and her destiny will be mine."

As she pronounced those words she had covered a considerable part of the distance that separated her from the main staircase. She turned round to see whether she was being followed. The drawbridge was raised again. At that sight her courage weakened; it seemed to her that everything was ended, and that she had just raised a barrier between herself and the world that she could no longer cross.

She would have liked to find herself transported suddenly into the middle of a wild forest, at the mercy of the most ferocious animals, during one of the most bitter nights of winter, but still free and mistress of herself; the walls of the castle weighed upon her, on the air that she breathed, and her compressed heart was near to bursting in her breast.

She approached the balustrade in order to lean on it and get her breath back. Her eyes were turned toward a ventilation shaft from which a faint light was emerging, which came to tremble at her feet.

After a few moments of vague and involuntary attention she thought that she could hear singular noises emerging from the subterrains of the castle, which put her in mind of the solemnity of certain religious chants. She thought at first that it must be the roar of the sea that was breaking at the foot of the mountain, but the sounds only reached her at intervals, and sometimes even appeared to cease entirely.

Antonia approached the shaft with an anxious curiosity. The sounds finally struck her more directly, to the point that she imagined that she could discern articulate sounds therein, and the name of her sister. Persuaded that the preoccupation of her mind might have produced that illusion, she knelt down on the edge of the shaft and, holding her breath in order not to lose the slightest sound that agitated the air. She continued listening.

"My sister is there," she said, aloud, incapable of moderating the sentiment that absorbed all her ideas and penetrated all her senses with an inconceivable mixture of joy and terror. She got up precipitately, and launched herself into a poorly-lit staircase that ought to lead into the cellars of the castle.

After countless detours indicated at intervals by pale lamps hidden in hollows in the wall, she slowed her progress, because the noise that had attracted her attention became closer, in such a manner as not to let her miss a word; but she no longer heard the name of Madame Alberti. It was only, as she had presumed, a chant similar to those of the church, intoned by a single voice and repeated in chorus.

Soon, she arrived in the very place of the ceremony, and, numb with fear, she glided like a specter between the high columns that sustained the vault at a prodigious height, hidden in the shadows projected into the distance by their enormous bases. All the columns were charged with sheaves of lances, scimitars and firearms, forming a kind of forest through which what was happening in the middle of the subterranean hall could only be distinguished confusedly.

Stimulated by her attachment to her sister, Antonia armed herself increasingly with a resolution previously foreign to her character. Every time the united voices filled the echoes with a prolonged sound capable of covering the noise of her footsteps, she flew from one column to another, and waited, before daring to turn her eyes toward the enclosure, for the universal silence that succeeded it from time to time, which the sight of her would doubtless have disturbed—which proved that she had not been perceived.

However, the delicacy of her eyesight prevented her from distinguishing objects, as if it had been intercepted by a cloud, and the blur that her imagination lent uncertain forms augmented the terror of the nocturnal scene.

On the side opposite to the entrance of the subterrain, a long sequence of angular arcades rose up, the points of which were lost in the obscurity of the vault, and which were only separated from one another by further groups of slender columns, blackened and worn away by time.

Mourning drapes cut the arcades at a certain elevation, and the brigands disseminated against the backcloth of that funereal decoration added to its mysterious horror. Some, motionless and meditative, were sitting in the depths of stalls hollowed out in the body of the columns, which might have been mistaken for sinister figures disposed by an atrabiliary sculptor; others were, standing around iron candelabras heating their daggers in the flames of torches; others were lost in the darkness of distant porticoes and braziers, who, through the mobile darkness from which their hirsute heads and bushy beards were alternately obscured and disengaged, resembled as many phantoms.

Among them there was one in particular who attracted Antonia's attention all the more intensely because she soon judged that he was unhappy and sensitive. His face was enveloped by a crepe that hid it completely. Kneeling on the first steps of a platform, the rest of which was hidden from Antonia's view, he was leaning on the hilt of his saber and weeping bitterly. The sound of his sobs was only interrupted by the firm and sustained voice of the priest who was presiding over the sacrifice.

Antonia, beside herself and driven by an invincible curiosity, made a movement in order to see the altar. It was a funeral bed, and on that bed a woman was lying, her head raised on a black velvet cushion, scarcely disfigured by the recent traces of death.

"My sister!" cried Antonia, and she fell.

It was indeed her, for the rifle shot fired at the boat had killed her, and Jean Sbogar's troop were rendering her the last honors.

XV

Why are you bristling thus your bloody hair while gazing at me? Why turn on me those eyes whose dry pupils have disappeared from their orbits? It is not me who killed you.
Shakespeare.

Shall I find you everywhere, shadows of the murdered, with your wide livid wounds? And you, tearful mothers, who are showing me those flames lighted by my hands, those flames whose horrible tongues are devouring the cradles of your newborns?
Schiller.

Antonia remained buried for a long time in a state that resembled slumber. She did not appear to experience any agitation, and that calm was so profound, and had to give way, according to all appearance, to such mortal anguish, that one trembled to see it end. However, she came round without manifesting any dolor. At the most, she seemed to be occupied by a trouble-some thought, an importunate memory, that she was trying to chase away. She paraded her gaze around her uncertainly, and passed her hand over her brow as if trying to take account of an anxious doubt.

"I know full well," she said, finally, "where she is. I shall find her again this evening."

Fitzer, the youngest of the brigands, approached her in or-der to inform himself of her condition. She smiled at him like a familiar person, because he was the one who had spoken to her the previous evening on behalf of Jean Sbogar.

"I've been waiting for you for a long time," she said. "I wanted to know with what torture you punish indiscreet persons who penetrate your celebrations without having been invited. I know a young woman . . . but I recommend that secret to you on the salvation of what you love the most in the world. Promise me never to speak of it to anyone."

The young man looked at her, his eyes moist with tears, because he perceived that her reason had gone astray.

"Wait," she said to him, in a tone of the greatest surprise, "those are tears! I didn't believe that anyone wept any longer. Don't hide your tears from me. For myself, I can no longer show them. I remember having seen another man, in a place where I did not expect him, a man who was also weeping. I think it might have been you, for his face was covered by a veil that prevented me from recognizing him."

"His features are unknown to me, as they are to you," replied Fitzer. "Few among us have perceived him other than through that veil or the visor of his helmet. Only our old warriors have seen him uncovered in battle, but he very rarely comes to Duino, and only appears masked since we have been traveling the Venetian provinces without danger. He's our captain."

"Where is he?" said Antonia coldly. "Does he not know that I'm here?"

"He knows, but he dare not present himself before you, dreading that his presence might alarm you and that you might impute to him the error that rendered you captive."

"Captive, you say? Antonia is freer than the air! This very night I have strolled far from here in delightful woods where one breathes an air so pure! I have never seen so many flowers! My sister was with me; she wanted to stay there. I went there more often when I was younger, but I never went there with my mother. My life has changed a great deal since then."

Antonia reposed her head on her hand and her eyelids lowered. Her complexion was animated by deep colors; her lips seemed desiccated by a burning fever. She was laughing and sobbing.

Antonia's destiny was accomplished. No other protection remained for her on earth but that of the enigmatic lover who had appeared to her mysteriously in the Farnedo, and who was Jean Sbogar himself. The love of Jean Sbogar was watching over her with a solicitude that would doubtless have astonished her if the disturbance of her reason had permitted her to reflect on her condition.

Young women had been summoned from the cottages of Sestiana in order to serve her and nurse her; celebrated physicians were summoned or abducted from nearby towns in order to give her the cares that her malady demanded. An ecclesiastic, a prisoner of the brigands for some time, the one who had just celebrated the funeral service of Madame Alberti in a subterrain that they had converted into a chapel for that ceremony, was watching next to the bed of dolor for the lucid moments that her illness allowed her, in order to bring her the consolations of Heaven. Those ferocious men, finally, whose souls had only conceived thoughts of blood until then, purified by the sight of such innocence and touched by so much misfortune, lavished the most delicate and tender marks of submission upon her. Antonia became accustomed to seeing them and to entertaining them with the bizarre illusions that succeeded one another in her sick imagination.

Only Jean Sbogar dared not present himself before her under the veil or the visored helmet that hid his features, except when she was asleep or delirium took away her consciousness of all objects, and he could nourish his gaze with the dolorous contemplation of the beloved object without the risk of inspiring her with dread or horror.

One day, however, prostrate at her feet and incapable of containing the sentiments that oppressed him, he cried "Antonia!" in a voice stifled by sobs. "Antonia! Dear Antonia!"

She turned on her side and looked at him tenderly. He hastened to draw away. She called him back with a sign. He stayed, his head inclined over his breast, in an attitude of obedience and attention.

"Antonia!" she said, after a moment of silence. "I believe that is, in fact, my name; I bore it in the house where I was born, and I was promised then that I would be happy. Listen," she continued, taking the hand of the thief, "I want to make you a confidence. From the time of my first youth, when I believed that it was so easy and so pleasant to live, when my blood did not burn in my veins, when my tears did not burn on my cheeks, when I did not see spirits running through the thickets, which open the earth by striking it with their foot, hollowing out abysms in it and causing wells of fire to spring therefrom; when the souls of assassins who have no refuge in the tomb did not come bounding around me and launching themselves with cruel laughter, and when, on awakening, I was not obliged to detach the viper enlaced in my hair, the viper whose head, foaming with a blue poison, reposed on my neck . . . in those days there was an angel who voyaged over the earth with features that would have stirred the heart of a parricide; but I only saw him, because God took him away when his felicity was jealous of mine, and I called to him: 'Lothario, my

Lothario . . .' I remember that we had a palace in far distant mountains. I was never able to find the road to it."

Although the brigand had not quit his veil, Antoina perceived that his tears had redoubled at those last words. She smiled at him then with a tender pity, and, taking his hand again, which she had allowed to escape and which had not dared to retain hers, she said: "I know that I am causing you pain, and I beg your pardon for that. I'm not unaware that you love me and that I'm your fiancée, the fiancée of Jean Sbogar. You can see that I know you and that I am talking reasonably today. Our marriage was arranged a long time ago, but I did not want to have any secret for you. In any case, Lothario might well not exist. I've seen so many people in recent days who only exist in my imagination and who escape me when I return to myself. I'm sure, for example, that you haven't known my sister?

"No," she went on, after reflecting for a moment, "if I had had a sister she would have taken the place of my mother, and we would be able to invite her to the celebration of our wedding. Tell me whether you have made brilliant preparations for that day. It's necessary, for the bride is a rich heiress. I have golden clasps and diamond rings to ornament myself, but I only want a simple garland of eglantines for my hair."

She interrupted herself again. Her aberration increased. A smile that was frightful to see paused on her mouth.

"It will be a beautiful celebration," she continued. "All Hell will be there. The wedding torch of Jean Sbogar ought to make the midday sun pale. Can you see the guests from here? You know them all. I haven't invited anyone. And there are some with limbs half calcined by the fire; old men and children whose shreds awakened alive in the fires that you have lit, in order to take part in your pleasures . . . And there are others who rose up in their shrouds, who are gliding to the banqueting table hiding bloody wounds . . . Oh my God, what monsters have killed that young woman? Poor Lucile! And with what name are they saluting me . . . Did you hear them? *Salut, salut* . . . ! I don't dare repeat it. *Salut*, they're saying, and they're all murmuring in unison the word that rallies the accursed, the cry of joy that Satan would have uttered if he had vanquished his creator, the secret word that an execrable mother pronounces who is about to murder her child in order to render herself deaf to his moans. *Salut to the bride of Jean Sbogar* . . ."

As she finished speaking, Antonia lost consciousness.

That crisis was long and terrible; for a long time there was despair for her life. For a week, the chief of the thieves, immobile at the foot of the bed on which she was lying, attentive to all her movements, was not occupied with any other care than serving her. He watched and wept.

When Antonia's condition had improved, certain that she had become familiar with the sight of him and that she saw him without fear, he continued watching.

That assiduity struck her.

The reminiscences she had of the past were too confused for the name of the man and the memories that were attached to it to inspire any continuous sentiment of horror in her. Only, from time to time, her soul revolted against the idea of depending on him, and his mere approach chilled her with fear; but, more ordinarily, abandoned like a child, by virtue of the absence of her reason, solely to the instinct of her needs, she no longer saw in the captain of the bandits of Duino anything but a sensitive and sympathetic creature who was striving to soften the bitterness of her suffering, and who anticipated urgently her slightest needs. Then she addressed tender and flattering words to him, which appeared to redouble the secret dolor by which he was devoured.

One day, among others, he was sitting next to her, veiled as usual, and attentive to protect her sleep against all the accidents that might trouble it. She suddenly woke up, however, with an abrupt movement, pronouncing the name of Lothario.

"I saw him," she said, sighing profoundly. "He was sitting in your place. I see him there often in my sleep, and I find myself very happy; but how is it that I also believe I see him sometimes when I'm awake, and when it seems to me that I'm not dreaming? It's there, behind that curtain, that he has the custom of coming. In those days of dolor . . . and hope, in which I sensed myself summoned to the eternal liberty, a stream of flame ran through all my limbs, my mouth was ardent, my fingernails blue and bruised. Everything here was full of phantoms. Asps of a brilliant green were seen here, like those that hide in the trunks of willows, and other reptiles far more hideous, which have human graces; immeasurable and formless giants; newly fallen heads, whose eyes full of life penetrated me with a frightful gaze; and you, you were also standing in their midst, like the magician presiding over all those enchantments of death . . . I cried out in terror, and I called to Lothario to protect me . . . Suddenly—don't laugh at my chimera!—I saw that veil fall, and in the place where you were standing, I perceived Lothario all in tears, who extended his tremulous arms toward me and named me in a moaning voice . . . It's true that it wasn't him such as I knew him, sad, careworn and severe, but beautiful with a celestial bounty! Defeated, livid, fearful, he was rolling bloodshot eyes; his beard was thick and hideous; a desperate laugh, like that of demons, wandered over his pale lips . . . Oh, you can't imagine what has become of Lothario . . . !"

The thief did not appear to have heard the name of Lothario. He was plunged in a profound silence. He stood up and marched back and forth in the chamber with precipitate steps, and then he came back toward Antonia and contemplated her for a long time. His teeth were gnashing violently. A horrible meditation seemed to occupy him entirely, to the point of not even allowing him to discern the ever-increasing terror that he was inspiring in his unfortunate prisoner.

Finally, she raised herself up on her bed, succeeded in sustaining herself on her knees, and cried out, her hand joined in a sign of prayer: "Mercy, mercy, forgive me! Have no fear of Lothario; he does not want Antonia. I gave myself to him and he refused me. Mercy again for this time, and I will never mention him again!"

Then she fell back, for her strength was exhausted.

Jean Sbogar flew to her feet, seized the extremity of the blanket that enveloped her, and which was dangling on the floor, pressed it to his mouth furiously, and fled.

XVI

For two months Antonia had been living in that manner among the brigands of Duino without her condition having changed, without it having given any hope. She had only recovered a little strength, and she liked to come and respire the evening air at her window overlooking the sea.

One day, none of the people who served her had appeared in her presence. It was the first time that had happened, but she scarcely perceived it. The noise of the cannon that was booming in the vicinity of Duino occupied her more, because the emotion that it caused her was repeated frequently. Desiring to see her companions, she went down the great staircase, went through the halls and the vestibules, and found the castle deserted.

The cannon fire drew nearer, and every shot was followed by a rumor similar to that of a tempest. Antonia went back up again, opened her window, and gazed at the sea. She noticed a large number of small boats similar to those of fishermen, which seemed to be circling the foot of the fortress.

All those impressions were quite sharp at first, but they were promptly effaced. Night had fallen, the air was serene, the waves tranquil, the sky populated with myriads of resplendent stars, as on the night when Antonia's boat had been stopped on the Istrian coast after emerging from the lagoons. She spent some time enjoying its contemplation.

Meanwhile, the noise she had heard was augmenting behind her in a menacing manner. She thought she could distinguish a clashing of swords, imprecations and groans, which gave way at intervals to a deathly silence. She was too unfortunate for dread, even if she had had the use of her reason, for her fate did not seem to be susceptible to changing for the worse; but she did not see in the announced catastrophe anything but the danger of suffering, and the plaints that reached her ears gave her a frightful idea of the dolors to which she was about to be exposed.

The galleries of the castle had not been illuminated and the obscurity had become profound. She engaged in them, however, and slid along the tenebrous walls, following them with her hand. When she reached the top of the staircase she listened. The courtyards were full of armed men, who were talking confusedly,

They were no longer fighting. Only the butts of rifles resounded in falling upon the paving stones.

Suddenly, she heard a horrible tumult, in the midst of which the name of Jean Sbogar rose up. A pursued man launched himself on to the stairway and went past her like lighting. A few torches began to gleam on the first steps. Bayonets collided. The stone steps resounded under the footfalls of soldiers. Antonia ran to her room and, as she entered it, it seemed to her that someone named her in a muffled voice.

"Who's there?" she said, trembling.

"It's me," replied Jean Sbogar. "Don't be afraid, Antonia. Adieu forever."

He had approached the window, and the troop that was searching for him already filled the far extremity of the gallery.

The thief came back toward Antonia and seized her.

"It's me, it's me," he said. "Adieu forever."

Antonia experienced a vague sentiment of horror and tenderness, which she did not understand.

Sbogar shivered.

He pressed her against his heart with one of his arms.

"Antonia, dear Antonia," he cried, "Adieu forever! Oh, for the last time, no more than this minute in all the centuries! Antonia, dear Antonia!"

His veil had fallen, but Antonia could not see his face. She touched it; she had felt the heat of his breath. At the same moment the brigand's lips were attached to hers, and imprinted a kiss thereon that spread an unknown intoxication through Antonia's senses, a devouring sensuality that participated in Heaven and Hell.

"Profanation or sacrilege!" said Sbogar. "You are my mistress and my wife, and may the world perish now!"

As he pronounced those words he set her down on the high step that rose up to the window and hurled himself into the sea.

The soldiers had arrived with their torches. They were astonished not to see the thief, and asked Antonia whether she had seen him.

"Peace," she said to them, applying her finger to her mouth. "He has gone first to the nuptial bed—and left behind there," she went on, pointing at the crepe that he had left at her feet, "is his wedding gift."

XVII

The one that the angel made me see then was mounted on
a pale horse, and dragging all the living in his wake.
His name was DEATH.
The Apocalypse.

The French troops had just entered the Venetian provinces. The first concern of the generals was to purge the country of the brigands that infested it, and who might have become the most redoubtable auxiliary of the opposing army. That was the motive that had determined the attack on the castle of Duino. Almost all the bandits perished, arms in hand. It had only been possible to capture a few alive, whose serious wounds had put them *hors de combat* or who had leapt into the sea and had been collected by the small boats that Antonia had observed. It was presumed that Jean Sbogar was among them, but as his features were unknown even to the brigands themselves, nothing was able to settle the victors' doubts on that subject. Fitzer, Ziska and the majority of the captain's principal affiliates had died at his side before he had reentered the castle.

The prisoners were sent to Mantua in order to be judged there. That rather distant city was preferred to any other because it put them out of the range of the attempts of their accomplices, and its fortunate military position defended it from attack. Antonia was taken there in a separate carriage. Her state of dementia being quite manifest, she was confined in a hospital under the care of a physician celebrated for the progress he had made in the knowledge and treatment of that sad malady.

His efforts were crowned with a catastrophic success. Antonia was cured, and understood the full extent of her misfortune.

During the time she had spent in that house, she had not ceased to be the object of the pious solicitudes of which religion alone can teach the secret to charity. As she had made herself known there and her mind, disengaged from the darkness that obscured it, had resumed the affable charm that enchains the heart, she had excited around her, especially upon the saintly women who served the hospice, a sentiment milder than pity.

She was loved.

As no affection recalled her to society, and that peaceful refuge was henceforth everything for her, it was easy to accustom herself to ending her life there. A little later, she was forced to resolve herself to it.

A few steps taken to reclaim her great wealth were futile. Avid relatives, who had arrived after the army, had had the death of Madame Alberti certified, had supposed her own, and had taken possession of her heritage. They were powerful. That spoliation rendered them rich. Antonia's claims were unheeded. She was no more in the eyes of men but an orphan without means and a vagabond.

That was the least of her misfortunes, and her heart only felt it in thinking about the good she might have done in her new way of life if she had brought the resources of opulence to it. Her jewels at least sufficed for her dowry and the distribution of alms that were to make it known to the poor that one benefactress more had come to the hospital of Sainte-Marie.

The day of her profession, long delayed because of her extreme weakness, had finally arrived when two sbires came to summon her in the name of the law.

The trial of the brigands had been completed. Forty of them had been condemned to capital punishment, but there was no proof that Jean Sbogar was among them and the terror of that formidable name still hovered over the Venetian provinces, where he alone could rally further bands as dangerous as the first.

In that uncertainty, they had recalled the young madwoman who had been found in the castle of Duino and whom all evidence accorded in presenting as the sole object that had ever softened the implacable ferocity of Jean Sbogar. It was thought that she would doubtless recognize him among his accomplices if he were among them, and that her first movement would indicate him in a certain manner; it was for that reason that they had thought it appropriate to place her in the main courtyard of the prison at the moment when the condemned men passed through it for the last time.

Antonia had donned the habit of her novitiate again; her hair was already attached by the virginal headband, the whiteness of which her pale complexion effaced; two sisters from the hospital accompanied her. Almost incapable of sustaining herself, she leaned on the arm of one of them; her hand was fixed on the shoulder of the other and her head was slumped over her breast.

Soon, a strange noise was heard; it was the exclamation of a horrible impatience that was finally about to be satisfied; she raised her eyes and thought she distinguished something extraordinary, but her eyesight was poor. An officer of the law who had perceived it advanced a few paces. She saw more distinctly, without understanding what she saw; there were men whose hideous costume sickened her with terror, who were advancing in a single line before a hedge of soldiers. Their paces were measured, their pauses frequent. At each one she sensed her frightful anxiety increasing; finally, she was struck by a frightful illusion, and believed that she had fallen prey again to the delirium from which she had been saved.

It was him.

It was the scene that had inspired such a profound terror in Venice, when Lothario's head appeared in a mirror above her red scarf.

She advanced of her own accord in order to convince or disabuse her eyes. His physiognomy had the same character. He was enveloped in a robe or mantle of the same color.

It was him.

"Lothario!" she cried, in a heart-rending voice, precipitating herself toward him.

Lothario turned and recognized her.

"Lothario!" she said, opening a passage through the sabers and bayonets, for she understood that he was about to die.

"No, no," he replied. "I am Jean Sbogar!"

"Lothario! Lothario . . . !"

"Jean Sbogar!" he repeated, forcefully.

"Jean Sbogar!" cried Antonia. "Oh my God!"

And her heart broke,

She was on the ground, motionless; she had stopped breathing.

One of the sbires lifted her head with the tip of his saber, and let it strike the pavement by abandoning it to its weight.

"This young woman is dead," he said.

"Dead," said Jean Sbogar, staring at her. "Let's go!"

APPENDICES

The Spalatin Bey[1]

The twenty-four grandsons of the Spalatin Bey, assembled at the foot of the high walls of the fortress of Zetim, gazed at them with bleak eyes, in a profound immobility.

They enclosed Pervan, chief of a thousand fanatical Heiduques, who had just descended with him from the summits of Zuonigrad, pursued by the vengeance and malediction of peoples.

After having ravaged the cheerful country of Castelli[2] and abducted beautiful young women from the banks of the Zermanga, celebrated for the freshness of its shores, the brigand had surprised the old castle in the obscurity of a stormy night.

The cries of the assailants and the victims were lost in the noise of the tempest, like the rumor of a distant torrent falling while groaning into the depths of abysms.

---

1 The authenticity of this "translation" is dubious, and it is generally supposed to be a literary hoax composed by Nodier, although the two items that follow are not suspected of being similar in nature. There was a craze for discovering the folk songs and epic poetry of exotic cultures in France in the early nineteenth century and Prosper Mérimée, a member of Nodier's *cénacle*, published "translations" of several "Morlach songs" allegedly collected by Alberto Fortis, which were actually his own compositions: classic examples of "fakelore."

2 Author's note: "This is the modern name of a delightful country that my noble friend, Comte Kriglianovich, has described with an inexpressible charm in his *Mémoires sur la Dalmatie*. The name has prevailed and the ancient name has disappeared from this entirely traditional poem. It is the same with several others, as I said in the beginning." The reference is to the dramatist Giovanni Kreglianovich Albinoni (1777-1838).

At sunrise, however, two hundred bloody heads, fallen into the ditches of the palace, told the tribe of the Spalatin bey that the foreigner had come.

The son of the old bey, the brave Iskar, had died with his soldiers; the terrible expression that remained in his features announced that he had been murdered in his sleep, and that his life had cost the enemy dear.

The beautiful Iska, his daughter, the unique sister of the twenty-four warriors, had fallen into the power of the tyrant, and the air brought from afar to her desolate brothers the groans of the dove captive in the claw of the vulture.

That is why, their eyes fixed on the inaccessible heights, they were meditating vengeance without daring to hope for it; some were tearing their breast with furious hands while criticizing Heaven;

others, overcome by a somber despair, were lying motionless on the ground and chewing it with their teeth. Weak and innocent children, the youngest were weeping.

Suddenly, here comes the old bey, his heart penetrated by a bitter dolor for the death of his son and because of the fate of his granddaughter, whom he loves more than all the wealth of life.

The elder of the tribe cleaves through the mute crowd of his children. He advances, crowned by his snowy hair, which floats above his venerable head like the pale mist that one sees suspended from winter moons.

His beard descends in a silvery fleece over his robust flanks, embraced by a broad strap. A hanzar[1] is hidden in the vast folds of his multicolored woolen belt. A guzla[2] hangs from his sash.

---

1 Author's note: "The Franks ordinarily said *cangiar*. In our old French, which has perhaps retained some of the traditions of the crusades, the word signifies a *serpe*; it is a large cutlass, ordinarily enclosed in a brass sheath garnished by fake gemstones."

2 Author's note: "An instrument in the form of an ancient guitar—which is to say, a hemi-ovoid with a shaft. It only has one string made of horse-hair."

He climbs with a stride that is still firm the perilous rocky path that he has seen under the laws of his tribe for eighty years. He stops before the impenetrable palisade of the gardens of Zetim.

There he detaches the melodious guzla, the majestic instrument of the poet, and, striking the string woven from the manes of the proud mares of Macarsca with a curved bow held in a bold hand, he begins to sing.

He sings the victories of the famous bey Skender,[1] who freed his fatherland from the terror of the enemy, the sweetness of the native soil, and the bitter regrets of exile; and every refrain is accompanied by a dolorous and piercing cry;

for the mourning song of the Morlach resembles that of the great white eagle[2] that soars in circles over the strand, and falls with a high-pitched shriek at the most advanced point of the Lissa, when it sees the immense wave coiling like a long serpent over the frightened water, turning in innumerable folds, rounding out, extending and raising a foaming and terrible head all the way to the nest of its chicks.

The soldiers of Pervan listen without suspicion, because they do not understand the divine language of the old man, and because the string of the guzla has not resonated at the feasts of their forefathers.

They looked at one another, they interrogated one another, they shouted, they tried to imitate what they heard by confounding discordant clamors with it, and danced, bewildered like the spirits of the tombs[3] at festivals of vengeance.

---

1 Author's note: "Scanderbeg."

2 Author's note: "I believe this to be the balbuzzard, *Alba busa*, Jean-le-Blanc." The bird known in French as the balbuzzard is the osprey, *Pandion haliaetus*; the speculative identification seems unlikely.

3 Author's note: "*Vudkodlaks*, nocturnal spectres that frequent cemeteries. The translator of *The Vampyre*, falsely attributed to Lord Byron, writes the word very differently. I have explained the cause of the variations in orthography elsewhere."

The captives are also summoned by the songs; one of them repeats them to her companions, who prostrate themselves, stand up, run in circles; then stop, prostrate themselves again, and run in the opposite direction with fantastic cries mingling dolor and joy.[1]

They gradually draw closer together, reassured by the intoxication of their guards, whose souls, alerted for the first time to the sublime power of poetic songs, are astonished to be sensitive.

Iska—how beautiful she is!—is wearing a tunic of red woolen fabric of Krain,[2] embroidered with threads of gold and closed by a double silver clip, for she has not been permitted to dress in the sad ornaments of dolor;

her robe falls in long coils, her hair as black as the plumage of the bird of ill-omen that maintains woes to come in the echoes of Nona; a necklace of glass of all colors shines on her dazzling shoulders;

rings of gold and copper incrusted with the purest tin ornament her slender fingers; on her thumb is a marquetried die of brass and silver, a glorious sign of her nobility;[3]

Iska, who has recognized the voice of her ancestor, launches forth, abandoning to the wind the waves of her hair, and knots her dazzling white arms around the narrowly united iron bars that close the elevated gardens of Zetim.

The old man seizes her then, and fixes his trembling limbs to the inflexible and immobile iron. He flatters her with his language and his gaze. He studies her with his eye like a prey. He sings and he weeps:

---

1 Author's note: "A description full of exactitude and naivety of the singular dance of the Narentines."

2 Author's note: "Carina, or Carniola."

3 Author's note: "The richness of the ornament appears to have consisted among primitive peoples of incrusting the less precious metal with one that was more so. *cf Song of Songs* 1:11 'We will make thee borders of gold with studs of silver."

"Unfortunate daughter," he cries, "it is no longer the day of our celebrations, when the pismé[1] resounded the delight that burst forth in the tribe, when your father wept with tenderness and joy on learning that a daughter had been born . . .

"Weep with me for the warrior who is no more, and the dolors of his children, and that of his aged father, who remains orphaned of the honor of his face, like a sterile oak spared because of its antiquity by the woodcutter's ax.

"Weep with me for beautiful Iska, the sweet flower of my life, the tender hope of my imprudent old age, weep for poor Iska, who will never be led to the altar by the acolytes of marriage,[2] for it is necessary to die!"

Meanwhile, the astonished soldiers assemble anxiously, and Iska, informed of her fate, turns upon them a gaze milder than the manna that flows from the beeches of Colovaz.

The old man lets the guzla fall, he draws his redoubtable hanzar, and Iska, who no longer retains herself, precipitates herself between two bars to offer her breast to death, smiling at him.

They are so tight, the menacing darts that bristle the ramparts of Zetim; the unhappy bey killed her with a sure hand, but he could not embrace her.

Then he descended slowly from the heights of the fortress, and more slowly, as the detours of the narrow path brought him back below the furious enemy, for his great soul was weakened in that sacrifice, and he wanted to die.

Two arrows attained him without felling him; one broke in his broad chest, the other trembled for a long time in his muscular leg; the blood ran without astonishing him; it was thus that he arrived in the midst of his children.

The sun finished its course, and Zetim rose above him like a thick cloud crowned with pale radiance. The plain that it covered with its elongated shadow resembled a funeral drape around which a few torches blazed.

---

1 Author's note: "Song, poem, the *poema*, the *psalmus*."
2 Author's note: "The *druch* and the *druchiza*, which we call the best man and the maid of honor in most of our provinces."

"Victory," said the old bey, "victory, children of the Spalatins, the daughter of the tribe is delivered from our tyrants; she is dead, and here is the hanzar that has killed her!" Afterwards, strength failed him, and he fell.

Informed of the loss of Iska, Pervan roared on the mountain like a she-wolf which finds, on awakening, all her children, without exception,[1] struck by the hunter's spear; he utters the war cry.

The doors of Zetim rotate on groaning hinges. The draw-bridges resound under the hooves of horses. Confused arms clash in the night, and the sound of alarm extends and grows like the voice of an approaching storm.

Suddenly the hill begins to brighten with the fires of the conflagration that devours in haste the most distant roofs of the tribe. The bandits, like menacing spirits, appear and descend into the midst of the flames.

Already the women and children, are fleeing in all directions with lamentable cries. The oldest carry in their arms images of protective saints, and the young women do not forget the beneficent Zapis,[2] which cures the wounds of soldiers.

The old bey raises himself up on his bloody mat at the sight of the unknown meteor that is reddening the nocturnal horizon. He recalls his senses and recognizes the vengeance of Pervan. He says: "That is good.

"Children of Spalatin," he cries, the mild shade of the river of the Castelli no longer belongs to us. It is necessary to knot the belt around your waist strongly and fix the traveler's opancke[3] to your feet with the straps that have never served. For the road of exile is very long'

"And you will leave behind you the mountains of Novigradi, which tear the sky with their unequal points, and the towers

---

1 Author's note: "La Fontaine says: 'If one alone remained to me, I would soften my lament.'"
2 Author's note: "A certificate that serves as an amulet."
3 Author's note: "A kind of brodequin of raw leather."

of Zermonico, which serve as a beacon to the wandering tribes of the desert.

"And you will follow for a long time the solitary boundary of the sad Aseria, which also once prosper saw a family celebrated for the successes it obtained in war, and for the number of its servants, and of which only one house remains.

"And from there, your gaze will extend over a host of enchanted islands favored by the mildest benefits of the sun; for the boscages of Zeni[1] undulate like a virgin's girdle, and the white hills of Capri resemble young lambs bounding in the new verdure.

"But stop on the hospitable banks of the Pago, where you will receive the ever-free boats of fishermen; for that independent people, who confide their destiny to the sea, has never submitted to the law of the foreigner.

"Only depart, my children, avoid slavery and the humiliation of saluting like vanquished the kalpach[2] of the enemy; and if you seek a fatherland I will tell you that you will find it where liberty is; that is the instruction I received from my forefathers.

"As for me, I order to you not to hinder the dolorous convoy of the tribe with the cadaver of an extinct warrior. Leave me on the threshold of the bed of the ancestors, for I have known many more men among the dead than among the living."

As he spoke, strength abandoned him again, and his eighty children, pious in their disobedience, formed a litter with a dozen crossed lances, which they covered with foliage.

Then they descended silently by the paths least practicable for the enemy cavalry, while Pervan's troop rolled a new cur-

---

1 Author's note: "There is a double wordplay here, which seems to indicate a knowledge of Greek etymology. Perhaps to the present names of Zeni and Capri are only translations of their Slavonic names. I will add that this itinerary of sorts is very equivocal in its exactitude, which probably comes from the arbitrary substitution of modern appellations from the ancient ones I have already mentioned.
2 Author's note: "Slavic toque or bonnet; we say colback."

tain of flame from village to village, over the flames of the conflagration.

When the fugitives, having stopped to take some repose, turned gazes of adieu to the horizon of the fatherland, pursued by the image of the desolated natal roof, they recognized again the form and the extent of its burning ruins.

It was in vain, however, that the route of the flight, abridged by the knowledge of places and by temerity, approached its goal. The cavalry of the Heiduques devoured in rapid detours the distance conquered in vain by fatigue.

Twice the morning dawn had brightened the shadows of the eastern mountains, and twice the black squadron had reappeared at their summit in a whirlwind in which the dust raised by the feet of the chargers was confounded with the fugitive dust of almost banished mists.

Often the foreigner's course, favored by a vast plain or a facile slope, had resounded over the footfalls of the tribe. Often they had only found between them the opening of a somber path,

or a ravine, an unexpected benefit of torrents, the thickness of a hedge cut by paths without issue, or a rock fallen from the mountain and hanging over the precipice. Such is the one that menaces the strait of Pago.

On one side falls a hazardous and terrible path where the human foot can scarcely fix itself; on the other extends a plain of sand as dazzling as powdered glass, which goes to die at the level of the sea.

From the brow of distant hills, the whiteness of the last limits of the beach can scarcely be distinguished from the whiteness of the first waves, and you would have difficulty saying whether the gull that is descending in a spiral, like the shuttle of a weaver, will alight on a reef or a wave.

The fugitive life of the old bey had rallied at the increasing sound of peril. He was astonished by the route traveled and conceived the peril to come; for they had arrived above the point of the cape, and the dust of Pervan's horses was drifting over the kalpachs of Iska's brothers.

"Children," he said to them, "you have disobeyed for the first time the elder of the tribes of the Kotar, but it was in the vain hope of saving his days. May the gaze of the savior God descend upon you, with his pardon.

"Only, put me down there for a moment, near the tip of that advanced rock that dominates the profound plain and commands the vast sea, in order that my experience can direct you to the place of exile." And they did as he had prescribed.

Then he continued in a soft voice, but full of authority, and said to them, while gazing into the distance: "I can see from here that the tribe has reached safety in the strait of Pago, and is agitating, impatient for your arrival, like a swarm of bees separated from its king[1] by the first drops of summer rainfall.

"Already the fisher's boats are bobbling on the waves that are rising around them, and summoning you from afar under their triangular sails, favorable to misfortune and protective of liberty.

"What will become, my children, of the tribe abandoned by its chiefs, and by what right will it go to share the tents of the islanders, if it cannot offer in exchange for hospitality, the vigilance of its pastors and the courage of its warriors?

"However, time is passing and since I have been speaking, here they are. The horses of Pervan have spread out in the plain; they are covering the area, the only area across which you might carry the wounded old man.

"Wounded without hope," he said, tearing off his apparel, "for your efforts have only ended in delivering to the Heiduques one more victim or slave. That is what I had to tell you.

---

1 Author's note: "Like many other peoples, the Dalmatians say 'the king of bees.'"

"Follow the narrow path of the rock, therefore, which no man can descend charged with the slightest burden. It will conduct you among your wives and your children, who are groaning at your delay because they anticipate the enemy's arrival. Descend and leave me!"

Struck by the somber silence of the warriors, he raised himself up effortfully, drew nearer to the menacing tip of the rock, threw the names of Iskar and Iska toward the sky, and hurled himself into the abyss.

A generous devotion that was the cause of the salvation of the tribe and of the prosperity of Pago, for the generations that emerged from the Spalatin bey extend as far as our days in grandeur and valor.

And the story of the Spalatin bey, his dead granddaughter and his liberated tribe, is the most beautiful that has ever been sung to the guzla.

Asan's Wife

Palestna pjezanza plemenite Asan-Aghinize, literally "the ballad of the noble wife of Asan-Aga," is one of the most celebrated poems of Morlach literature. It appears to me to be superior to all those that are known, by virtue of the truth of its mores and the pathos of its sentiments. I do not believe that it exists in any translation other than that of Fortis in the *Viaggio in Dalmazia*.

What dazzling whiteness burst forth in the distance on the immense verdure of plans and boscages?

Is it snow or a swan, that brilliant bird of the rivers that effaces it in whiteness?

But the snows have disappeared and the swans have resumed their flight toward the cold regions of the north.

It is neither snow nor a swan; it is the tent of Asan, the brave Asan, who is sorely wounded, and is weeping even more in anger than of his wound.

For this is what has happened. His mother and his sister have visited him in his tent, and his wife, who had followed them, retained by the decency of duty,[1] has stopped outside,

---

1 Author's note: "A Morlach woman cannot enter the tent or bedroom of her husband without being summoned."

because he had not summoned her to him. That is what causes Asan's pain.

However, when the dolor of his wound had calmed, he writes to his sad and faithful friend: "Daughter of Pintor, you will no longer present yourself in my white house,[1] nor in my house, I tell you, nor in that of my relatives."[2] On reading that terrible edict, the unfortunate woman was devastated.

Since that day of dire memory, she has been listening, preoccupied by thoughts of lost happiness . . . one day, her ear is struck by the resonance of the ground under the hooves of horses.

She launches herself desperately toward the tower and seeks to gain its summit, where she can embrace a certain death, for she thinks that it is Asan, coming to pursue her with his reproaches; but her trembling granddaughters have attached themselves to her footsteps. "O my mother," they cry, "O my mother, cease to flee, for it is not our beloved father; it is your brother, the bey Pintorovich."

Thus reassured, she descends and throws her arms around the neck of the prudent old man. "Alas," she says, "you know him and you know my shame and that of our race. He has repudiated the wife who has given him five children."

The bey is silent, and does not respond,[3] but he takes from his vermilion silk purse the solemn title that permits his sister to crown herself again with the garlands of a bride, after she has trodden, on the threshold of the natal house, in the footprints of her mother.[4]

---

1 Author's note: "Is this an epithet particular to the house of Asan? Is it, as I think, one of those figures so common in the Slavic language, which expresses its illustration? However, Fortis, whom a long usage must have initiated into the finesse of the original literature, translates it as *cortile bianco*."
2 Author's note: "A formula of repudiation."
3 Author's note: "*Boxe muci; ne govorni mista*. Fortis translates it as *Il Begha null respondo*, in order to avoid the pleonasm, but pleonasm is one of the distinctive characteristics of primitive literatures."
4 Author's note: "*Da gre d'gnime majci u zatraghe*. This condition of divorce among the peoples we call barbaric has something sublime about it. It sup-

Scarcely has the unfortunate wife of Asan let her eyes fall upon that script than she gazes, she hesitates, she waits and then she submits, for the ascendancy of her brother dominates her.

Ready to quit them, she kisses ardently the foreheads of her two young sons. She presses with her lips the fresh and colored cheeks of the little girls, who weep without understanding completely the reason for their dolor; but she cannot tear herself away from the cradle where the last-born of her children is lying. She stares as if to draw the child with her.[1]

Her brother seizes her with a severe hand, pushes her toward the rapid charger, and flies with her to the house of Pintor.

She did not stay there for long. The week was scarcely over when a woman so beautiful and of such a noble family is sought by the illustrious judge of Imoski.[2] She falls at her brother's feet, weeping; she moans and she pleads: "Alas," she says, "don't give me for a wife to anyone, I implore you that by your life, I beg you on my knees! My heart will burst with dolor if it's necessary for me to renounce embracing my poor children again!"

The bey, deaf to her voice, has resolved to unite her with the noble Kadi. Devout, she prays again. "At least," she says, write in these terms to the husband you have chosen for me. Listen carefully:

"Kadi, I salute you. I am writing to you without having consulted my sister in order to obtain from you two mercies in her favor that would be dear to her: the first is to bring her, when you come with your friends, a long veil that can hide her from all eyes; the second is to avoid, in taking her to your house, passing

---

poses the unmerited misfortune of a wife who has incurred the disgrace of her husband without ceasing to be worthy of her mother."

1 Author's note: "A repudiated woman who remarries does not have the right to see the children of her first marriage again."

2 Author's note: "Imoski is the Emota of petty Greek geographers."

before Asan's, in order that she does not have the dolor of seeing the dear children that she must renounce forever."

Scarcely had that letter reached the Kadi than the latter gathered his friends to be witnesses at that celebration. They come, and present to the bride, on behalf of her new husband, the long veil she has requested; she covers herself with it and is accompanying them, glad at least to hide her tears, when cries coming from outside Asan's house inform her that the Svati guiding the nuptial cortege has mistaken his route, for her children have seen her and have launched themselves into her path.

"Beloved mother," they cry, "come back to your poor children, since it is the time of the repast when we appeal to you every day."[1]

At the voice of her children the unfortunate wife turns to the old bey. "My brother," she says to him, "permit your horses to pause for a moment before that house, in order that I can give a few more pledges of love to those innocent orphans, delorable fruits of my first union."

The chargers remain motionless while she goes to divide between her cherished family a few jewels or garments, the last testimonies of her tenderness; fine cothurnes woven with gold for the boys; for the girls, long and floating tunics, and a tiny robe for the one asleep in the cradle, whom she dared not awaken with a kiss.[2]

---

1 Author's note: "The original says *uxinati*, breakfast, a naïve expression that suits the mores of that people and the simplicity of their poetic language, but which we have dared to translate by a periphrase because we are translators. We beg poets to say frankly 'because it is time for breakfast.'" At the time when the story was written it was conventional to have two meals a day, in the morning and the evening, but when it became conventional to have three, the term *déjeuner* changed its implication, usually referring to the midday meal, and hence translatable as "lunch" while the first became *petit déjeuner*, or breakfast.

2 Author's note: "This lesson is not quite the same as Fortis', but I have collected it more frequently from the mouths of Dalmatian women and I find it much preferable."

Suddenly, a voice bursts forth in the next apartment, that of Asan recalling his children: "Return to me, my dear orphans, return to me! The iron heart of the cruel woman whom you are embracing will no longer soften for you; she is the wife of another."

She listens, her blood freezes, she falls, and her head, covered with a mortal pallor, strikes the earth resonantly; at the same moment, her heart breaks and her soul flies away in the footsteps of her children.

The Firefly[1]

An Idyll by Giorgi

The poem is entitled *Svjetgnack*, the Illyian name of the firefly, or winged glow-worm, which is described there, in my opinion, with an incomparable charm.

Giorgi is the Anacreon of the Morlachs.[2] The reading of the classics and the frequentation of cities has imprinted on his style something of the brilliant research and hyperbolic enthusiasm of his Italian neighbors. That is what I have not wanted to dissimulate in my feeble imitation. Such as it is, Giogri's *Firefly* nevertheless appears worthy to me of sustaining comparison with Madame de Krudener's *Sphinx* and Goethe's *Violette*.[3]

The original, which I have taken from the savant Memoirs of

---

1 This translation was first published in 1813 as "Le Ver luisant," and revised when published as an appendix to *Smarra*, as "La Luciole."

2 Ignazio Durdevic or Ignazio Giorgi (1675-1737).

3 "Madame de Krudener" was the signature used in France by Barbara Juliane von Krüdener (1764-1824), a much-traveled German baroness whose estranged husband was a diplomat. In Paris in 1789, she was an enthusiastic supporter of the French Revolution. She returned again in 1803, when she met Chateaubriand and published a sentimental romance, *Valérie*. She subsequently became a religious mystic, and issued prophecies that allegedly had a powerful influence on Tsar Alexander I of Russia. Cénacle-member Paul Lacroix, alias P. L. Jacob le Bibliophile, edited a collection of her unpublished works, which might contain the obscure poem to which Nodier refers. "La Violette" is the title of a French translation of Goethe's "Das Velechen" (1773), which was famously set to music by Mozart.

Appendini[1] on the antiquities of Ragusa and Illyrian literature, is often cited as classical authority in the useful Italian-Illyrian dictionary of Père Adelio della Bella. cf *Lucciole o Lucciola* p. 80, vol, II.

The Slavic poem is divided into quatrains. I have marked by ruled lines the division of the strophes.

The Firefly

Already the humid night is deploying the immense flight of its silent wings, and the mysterious chorus of the stars, accomplices of the tender larcenies of amour, is commencing a magical dance in the plains of the sky.

I, who am only thinking of my beauty, profit from the nascent obscurity to glide through the shadows of the house she inhabits. From her balcony, on the extremity of a silken thread, a white sheet of paper descends, swaying in the wind. Alas, I still hope!

The impatience at least to recognize in that note the thoughts of the one I love causes my heart to palpitate and quiver, but the night has grown darker and darker, and in the profundity of its obscurity I ask my beauty's secret message in vain for the invisible sign that she has confided to me.

---

1 Francesco Maria Appendini (1758-1837), a Ragusan student of Slavonic languages. He was rector of the college of Dubrovnik while Nodier was in Illyria, and had published a grammar of the "Illyrian language"; Nodier would surely have met him.

Impotent efforts! Futile laments! The dazzling tresses of the moon only float as yet in silvery waves over the summits of the mountains where that nymph seats her throne. The torches of the sky are burning too distantly for my eyes.

I am borne away in reproaches against the night, which a few moments before I was criticizing foolishly for slowness. I am indignant at the repose of the elements, which refuses me even the lighting of tempests . . .

I would like to see storms illuminate, and read by the triple fires of thunderbolts balanced over my head the adorable characters that my beauty's hand has traced . . .

Who would believe it? Among a few sparse tufts of sterile grass on which I nearly trod, a brilliant insect[1] suddenly produces a spark, which flies in rapid and multiple circles at the tips of eaves that it caresses and tears.

The hearth of a vivid and mobile flame that burns in its bosom extends and radiates over its agitated wings, flooding in ardent darts all the segments of its flexible body and illuminating it with an aureole of dazzling light.

---

1 Author's note: "A wasp in the original."

I seize with an avid hand the insect favorable to my prayers, the insect to which protective amour had confided a light easy to hide, by turns tutelary and discreet, to embellish the evenings of lovers.

I approach the cherished letter to it, making the agile insect pass over all the points of every line, over which its capricious gleam wanders and trembles. None of its radiant jets is lost to my eyes; none of the sweet confidences of the beloved will be lost to my heart.

Thanks be rendered to your fortunate aid, beneficent star of the meadows, tender firefly with wings of flame, the most beautiful and most innocent of all the animals of the earth and the sky, imperishable radiance of amour!

How can I express the happiness that I owe to you? How can I depict your charm and grace, pretty firefly, the most ravishing of the mysteries of a beautiful night, who renders hope to anxious amour, who lends consolations to jealous amour!

When the sun descends into its magnificent palaces of the Occident, it leaves you behind for the enchantments of summer nights. It leaves you, like an atom of its immense splendor, and confides you to the protection of the verdure and amour of flowers.

Compared with your brightness that of gold pales, that of pearls is extinguished; one can only compare it to the fire, vanquisher of darkness that scintillates and springs forth in profound darkness from the bosom of the oriental carbuncle.

You are, in the delicacy of your beauty, modest star of the bushes, the image of a timid virgin who illuminates involuntarily the secrets of the night with the fire of her gaze, in seeking the trace of the friend whom she loves.

Ah, may you, charming Firefly, collect the price of what you have done for me, may the meadows lavish you at all times, beneficent Firefly, with the embalmed nectar of their flowers, and the sky with the inexhaustible sweetness of its dew!

A PARTIAL LIST OF SNUGGLY BOOKS

JASON ROLFE *An Archive of Human Nonsense*

MARCEL SCHWOB *The Assassins and Other Stories*

MARCEL SCHWOB *Double Heart*

CHRISTIAN HEINRICH SPIESS *The Dwarf of Westerbourg*

BRIAN STABLEFORD (editor)
    Decadence and Symbolism: A Showcase Anthology

BRIAN STABLEFORD (editor) *The Snuggly Satyricon*

BRIAN STABLEFORD *The Insubstantial Pageant*

BRIAN STABLEFORD *Spirits of the Vasty Deep*

BRIAN STABLEFORD *The Truths of Darkness*

COUNT ERIC STENBOCK *Love, Sleep & Dreams*

COUNT ERIC STENBOCK *Myrtle, Rue & Cypress*

COUNT ERIC STENBOCK *The Shadow of Death*

COUNT ERIC STENBOCK *Studies of Death*

MONTAGUE SUMMERS *The Bride of Christ and Other Fictions*

MONTAGUE SUMMERS *Six Ghost Stories*

GILBERT-AUGUSTIN THIERRY *The Blonde Tress and The Mask*

GILBERT-AUGUSTIN THIERRY *Reincarnation and Redemption*

DOUGLAS THOMPSON *The Fallen West*

TOADHOUSE *Gone Fishing with Samy Rosenstock*

TOADHOUSE *Living and Dying in a Mind Field*

RUGGERO VASARI *Raun*

JANE DE LA VAUDÈRE *The Demi-Sexes and The Androgynes*

JANE DE LA VAUDÈRE *The Priestesses of Mylitta*

JANE DE LA VAUDÈRE *Syta's Harem and Pharaoh's Lover*

AUGUSTE VILLIERS DE L'ISLE-ADAM *Isis*

RENÉE VIVIEN AND HÉLÈNE DE ZUYLEN DE NYEVELT
    Faustina and Other Stories

RENÉE VIVIEN *Lilith's Legacy*

RENÉE VIVIEN *A Woman Appeared to Me*

TERESA WILMS MONTT *In the Stillness of Marble*

TERESA WILMS MONTT *Sentimental Doubts*

KAREL VAN DE WOESTIJNE *The Dying Peasant*

www.ingramcontent.com/pod-product-compliance
Lightning Source LLC
Chambersburg PA
CBHW020356110726
47899CB00006B/1735